I'm Going To Find You

I'm Going To Find You

J D PULLAN

Matador
9 Priory Business Park,
Wistow Road, Kibworth Beauchamp,
Leicestershire. LE8 0RX
Tel: 0116 279 2299
Email: books@troubador.co.uk
Web: www.troubador.co.uk/matador
Twitter: @matadorbooks

ISBN 978 1 8004 6526 8

British Library Cataloguing in Publication Data.
A catalogue record for this book is available from the British Library.

Printed and bound in Great Britain by 4edge Limited
Typeset in 10.5pt Minion Pro by Troubador Publishing Ltd, Leicester, UK

Matador is an imprint of Troubador Publishing Ltd

For Andy

PROLOGUE

FRIDAY 27 AUGUST 2010

Emily's car screeches to a halt, coming to an awkward stop with one tyre hanging precariously over the kerb. Oblivious to the surprised looks in their peaceful cul-de-sac she glances again at the message on her phone. Why, oh why, had she turned it off just because the infuriating battery was running low?

11:06
YOU SILLY GIRL. I WARNED YOU. YOU'D BETTER GET HOME. NOW!

Five hours ago. You stupid, bloody idiot. She screams silently, thumping the steering wheel.

Within weeks she has become so ridiculously obsessed she has forgotten to consider anyone, or anything, else. The drinking. The lying. The cheating. All traits she completely despises in anyone.

Her hands shake so much she can barely turn the key, yet her senses are on high alert. Marcus' car isn't on the drive. She chokes on her breath. Everything around her seems perfectly normal; birds singing, lawnmowers whirring. A typical Friday afternoon before a bank holiday. The afternoon sunshine making promises it probably won't keep for the weekend. Yet her whole being is telling her everything is far from normal.

She's greeted by a deafening silence. Her footsteps echo eerily off the wooden floor as she runs along the hall.

'Marcus, I'm home,' she calls. The kitchen chairs are askew; three bowls of half eaten, congealed breakfast cereal on the table. Her daughter Molly's beloved but battered old teddy bear, Peanut, lies in the corner of the room. Flat on his back. Four limbs stretched out towards her as if desperate for a hug.

Oh, come here precious. She silently cries. They must have left in one almighty hurry to leave him behind. Grabbing Peanut she holds him tightly to her face. Tears roll down her cheeks. The scent of her little girl's favourite bubble bath in his tatty fur overwhelms her. A tsunami of terror rises up through her body. Frightened and alone she has no idea what to do.

Oh dear god, please, please help me. What have I done? She knew the threats had become increasingly sinister, but she didn't think, whoever it was, had really meant it. They were just trying to scare her.

'Marcus, Molly, Jack, I'm home!' she screams at the top of her voice. A surge of hope powers her up the stairs two at a time. Just in case, by some miracle, they are playing quietly in their bedroom.

Emily checks every room. Nothing.

She calls Marcus. "Low Battery Mode" pops up as it cuts straight through to his voicemail.

She tries again. And again. And again. Then it runs out of power altogether.

Not knowing what else to do she curls up in a ball on the floor. Hugging Peanut, so tightly his innards are about to explode, she sobs her heart out until she has no more tears left to cry.

NINE WEEKS EARLIER: JUNE 2010

'Come on you two – get a move on – what's keeping you?' Emily teases, as Molly and Jack attempt to carry the luggage to the car. Marcus has his head in the boot trying to fit everything in. Desperate to help, their little arms can barely drag the suitcases along the hall. Excitement kept them awake most of the night and they hardly touched their breakfast in the rush to get going.

'Daddy, my arms are aching,' whines Molly looking up at him with her huge brown eyes, through a mop of curly dark hair. Molly and Marcus are two peas in a pod. Jack is more like Emily, with blond hair and a freckly nose.

'You need to eat your crusts!' he jokes, taking the suitcases from them. 'That would give you muscles.'

Emily smiles as she watches. Little Miss Chatterbox Molly giggling, as she helps her dad and younger brother. Always full of questions and curious about everything and everyone. She's thrilled at the thought of a week's holiday in North Cornwall with the three of them. She spent so many happy, carefree childhood summers in the same area. Learning to swim in the sea, searching for multicoloured marine life in the magical rock pools and long, exhilarating walks along the cliffs spotting grey seals and peregrine falcons. She can't wait to do the same with Molly and Jack. To share their childish delight in doing everything she had.

A week off work too. No deadlines or office politics. No press releases to write. As much as she loves her job she needs a break. Jo, her job share partner, will take care of everything while she's away. With two children the same age as Molly and Jack it's an ideal arrangement; not only do they share an inbox but the challenge of being a working mum as well.

Who'd have thought it? Mrs Emily Harrison, Senior PR Executive. It makes her laugh out loud. How come anyone who works in PR or marketing becomes an "executive" just like that? Junior executives, senior executives, content executives, media executives – what nonsense. You never hear of an "accounts payable executive" in finance, or a "customer service executive" in the admin department. They are just humble representatives or assistants. Still it sounds very impressive on her business card. It makes her feel far more important than she truly is.

She watches Marcus playing with the children on the drive. He looks tired. He needs a break too. The IT software company he works for is rapidly expanding and, as one of their senior project managers, he's certainly got his work cut out. He's been working his socks off since being promoted six months ago.

She whizzes around the house for the final check. Everything turned off, doors and windows shut.

She strokes the shiny, oak banister as she goes back downstairs. She still loves this house. It felt enormous after their trendy waterside apartment in Bristol city centre. A brand new four bedroom detached, with an enormous mortgage to match. She remembers the brochure detailing the "stunning new development in the wonderful market town of Thornbury, just north of Bristol". They had only gone out of curiosity but the show home was amazing and they signed up on their first visit. Closer to her parents too, without being right on their doorstep, it was perfect. They moved in when she was expecting Jack. The flat had been perfect for a young couple, but it was very cramped when Molly arrived and would have been impossible with two.

As much as she's delighted she feels a tiny bit uneasy about going to Cornwall, but Marcus booked it as a surprise to celebrate her birthday. No, she *is* delighted. How could she not be? Maybe it was her mum. *"Are you sure?"* she'd said kindly when Emily had told her parents where they were going. Then quickly followed up *"Oh, I'm sorry love, don't worry. I'm sure it'll all be fine."*

Emily can't believe it's her 40th birthday. It seems like only yesterday she and Marcus were graduating from Warwick University. 1991. Almost twenty years ago. She can remember the day they met so clearly. She, quite literally, bumped into him. Late for a lecture, and running hell for leather, she didn't see him walking towards her. The collision was so severe all his papers flew up into the air, and then floated to the ground. Seemingly in slow motion, before landing in a puddle of rainwater. Momentarily lost for words she was horrified as the ink of his notes irreversibly turned into illegible splodges. She had to do something so, by means of apology, she asked him out for coffee. Marcus, annoyed at the loss of his notes, whilst simultaneously mesmerised by her beautiful but embarrassed smile, from her very unladylike position on the ground, simply couldn't refuse.

Now here they are. Nearly two decades later. A hardworking, devoted mum of two. A family of four. She's scared her life is accelerating too fast. She'd love to slow it down, to make sure they don't lose sight of all their dreams together.

'Muuuuum, we're ready!' screeches Molly. Emily returns to the present with a jolt.

'OK… I'm here. Have you got Peanut and BB?'

'Peanut's here,' laughs Molly, hugging her beloved teddy bear. Jack's blue blanket, called BB for short, is lying on the back seat. They would both be completely lost without them.

'That's it then, we're ready!' Emily kisses their foreheads gently as she fastens their seatbelts, grateful to get a head start on the traffic heading south on the M5.

How wonderful. A sunshine filled holiday with Marcus and their two gorgeous children. Building sandcastles, eating ice cream and nestling up in the beautiful cottage they've hired for their stay. Maybe even a glass or two of something bubbly too. She can't imagine a better way to celebrate her special birthday.

*

After setting off in drizzly rain the sky turns brighter the further they drive. As boredom creeps in they pass the time playing "I spy" and seeing who can count the most caravans, with extra points if the caravan is being towed by a red car.

'I spy something beginning with H!' Molly says, grinning from ear to ear.

'Handbag,' replies Emily.

'Head,' giggles Jack, which Emily thinks is actually a pretty good guess for a four-year-old.

'Handbrake?' suggests Marcus.

'No, I don't even know what that is!' squeals Molly; eventually saying the answer is horse.

'But that's not fair – I can't see a horse,' whines Jack.

'Not now, stupid,' says Molly, in a strop '… but there was one in the field when we started.'

'Mum, that's not fair. I want to play a proper game,' Jack continues to whine, kicking the back of Emily's seat for the hundredth time. Her patience is wearing thin. Marcus grins and strokes her leg in empathy.

It's three o'clock when they pull up outside the quaint holiday cottage in Port Isaac. A brief pasty stop in Tintagel had temporarily revived them but, with two grizzly children, tempers are starting to fray. Traditional Cornish stone, complete with slate roof, it is small but immaculate. Two cosy bedrooms, a modern bathroom and an open-plan downstairs with a homely wood-burner.

'Wow, this is absolutely amazing!' Emily admires the blue and white, maritime inspired décor. She falls onto the "sink into" settee and strokes the velvety arm, immediately feeling more relaxed. The French doors open onto a flagstone terrace. As Marcus opens them the sounds of summer rush in. A stunning view of the harbour, full of gently bobbing boats. And, just beyond the sea wall, a tantalising glimpse of the Atlantic Ocean between steep headlands on either side. The bright sunshine reflects on the gently swelling sea. Twinkling, like diamonds.

*

Tired after an early start they have a quick mooch around the ancient, cobbled streets of Port Isaac. Such a picturesque village, full of hustle and bustle. Dozens of souvenir shops, ice cream parlours and bakeries, plus a small newsagents-come-corner shop. Stacks of the local paper sit on a wooden stand outside, some still tied up with string. Emily reads the headline as Molly and Jack skip past, making a beeline towards the fish and chip shop. "Police re-open decades old case". *Strange*, she thinks to herself. *Wouldn't have thought much happens around here.*

They are the freshest fish and chips they've ever had. Sitting on the harbour wall they try not to burn their mouths on the scalding hot batter. Totally delicious. But rather too tempting for the local bird life. Marcus flaps his arms, trying to fight off a flock of expectant, greedy seagulls that are intent on having far more than their fair share.

But it's fun. An alfresco supper watching the passers by. Two young boys look hopeful, their fishing rods dangling over the sea wall. A tabby cat meows gently, rubbing up against their bucket, not realising they haven't caught anything yet. Young couples walk arm-in-arm with evening ice creams. A group of lads enjoy a noisy beer outside the pub.

What a fabulous start to their week. Sitting here on the sea wall it all seems strangely familiar to Emily. She can't wait to explore even more tomorrow.

JUNE 2010

The following day is blissful. Lazing on the golden beach at Polzeath, building endless sandcastles and swimming in the sea. In between marvelling at the multitude of surfers catching the waves, and watching the world go by with an ice cold drink in the little café next to the sand. At low tide the beach stretches for miles. Then, as the tide comes in, it all but disappears. The myriad of beautiful sandcastles created by each family gradually dissolves into the sea, to be transformed into another work of art the following day.

Emily loves the view from this beach. Acres of golden sand framed by the magnificently blue sea. It's two beaches really. They just merge into one vast, extra wide beach at low tide. She can remember the windbreak her dad would insist on knocking into the sand, with the largest pebble he could find. No one seems to have windbreaks these days. Then the majestic headland of Pentire Point. A giant rock jutting out into the sea, like an enormous sentry guarding Polzeath from unwanted invaders.

And the ice cream van. Still in *exactly* the same place, on the road that runs along the cliff front overlooking the sea. 'Now, that's what you call a fabulous view from your office,' she'd joked to Marcus when they passed it earlier. She can remember many an occasion when she and sister Debbie pleaded with their dad to buy them ice creams. He'd eventually relent, only to pretend to complain as he traipsed up the steep, stony path from the beach. How she remembered that path too. At the top was an evergreen shrub, in the corner of a front garden. It had such a strong, overpowering scent. Emily thinks it is myrtle. She'd smelt it again today. Straight away it took her back to her childhood holiday. Clambering back up from the beach, sandy and wet, legs aching, dragging her bucket and spade. The heady smell would fill her nose – she wasn't sure if she actually liked it or not – but when it did she knew she was near the top.

Molly and Jack screech as they spot a crab scurrying across the sand, not sure whether to be excited or scared. Then, equally bemused as it quickly buries itself. Emily rests her head back on her towel, staring up at the sky. Debating silently whether to have another dip in the sea or not.

'Don't forget we've got to be back by three o'clock,' Marcus reminds her.

'How could I forget? We'll pick up some refreshments on the way.'

Emily could easily stay much longer on the beach, but England are playing Germany in the World Cup and they both want to watch the game. They had considered going to a local bar but Molly and Jack would get ridiculously bored; they're already threatening to squabble over a sandcastle. So it's back to the cottage with a few bottles of beer.

'Come on Ennnglannnd,' Marcus shouts at the screen as he jumps around the room. Molly and Jack join in, thinking it hilarious. England are 2-1 down at half time but there is still hope. 'Oh no! I can't bear it, pass a cushion Em, it's too painful to watch.'

Marcus is more sedate as the game goes rapidly downhill in the second half. Germany score twice in three minutes and England go crashing out with a 4-1 defeat. What a disappointment. Emily wishes they had stayed on the beach.

By evening Molly and Jack are exhausted. The fresh sea air has them almost falling asleep face first in their supper bowls. Pasta with tomato sauce topped with lashings of grated cheddar cheese; staple food in the Harrison household. Followed by a Gruffalo story, still their joint favourite luckily, especially with all the sound effects and embellishments Marcus adds in. It makes it easier come bedtime. Only one book to read not two. They settle down, snuggled up with Peanut and BB, with none of their usual resistance.

*

'So, Birthday girl, what do you fancy doing for the big day?' Marcus asks later as they sip a delicious, chilled Chenin Blanc on the terrace.

Emily considers carefully, resting her feet on Marcus' lap. *Who ever thought playing on the beach could be so tiring?* The school holidays haven't even started, but the beach had still been packed with holidaymakers. Plus an assortment of inflatable dinghies, surfboards, beach balls, rubber rings, deck chairs and essential paraphernalia that goes with a day at the seaside. They had tried every possible design of sandcastle and explored every single rock pool.

'I'd love to go to Lundy Bay,' Emily smiles wistfully as she reminisces. 'I went there as a child and it was brilliant. It's just along the coastal path from here – past Rumps Point, towards Port Quin.'

'I'll take your word for it,' laughs Marcus. He has no idea where she is talking about. Emily can remember perfectly, so many childhood memories indelibly recorded in the cliffs.

'I always thought Rumps Point looked like a giant dinosaur when I was little,' she giggles. 'I'll show you tomorrow. From a distance the rocky headland looks like a jagged backbone and the sea its runny nose. We'll need to check the tide times as the beach completely disappears at high tide, but there's a car park so it's easy to carry everything.'

Emily remembers clambering down the steep, dusty footpath wearing her hateful flip-flops. The coarse sand scraping between her toes. It was tough going, but worth all the effort when she reached the beautiful beach at the bottom.

She moves inside for a top up of wine as the light fades on the terrace. The sun is setting slowly over the silver-gilt ocean. The TV is on quietly in the background, so they can check the weather forecast.

'… Cerys' parents have never got over the pain of not knowing what happened to their daughter. Mr and Mrs Morgan are in their seventies and in failing health and are desperate to find closure before it is too late for them both.'

The newsreader looks earnestly at his audience from the other side of the screen.

'It will be thirty-four years tomorrow since Cerys disappeared in the summer of 1976, whilst camping in North Cornwall with three girlfriends to celebrate the end of their A levels.'

The screen switches to a view of Cerys' parents, sat at a table. Their faces forlorn, they are flanked by two police officers, talking to a room full of journalists. The newsreader continues.

'On Tuesday 29th June she was due to call home but never did. No trace was ever found, other than her wristwatch near the telephone box. Despite an extensive police search, helped by hundreds of local people during the heatwave, they never found Cerys. Her disappearance remains an unsolved mystery to this day.'

A photo of the young, beautiful Cerys in a floaty summer dress and sun hat fills the screen. Although black and white

Emily can tell she has long, wavy golden hair with cool blue eyes and a sun kissed complexion. She looks so happy.

'Police are appealing to anyone who may have information to contact them on the following number. Any details will be taken in the strictest confidence.'

Without warning Emily feels the blood drain from her head. The room is spinning.

'What is it Em?' but Marcus is too late to catch her. Emily's glass shatters at her feet as she collapses in a heap on the floor.

JUNE 2010

'Em, wake up,' Marcus leans over her. 'One minute we're watching TV and the next you're out cold on the floor?'

It really couldn't be, could it? The mermaid girl. That photo, it really couldn't be.

With Marcus helping, Emily slowly pulls herself up to a sitting position, trying to avoid the shards of glass on the wooden floor. She brings her knees up, her back leaning against the settee. She's still dizzy.

'The awful nightmares,' Emily holds her head in her hands. 'I told Mum and Dad but they wouldn't believe me.'

'Hey, it's okay Em.' He strokes her head, gently kissing the top of her hair.

'It's not possible Marcus. It really isn't possible,' Emily's eyes fill with tears.

'Hey, it's okay, take it easy Em.'

'You'll only think I'm stupid too. Everyone did. But I saw her. I *saw* her… the mermaid.' She rubs her watery eyes. She can see Marcus has the same disbelieving look.

'Em, come here,' he guides her up on to the settee, plumping up the velvety cushions behind her. 'Take your time.'

God, where do I even begin? Emily thinks. Despite the warmth of the evening her whole body shivers.

'Em, don't worry. You've had a shock.'

Marcus strokes her back as Emily fiddles with her tissue.

'… We were on holiday. The evening we arrived Dad took Debbie and me to the beach while Mum unpacked. He told us a wonderful story about a beautiful mermaid.

'She would swim onto the rocks at high tide to make sure the ships didn't run aground. She had long, golden hair and a wonderful tail covered in shiny, silver scales that glistened in the sun and the moonlight. She would comb her hair, singing, until the tide went out, then dive back in the sea.'

Emily pauses.

'Carry on Em, I'm listening,' Marcus says softly.

'I truly believed him. The next day, on the beach, I saw her. She was the most beautiful girl I had ever seen.' Tears, now rivulets, roll down the contours of her face.

'She was sitting on the rocks looking out to sea. Singing to music on a cassette player, while playing absentmindedly with her shell bracelet. She was crying.'

Emily shuts her eyes. She is back there. She can hear the seagulls calling overhead, the rhythmic swoosh of the sea. She can smell the salty seaweed.

'I was so captivated. I dropped my bucket and water poured everywhere.'

Emily breathes in hard to stop her tears.

'I said to Debbie, "Look, it's the mermaid Daddy told us about" … but she laughed and said they didn't really exist. That Dad had made it all up.'

'Oh Em, it doesn't matter, you were only little, of course you believed him!' Marcus reasures her as he gently strokes her back.

'… Then Debbie told her I thought she was a real mermaid! I remember her laughing, not *at* me but just in a really kind way. Like she found it funny. She was so nice. I asked if her bracelet was made of real shells.'

Emily strokes her wrist, as if she is wearing it, and a tear drops onto her hand.

'She said it was a hair band. She'd made a hole in each shell with a pin and threaded them on. She held out her hand for me to look closer. Her skin was so soft. I told her the bracelet was really pretty... and then she said I could have it.' Emily smiles at Marcus as she remembers.

'I was over the moon and put it on straight away, then my shyness got the better of me. I grabbed Debbie's hand and we ran off.

'I still have the bracelet in my jewellery box, I'm sure I've shown it to you.'

'Wow, Em, that's such a sweet story.' Marcus picks up pieces of shredded tissue. 'Why did it give you nightmares?'

Emily's shoulders tremble. Surely it couldn't be? The true awfulness of what happened seeps through her body. Perhaps she knew all along. Perhaps she had subconsciously tried to convince herself otherwise. Put it in a box at the back of her mind, hoping it would go away.

'That's the thing. The next day was my sixth birthday. After a picnic we played hide-and-seek. I thought I was really grown up and went up the cliff path, all by myself, to hide. There were some fabulously big boulders and it would take them ages to find me.

'When I reached the top I felt amazing.' She can remember being lost in her own little dream world, the sound of the seabirds and the buzzing insects in the grass. 'Then I hid behind a rock and waited for them to find me.

'After a while I got nervous so I peeked over the top,' Emily shuts her eyes '... when I did she was there. The mermaid. She was arguing with someone. They hadn't seen me so I ducked back down.'

Marcus is deathly quiet. Intrigued.

'I didn't want them to notice me, and I knew Mum, Dad or

Debbie would come looking for me any minute. I eventually got the nerve to look again and they were really close. The mermaid looked straight at me.'

Emily covers her face with her hands. 'I *know* she recognised me. She looked me right in the eye. I'll never, *ever* forget that look Marcus. She was terrified.

'I put my fingers to my lips to say "shhh" so she wouldn't give my hiding place away.

'Then she disappeared. Literally. She vanished. I must have screamed as the other person turned around just as I hid again, behind the rock.'

She wipes her cheeks with both hands.

'Go on, Em, what happened?'

'Then Mum found me. She was angry, but it was my birthday so she tried not to be.

'I told her I'd seen the beautiful mermaid girl. That she had vanished right in front of me. Mum just said my father had filled my head with silly stories, then held my hand really tight as she marched me back to the beach.'

Emily feels Marcus' arm around her shoulder, his thumb caressing it gently. They sit motionless for a while. Marcus silently encouraging her to tell him. To tell him everything.

'The strange thing is, I remember other things too. Vague snippets of conversation… in the shop… on the beach. People talking about something *awful* that had happened in hushed voices.

'Then a photo of the mermaid girl, a headline on a newspaper. Probably in a garage forecourt on our way home. When I said it was the mermaid Dad got really funny. He just snapped that "mother was right and I'd been letting my imagination play tricks with me"… and I wasn't to *ever* mention it again. I was only six so I didn't understand why.'

Still sobbing Emily nestles into Marcus' shoulder; the comforting scent of his aftershave soothes her. Although his embrace is calming, she involuntarily trembles as he holds her in his arms.

'That's why, when I saw her tonight, I knew it had to be her. The newsreader said it was thirty-four years ago, so that would have been my sixth birthday. The exact day.'

She sighs, taking a long, deep breath.

'Oh Marcus, what am I going to do?' She cries. 'I used to have nightmares about the look she gave me. The fear in her eyes. It haunted me for years. Over and over. Now I know why.

'I may only have been six but I was the last person to see her alive.'

SATURDAY 19 JUNE 1976

'Oh my god, I can't believe it!' screams Cerys, flicking her long blond hair out of her eyes. She tries to shut the straining zip on her bulging travel bag for the tenth time. 'We're on our way!'

'I know,' screeches Pip, even louder and always the extrovert. 'Sun, sea and sand here we come… and a bit of partying, and some boys… and a bit more partying!'

'Sounds like a plan.' Vicky and Amy laugh in unison.

'Hey, keep the noise down guys, the other passengers will complain,' shrieks Cerys. Then, like a magician with a rabbit, she pulls a bottle of Cinzano from her bag to the delight of the others.

'Yay!' shrieks Pip. 'What are your parents going to say when they find *that* missing?'

'Same as they do when they find this missing too,' Cerys laughs as a bottle of Dubonnet appears as if by magic too. No wonder her bag had been so heavy.

'Pass it over, Cerys,' motions Pip. 'I can't stop panicking about my grades at the moment so let's drink and be merry. Let's toast our holiday and forget about exams for two whole weeks.'

'Here's to the weather forecast too,' chips in Amy. 'Have you seen it? It's going to be hot and sunny for *at least* the next week.'

'Yay! YAY!' shrieks Pip, now completely over-excited. 'I'm going to get my best sun tan ever *and* we're going to get there in time for the solstice, which will be *in-cred-i-ble*!'

'Too right but we'd best get our tents up first,' agrees Amy, always practical, taking a swig from both of the bottles as they share them round.

It had been Cerys' idea to go on holiday, although the others had not taken much persuading. After being stuck inside for what seemed like an eternity reading, re-reading, revising, re-revising and practising exam questions until she felt like she was going to internally combust she was desperate to get away and shake off all the cobwebs. Her very first holiday without her parents too.

Enjoying the sweet taste and fizzy sensation of the Cinzano, now mixed with a splash of lemonade in a plastic cup after a trip to the buffet car, Cerys closes her eyes and silently relishes the thought of two weeks of fun.

'So it's final then, I'm sharing with Amy and Pip's with Vicky?' she asks, finishing off her drink in one large gulp and putting her hand out for a refill. A rhetorical question, as she knows they have already decided.

'If I must – just don't snore too loudly,' laughs Amy. She and Cerys have been best friends since primary school. The four of them have stuck together through thick and thin over the years. After moving to the comprehensive in Haverfordwest they still travelled the twelve miles each way by bus together, catching up on all the juicy gossip every day.

'Did you see Phil yesterday?' Vicky asks Cerys, changing the subject.

'He popped over,' she shrugs her shoulders. 'Now he's passed his driving test he just wants to be in his car all the time, either driving it or tinkering around under the bonnet. I'm glad really, it will give him something to take his mind off me being away.'

'Hey, we'll have none of that you know. You're not going to mope around all lovesick,' Pip feigns a theatrical swoon. 'You can still have a great time with us girls. Absence makes the heart grow fonder, so he'll still be there when you get back.'

'I know, I know,' grins Cerys. 'It's just weird, I'm so used to him being around, you know, *all* the time. Anyway, what about you Pip?'

'What about me?' Pip raises her eyebrows.

'Well, I think we should make sure you have a holiday romance. Neil was such a prat doing what he did just before our exams started,' Cerys follows up sympathetically.

'I know. I should never have trusted him – that bitch in the lower sixth had been flirting outrageously with him for weeks.'

Pip's put on such a brave face, Cerys thinks to herself. *I'm so pleased to see her back to her normal self. Her crazy, wild normal self.* Secretly envious of her stunning, shoulder length red hair and green eyes – with the longest lashes Cerys has ever seen – it was only a few weeks earlier she had been utterly distraught. Always the drama queen she had threatened to not sit her exams, with a few more histrionics thrown in for good measure.

'So yes, I'd be delighted to find a very handsome, suntanned surf-dude or two if I can,' Pip laughs, playing with her hair as she twists it up into a ponytail.

'Not if I find them first,' Vicky adds, pretending to be put out. 'It must be my turn. Especially now I've got my new trendy haircut!'

'Too right,' says Cerys. 'I absolutely *love* your hair. It *so* suits you. I think you were really brave having it all cut off, I would never have the nerve to do that myself.'

It was true. Until recently her dark hair had been so long

she could sit on it. Then, on a whim, she visited the hairdresser to have "a little trim" for their camping trip and ended up having a complete restyle on the spur of the moment.

'I am so glad I did – it feels very glamorous and chic – very Parisian,' Vicky laughs, posing like a Vogue model with her trendy, short bob and catching her reflection in the window.

Cerys thinks how apt it is. Vicky is so passionate about languages, and plans to take a gap year to travel around France and Italy.

'I know you always say I try too hard, *whatever* that actually means,' Vicky continues with yet another pose. 'But I have a feeling my luck is going to change in Cornwall. Big time. There's a dreamy holiday romance waiting just around the corner, with someone tall, dark and *extremely* handsome.'

'To Cornwall!' They sing, waving their plastic cups in the air. 'Here's to the best summer holiday ever!'

*

Almost five hours, and three weary train changes later, Cerys is relieved to see Bodmin station appearing in the distance. Fun to begin with, once the enormous picnic Pip's Mum had made them and the alcohol had run out, the journey became tedious. The rolling West Country scenery – spectacular as they sped further away from first Cardiff, then Bristol and finally Plymouth – made Cerys feel like she had been parachuted into an Enid Blyton adventure. The bright, azure blue sky and green fields making her want to be at their final destination even sooner. To be fully immersed in it, not just observing, through a rather grimy train window.

At some point, between singing along to The Wurzels – she can't believe "Combine Harvester" is still Number One in the charts – followed by Queen's *Night at the Opera* album, Cerys dropped off to sleep. She had woken up, her cheek numb and clammy where it had been pressed against the glass. Pip was shouting to pull the emergency cord, and Cerys, still half asleep completely freaked out. An elderly gentleman looked up from his book, over the wiry spectacles perched on the end of his nose and calmly pointed out the track runs adjacent to the sea near Dawlish. There was no need to panic. They weren't about to drown.

*

'Phew, that's the lot girls.' The taxi driver squeezes the last of their luggage into his six-seater. 'How many months are you staying for?' he teases. Years of practice at working out the best way to fit huge amounts of baggage in his boot has paid off. He slots everything in place within the blink of an eye. He doesn't chat much but has a gentle Cornish burr when he does. Cerys senses he is keen to drop them off as quickly as possible so he can get back for his next passengers. Even with his foot hard on the accelerator it is gone four o'clock by the time they get to the campsite. Cerys is exhausted. And they've still got to put their tents up.

'Hi girls, come on in, it's great to see you,' welcomes Donald. The proud owner of the Atlantic View campsite and dairy farm, about half a mile from Polzeath on the road to St Minver.

'It certainly is,' echoes his wife Beryl, as she scrapes mud off her boots. 'You must have been travelling for hours, come on in and make yourselves at home.'

'Hi,' says Cerys. 'I'm Cerys and this is Vicky, Amy and Pip. You must be the lady I spoke to over the phone... we're so excited to be here.'

'And so you should be, I am sure you'll all have the most wonderful time. I'll just check you in, give you a quick tour and then leave you in peace to get yourselves sorted.'

Wow, what a lovely welcome. Cerys remembers how friendly Beryl had been on the phone when she booked. *Definitely a good choice to stay here.*

Almost twenty pitches in total, Beryl shows them around. She points out the newly built bathroom block – with modern showers – plus a small kiosk where they sell "emergency" supplies. Milk, eggs, cream, bread and even toothpaste. The girls have two adjacent pitches in the far corner of the campsite. *Great, more private and we won't disturb everyone there,* thinks Cerys as she takes it all in. The air smells so pure. No traffic fumes, just fresh, country air. Good for the body and the soul. She can hear her grandma say.

Most of the other campers are out for the afternoon. Just two couples, sitting in deckchairs and soaking up the sunshine, drinking cups of tea and reading Sunday newspapers. She stifles a giggle as she spots a middle-aged gentleman with a handkerchief over his pink face. It floats up and down rhythmically, in time with his snoring.

'I'll ask our boys to pop over shortly too. They're back from university for the summer. If you have any questions about anything, anytime, just ring the bell in the office, there's always one of us around if you need us.'

'That's great, thank you so much,' says Cerys as Beryl disappears, before laying down the gauntlet. 'Come on Amy, I bet we can get our tent up before Vicky and Pip!'

The practice runs in the garden prove to be a waste of time. It takes them an absolute age. Just as they think they have succeeded Vicky and Pip's tent starts to collapse. Quickly followed by the four girls, who collapse in fits of laughter. Or possibly hysteria, given how long the tent-building debacle has already been going on. There is much tut-tutting from the middle-aged couple with the handkerchief. They have been discreetly watching their progress from behind their gin and tonics. Cerys is envious. Their tent looks huge. It's a small bungalow. It's even got a porch and see-through plastic windows.

On their other side is a young family with twin boys of about five. They're identical. Little cherubs, with white blond hair. Their dad kindly offers help "should they need it" but Cerys is not sure he really means it. He and his wife are clearly finding it all quite entertaining. Barely stifling their giggles as they pretend to play with their sons, while watching the pantomime unfold.

Sufficiently recovered from their hysteria the next attempt goes more smoothly.

'Oh my god, that was such hard work,' Cerys mops her brow. 'I need another drink... Hey, you lot, what are you looking at?'

She throws her arms up, perturbed by the other three. They're all staring at her. Eyes open wide, with a weird, bewildered look.

'Hi! Mum asked us to pop over,' says a deep voice from behind her.

Cerys spins around.

'Do you need a hand?'

Wow, Cerys thinks. *Now I know what they're staring at. Beryl's two sons. And they are both absolutely gorgeous.* She guesses from their less than subtle reaction that Pip, Amy and Vicky are thinking exactly the same.

'I'm Richard and this is my brother John. Well, technically Robert, but we use his middle name as it's less confusing. Too many "R"s otherwise,' he grins.

Cerys looks at John, trying not to make it too obvious. Slightly taller than his brother, they're very alike. John's hair marginally darker but both suntanned with a rugged, healthy complexion; what she would call an "outdoorsy" look.

She feels John's gaze. He lets Richard do all the talking. *Perhaps he's shy.* She catches his eye and feels her cheeks glowing. He smiles at her, then looks coyly at his feet.

They are so obviously brothers with their identical, friendly smiles.

'Well, talk about good timing,' says Cerys, eventually breaking the near-awkward silence. She has never known the other three girls to be so quiet.

'You've arrived just as all the work's done. Where were you thirty minutes ago?'

JUNE 2010

Emily fidgets all night, trying hard not to disturb Marcus. As the night wears on she gazes at the stars. They wink back at her through the open window. She would love to see a shooting star but no luck at the moment. Just a satellite slowly orbiting earth in a steady, precise arc. Then, as day breaks, the stars are replaced by the flashing lights of aircraft heading towards Heathrow for an early landing.

The gentle sea breeze, with its salty freshness, wafts in and out. The curtain moves softly. She imagines it to be Neptune himself, breathing gently as he slumbers before another sun-filled day.

With her head full of ideas for their holiday and places to take Molly and Jack she realises it wasn't only the anticipation of her birthday that kept her awake. It was the missing girl. The nightmare of the disappearing mermaid from her childhood has returned. Disturbingly vivid. Intermingled with images of Molly and Jack eating chocolate birthday cake.

Cerys. She has a name now. A real person. Flashbacks of the newspaper headlines and snippets of local gossip, spoken in hushed voices, fill her head.

Marcus starts to stir as seagulls squawk incessantly about

their exciting day ahead, already on the hunt for breakfast. Emily knows it won't be long before Molly and Jack are up. *The peace before the storm, enjoy it while it lasts* she thinks, rolling over to snuggle into Marcus. Sure enough, within seconds, she hears squeals from their room and the patter of bare feet heading their way.

'Happy Birthday Mummy,' they yell in delightful unison. 'We want to see you open all your presents.'

Emily knows what they really mean is they want to open her presents for her, but she doesn't mind. It's much more fun that way.

Marcus and the children insist on bringing her tea in bed before serving breakfast on the terrace. Piping hot when it leaves the kitchen, by the time they carry it upstairs – trying not to spill any under Marcus' watchful eye – it is decidedly tepid.

'Mmmm,' she pretends. 'The best cup of birthday tea ever!'

Marcus winks without them seeing and Emily delights in an extra fifteen minutes to wake up. She must stop thinking about the mermaid girl. She mustn't let it spoil the day. Instead, she enjoys the sea view and decides what to wear to the beach. Before wandering downstairs for hot croissants, strawberry conserve and freshly squeezed orange juice. Delicious.

It is rapidly turning into another sunny day so any birthday presents can wait. She can't wait to see Lundy Bay again, and Molly and Jack are excited too. The tide will be out by now so, armed with a picnic and cold drinks, they head off. The car boot still overflowing with all the beach essentials from the day before.

They park in a shady spot, the best one out of the few spaces left, and put their money in the honesty box. It's an exhilarating fifteen-minute walk from the car park. After crossing the road they follow the edge of the field opposite. The view over the hawthorn hedge teases them. Intermittent glimpses of softly breaking waves and the blue sea get closer and closer. They stroll through a beautiful wildflower meadow then clamber over a stile onto the high cliff path, before turning sharply down a steep, dusty path by the sign pointing to the bay. Almost hidden by vegetation Emily hopes other people will miss it so they can have the beach all to themselves.

A recently added wooden staircase hugs the cliff and makes the final and steepest part of the descent a lot easier than when she had been a child, although they still need to scramble over the rocks at the bottom to reach the sand.

It is a picturesque cove. Unique. With a narrow waterfall tumbling over the cliff. They watch the big rollers further out to sea careering past, and enjoy the swoosh of the smaller waves as they gently roll onto the sand and shingle. The musical jingling of tiny shells. Tossing and turning as the water runs out of puff, after seeing how far it can stretch up the beach.

It's busy but not crowded. Families with toddlers make sandcastles and shrieking teenagers play frisbee.

'Hey, Marcus, I must have left some of the picnic in the car.' Emily says, rummaging in the hamper. 'I'll pop back and get it before it's ruined in the heat.'

'Sounds good. I must admit I'm starting to get peckish,' Marcus grins cheekily. 'I'll keep an eye on M & J, they're fully occupied exploring rock pools at the moment.'

Emily feels the pull in her calves as she climbs back up the steep path. *I must get fitter,* she thinks to herself. *Forty and fit, not forty and fat.* Although she is hardly the latter. She knows she could definitely exercise more, especially as she puffs a bit too. At least she doesn't have to wear those awful flip-flops anymore.

*

At the top she feels like her young six-year-old self again. She stops to enjoy the moment. Lying down with her eyes shut and the beautiful Cornish sunshine on her face. All she can hear is the musical buzz of insects in the grass, the long call of the gulls and the hypnotic sound of the sea. All she can smell are the flowers and the salty sea air. Magical.

Emily is motionless for at least ten minutes, drifting off into a wonderful place. She rubs her eyes as she comes round. She needs to get a move on otherwise Marcus might wonder where she is. As she readjusts to the brightness she feels a cold shiver run right through her bones, despite the warmth of the mid-day sun.

Emily does a double take. This is the very place. The very rock she was hiding behind when she saw the mermaid.

She slowly moves across the grass and sits behind the boulder, her back leaning against the warm stone. It is all so familiar. The view of the sea. The coastline gently winding into the distance towards Rumps Point. The view that has appeared to her so many times in her dreams. Her nightmares. She is instantly transported back to 1976 with the mermaid – Cerys – right in front of her, looking deep into her eyes.

Without thinking Emily puts her fingers to her lips and says 'Shhh'. Her heart lurches. The significance of that fleeting moment once again fully dawns on her. Shaking, Emily feels sick, acid bile gathers at the back of her throat.

A barking dog brings Emily abruptly back.

'Sorry love,' the owner says, walking briskly past. 'I didn't mean to startle you – lovely day.'

She has no idea how long she has been in her other world. Brushing the grass seeds and dust from her legs she stands up. Her knees still weak. She needs to get back to the car and fetch the picnic or Marcus will be sending out a search party.

*

Later, as the tide turns and starts to gather pace, they make tracks back up the cliff. Years ago, when it was just the two of them, they would have tested their nerve, but not any longer. She doesn't fancy being stranded on the rocks. Plus there is a bottle of chilled champagne waiting at the cosy little pub in Port Gaverne where Marcus has booked a table. The landlord knows it is her special birthday so they can't possibly be late.

*

'Happy Birthday Ems!' Marcus clinks her glass and kisses her gently on the lips. 'To the best wife and Mum in the whole, wide world'.

'Ughhhh,' Molly and Jack cover their faces in mock horror, full of giggles after the tiniest sip of champagne. Luckily they decide it is disgusting, and leave the rest for Emily and Marcus to enjoy.

A huge, shared pudding follows delicious sea bass. Fruit salad with vanilla and strawberry ice cream topped with crushed meringue, chopped nuts and a rich chocolate sauce. It is utterly unhealthy, yet totally scrumptious. Molly and Jack absolutely love it. They dig in as deep as they can with the specially designed, long handled spoons. The fun of eating the molten puddle of flavours far surpasses savouring a delicately constructed dessert.

'So, Mrs Harrison, there is just one more thing we need to do!' Marcus laughs, both of them feeling rather too full, as he pulls a small velvet box from his pocket.

Emily carefully unwraps it. An exquisite eternity ring. A delicate row of six perfect diamonds set in a simple band of gold.

'I love you with all my heart. I always have and I always will,' Marcus says with tears in his eyes. 'You, Molly and Jack are my world.'

Emily is overwhelmed, but she knows what he is referring to. Not that they ever discuss it any more, there is no need.

They lost their way a bit after Molly was born. Suffering from post-natal depression after a protracted, traumatic birth she hadn't realised he was going through a tough patch at work too. They were both preoccupied. Struggling to manage the demands of a new baby, whilst juggling other commitments. The inevitable happened and Marcus found solace in the arms of a pretty, young female colleague called Juliette. The sister of a boy he knew from school. He was just "helping her settle in" when she joined the same company he worked for.

Emily had been heartbroken. They hadn't even got to the end of her maternity leave. "A cross between Baby Spice and Holly Willoughby" he said, when she made the mistake of asking him what she looked like. Lucky him. She hadn't been able to watch either of them on television since, without her heart breaking into smithereens all over again.

But it certainly explained all the obvious lies and increasingly emotional distance that had grown between them. She still kicked herself for not saying something sooner. Each time an alarm bell had rung – "you know I love you, don't you?" he used to say, over and over – why? He had never done that before. It turned out Juliette had recently moved to a new flat and he was helping her to "settle in" there too, during their extended lunch breaks.

Hard as it was they somehow made it through the heartbreak. Then Jack arrived a year later.

He wouldn't ever do it again though would he?

'Hey gorgeous, come back.' Marcus jokingly clicks his fingers, like a hypnotist.

'Oh, I'm sorry, I was miles away.' She laughs, trying hard to eliminate her negative thoughts. 'It's just so beautiful. What a lovely surprise, I'm truly speechless.'

Emily slips it onto her wedding finger. It sits perfectly against her engagement ring. What a wonderful way to end her special day; all she wants now is to get back to the cottage so they can settle the children in bed, and have a romantic evening watching the sunset.

What an amazing day, she needs a moment to take it all in. And to clear her head of the awful, recurring image of Cerys. In her summer dress walking across the wildflower meadow all those years ago.

30 JUNE 2010

The smell of fish hangs in the air.

Trawlers unload their catch of the day in Padstow harbour. Emily daydreams as she watches them. They're already halfway through their holiday.

'Penny for them?' asks Marcus as he rescues Molly and Jack from the imminent, and messy, collapse of their cones. The ice cream is rapidly melting in the afternoon sun.

'I just can't get her out of my head, Marcus. I feel like I'm going insane. She's in my mind *all* the time. The look in her eyes …'

'You mustn't let it get to you,' he reassures. 'It was years ago, you weren't to know.'

'But it does bother me. I've *got* to do something to help.' She watches a small boat pass by, the ropes on its mast flapping noisily in the wind. Then flinches as a seagull swoops low, right over their heads. Its beady eye checking out their ice creams. Marcus waves it off as Molly and Jack squeal.

'But I don't know what… what would we do if it was Molly who had gone missing?' She wipes a blob of ice cream from Jack's chin with her tissue. 'As parents I can't even begin to imagine what pain and suffering her parents have gone through.'

'Shush, don't say things like that.'

'I'm sorry, but you know what I mean. She would have been in her fifties by now. With children – even grandchildren – of her own. She was robbed of all that… and just living a normal, happy life with her family and friends. Everything we take so much for granted.'

They are soon on the ferry back to Rock, the engine chugging rhythmically in time to the gentle swell. More ever-hungry seagulls circling overhead, just in case the wake should bring any more fish to the surface. Molly and Jack, somehow, mastered walking along the narrow, wobbly boarding plank and are excited about doing it again when they disembark for a walk around the headland to Daymer Bay.

They sit in a row on a hard wooden seat along the edge of the boat. The sea breeze tangles their hair. Even with sunglasses the strength of the sun reflecting on the water makes them squint. Emily has her arm around Molly and Jack. They marvel at the windsurfers performing their acrobatic feats and look in wonder at graceful yachts, gliding across the shimmering sea.

It's a beautiful stretch of the coast, with sand dunes running immediately behind it. Just a short distance inland sits the picturesque church of St Enodoc where Sir John Betjeman is buried. Emily tells them the story of the ancient slate roofed building that nestles so snugly in its surroundings.

'Hundreds of years ago the church was virtually buried by sand, blown in from the dunes, so the locals called it Sinking Neddy,' she laughs. 'The vicar had to climb in through a hole in the roof until it was dug out again years later!'

Imagine that, what a brilliant story; you can't make something like that up. Immediately her thoughts go back to Cerys and what she saw all those years ago. It couldn't have been her imagination, could it? *You can't make something like that up.*

'Let's talk about it tonight after the kids are in bed,' Marcus whispers in her ear. He instinctively knows what she's thinking about.

'Thank you.' She squeezes his hand. 'Do you think it's all just a strange coincidence? Would the police even be interested in something a six-year-old saw such a long time ago?'

*

Later, after a simple supper and the usual Gruffalo story routine, Emily relaxes with Marcus. A sea mist is rolling in and Emily, desperate to talk about her dilemma, has moved inside.

'It's all so weird Marcus. Yesterday when I went back to the car I recognised the exact spot where it happened.'

'Why didn't you say anything?'

'I couldn't. It made me feel sick and I didn't want to spoil our day. I don't know what to do Marcus. I can't explain it; I just feel I *must* help Cerys' parents get closure.'

She takes a deep breath.

'But then I don't even know if it *would* help. Would anyone actually believe the recollections of a six-year-old child? Do *you* think it was all just my imagination? It all just keeps spinning round and round in my head.'

Emily looks at Marcus. He sits quietly, listening intently. Surely he knows her well enough to realise she isn't making this up. She knows it all sounds incredulous. It's taking over their holiday.

'OK. I'm certainly no expert in this field,' he eventually says. '...Don't laugh, but if it helps, why don't you look at it from a different point of view? You know, like a project or something?'

Emily raises her eyebrows.

'Perhaps if you consider all the "pros and cons" of what you're thinking?' he suggests, doing his supportive best.

'I'm happy to try anything Mr Senior IT Project Manager,' Emily teases, pushing him in the ribs. 'Carry on!'

'Well, there was a telephone number to ring. I didn't take any notice at the time, but I'm sure we could find it again? Then you can call. At least then you will know you have done something?' he adds encouragingly.

'What if I don't call?'

'Well, I'm not going to tell you what to do Em. Only you can decide. But, if we go home and you haven't, how are you going to feel?' he continues, his arm around her shoulders.

'I would definitely regret it,' she says, without any hesitation. 'I know that if there is even the *smallest* fraction of a chance that I can help her parents, then I must.'

'There you go then. Decision made.'

Rummaging through the recycling Emily soon finds the *Pentire Post*, a free weekly newspaper. It had been on the doormat when they arrived. The police information line is in bold on the front page, under a photo of DI Davis who is leading the reopening of the cold case. Before she can doubt her decision Emily tentatively dials the number. She takes a deep breath.

"Thank you for calling the Devon and Cornwall Police information line. You will now be prompted to answer a few questions and all responses you provide will be treated in the strictest confidence. This information line is monitored on a regular basis and we will be in touch in due course."

Damn. She had expected a real person. She sits down, preparing for the questions. Concentrating hard, so she doesn't miss anything.

"After the tone please leave your full name... beep."

'Emily Harrison.'

"Thank you. After the tone please leave your contact telephone number… beep."

Emily leaves her mobile phone number. Twice. Just to be on the safe side. She gets to her feet. She learnt years ago that you sound more confident if you stand up whilst talking on the phone, rather than sitting down or slouching.

"Thank you. After the tone please leave a brief message outlining the reason for your call and press star when you have finished… beep."

'Er… I think I may have information relating to the Cerys Morgan case in 1976. I was on holiday with my parents at the time and… um… I believe I *may* have seen her. On the day she went missing.'

Silence.

God, what else shall I say?

'Er… I've considered it very carefully, and I feel it is important I talk to someone… just in case the information I have is useful to the investigation.'

More silence.

'I… I… I know it's a long time ago but I'd really like to help if I can.' Emily carefully presses the star button on her phone. Her hands are trembling.

"Thank you for your call, it is important to us. Please note we treat all messages in the strictest confidence and will let you know if we need to get in touch to discuss further."

Then the line went dead.

MONDAY 21 JUNE 1976

'How early is early?' asks Cerys.

'The sun will rise about quarter to five so you need to be up… well, I'd say three thirty at the latest,' John replies, in a matter-of-fact sort of way.

'Personally I'd love to,' says Cerys. 'What about the rest of you? We can cook breakfast on the camping stove afterwards. It'll be a fabulous start to our holiday.'

'I'm in!' says Pip and the others agree.

Cerys is so glad they did. Still half asleep, luckily they don't have to walk far. Just to the edge of a field, where there's a low stone wall to sit on. The view is incredible, they can see for miles and miles. What an absolutely amazing sunrise. She's not sure if it is the anticipation – and excitement – of their holiday, meeting John and Richard, or just being away from home on her own for the first time. The salty, sea air makes the sunrise extra special in the way it diffuses the light. The stillness and silence of the morning takes her breath away, as the birds start to sing their dawn chorus.

Declining the girls' breakfast invitation the boys set off to work on the farm whilst the girls enjoy some tasty, but distinctly burnt, bacon and eggs. Cooking on a camping stove is definitely going to require a little more practice. Drinking the last dregs of her tea, Cerys heads off to find a phone box to call her parents. She's promised to do so every other day and her mum will be beside herself with worry if she doesn't.

'Hi Mum, it's me!' she calls down the handset, frantically pushing coins into the slot so she doesn't get cut off before she has even started.

'Hello darling, how are you?' her mum is delighted to hear from her. 'I hope you're having a great time?'

'It's brilliant, the tents stayed up all night and we got up to watch the sunrise – it was amazing. I've never seen one like it before.'

'That's because you're never up early enough,' her mum teases. 'But that does sound wonderful. Your father's listening over my shoulder and he says you really ought to see it set this evening if you can too, love. It'll be spectacular looking west from where you're staying.'

'Ooh, I hadn't thought of that. I'll have to let the others know… If we can stay awake long enough after being up so early.

'Better dash though Mum… the others will wonder where I am, and I need to save enough change for my next call. Love you lots… and Dad and Ella the dog.'

*

Smothered in baby oil to kick-start their suntans the girls work up a thirst simply lazing on the beach. The Doom Bar perched high up on Polzeath sea front is too good to miss. It's decorated like an old sailing ship, with fake portholes, ancient black and white photos and historical texts adorning the walls. So much history.

Fascinated, Cerys learns the Doom Bar is actually a notorious submerged sandbank where the River Camel meets the sea. It continuously moves and can shift so rapidly in stormy weather it has caused dozens of shipwrecks, hence the name.

Seems the most unlikely name today, Cerys thinks, as the girls sit in the sun-drenched, crowded beer garden. The main topic of conversation being what to do that evening. George the surf-dude barman introduces himself. It's so close to the campsite they are sure to come back so it will be good to get to know him. Cerys nudges Vicky as she notices his sun-bleached hair and cheeky grin, although Vicky has clearly already noticed for herself.

It's unanimous. It would simply be the best first day *ever* if they saw the sun set as well.

Back at the campsite Vicky is full of excitement as she returns from the kiosk, laden with chocolate and other treats.

'Hey, you'll never guess what,' she gasps, out of breath. 'I've just seen Richard. He says we should go to Pentire Point to watch the sunset… oh, and he and John are coming too. We're meeting them at seven thirty by the farmhouse, hope you don't mind.'

'Wow, that's brilliant. Of course we don't mind, why should we?' laughs Pip. 'Two gorgeous blokes coming with us *and* now we won't get lost either!'

'You too are unstoppable,' giggles Cerys. 'We've been here less than twenty-four hours and you're already getting your claws into the local talent.'

*

The walk to Pentire Point is strenuous. Fortunately, the brothers know the best shortcuts. Left to their own devices the girls would have zigzagged up and down, in and out, along the coastal path, making it even longer.

On reaching the headland the six of them settle down. Laying out their blankets, before adorning them with all their refreshments. A selection of Salt'n'Shake crisps, Wagon Wheels and Mint Choc Viscount biscuits plus cans of lager and cider to wash it all down.

The sun sets slowly, iridescent light shimmering across the silver blue sea. Cerys still can't believe she is actually here. It is the most beautiful warm, balmy evening. Just the occasional seagull or cormorant passing overhead, and the hypnotic rhythm of the waves crashing against the rocks far below.

'So what are you all planning to do after your holiday?' John sips cider from his can.

'Well, Cerys is the sporty one and is going to Loughborough,' explains Pip. 'Vicky is taking a gap year around Europe, I'm planning to do economics in Cardiff and Amy – the super clever one – is going to Bristol to be a vet.'

'Gosh what a mixture. I'm at Manchester,' Richard explains. 'John is in London. He graduates next year and me the year after.'

'What will you do then?' asks Cerys.

'Not sure really. Mum and Dad want us to come back to run the farm, so they can take more of a back seat, but I definitely want to see a bit more of the world first.'

'Well I guess you can do both,' says Cerys. 'It would be absolutely amazing to live somewhere like this, you're lucky to have the choice.'

'I know. I can't imagine not being near the sea. Hey, I don't know what your plans are, but how about coming to our sailing club sometime this week? What do you reckon John?'

'Great idea! We can teach you how to sail… or windsurf?' John replies. He finishes off his cider and opens another can with a loud pop.

'Oh my god, that would be amazing,' says Pip excitedly. 'Just tell us which day and we'll be there!'

Cerys is thrilled. It's only the first day of their holiday and it has already exceeded all her expectations. Leaning back on her elbows she sips her drink, watching the golden sun disappear behind the horizon.

Cerys shuts her eyes to listen to the sound of the ocean. Lost in her daydreams, she's so excited about the next two weeks. She feels something touch her arm, and goes to brush it off, thinking it's a blade of grass.

It's John. His fingers touch hers gently.

'Just checking,' he whispers, so the others won't hear. 'I thought you'd fallen asleep?'

Cerys blushes. She had been so deep in her thoughts. His hand is still resting softly on her arm.

'It was a near thing.' She giggles, trying to spare her embarrassment. 'But thank you – I don't want to miss anything.'

The walk back seems quicker despite the darkness. Cerys feels exhausted. Even their amateur tents now seem extremely inviting for a night's sleep. Tired, she stumbles on the uneven path, almost falling flat on her face.

'Whoa, steady there Cerys,' John grabs her hand.

What a gentleman. Cerys blushes again, unseen in the moonlight. She feels a wave of emotion as he brushes against her. She feels quite confused. *Perhaps it's the amazing sunset. Or maybe just the cider.*

Back at their tent Vicky is not amused.

'Why did you do that?' she glares at Cerys.

'Do what?' Cerys replies innocently.

'You know *exactly* what,' Vicky says sternly. 'You were being so, so… I don't even know what the word is… but you know what… with John!'

Cerys is dumbfounded. 'With John? I didn't do anything. He just stopped me from falling over, I didn't ask him to.'

'Yeah, well,' Vicky replies. 'You didn't exactly try to stop him either, did you?'

Cerys looks at the other two for moral support. It isn't forthcoming.

'God, you lot.' She is exasperated. 'I'm sorry. I slipped. He caught me. End of.'

'That's enough everyone,' chips in Pip. 'We'll wake up the whole campsite at this rate and it's only our first day. We've had a fantastic time and we're tired. Leave it. We've got another day of serious sunbathing on the beach tomorrow.'

Cerys knows Pip is right but it doesn't stop the aching hurt she feels.

Vicky is probably just jealous. But come hell or high water, she's not going to let her spoil their holiday.

THURSDAY 1 JULY 2010

Emily hasn't heard back from the police. It's only been a day since she called but feels much longer. The mobile phone signal isn't great where they are, so she tries to put it to the back of her mind and enjoy herself, especially as their holiday is almost over. She doesn't want to waste their last two days worrying about whether she left a sensible message or not. *They'll call you if they think you have something useful,* she keeps telling herself.

Sure enough, as they drive back to the cottage later that afternoon her phone starts to buzz. Five messages and two missed calls. A voicemail from her mum saying she hopes they're still having a lovely time. She has phoned every day and is obviously missing them. She had offered to come along, to babysit so Emily and Marcus could go out in the evenings, but they decided for this particular holiday they just wanted it to be the four of them. They would hire a larger cottage somewhere else next time.

The very last message is the one Emily has been so eagerly waiting for. She is almost too nervous to listen to it.

'Good afternoon. This is Detective Inspector Davis from Devon and Cornwall Police.' The official sounding voice introduces himself.

'Thank you for leaving your message on the information line. I am interested in talking to you further regarding the information you have relating to the Cerys Morgan case and will be available on Saturday morning. If you could please call me back, perhaps we can arrange a mutually convenient time for you to pop in to see me at Bodmin Police Station.'

Emily listens to it again in case she missed anything. Trying to concentrate as the children chatter in the back seat and Marcus curses quietly. The narrow, twisting country lanes were not designed for modern day volumes of holiday traffic. He reverses out of the way for at least two caravans to pass, getting increasingly impatient. As soon as they get back to the cottage she calls DI Davis from the terrace. They need to be out of the holiday let by ten o'clock on Saturday morning so she agrees to meet him at eleven. Marcus will drop her at the police station and then have a wander around Bodmin with Molly and Jack. They can spend their holiday pocket money. Bar a couple of minor exceptions, they've been well behaved all week and it'll be a treat for them to see what toyshops there are.

*

After spending their last day on the beach at Polzeath they go to the Ship Inn in Port Isaac to celebrate the end of their holiday. The weather has deteriorated, with a strong easterly breeze. But it didn't stop them going in the sea, determined to make the most of it.

Ben behind the bar is great with children. He keeps Molly and Jack entertained with magic tricks, just like Emily's grandfather used to. Finding pound coins behind his ear or up his sleeve. They are so enthralled; their little faces look up at him in amazement.

'So how's your week been?' Ben asks, as Molly and Jack

giggle at his latest tease, and Emily orders another round of dinks.

'Wonderful,' replies Emily. 'Just what we all needed. Lots of fresh sea air and hundreds of sandcastles.

'I used to come here as a child. Marcus booked it as a surprise for my birthday so we could bring Molly and Jack – they've loved it!' she laughs as the children, still mesmerised by Ben, watch him closely.

'It's weird though; I saw an article on TV this week about the missing girl from 1976. I was here on holiday with my parents when it happened.' Emily stops. *Why has she even mentioned it?*

'I don't remember it myself,' Ben replies. Taking a break from magic tricks, he dries some beer glasses and hangs them up above the bar. 'I was born the following year, but my dad knew about it. He worked in a bar in Polzeath at the time she went missing. It was really close to the campsite where she had been staying.'

'Gosh.' Emily tries not to look *too* interested, Ben might think it weird. 'Did he know her?'

'I've no idea; my parents never talked about it much. It had a huge impact on the locals. It was very sad that she was never found. My grandfather owned this pub then and my dad – George – took it over a few years later with his sister, Aunt Lisa.

'The Inn has been in our family for generations, but I'm still very much the apprentice in my dad's eyes.' He laughs.

Hearing Ben talk about it makes her feel more nervous about meeting DI Davis the next morning. She decides to just enjoy her glass of wine rather than push him for any more information about Cerys.

He doesn't seem to know that much.

SATURDAY 3 JULY 2010

Emily arrives early at the police station. She introduces herself to the person on reception, takes a seat and waits. Butterflies flutter in her stomach.

They had been packed and ready to leave the cottage in plenty of time. All the rooms checked, double-checked and triple-checked to make sure they didn't leave anything behind. Impatient, Emily had rushed them all out the door. She didn't want time to think. She can't get cold feet now.

Too late to make a run for it, she thinks as DI Davis appears. She recognises him from the newspaper as he greets her with a big smile and a firm handshake.

'Good morning Mrs Harrison.'

'Good morning, it's really nice to meet you,' Emily replies, trying not to appear nervous. He looks very young to be a DI.

She follows him into a simply furnished room at the back of the building. Bare walls, apart from a clock, with a square table and four upright chairs in the middle of the floor.

'I've only recently taken on this case,' DI Davis explains, in a formal but relaxed manner.

'As you already know it dates back many years. I am

currently familiarising myself with all the details from the archived records.'

He talks calmly, putting Emily at ease. Chatting a little before asking any specific questions.

'It was a long and complex case for the Devon and Cornwall Constabulary, which saw a lot of media coverage both locally and nationally.'

She can't help noticing how he moves his hands around a lot while talking.

'The force hadn't been used to such newsworthy events in North Cornwall. Back then any big, juicy stories – and even then there weren't many – would be in Exeter, Plymouth or Truro, certainly not around here by the seaside.'

He smiles at Emily as he straightens out his files on the table.

'There was huge disappointment it was never solved. The search lasted months. A number of people were interviewed, but no substantial evidence was ever found.

'So my job is to go through all the details again, as thoroughly as I can, and see what new leads there may be. There are various avenues to follow. At the moment I'm focusing on Mr and Mrs Morgan's recent TV appeal in case it has jogged someone's memory.'

Emily, still nervous, can see DI Davis is clearly doing his best to help her relax. He's obviously done this sort of thing many times before. She bites her lip; she knows she'll have to start talking soon.

'So, when you left your message and said you may have some information relating to the case, I was definitely interested in finding out more. You mentioned you were on holiday with your parents in the area. You may even have seen her on the day she went missing?' He asks inquisitively.

'What I need to ask you to do Mrs Harrison – Emily – is simply to share with me whatever it is that you can remember, in your own words.

'Please take as much time as you need. I do need to let you know, however, that I will be recording our conversation. I will also take notes, so I can refer back to these as and when necessary, should it help to progress the investigation.

'I may also ask questions as you talk, but again this is nothing for you to be worried about. It is purely to ensure I totally understand everything you tell me, and there is no ambiguity.

'Please let me know if you have any questions before we start – would you like a glass of water?' he asks kindly.

Emily accepts, and tries to relax as she takes a small sip. She has practised in her head what she is going to say, but is worried it will come out in a garbled rush. She takes three silent, deep breaths. She always does this at work before a client presentation. It usually works so fingers crossed. Composing herself she slowly starts to speak.

'It was my sixth birthday. So I know it was the exact date she went missing,' she begins. 'Likewise, I know the exact location as we – that is my parents, myself and my sister Debbie – spent the day on the beach at Lundy Bay.'

DI Davis listens intently. Emily watches as he takes longhand notes. He lets her talk without interruption.

'She was the most beautiful girl I had ever seen.' Emily continues, staring at the tabletop. 'I know I remember her because we, Debbie and I, spoke to her the day before too. She had been sat alone on the beach listening to music on a cassette player. Our dad had been telling us stories about mermaids and me, being only six, was convinced she was a real-life mermaid with her lovely long blond hair.'

She looks up at DI Davis to check he isn't looking sceptical but his expression has not changed.

'She gave me her bracelet. She'd made it herself using shells from the beach and it was so pretty. I still have it,' she adds, as if trying to convince him that her story is true.

'So when I saw her on my birthday, I knew it was her, the girl we'd met on the beach.'

Emily's mouth is dry. She takes another sip of water.

'We played hide-and-seek after a picnic lunch. Having just turned six I thought I would be big and brave and go up the steps, away from the beach, all on my own. I thought it would be harder for them to find me. I went up to the top and hid behind a big rock. That's when I saw them.'

'Saw *them*?' asks DI Davis, speaking at last. 'Was she with other people?'

'Just one other person. I couldn't see them so well – they were wearing a baseball cap and the sun was really bright – but it was definitely her, the mermaid girl. She had long, wavy golden hair. They looked like they were arguing; they were waving their arms around. Neither of them had seen me, and I suddenly felt like I shouldn't be there, so I ducked back down behind the rock again.'

DI Davis stays silent again now, not wanting to interrupt her train of thought.

'I didn't want them to notice me so I kept down, completely forgetting that Mum, Dad and Debbie would come looking for me any minute. When I looked back up they were really close to me.' Emily's eyes begin to fill with tears.

'The other person, with the cap, had their back to me... but Cerys was looking straight at me. I know she recognised me from the day before because she looked me right in the eye. I put my fingers to my lips to say "Shhh" because I didn't want her to give my hiding place away.'

Emily sighs; her heart feels so heavy when she talks about it.

'That was when she disappeared. Literally. She just vanished into thin air. We weren't by the edge of the cliff or anything, but she disappeared right before my eyes. I knew then that mermaids were truly magical. I must have screamed, as the other person spun around, just as I hid back behind the rock. Then I heard Mum shouting as she came up the path from the beach. I just sat there. Frozen.'

DI Davis pushes a box of tissues in her direction without saying a word. She carefully pulls one out.

'By the time Mum got to me the other person had walked away. It's weird now. It's as if I knew something really bad had happened, I just didn't know what.

'I told Mum about the vanishing mermaid, but she told me off for making up stories and having too much of an imagination.'

'Did you hear Cerys, or the other person, say anything?' asks DI Davis.

'Not really, their voices were muffled, by the sound of the waves and the seagulls. But they did seem to be arguing. I don't think they were shouting, it's just they seemed... I don't know... just *unhappy* somehow. I think the other person may have held her wrists at one point – like they were trying to hold her hand or something – but she didn't want to.'

'Is there anything else you can remember, maybe some distinguishing features or details about either person that may be relevant?' asks DI Davis.

Emily sips her water again. Apart from the tick of the clock the room is quiet. She tries not to swallow too loudly.

'Cerys was wearing a summery white, floaty dress and strappy sandals,' she continues. 'The other person was in T-shirt and shorts. Their T-shirt had some initials on it. Three I think. I've been trying desperately to remember what they were.'

She shuts her eyes, hoping it will help to make it clearer.

'I know it sounds daft, but I have a feeling the letters were possibly something to do with the theatre. Although I have absolutely no idea why. Some sort of logo with three big capital letters, maybe an S... or a C?'

She looks at DI Davis again. He still has the same expression. He's still making notes.

'I think they had a tattoo, or mark of some sort, on their arm too. The sun was in my eyes so it was difficult to see properly. On their forearm, below the elbow; it looked like a smiley face.' She stroked her own arm absentmindedly, to show where she meant.

'Did you see what colour hair they had?' asks DI Davis.

'As far as I could tell they had dark hair, but I could only see a little bit under their hat.'

Without smiling, or frowning, DI Davis manages to maintain a very supportive expression. Looking up at the ceiling Emily shuts her eyes again. Partly to fight back the tears, partly to help her remember. She must tell him absolutely everything; this is her chance. She imagines herself back in 1976, like a video recording playing before her. She doesn't want to get over-emotional in front of DI Davis, but she must do her utmost best. To clarify what she *felt* as much as what she saw. The mind numbing sensation that something unbelievably bad had happened right before her eyes. That she had intruded on something and she shouldn't have been there, or watching them.

'I don't think I *saw* anything else,' she realises she has screwed her tissue up into a ball. 'It's just the *feeling* I had at the time and have never forgotten. Seeing the TV appeal made it all come flooding back. The nightmares I had afterwards, night after night.

'That's why I called. Why I wanted to see you today. I can't go home knowing I might have something vital to your investigation… and which might help Cerys' parents to find out what happened to their daughter.'

Emily feels exhausted. The colour has drained from her face.

'Mrs Harrison – Emily – I am genuinely grateful for your

honesty in telling me everything. Please take some time to just relax, and think carefully in case there is anything else. However small or trivial it may seem.

'If you'd like a short break, or a cup of tea or coffee, you are very welcome. I am more than happy to wait while you consider everything,' DI Davis adds, genuinely interested in what she has to say. Genuinely concerned for her.

He gives her time to reflect, then reads his notes back to her. He confirms the location, time of day and date. He thanks her again for coming to the station and says he will review everything she has told him alongside the information from the original files.

'Do bear in mind the investigation will take some time.' He brings the discussion to a close. 'Police processes have advanced massively since 1976 and we will leave no stone unturned. However, everything you have told me will be extremely useful and, please be reassured, it will all be treated in the utmost confidence.'

There's a knock at the door.

'Please excuse me for a second.'

DI Davis stands up. Emily can see it is one of his colleagues. Mid-fifties but no uniform. Must be CID. They talk quietly and she can't help but eavesdrop, making out the odd word. Something about a serious incident in the cells the night before. Whoever it was is now comfortable and all the paperwork has been completed. Nodding of heads. Hopefully Saturday night would be quieter. Then DI Davis says her name – *Emily Harrison* – she sits up and listens even harder.

'Well, good luck with that,' the other person says, more audibly. 'I'm surprised it's being dug up again after so many years. I thought it had all been put to bed a long time ago.'

'Apologies.' DI Davis closes the door gently behind him as he returns. 'That was Dr Bob... well, Dr Trevelyan actually,' he laughs. 'Affectionately known as Dr Bob round here. He's a local GP and one of our police doctors. He's been sorting out a few things, after a busy Friday night in the cells.' He explains to justify his momentary absence.

'That's fine,' smiles Emily. 'You must be very busy.'

DI Davis shakes Emily's hand and bids her a safe journey home. He says he'll be in touch if he needs anything more.

As she leaves the station Emily feels a simultaneous sense of relief and pride. Why had she worried so much? DI Davis was so easy to talk to. She's definitely done the right thing.

As she walks through the reception, eager to meet up with Marcus and the children, the police doctor is now deep in conversation with another colleague at the front desk. He nods his head slightly to acknowledge her and she smiles back politely.

Emily is on a high. Wouldn't it be amazing if DI Davis can find out what really did happen to Cerys. And for her parents to get closure.

10
FRIDAY 9 JULY 2010

Emily can't get Cerys out of her head.

It's Friday evening. She and Marcus have been back a whole week already. Sports day and parents' evening have come and gone – they've even met Molly's new teacher for next term – and it's only days until her school breaks up for summer.

Six weeks of juggling childcare. Emily has it all meticulously planned. Hopefully they can squeeze in another short family holiday at some point. They'll take it in turns to have time off work, and Molly and Jack love staying with both sets of grandparents too. How lucky she is, they never complain about having their grandchildren or helping out.

Not a lot has changed at work in the week she has been away, although it feels considerably longer. She struggles to concentrate and keeps thinking about Cerys. The nightmares are back with a vengeance. She met with Jo her job share partner for lunch in the week, trying to be interested in everything that has been going on. But Jo got frustrated when Emily was continuously distracted. In the office it's the same. She pores over news websites for Cornwall over and over again to see if there are any updates. Perhaps DI Davis' investigation will just fizzle out and Cerys' elderly parents will be left none the wiser.

Surely there must be more she can do to help?

'You've done everything you can Em, you know that,' Marcus says to her one morning. He knows the nightmares have returned. 'DI Davis just needs time to work everything through. Like he told you he would. You need to be patient. Let him do his job.'

'I know,' she says wistfully. 'It's just that I want it to be sorted for her mum and dad. Once and for all... and for the nightmares to stop.'

'They will Em, they will,' he says reassuringly, just a hint of impatience.

But Emily isn't sure. She knows Marcus doesn't want her to worry over something she can't do any more about. It keeps cropping up. *You did the right thing Em,* he repeats again and again. *There's nothing more you can do. Leave it to the experts.* She knows he's right. *There's no point in meddling in someone else's problem.* He says. But she isn't meddling, she's helping.

Emily understands his point of view but it doesn't stop the gnawing pain inside telling her she must do something.

She owes it to Cerys.

Cerys looked her straight in the eye and didn't give her hiding place away.

Cerys gave her the beautiful handcrafted bracelet she still has in her drawer. She keeps holding it, turning the shells in her fingers. Maybe it will be a lucky charm.

She simply *must* do something to help.

Then she has a brainwave.

'So how about another sisters' weekend away Debs?' Emily talks excitedly on the phone, once Marcus is out of earshot. 'I haven't seen you for ages and you must need a break from that crazy law firm of yours. I've found a great campsite in Cornwall with the most amazing, brand new shepherd huts – you'll love them.'

'I'm up for it – sounds brilliant!' Debbie replies without

a moment's thought. 'I am a bit stressed, you're right; I could definitely do with some serious relaxation. I've got a big case looming too, so it would be better to do it sooner rather than later.'

'Leave it with me big sis. I'll book something and let you know as soon as possible.'

Twenty-four hours later it's sorted.

Richard, owner of the Atlantic View campsite, confirms they have vacancies for a long weekend, either "traditional camping" or one of their shepherd huts, brand new and available for the first time this season.

Without hesitation she books one. *Glamping at its wonderful best!* Their website says. Complete with shower room, twin beds and an open-plan kitchen-come-diner-come-sitting room. The photos look brilliant. Debbie will absolutely love it.

'Why Cornwall again?' Marcus asks, raising his eyebrows.

'Debbie chose it,' she lies, thinking on her feet. 'I'd suggested the New Forest or Cotswolds, but a friend of hers recommended it. It looked so amazing I told her I didn't mind going again so soon.'

Phew. Emily feels bad. She normally tells him everything. She can't risk him thinking she's planning anything other than a fun, relaxing weekend with her sister.

Debbie is even more excited than Emily. She will catch the train from Paddington via Bristol Parkway so Emily can join her from there.

'We won't need a car in Cornwall, and there's nothing worse than joining the hordes of holidaymakers heading to the south west on a Friday evening in the summer,' she explains.

Only two weeks to wait. Six working days makes it sound less. Perfect. Emily is desperate to get back down to Cornwall, but is pleased she also has time before then to plan her approach. That way she can make sure she does everything she possibly can to find out more about Cerys, and what happened to her, when they are there.

Emily will explain to Debbie when they're on the train. She hopes her sister won't mind a few extra-curricula activities.

11

'Aaaaaaaagh!' screams Cerys, falling into the water yet again with an enormous splash, as John and Richard take it in turns to teach them how to sail a mirror dinghy. 'That's it – I've had enough. I'm going to stick to sunbathing from now on.'

'Don't be such a drama queen,' laughs Pip. 'That's my job!'

'You just need to keep an eye on where you're going more,' suggests John. 'Don't make such jerky movements, otherwise you make it unstable.'

'I think she'd be better suited to one of those,' Vicky points at some stunning yachts. 'With her own personal crew and a butler for serving drinks.'

'Now you're talking,' giggles Cerys. 'That sounds ideal.'

They are at Rock Sailing Club. Richard and John invited them the previous evening as they polished off two packs of Babycham, sitting on the grass beside their tents. It had seemed a good idea to Cerys at the time. Terra firma now seems far more appealing.

All four girls are settling into life on the campsite. Hot, sunny days on the beach – smothered in baby oil to enhance their suntans – followed by warm, balmy evenings.

They check the latest offers in the charming little grocery

store in Polzeath every afternoon, conscious of making their money last. They've found some excellent bargains, just before it closes, for food near its use by date. Or beyond in some cases. Then have fun cooking it on the camping stove. Although "heating up" or "warming through" is probably more accurate. With the exception of some wonderful local, free range eggs that got well and truly scrambled. It doesn't matter to the girls; with so much fresh air and swimming everything tastes completely delicious, washed down with something alcoholic.

Cerys is soaked.

'Look at you,' says John, tipping his head back in laughter. 'You need to dry out. How about I drop you back to the jetty and then Vicky can have a go?'

'Yes please!' Cerys doesn't want to sound ungrateful for their hospitality but is desperate to get back to dry land. She can also see Vicky is eager to have another go and the opportunity to spend more time on her own with John on the boat.

'We've been so lucky,' Amy sips a cold drink as she and Cerys watch from the terrace in the sailing club bar. Pip and Vicky are doing well, manoeuvring the small boats under the careful tutorship of Richard and John.

'I know,' smiles Cerys. 'Who would've thought we'd be living it up at a yacht club on day three ... and with two good looking guys.'

'Do you fancy John?' Amy asks. 'You seem quite taken by him?'

'I wouldn't say I *fancy* him, but he is very nice... and he and Richard have been so welcoming to all of us.' Cerys avoids giving a straight answer. She's struggling to understand her own feelings, let alone explain them to someone else.

'I'd be careful if I were you Cerys,' Amy continues. 'We know each other well enough to talk about these things ... just beware. I think Vicky is incredibly jealous. I may be wrong but

I think she *really* fancies him. She's watching you both like a hawk all the time.'

'Really?' Cerys looks at her open mouthed. 'Are you sure?'

'C'mon Cerys, surely you've noticed? It's *so* obvious. I think he likes you. If I were you I'd give her – and him – a bit of space. It would make Vicky so happy if he did fancy her… and you do have Phil at home.'

Cerys tries not to react to her last comment. What exactly does she mean? She hasn't done anything? She bites her tongue, watching Vicky sail the boat with John. She can see Amy is right. Vicky is trying so hard to make a good impression. She can't take her eyes off him.

*

'Wow, thanks.' Richard takes his pint when they eventually rejoin them. 'Just what I need after a hard day's sailing. It's thirsty work teaching you girls.'

'Only because you've been shouting instructions at us all day!' laughs Pip.

'Cheers everyone!' John clinks glasses with everyone. 'Here's to another sunny day tomorrow – we'll make sailors of you all yet.'

What a perfect way to round off the day, Cerys thinks, as the last of the boats make it back to their moorings. Recounting all the escapades of the day and comparing capsizes and near misses, John presents Vicky with a beer mat as her prize for being "star pupil" of the day. Cerys knows he's only joking, but Vicky is chuffed to bits.

*

They meet at the Doom Bar again that evening. After a feast of spam fritters and spaghetti hoops followed by a large slice of arctic roll. The dessert was a too-good-to-miss bargain. It tasted like summer on a plate, washed down with Martini Bianco and lemonade, despite being thawed beyond all recognition in the heat of the tent. Not particularly nutritious it hit the spot and would tide them over until breakfast. And, even if it didn't, they have salt and vinegar flavour Chipsticks and orange Club biscuits stashed away for emergency purposes.

'Hi Mum,' Cerys calls home again on her way to the pub. 'It's me!'

'Hi Cerys,' her mum always sounds so pleased to hear her voice. 'How are you love?'

'I'm fine Mum, we're having such good fun.' She gushes, one hand holding the handset, the other waving around the call box. 'You'll never guess but we've been sailing today with some boys we met at the campsite and it was brilliant… although I was rubbish.

'We've just had supper and we're going down to the pub in Polzeath for a bit.'

'Gosh, you're packing a lot in,' her mum replies. 'Phil was here earlier but he's just left. I'll tell him you've phoned.'

'Aw, thanks Mum, I'll call him tomorrow. We've been so busy I haven't had a chance yet. Must go though, the others will be waiting for me. Speak soon, love you lots.'

By the time Cerys joins the others the Doom Bar is bursting at the seams. The chatter and background music is deafening after her peaceful stroll through the farm and down the lane. George the barman is rushing around madly but appears to have two helpers tonight.

The brothers buy them all bottles of local Spingo Ale, brewed in Helston. A lovely sweet tasting beer. So the label says. Originally made to welcome the men home from the First World War.

Probably doesn't mix too well with the earlier Martinis, thinks Cerys. But it quenches her thirst, and drinking pints saves having to queue again too soon. George manages to chat whenever he can as he collects tray upon tray of empty glasses.

'So, have you set a date yet George?' asks Richard.

'October mate, before Sue's too far gone, and still trying to save up – that's why I'm working all hours in here. No rest for the wicked!' He laughs.

'Bit sooner than either of us planned to be honest but these things happen. Sue's really excited about the baby now… I am too, just takes a bit of getting used to,' he adds, as if trying to convince himself.

Cerys thinks George is great fun. He knows Richard and John from school and is a typical beach loving surf-dude, with a golden tan and sun kissed blond hair. Shoulder length and unkempt in a fashionable way. Even though he's hopelessly handsome he isn't pretentious or full of himself. If anything he's the opposite. He uses his role as barman to give him confidence to talk to people he wouldn't otherwise have the courage to chat to.

The girls are the last to leave. The starlit sky adds to the atmosphere as they wander back to the campsite. Vicky is openly flirting with John. The Spingo has given her extra courage. Cerys, fuzzy headed herself, is mindful of her earlier chat with Amy and is discreetly watching. She can see John isn't interested. His body language says it all. Poor Vicky is too smitten to realise.

They fumble helplessly as they negotiate their way back to their corner of the campsite. Unfortunately in one tent someone is snoring for the Guinness Book of Records and, despite trying to be as quiet as possible and suppress their giggles, they simply can't. They stagger the rest of the way trying not to fall over any tent pegs or ropes but can barely see where they're going through tears of laughter.

'Looks like you've had a good evening,' the twins' dad remarks. He and his wife are having their usual nightcap now the boys are asleep. They don't seem to mind the girls enjoying themselves at all; Cerys thinks they find them a source of entertainment.

The middle-aged couple on the other side are quietly amused, they do their usual tut-tutting, as they sip hot chocolate in their posh porch. Cerys has decided they're not actually married at all and are having a raunchy, clandestine affair where no one knows them. So, to liven things up a bit and make them more interesting the girls now call them the Loveshack Smythes.

*

The following morning the girls are late rising. The warmth of the sun bursting through the canvas and the clatter of other campers making breakfast eventually wakes them up.

Cerys is tired and grouchy. She hasn't slept well. The tent is incredibly hot and sticky, plus her head is still spinning from the previous night's alcohol. And her confused thoughts of John and Phil. None of the girls are in a hurry to get up, so she heads off for a shower to wake herself up. She isn't used to drinking so much but doesn't want the others to know she is feeling a bit jaded, to put it mildly.

She has the bathroom block all to herself and treats herself to a blissfully long shower. The campsite generously provides towels for guests to use. As no one else is around she greedily uses two; one to dry her body and the other to wrap around her hair, in a big twist on top of her head.

She can see her skin is starting to tan and has a healthy glow. It makes her feel good as she looks in the mirror. She does a few different poses just to check what she looks like, to make sure she hasn't put on any weight. She'd read in her *Jackie* magazine that beer has loads of calories and she'd drunk far too much Spingo. She rubs her hair dry; it is so much easier in the summer when she lets it dry naturally. Knowing she is alone Cerys stands naked for a while to let her body "air dry". She hates getting dressed with that immediate post shower dampness. She feels so refreshed as her skin cools down.

Something startles her. A reflection in the mirror. Not hers. She screams so loudly she thinks the whole campsite will have heard. Her heart is thumping. It's the twin boys' dad. She scrabbles around clumsily with her towel to cover her nakedness, as he stands staring at her, for what seems like an eternity. She is paralysed with fright.

'I'm so sorry,' he smirks, not giving the impression he is genuinely sorry at all. 'I didn't mean to startle you… I… I… um… I just wanted to check you were OK. You've been in here for ages… but it certainly looks like you are,' he adds, still leering at her, as he scuttles out.

Cerys is shaking. He has seriously freaked her out. What in heaven's name was he doing there, why was he looking at her so weirdly and how long had he actually been watching her? He must have seen her stark naked. He was looking at her with a horrible, lopsided expression.

It makes her feel sick. She quickly pulls on her shorts and T-shirt and stands, trembling, with both hands leaning on the basin to calm herself down.

Cerys doesn't know how long she is there, her hands gripping tight, when two women she vaguely recognises arrive. They smile and say good morning, but are too busy gossiping to notice how shaken up she is. She doesn't mind. Just their presence is enough for her to muster the courage to gather up her toiletries and walk slowly back to her tent.

'Hello stranger,' Amy says when she gets back. 'We were about to send a search party. Where have you been? Your cup of tea is getting cold.'

Cerys doesn't know whether to laugh or cry. She is so relieved to see them her eyes well up with tears.

'Oh my god. Oh my god... You won't guess what just happened.' She garbles as she ushers them to the back of their tents, away from the twins and their family.

'The twins' dad was spying on me in the shower. I was getting dressed and there he was. Staring at me. He must have been there for absolutely ages... I was completely naked. Nothing on except a towel on my head.' She shivers, as she realises what she is saying.

'Bloody hell, that's awful.' Pip hugs her with both arms as Cerys starts to cry on her shoulder. 'I knew there was something weird about him right from the start. The way he was watching us putting up the tents, now we know!'

'Shush,' says Cerys through her sobs. 'He'll hear you. He said he wanted to check I was OK because I had been in there so long. He must have seen me go in and was waiting.

'Oh my god, I don't know what to do, it's really freaked me out,' she wails.

'My mum said to look out for campsite weirdos,' says Amy, giving Cerys another reassuring hug. 'She was right. Are you sure you're OK? Did anyone else see him?'

'I don't think so, two ladies came in but he had gone by then.'

'Well, we'll just have to make sure we go to the bathroom in pairs from now on,' says Amy. '... And keep an eye out for the Campsite Creep in case he tries anything else.'

12
JULY 2010

Since booking their sisters' weekend away time has dragged unbelievably slowly. Emily can't wait to go back to Cornwall. She's undertaken hours and hours of research. Making the most of a lull in her workload, with so many colleagues away on their summer holidays. She is spending every moment she can in the office to search online, to make sure Marcus doesn't know.

She is convinced Richard – the owner of the campsite – will be able to help. She has studied their website so many times they're probably wondering why the farm is suddenly getting so many hits. It has been in his family for at least two generations and the campsite was established in the late 1960s. Looking at the photo gallery he must be in his fifties. Plus news archives she has found about the Cerys Morgan case mention the campsite owners Donald and Beryl Trevelyan and their two sons so, by her powers of deduction, he *must* be one of them.

Emily meets Debbie at Bristol Parkway as planned. Sharing a bottle of wine they don't realise it is the same train journey Cerys and her friends made all those years ago.

'It's weird being back here,' says Debbie. 'Seeing all the

signposts to Chipping Sodbury – or Sodding Chippery as Dad used to call it – and Wickwar.'

'I guess so for you,' replies Emily. 'I drive past them every day. I still love Wickwar though … I work with some of the people we went to primary school with, although we all look a bit older now.

'I especially love the Holy Trinity church perched at the top of the hill in the village, where Marcus and I got married. Do you realise it'll be fifteen years in September? Where has that gone?'

'God, that's amazing. It's so lovely to see you again Em, we must do this more often.'

The train, packed with passengers, glides along the tracks parallel to the stop-start traffic on the motorway as they drink their wine. Emily knows they made the right decision.

'I hope you don't mind Debs, but I've got a dilemma I need to talk to you about.' Emily wants to make good use of all the time they have en route to bring Debbie up to speed.

'You know I was in Cornwall with Marcus and the kids for my birthday,' she continues. '… Well, I sort of got caught up in something that I can't stop thinking about.'

'Wow, you've got me intrigued,' Debbie laughs, taking another large swig of wine. 'Tell me more.'

'Do you remember the story of the mermaid Dad told us about, and then the beautiful girl we met, when we were on holiday in Cornwall all those years ago?'

'God, yes, of course I do. You *completely* believed him and thought she was a real mermaid!' giggles Debbie. 'Absolutely nothing was going to convince you otherwise. Mum kept telling Dad off for filling your head with rubbish.'

'I know. But do you remember the shell bracelet she gave me?' Emily can see Debbie nodding in fascination. 'Well, I've still got it so she was definitely a real person.'

'OK, the *girl* may have been real but she wasn't a real

mermaid.' Debbie laughs. 'But, anyway, how does that fit in with your birthday trip with Marcus and what's the dilemma?'

'Well, the day after you and I spoke to the mermaid girl, it was my birthday – do you remember… we played hide-and-seek on that same beach? When it was my turn I thought I was really brave and went up to the top of the steps and hid behind a rock, thinking you would never find me.'

'Oh my god – you did. Mum and Dad were so worried about where you were.'

'That's when I saw her again. She was with someone; they looked like they were arguing. She was there right in front of me Debs as I hid… and she looked straight at me.' Emily looks plaintively at Debbie, scared she won't believe her. 'It was definitely her Deb, honest… and she looked straight at me. I put my fingers to my lips to say "shhh" so she wouldn't give my hiding place away.

'I didn't know what to do. I knew one of you would soon come looking for me, so I ducked down… then, when I looked back up again she was gone.'

'What do you mean she was gone?' asks Debbie, eyes open wide.

'Exactly that. She had completely vanished before my very eyes. Completely. Vanished.' Emily gets more animated the more wine she drinks.

'I remember telling Mum and Dad about it but they wouldn't believe me. Mum just said I had too much imagination. I had nightmares for ages afterwards,' Emily sighs.

'Oh my goodness, Em, I do remember that, but I had no idea that was what they were about… So how is this linked to your holiday a few weeks ago?'

'We were watching the local TV news. An elderly couple from Pembrokeshire were asking for anyone who had any information about their daughter to come forward.

'Their daughter had gone missing thirty-four years ago

– *on the very same day as my 6th birthday,*' Emily lowers her voice as it starts to waver. 'But she was never, ever found. No one has ever been charged with abducting or murdering her… or anything. Nothing. Her poor parents never found out what happened.

'And then they showed a photo. I knew straight away it was her.'

Emily's eyes fill with tears. She looks out the window and blinks hard, in a vain attempt to stop them.

'Oh Deb, I promise you it was her. It really was her. The mermaid girl we spoke to on the beach, who gave me the bracelet.'

'Hey, Em, don't get upset, it was a long time ago.' Debbie holds her hand, trying to calm her.

'After going over and over it in my head – and talking to Marcus – I called the police helpline. I went to the police station and spoke to the DI on the morning we came home.'

Emily inhales slowly, still fighting her tears. 'He was so nice. He explained how the case has been reopened and they are hoping the TV appeal might jog someone's memory. Give them some new leads. So I told him everything I could remember.'

'Wow Em, that's amazing,' says Debbie giving her a kiss on the cheek. 'Good for you. You never know, the things you told him may be just what they need to find out what really happened. I remember talking to the girl on the beach but I honestly can't remember anything about her going missing.'

'I think it only made it into the newspapers after we returned home,' Emily continues. 'I remember seeing a headline, I think it was at a garage, when Dad was filling up with petrol. But that's about it. Although I do remember Dad getting short tempered when I mentioned the mermaid girl that had vanished. Maybe they *did* know about it but just didn't want us to.

'The thing is Deb, since I went to see DI Davis, the nightmares have come back. I can't get the mermaid girl out of my mind.'

Emily pauses briefly.

'That's why I wanted to come back down and see what I can do to solve the mystery myself. Marcus has made it clear he doesn't want me to, he's really happy I went to the police, but doesn't want me doing any more.

'I totally understand why he feels like that, but I just need to do something… Deb, do you understand?' Emily looks for affirmation.

'God Em. What a story, I most certainly do. But I have to be honest, I do get Marcus' point of view too. It's only because he cares for you silly, and it's such a tragic story.'

Debbie smiles at her kindly and squeezes her hand.

'Look, if it helps, I'll do what I can to help you this weekend. Then you can go back home, knowing you've done your bit, and get back to normal. Three days should be more than enough for us to see what we can do. I can use my lawyer skills too if needed.'

'Aw, Debs, you're an absolute star. The best ever big, old sis.'

'Less of the big – or old for that matter,' Debbie giggles. 'I'm only two years your senior!'

'… I thought if we did our "research" in the mornings – we could go to the library for starters – and then sunbathe in the afternoons?' Emily isn't letting up. '… And then just chill out in the evenings over a nice meal and glass of wine or two somewhere. What do you reckon?'

'It doesn't sound as if I have a choice,' laughs Debbie. 'That's so like you, little Miss Organised. Now I know why you were so dead set on coming here, you had it planned out all along.

'Seriously though, of course I don't mind. It all sounds rather fascinating. If I can help in any way I will, as long as we still do all the other sisters' stuff too … and make sure we have another glass of vino right this minute.'

'Deal!' says Emily, as she tops up her sister's glass and gives her a high five.

13

'So what have you found out so far?' Debbie looks back at Emily.

They've both been silent. Staring out the window for a few minutes.

'Knowing you, like I do, I'm sure you've already done lots of research and you may as well bring me up to speed before we get there.'

'I may have done some,' Emily laughs, she's never been able to get much past her sister.

'I've studied all the old newspapers I can find online. The best reports have been in *The Western Morning News*. They ran with the story on the front page for weeks, until the police decided there were no new leads to follow up.

'It was the year of the amazing heatwave – do you remember the standpipes we had for a while?' Emily reminisces. 'I found so many other interesting stories too. The parched reservoir at Burrator in Devon, which began to expose the drowned dwellings. They hadn't been seen for almost eighty years since the dam was constructed. It even said the church bells started ringing again. It was amazing – although I'm not sure that bit was true.'

She glances at her sister again, making sure she's still interested.

'... About Cerys though, a few people were taken in for questioning, but they were all subsequently released without charge. The search took place day-in-day-out for weeks.

'She – Cerys – had been camping with three friends Amy, Vicky and Pip. They all gave witness statements, as did the campsite owners Donald and Beryl and four local lads, including Donald and Beryl's two boys Richard and John.'

Emily laughs.

'I hope you're taking this in!'

'Oh yes, trust me Inspector Morse,' Debbie nods her head. 'I'm all ears. This is truly fascinating, you've obviously been *very* busy at work recently!'

'... Well, the other two lads were a chap called George Pengelly, who was a barman who worked at the Doom Bar in Polzeath, and his best mate Barry Hammett a mechanic. Apparently the four of them went to a barn dance with the girls the week before Cerys went missing. They had got to know them well.'

Emily is in full flow.

'I worked through the papers in date order. There was so much speculation about what happened, or who did it; some of it was really grisly. Various people were questioned but later editions reported they all had strong alibis. Then, as her body was never found – or any specific evidence – the police were never in a position to make an arrest.'

Emily's research is correct. Hundreds of local residents joined the search party. They were devastated. That a young, innocent girl should come to their beautiful part of the world to meet such a dreadful fate. There were all sorts of theories. They varied hugely from one day to the next. Firstly she had been abducted or murdered, dismembered and buried in the campsite. Another, that she decided of her own free will, to disappear and start a new life somewhere else. A third claimed that one of the other girls had accidentally killed her after drinking too much, or all three had ganged up on her for some reason and it had all got out of hand. All the variations seemed equally incredulous. However, as no body was ever found what really happened is anyone's guess.

Police divers checked the coastline daily. They know the local tides and currents and where bodies get washed up, generally within a week or two of falling in the water. But with no body the disappearance of Cerys Morgan became increasingly mysterious as each week passed.

Just as Debbie thinks Emily has finished she starts again.

'There was one thing I found. A few weeks into the search her wristwatch was found, in a grass verge near a phone box in Polzeath. She had been using it to call home every other day. Various newspaper stories speculated about how and when she had mislaid it, but the last call her parents received was on the afternoon of Sunday 27 June. Two days before she went missing – so I think the police assumed she dropped it then.'

'God, Em, I can't believe all this was happening when we were there with Mum and Dad, and we had no idea,' Debbie says quietly, trying to take it all in.

'I know, it makes you feel funny inside doesn't it.' Emily shudders. 'Apparently that day she told them she was really enjoying herself, so there was no reason for them to be concerned. But what if she *had* gone two days later Deb, for her regular call, and for one reason or another not been able to get to the phone? Maybe that's something we need to look into?' Emily looks at her sister to check she's keeping up.

'Plus I really want to talk to Richard at the campsite to see what he knows too. I reckon he *must* be the son of Donald and Beryl, the owners at the time. I just have a gut feeling he knows something. Perhaps we can catch him on Sunday morning after we've been to the library on Saturday.'

Emily waves her arms around enthusiastically, but senses it is now time to shut up.

Debbie, initially interested, looks overwhelmed. Emily doesn't want her to think she tricked her into coming down purely for her own selfish reasons.

*

Finally they make it to Bodmin Parkway and are relieved to stretch their legs. The row of waiting taxis is a welcome sight and they jump in one, before anyone else can grab it.

'Michael!' The cheery taxi driver introduces himself, as he swiftly puts their luggage in the boot and jumps into the driver's seat. 'So what brings you two lovely ladies down to these parts?'

'Hi Michael, I'm Emily and this is my lovely sister Debbie. We're down for a weekend of fun, sun and relaxation,' replies Emily.

' ... And lots of Prosecco!' laughs Debbie.

'You and half the population of the UK,' he replies. 'It's certainly the best place in the world to do all that. I've lived here all my life and wouldn't ever move anywhere else.'

'We're going to do a bit of detective work too,' chips in Emily, although she really isn't sure why she is telling him. It must be the wine.

'I heard recently about the girl who went missing back in 1976 and who was never found. Debbie and I were both here on holiday with our parents back then, the very week it happened.'

Debbie rolls her eyes at Emily, but it is too late.

'Well, love, I was a teenager back then but I remember it all happening as clear as day.'

Michael looks left and right as he pulls out at a junction. 'I lived here in Bodmin, a few miles away, but hundreds of locals helped with the search. It was in the news for months and months.'

The rest of the short drive is spent in silence until they pull up at the farm entrance. Michael hands Emily one of his business cards ready for their trip back.

'Cornish Fairways!' He jokes with the same huge grin. 'Proud of that. Me and the wife took ages to come up with a name for our business. We do a lot of work with the local hotels that specialise in golf tours. We ferry golfers here, there and everywhere.

'It was going to be British Fairways or even f-a-r-e-ways at one point,' he continues, spelling out the word letter by letter.

'But we thought people might get us confused with British Airways, and we didn't want them suing us or anything.'

Highly unlikely. Emily winks at Debbie the lawyer as he carries on chuckling at the story he no doubt tells all his passengers every day.

'Word of warning, though, about the missing girl – don't go fishing too deep,' he says in a hushed voice. 'I wouldn't be surprised if there's folk round here who do know what happened and have kept quiet. There was a lot of speculation at one time, you know, that there may have been a cover up.'

Emily glances at Debbie, she is sure he nodded his head, just slightly, towards the farm sign. She wonders if her sister noticed too. Then he stops talking, to check the boot is locked.

'Mark my words love, just be careful. You probably don't want to go poking your nose in where it's not wanted.'

14

THURSDAY 24 JUNE 1976

Cerys, Amy, Pip and Vicky are having a crazy but fun afternoon trying on all their new clothes and make up. They've been invited to a Young Farmers Barn Dance and have already spent at least two hours getting dressed. Their excitement and enthusiasm steadily increasing, in direct proportion to the amount of Dubonnet and lemonade they drink.

John's driving. He and Richard have to be up early tomorrow, but George has a night off, so he and his best mate Barry are also coming. George's fiancée was going to join them, but is still suffering badly with morning sickness. She's decided dancing a hoe down in her condition is probably not the best idea.

The annual dance raises much-needed funds for numerous local charities. The brothers know the farmer who organises it, and his family, well. Tickets are an incredible £1 including a free drink on arrival *and* a barbecue. *Amazing value plus we don't have to cook on the camping stove, an extra bonus!*

It's another gloriously sunny day and promises to be a warm, balmy evening; just perfect for dancing under the stars. The girls look stunning in their shorts and hot pants. The marquee will be so humid the thought of denim jeans makes them wilt. Miraculously they have had the bathroom block to themselves all afternoon. They have tried on every possible permutation of their wardrobe to decide what – or what *not* – to wear.

'Make sure we keep an eye out for the Campsite Creep,' laughs Cerys, trying to make light of the incident earlier in the day.

'Yeah, he may be lurking outside watching us,' Vicky pretends to look outside.

'Don't make fun of it you guys, it seriously freaked me out!'

'God, he wouldn't know what to do with himself, if he was out there watching all four of us getting undressed.' Pip pulls a face of pure disgust. 'I wonder if his wife knows what he does when she isn't looking?'

'Ooooh don't say that, you'll spoil the fun of getting ready!' Amy pretends to slap her on the head. 'Anyway, I need a top up, who's got the bottle?'

'Sounds like a very good idea to me,' Cerys tops up all their glasses. 'What do you think of this combination by the way?'

After much deliberation Cerys is wearing her navy hot pants with a multicoloured, silky blouse tied at the side.

'Wow, you look absolutely fabulous Cerys!' Pip is right, Cerys looks radiant.

'You do too,' replies Cerys, blushing. 'I just love your hair like that and that top is so trendy, I love it – I might have to borrow it!'

Pip does look stunning, her shiny red hair flicked up at the sides in a Farrah Fawcett-Majors type of style set off beautifully by a pale green cheesecloth top that she had rolled up and tied in a knot under her ribs. All the craze and which shows off her tiny waist teamed with her denim shorts and wedge sandals.

'Hey, you two, what's this? The Cerys and Pip mutual appreciation society?' giggles Vicky. 'What about me and Amy, don't we look good too?'

'You most certainly do, we'll have to make sure we get a photo of us all together later,' says Cerys. 'I'm sure the boys will take one for us.'

Vicky has a strappy, ruched cerise pink top with faded denim shorts that are a little frayed around the edges. The nautical headscarf tied under her dark hair really suits her. Amy is in bright red hot pants with a linen, wrap around top. The four girls look like they have stepped out of a *Vogue* magazine.

*

Avalon Farm is a quintessential, sprawling Cornish homestead. It nestles into the surrounding landscape perfectly. Built out of local stone, with an undulating slate roof, the idyllic scene this evening has no doubt experienced many storms over the centuries.

Cerys wanders around the huge marquee, enjoying her free welcome drink. A delicious, fruity punch. She watches the ever-growing crowd of people, glad they got there in plenty of time. She loves the colourful bunting interlaced with fairy lights. The overall effect is magical. She sips her punch and gazes up at the patterns. It's like standing inside a giant kaleidoscope.

Hay bales double up as tables and chairs. Cerys jumps as the band suddenly start warming up. Ear bashing, off-key, squawky notes while they tune their instruments. They'll be starting soon. She'd better get back to the others before she loses them in the hordes of people.

George and Barry have arrived and are enjoying their free drinks. They're already deep in conversation and laughing with the others. Feeling thirsty and devious Cerys sneaks back to the bar to wangle another glass of punch. The bartender gives her a doubtful look, but she flutters her eyelashes just enough to convince him she's only just arrived. She's looking forward to meeting George properly, away from the Doom Bar. It's great to see him enjoying himself as one of the gang rather than rushing around sorting out orders and clearing glasses for other people.

The compère, clad in a summery Hawaiian shirt with a bright, tropical fruit print, taps the microphone. It pops and crackles. Echoing off the canvas walls.

'Good Evening ladies and gentlemen!' Another tap and crackle. 'Welcome once again to the wonderful Avalon Farm; please collect your drinks and be ready for dancing in five minutes.'

He's gone as quickly as he started, and the background hubbub of noise once again takes over.

As Cerys watches John her heart misses a beat. She's so confused. She can't help being really attracted to him, even though she's trying so hard not to be. She just wants to enjoy herself, to be friendly with him. Nothing more. She has Phil at home, she loves him. But each time she sees John her heart does another little skip. She has to admit she really likes the feeling.

Just relax, she tells herself. *Have a good time, dance and enjoy the music.*

'... So this is Barry my best mate... and this is Vicky, Pip, Amy and Cerys.' George, introducing them all, feels pleased with himself for getting their names right. They give him a round of applause and he takes a mock bow. Cerys can see the remnants of engine grease under Barry's fingernails.

They're chalk and cheese. George the sun tanned, blue eyed, blond surfer and Barry the olive skinned, dark haired footballer with hazel brown eyes and exquisite cheekbones.

How come all the men are so drop dead handsome around here?

She can see Vicky is in heaven. But the fact they are with

four very attractive young men isn't lost on Amy, or Pip, either.

Curnow Ceilidh are brilliant. Their caller leads the steps so anyone – and everyone – can follow the dances whether or not they have done them before. Young and old all join in. Cerys loves it. It doesn't matter that she has no sense of rhythm whatsoever. She just follows the instructions, trying her best not to go the wrong way, or knock anyone over.

The beat of the music and the thump of feet on the ground pulsate through her body. She feels pleasantly giddy as she tries to follow what the caller is saying. And to remember her left from her right, clockwise from anti-clockwise. Aided by several glasses of punch she throws herself into all the spins and turns, as she and the other girls move up and down the rows of dancers. A Barley Reel, Cornish Six Hand Reel, The Oak Tree, The Ploughboy. The uneven ground makes her wish she'd worn flatter shoes. She'll twist her ankle if she's not careful. It's great fun, the eight of them make a perfect group for dancing, and Cerys loves mixing with them all including Barry. He's friendly and chatty like George and has a great sense of humour.

Cerys' head spins. The deliciousness of the punch and the rotation of the dances make her giddy. The music is so inviting. She do-si-dos, elbow swings and promenades with her partner, up and down the marquee, under and over the other couples. Her skin is tingling where she has caught the sun on her back and arms earlier in the day. She is glad she wore a floaty blouse. The silky material feels really soft and gentle, soothing her skin.

As the first part of the evening concludes they all clap and cheer, the delicious aroma of the barbecue now wafting through the marquee. Cerys feels a hand on her back. A tiny, gentle but deliberate caress. Soft and tender through her flimsy blouse. She turns to see who it is but they pull away.

George. Barry. John. Richard. They're all close, or was it just an innocent passer by, pushing their way to the bar? It is so crowded she can't be sure.

But she is sure about something else. Vicky's look of pure venom.

15

'We've got four brand new shepherd huts each named after a Cornish village, yours is Porthleven,' Liz hands over the keys. 'Make yourselves at home, and if there is anything you need just give me or Richard a shout.'

'Wow, this is brilliant. Thank you,' says Emily. 'It's even better than the photos. My two kids Molly and Jack would love this, they'll be so envious when I tell them.'

'Well, I hope you both have a lovely weekend – make sure you pop in to see us before you go.' Liz disappears to deal with the next arrivals.

Emily and Debbie are blown away. There is even a welcome card in the hut, balanced on a small wicker basket full of groceries and two complimentary postcards. Plus local milk, eggs, cheese and butter in the fridge.

How thoughtful is that. Soft close drawers and cupboards too.

The girls quickly unpack what few clothes they have brought and hang them up, so they won't be too crumpled. Everything has been thought of in the hut. There are little cubbyholes and storage spaces for everything, even shelves for toiletries and toothbrushes in the compact and bijou bathroom. What an absolutely heavenly place.

Emily and Debbie are up bright and early on Saturday, despite polishing off a further bottle of Prosecco the night before. They have breakfast outside, on a small rustic wooden table and chairs with co-ordinated cushions. Each shepherd hut has a private, decked area at the bottom of the steps that lead down from the stable door.

Emily has already called Marcus. He and the children are in a rush to go swimming, get back for a picnic lunch in the garden, and then take Molly to her friend's birthday party in the afternoon. Typical weekend. Molly and Jack have a far more varied social life than she ever did at their age. It's a non-stop whirl of swimming, ten-pin bowling, dancing, parties, nail painting, face painting and sleepovers. You name it. But they're happy and not missing her at the moment, which is good. It means she can relax with Debbie, without feeling guilty about leaving them.

They have a bowl of sugary cereal – topped with sliced banana to convince themselves it's healthy – and two cups of strong coffee, then collect their hire bikes and set off to the library. They cycle three meandering miles to Rock, along narrow lanes, and time it perfectly – more by luck than judgement – as the ferry is just boarding. They hop straight on, and are halfway across the estuary to Padstow within minutes. From there they head down the Camel Trail to Wadebridge. The converted railway line is flat and fun to ride after the winding lanes playing dodge the caravan. When they head back later they can always stop in Rock, Daymer Bay or Polzeath depending on how their legs are holding up.

The library is a gem of a place. Immaculately tidy. Two storeys packed with an amazing array of books, six computers for visitors to use and a range of daily newspapers. If Emily wasn't so intent on her "research" she would love to just browse. But it shuts at one o'clock on Saturday, which means they have a maximum two hours to see what they can find.

The librarian gladly retrieves what boxes there are from 1976, albeit not much. She explains most of it is now online, but they are welcome to look through what is available. They don't say what they are specifically looking for, nor has the lady been particularly interested in quizzing them about their motives. She is just happy to be of assistance and continues serving other visitors behind her desk.

Emily and Debbie settle down at one of the wooden tables.

'Let me know if you find anything,' Emily whispers. She is keen to jot down any notes that may be useful and is really excited about what new information they will find.

Two frustrating hours later the librarian walks a lap of the building to let everyone know there are only ten minutes left. They haven't completely wasted their time. They enjoyed thumbing through all the old newspapers, and confirmed facts Emily has already found, but no new or important details have come to light.

Emily cannot disguise her disappointment. Debbie reassures her that so much is online it is hardly surprising she has already gathered all the critical information. Also, if there had been anything vital – that was so readily available – the case would no doubt have been solved many years ago.

Emily reluctantly agrees. She knows Debbie is right. But the more articles she reads the more curious she becomes. What exactly did Cerys and her friends do each day of their holiday, and who did they become friendly with? There simply must be some other people, who met the girls and got to know them during their trip. She was determined to see what else she could find out.

Relieved to see their bicycles still chained up where they left them they start their return trip, along the cycle trail, towards Padstow. They grab the opportunity for a delicious crab sandwich on the harbour, watching the boats sailing in and out, before catching the ferry back to Rock.

It's such a fabulous place to just sit, relax and watch the world go by. There are holidaymakers, like ants, exploring all the little streets and alleyways. Fishermen sort their catch with raucous seagulls continually circling above them. Day cruisers sail up and down the estuary, with passengers armed with binoculars, hoping to spot a seal or two. They could spend all afternoon on the quayside, but agree it's best to catch the ferry back sooner rather than later. If they miss the last ferry it's a long way to cycle back. They would have to return to Wadebridge first and then go north along the country road towards Polzeath. Even thinking about the prospect makes their legs ache.

Rock is busy too, different in character to Padstow. Trendy waterfront bars and cafés, full of hustle and bustle. Surfboards and wet suits. They keep moving. Emily fears if they stop again their legs won't manage to cycle another three feet, let alone another three miles.

It certainly seems longer on the return journey than it had in the morning, and the last stage of the cycle ride back to the campsite is the hardest. Their legs, now massaged by the salty sea after a refreshing dip at Polzeath, are too relaxed for another hill, however short.

Emily knows she is struggling. Her bicycle weaves from side to side, but she's determined to get back as soon as she can. Not far to go now.

She swings from right to left. Huffing and puffing, like a metronome in overdrive. A silver BMW comes up so close from behind it takes her breath away. She can feel the pull of the metal as it passes her by. It misses her by millimetres.

'Gosh… that was close,' shouts Debbie. 'Some drivers have no idea. Go steady Em, we're almost back. I'm right behind you.'

'I feel like I've been training for a triathlon,' Debbie jokes, when they finally make it back and both hobble to the shepherd hut. 'All we need now is a quick ten mile run and we'll be sorted.'

'Don't ever trust silver BMWs though,' giggles Emily. She's still shaken although she doesn't want to show it. 'I think the driver wanted to see what I had in my rucksack.'

16

JULY 2010

It is an easy decision to go to the Ship Inn in Port Isaac for supper. Emily has told Debbie about the delicious meal she had there with Marcus, and how Molly and Jack had loved Ben's magic tricks.

Even better, Richard runs a "taxi" service on Saturday evenings in his beloved converted VW camper van, known as Maisie. Classic orange and white. So now they'll meet him. For a small fee he drives a circular route from the campsite taking in the local pubs and restaurants. A few trips early evening, and then again at closing time, to make sure everyone gets back. Brilliant.

By the time they climb into Maisie their legs are stiff from their cycling but the drive is fun. Richard entertains all his passengers with funny anecdotes about landmarks they pass and local myths. Emily is disappointed she doesn't get a chance to talk to him properly, there are too many other people. She can see it's really an excuse for him to drive Maisie but the unique taxi service is extremely popular, just as well they booked two seats.

The Ship Inn is packed to the rafters, but luckily they find a small table for two, squeezed in the corner. Near enough to the bar but not too close to the live band so they will still be able to talk. Ravenous after all their exertions they waste no time ordering their meals along with a bottle of organic Sauvignon Blanc.

'Here you go ladies,' Ben smiles as he delivers the food to their table.

'Enjoy!… Hope you don't mind me saying but I'm sure I've seen you guys somewhere before, but just can't place it?' he looks at Emily with a puzzled expression.

'I was here a few weeks ago,' she laughs. 'With my husband and two kids – Molly and Jack – you did some magic tricks for them and they loved it.'

'I knew I wasn't going mad,' he nods his head and puts the empty tray under his arm. 'I remember now – they were fascinated by the fifty pence piece appearing behind my ear – their little faces were a picture. So what brings you back to these parts?'

'We're here for a sisters' weekend,' Emily introduces Debbie. 'We decided we needed some sunshine and relaxation. I had such a lovely time here the other week we decided to come back.'

'Well you've come to the right place, the sun always shines in Port Isaac!' He grins as he disappears into the crowd to collect another order, promising to catch up with them again later.

It's just like old times. The sisters savour their meal and chat about anything and everything. Feeling relaxed they order another bottle of wine, it's going down well, and they convince themselves organic wine doesn't give you a hangover, so they won't regret it in the morning.

The band is great too. A few people are dancing – normally Emily and Debbie would join in – but tonight they're just content to chat.

Not sure my legs could manage it either, thinks Emily as she people watches.

'Gosh I'm tired.' Ben wipes his forehead as he sits down next to them for a few minutes. The inn has thinned out a little and he's winding down after a busy evening.

'We've been rushed off our feet all day. One family even managed to spill not just one but *three* of their drinks in one fell swoop of the dad's arm… all over the floor *and* in their food.'

'Well our meal was delicious… and filling,' says Emily rubbing her tummy in mock appreciation. 'And we've been kept entertained by the people trying to play darts and failing miserably. I don't think I'd want to be sat on the table next to the board – it's definitely in a danger zone!

'So anyway, how have you been the last few weeks since I last saw you?' asks Emily.

'All good, and very busy now the school holidays have started,' he smiles. He must be at least six foot two. Emily can tell Debbie also thinks he's handsome, with his sun-bleached hair and blue eyes.

'But I don't mind. I'm single again now. Mandy and I decided to call it a day a few weeks back so I'm throwing myself into my work at the moment. In between surfing, obviously.'

'Aw, I'm sorry,' says Debbie. 'I hope you're OK?'

'Me? Yes, I'm absolutely fine. It had been pretty on-off lately and it was getting us both down. I'm just happy to have the freedom to go surfing whenever I want … and working in the pub I get to meet all sorts of new people.' Ben winks at them both.

And to have the freedom to flirt outrageously with all his female guests, Emily thinks to herself. Although she doesn't mind, he's so easy to talk to and he was so good with Molly and Jack. She enjoys the attention as much as her sister.

'So is your dad still here too Ben?' Emily changes the subject, sipping her wine although she has already finished it long ago. She remembers Ben telling her last time that his father George had suffered a stroke a few years ago but still lived in the pub, along with his Aunt Lisa, who did all the cooking.

'Yes, although he's not in the bar tonight, he'll probably be around tomorrow. A few of his old pals usually pop in on a Sunday night and he likes to see them all.

'He was the life and soul of this place before his stroke, such a shame. Always a bit of a party animal by all accounts. He worked as a barman in Polzeath before he got married then took over the Ship from my grandfather. Seems like he always had a reputation for being a bit of a ladies man. How true that actually is I don't know, but I've heard plenty of stories from the locals, so there's probably something in it.' Ben laughs.

'He still loves it here. He isn't well enough to work full time but does "light duties" as we call them, so he still feels involved.

'He loves just sitting in the bar chatting to people, always did! My mum died when I was ten and he's never met anyone else so his life has evolved around The Ship for well over twenty years.'

'Oh Ben, I'm so sorry,' says Emily. 'That's so sad, for you and him. She must have been so young.'

'I know, she was. We still miss her loads. But my Aunt Lisa is amazing; she's like a second mum to me and has been brilliant looking after Dad since he was ill *and* doing all the cooking and stuff she does here. She got divorced years ago and, like the rest of the family I guess, just feels like The Ship is part of her DNA.'

'Well, I think it's amazing. What a lovely place to run and keep in the family. Do you intend on staying here yourself Ben?' asks Emily.

'Oh definitely. Well, that's the plan anyway. You never know, I might meet the right young lady one day too, then we pass it on to the next generation as well.'

'Oh you will Ben, a handsome young man like you must have the girls falling over themselves,' Emily laughs.

'Now now Em, you're a married lady you know,' giggles Debbie.

'I know, I know,' Emily blushes, it must be the wine talking. 'I'm just giving Ben some moral support that's all. Not offering my own services!'

They're so busy talking Emily and Debbie nearly miss the last Maisie pick up at eleven thirty.

'See you tomorrow night?' Ben gathers up more empty glasses while they hastily grab their bags.

He all but pushes them out the door. 'Best to book a table if you do, the kitchen shuts early on Sunday evening. It'd be good to see you… tell you what though, there's no campsite taxi on a Sunday either so if you walk down I'll give you a lift back. If you don't mind waiting for me to finish up that is.'

*

Maisie's engine makes the familiar VW tickety-tick sound as they pull away up the hill back to the campsite. Emily watches the headlights, throwing shapes and shadows, along the dark lanes with the high hedges, grateful they didn't have to walk back.

'Look, I know we promised faithfully not to talk about Cerys tonight,' Debbie suddenly blurts out, seconds after jumping out of Maisie, as they make their way back to Porthleven the shepherd hut. 'But we definitely need to talk to Ben's dad George you know.'

'Why's that?' asks Emily, grabbing Debbie's arm to steady herself.

'C'mon Em, have you seriously not worked it out for yourself?'

'Worked out what?'

'Well, he *must* have been the George Pengelly in the newspaper from 1976.' Debbie looks at her, eyes wide open.

'How do you know that?' Emily is intrigued. 'How do you even know his surname?'

'Well, when Ben mentioned his dad worked in a bar in Polzeath before he married I got curious. I checked the proprietor's name above the door to the pub when we came out – it's Pengelly. There can't be that many people called George Pengelly around here, who just happened to be working in the very same bar, that very same summer – and even his own son says he was a ladies man!'

'Oh my god. Debbie, why didn't you say something before?' shrieks Emily.

'Shush, you'll wake everyone up … and I couldn't, stupid, not in front of him, or Richard in the taxi.'

Wow, Debbie is so clever, it hadn't even occurred to Emily. They can't miss this opportunity. If he's the George Pengelly who gave a witness statement to the police then he will definitely be able to help.

'Bloody hell, Deb. I can't believe it. We've got to go back to the Ship tomorrow now… and see Richard in the morning too. I'll figure something out.'

What an evening. Emily's head is overflowing with a mixture of organic Sauvignon Blanc, and a variety of imagined possibilities about what could have happened to Cerys.

Cerys.

She's back again.

Her head sinks into the pillow as she tries to find the "off" switch for a few hours.

THURSDAY 24 JUNE 1976

Cerys jostles her way to the front of the queue. Sausages, burgers, chicken pieces and salad. It looks and smells delicious. The servers are rushed off their feet. Beads of perspiration adorn their foreheads as they try not to get in each other's way. Cerys isn't going hungry tonight and is determined to get her money's worth. She's craving some decent food; their campsite meals haven't been remotely close to this standard. Their repertoire is definitely limited. Significantly constrained by both their budget and cooking skills.

ABBA and The Beach Boys blast through the loudspeakers as the band take a breather. Cerys has barely swallowed her last mouthful of food when John asks her to dance. Without hesitation she agrees. She is having such fun, it will be great to have a disco bop before the barn dancing starts again. Still mindful of what Amy mentioned she pulls at Pip's arm, to get all the others to join in as well. At least that way Vicky won't get jealous.

After doing all the actions, as best they can and usually a beat or two behind – or three in some cases – to Brotherhood of Man's "Save Your Kisses for Me" they all decide it's time to get another drink before the band start up again.

'I really hope you will,' John whispers quietly in her ear.

'Will what?' Cerys asks, bemused.

'Save your kisses for me?' he smiles at her, as Cerys slowly realises what he is saying.

'I'm very flattered but I bet you say that to all the girls,' she blushes, trying to laugh it off. 'You're nothing but a flirt!'

'No, not me.' He replies earnestly. 'I really mean it Cerys. Honest.'

Flattered, but self-conscious, Cerys sees an escape route as the song finishes. Richard is taking orders for the next round of drinks and she offers to help carry them. She is even more confused now. She really does like John but she mustn't hurt his feelings by giving him any false impressions.

Maybe if I just enjoy the barn dance with him and then tell him about Phil tomorrow. Cerys plans to herself as they queue. *It's too noisy to talk properly and I don't want to embarrass him in front of everyone. Or make a scene.*

The bar is at least eight people thick now. Richard and Cerys fight their way through and reappear with a tray of drinks for everyone, plus a large jug of punch. Cerys laughs with the others, trying to stop thinking about John and Phil. Perhaps she's making a mountain out of a molehill. She clinks glasses with the other girls, feeling distinctly lightheaded. She's certain the punch is getting stronger, as they gear up for the next round of dancing.

Cerys manages to cleverly manoeuvre herself so she is partnering George, Amy is with Barry and Pip and Vicky are with Richard and John. Amy winks discreetly at Cerys. She can see what she is doing but no one else seems to notice other than Vicky who is beaming as she is now next to John.

The caller taps his microphone to get everyone's attention and with the same crackle and pop welcomes them back for "Round Two".

'This is going to get messy if everyone else has had as much punch as we have,' laughs Cerys to Amy.

'I know, look at them over there,' giggles Amy pointing at a group of rosy-faced young farmers lolling about on some dishevelled hay bales. Beer slops from their tankards as they wave them around in heated discussion. 'They're in a far worse state than us. At least we're still on our feet and dancing!'

The whole marquee erupts, cheering and clapping, as the band strike some chords and start the next piece of music. They begin with some of the earlier dances in the hope they would be vaguely familiar and then move on to some far more complicated routines. The caller demonstrates first then lets them have a go. The reels get faster and faster. Tipsy dancers spin dangerously all over the place.

'Vicky is loving it,' Cerys whispers in Amy's ear as they dance past one another. 'Just look at her doing those elbow swings with John.'

'You did well to swap things around,' smiles Amy. 'Although she's going so fast she'll probably fall over deliberately so he'll sweep her up off her feet!'

'Now, now,' Cerys laughs. 'No bitching, as long as she's happy that's good.'

The night ends with a Farmer's Gallop. Everyone in the marquee forms a huge circle, then they step in and out. In and out. Cerys follows the caller as she elbow swings and skips diagonally with her partner around the circle, then repeats the same sequence over and over until she ends up exactly where she started. Brilliant.

'Just one more; just one more,' everyone chants and the whole marquee claps. Hands above their heads.

The band are bidding everyone a good evening and safe journey home, but the boisterous audience aren't taking no for an answer. After a couple minutes of noisy persuasion the band reluctantly agree to play just one more dance to keep them happy.

The crackle and pop compère announces the bar will remain open for another thirty minutes.

'We don't want any beer left over and it's all for charity.' He thanks everyone again for coming.

'What an amazing evening!' Cerys shouts over the hubbub of noise. 'I had no idea barn dancing could be such great fun. I don't want to stop, I hope they play some more disco music now.'

Cerys can see Vicky hovering near John in the hope that he will ask her to dance this time. Part of her wants him to, but she has to admit she really wants to have another dance with him herself.

Just for tonight, then I'll tell him tomorrow.

She empties the last of the jug of punch into her glass, as she does so George makes a beeline for Vicky.

'Howdy partner,' he jokes, trying to do a cowboy sort of look. 'How do you fancy a quick do-si-do to the sound of the Beach Boys?'

Cerys watches over the top of her glass. Poor Vicky. Her disappointment cuts through the air, despite the sticky, hot atmosphere of the marquee. She knows Vicky would never be rude and say no. Although from the look on her face it clearly crosses her mind for a brief moment. Vicky nods and manages to smile at George, glancing over her shoulder towards Cerys, then joins him on the dance floor. Cerys knows there is absolutely nothing she can do now to stop John asking her.

Just enjoy the dancing and tell him tomorrow. She tells herself again.

They're all up dancing again now, Cerys makes sure she isn't getting too close to John. But as a couple slower songs are played to round off the night – and let everyone know it's almost closing time – John moves towards her. She can't resist.

They hold each other tenderly on the dance floor to the "Theme from Mahogany (Do You Know Where You're Going

To)". Cerys really doesn't know anymore. Instead, she lets herself relax into his tender embrace. It feels like the most natural thing in the world. Diana Ross's amazing voice fills the marquee; it's such a beautiful song. Cerys loves it. It was number one in the charts for absolute ages earlier in the year. She rests her chin on his shoulder, as they sway slowly to the music.

Cerys can see Vicky watching her with John. Her heart pounds. She tries not to let it show, or allow her body to tense up, in case John wonders what is going on.

She and John move slowly around the dance floor. She loses sight of Vicky and George.

That's better. Enjoy the dance and sort everything out tomorrow.

When she dances with Phil they always step on each other's feet. This is different. It's wonderful. It's natural.

John strokes her back and holds her close. 10cc's "I'm Not in Love" starts and he pulls her into an even closer embrace.

'Trouble is I think I might be.' He whispers so tenderly in her ear she can barely hear.

Oh god, I've got to stop this. Cerys panics. 'No John, it's the punch, it's clearly gone to your head,' she giggles, except he's the driver and the only sober one among them.

They continue to dance slowly when she catches sight of Vicky again. Oh dear. Vicky is looking around surreptitiously, peering over George's shoulder. Cerys can see him singing quietly to her but Vicky barely notices. She's too busy watching Cerys. Looking furious.

Oh shit, thinks Cerys. *I've gone and done it now. I've never seen Vicky look so angry.*

Cerys shuts her eyes hoping she imagined it, dreading the music coming to an end.

John whispers in her ear and kisses her neck lovingly. She holds on to him as tightly as she can. Partly to make the moment last as long as possible. Partly in fear of what Vicky will say when it's all over.

And then he kisses her. A gentle, tender, slow kiss on the lips. Cerys is in pieces. She wants him to stop. She doesn't want him to stop. She's falling for him. She knows that now, but she mustn't let herself. She mustn't let herself because of Phil. She mustn't let herself right in front of all the others.

'Hey, what's up gorgeous?' whispers John, as he senses her tense up.

'Oh, nothing,' she lies. 'I just love this song.' And she nestles back into him as she tries her hardest to stop thinking about the consequences.

But they are soon distracted. Proceedings come to a very abrupt end as Amy, the sensible one, attempts to sit on a hay bale, misses completely and ends up in a bedraggled heap on the floor. The carpet of stray hay covering the ground fortunately ensures a relatively soft landing. Only her pride is hurt. Cerys runs over to check she's OK. Once she, and all the horrified spectators, realise she is unscathed the girls end up giggling hysterically as she looks up at everyone, mightily embarrassed.

'Something tells me it might be time to go home,' laughs Richard, scooping her up with his arm and brushing strands of hay off her back.

George and Barry head off home to St Minver. The rest of them squeeze noisily into John's car. He and Richard seemingly unfazed by the four decidedly tipsy girls in the back of their car, or the barbed atmosphere between them. Amy and Pip can tell Vicky is fuming but they don't know what it's about. They continue their hysterics about Amy's fall in a feigned bid to disguise the mood. The shock intake of fresh sea air in contrast to the humidity of the marquee has made them all realise just how much punch they have drunk. Almost falling out of the car, John holds Cerys' hand affectionately, as she takes his arm to pull herself out the car. She smiles goodnight and the two of them share a quick kiss clearly thinking no one else can see.

Vicky is appalled. The girls, exhausted and feet sore from dancing, struggle to find their way back to their tents, and she finally loses control. The intense jealousy that has been building all night can no longer be contained.

'Well, I hope you're proud of yourself Cerys Morgan.' Vicky shouts, arms waving. 'What the bloody hell do you think you were doing with John back there? You've been all over him all night. And then, smooching and kissing on the dance floor as if you thought no one would notice!'

She taunts Cerys, puckering up her lips and wrapping her arms around herself in a pretend hug.

'Hey, Vicky, stop it,' says Pip. 'Keep the noise down, at least get back to the tent first.'

'No I won't Pip, and don't tell *me* to stop!' Vicky yells as she staggers. 'It's Cerys you should be telling to stop. She is such a cow – didn't you see her? – well, didn't you?'

Vicky points her finger angrily at Cerys. 'I think it's absolutely disgusting. You've got a boyfriend at home and you go and treat him like this. We've only been here four days. It didn't exactly take you very long did it?' Vicky prods Cerys in the arm, still swaying from the alcohol.

'The first boy that comes along and you're … you're all over him. I've a good mind to telephone Phil tomorrow and tell him everything. Everything! That would teach you … you stupid, horrible bitch.' Vicky bursts into tears as her drunken tirade comes to an end.

Amy and Pip are speechless. Cerys stands motionless, looking for the right words.

'Well, that's just so kind of you Vicky,' she eventually says. Quietly and calmly.

'So thank you. Thank you for being so *incredibly*

thoughtful. You really know how to ruin everyone's evening. I was only dancing with John. I didn't know he was going to kiss me. I have already decided to tell him about Phil, it just didn't seem right to do it tonight, in front of everybody.'

'I bet it didn't,' Vicky comes back, still pointing her finger at Cerys, spittle forming at the corners of her mouth.

'But you didn't make any attempt to stop him did you... and it seemed perfectly okay to you to smooch and snog with him in front of everybody. Talk about double standards, you should be ashamed of yourself.'

18
JULY 2010

'Hi Ladies, come on in…' Richard ushers them into the office with a huge smile. 'I hope you've enjoyed staying in the shepherd hut and aren't coming to see me with any problems.'

'Oh, totally,' Debbie gushes. 'It's been an absolutely heavenly place to stay, we only wish we could stay longer.'

Emily had woken in a panic so she's glad he is so receptive. Only twenty-four hours left of their mini-break and she hasn't made any progress at all. Her idea of a weekend sleuthing has so far been a complete waste of time.

Panic had then quickly turned to despair. What had she honestly hoped to achieve. The police had looked for Cerys for weeks. Months. Why should she expect to come waltzing in thirty-four years later and solve the mystery, hey presto, just like that?

'Definitely,' agrees Emily, looking around judiciously. The room is cluttered with family pictures. Old and new. The ribbon cutting ceremony *must be his parents* she thinks, when the campsite first opened. Others she assumes are Richard, and his brother John. In their boy scout uniforms. Various athletic and sailing trophies. School photographs. All with self-conscious, lopsided smiles. They are very alike.

A variety of wedding and graduation mementoes too. Emily feels rude staring so intently at them all, but is equally fascinated by them.

They wouldn't put them out on display if they didn't want visitors looking at them.

'Coffee ladies?' Then without waiting for a response, he shouts through an open door. 'Liz love, make that four.'

'No problem, just seeing John and Mary off, won't be long,' a voice calls from a distance, as a car slowly turns around in the car park.

Jesus, is that his brother John too? thinks Emily. *Damn. If only she'd known.* Craning her neck without making it too obvious she sees a car pull away. All she catches is a dog-eared South West Air Ambulance sticker in the rear window and a cloud of dust.

Emily hears Debbie cough.

Pay attention.

Emily's embarrassed and temporarily thrown. There's an awkward silence. After the usual pleasantries she doesn't know what to say next.

Think Emily, think.

Then all three of them talk at once.

'You first!' laughs Richard, motioning to Emily.

Oh shit, now I really do have to say something.

'Oh, gosh, I'm sorry… it's just there's something else I really wanted to ask you about,' Emily wavers. In for a penny, in for a pound. All the plans she and Debbie agreed about playing it cool go straight out the window.

'I don't really know where to start, so I may as well just blurt it all out.'

'Well try me,' Richard is amused; he runs his hands through his hair. 'You wouldn't believe some of the things guests ask us about.'

'A few weeks ago I was on holiday in Port Isaac with my

husband and two children,' Emily explains, trying not to let her voice quaver. 'While we were there we saw a TV news article and it triggered some memories from when I was a child.'

Emily is ultra careful now. She doesn't elaborate further about exactly what she saw all those years ago. Debbie has warned her to avoid this at all costs.

You can't be sure who you're talking to, she told her. *Or whether they know anything.* Then she'd added, *don't get into a tricky situation by revealing too much information to the wrong person by accident,* and then *remember what the taxi driver said.*

Debbie's multiple warnings silently ring in her ears.

'The thing is, I feel like I want to help her parents. It was heartbreaking watching them on the television. Being a mother I can't imagine what it must be like to lose your only daughter in that way. I just wondered if you were here on the campsite when it all happened?'

The power of his reaction takes them both by surprise. Richard, white as a sheet, sits down with a thump, grabbing both arms of his chair to steady himself.

'It's not something I ever talk about,' he shakes his head in disbelief. 'It was an awful time for my parents. The campsite was in the news for weeks and for all the wrong reasons. It took them months – if not years – to get over it.'

Emily plays with her sleeves. She always does when she's nervous. She was prepared for an awkward conversation. Now she feels really errant.

'I totally understand. I really don't want to make you feel awkward or discuss anything you don't want to. I just wondered if you had the names of any other campers or people Cerys may have got friendly with whilst she was here that I could follow up?' Emily can sense his reticence.

'Why on earth should I share details like that with you? The police weren't able to do anything when they were privy to all the information all those years ago... what makes you think you can do anything different?' He snorts his disapproval. His smile erased.

'Coffee!' calls Liz as she reappears round the door with a jolly smile. It eases the tension. 'Help yourselves and I'll be back with some biscuits.' Then she's gone again.

Emily feels awful, but she can't waste this opportunity. Perhaps if she tries again in a moment over their coffee, then she will call it a day. She hates making him feel so uncomfortable after such an amazing time in the shepherd hut. But he must know something. He *must*.

Lost in her thoughts Emily jumps as Richard speaks.

'I'm sorry ladies but I really, really don't want to talk about this. The recent TV appeal was a complete surprise to us. Reporters have been snooping around the farm again, bringing it all back.'

He sighs.

'My brother and I were questioned by the police because we got to know the girls when they were here. We were home from uni for the summer. The four girls were really good fun and, yes, we spent a bit of time with them. But, I can assure you, that we had absolutely nothing to do with her disappearance.'

He holds his hands together, in front of his face, as if in prayer. His nose resting on his arched fingers.

'It was horrendous. The blatant gossip. The speculation. John and I went back to our studies in the autumn and tried to forget all about it. Our poor parents, however, struggled for a very long time afterwards. Even our father was questioned, god rest his soul.'

Richard looks at the floor shaking his head slowly from side to side.

'I'm sorry. Just talking about it now brings back the awful feelings of helplessness. We wanted to help find her, we really did. John and I both helped with the search for weeks. But, at the same time, we were almost being accused of some awful crime. It wasn't just us either, there were so few leads for the police to work with. They questioned people but there was never sufficient evidence to arrest anyone.'

'I'm so sorry,' Emily feels utterly reproachable for making him feel so uncomfortable.

'I'm sorry girls,' Liz has now sat down as well. 'I hadn't realised what you were talking about. I would have explained sooner. The events of that summer still upset us.'

She talks very softly. Emily can see Richard relax. Liz has no doubt dealt with many similar situations, over the years.

'That was his brother John in the car,' Liz continues. 'He was here that summer too. Neither of them talk about it. They're still close mind. John didn't want to take on the farm, but he does have a financial interest in the business, just in case our nieces ever decide they do.'

She smiles now, as if amused by the thought of it.

'We don't have any kids of our own you see, but we do dream of it staying in the family.'

Emily breathes a sigh of relief. Bless her. Liz has diffused the tension in the air but she still feels awkward. Every sip of her coffee seems too loud. She rattles the saucer as she replaces her cup. As she bites into her biscuit it collapses and crumbs fall everywhere. Embarrassed she tries to brush them up, but just makes it worse.

'I'm sorry ladies,' Richard says again, looking contrite. 'I didn't mean to be rude. It's just been a difficult few weeks since the TV appeal. John and I helped on the campsite but we didn't know all the campers, not like our parents did. I remember there was a young family next to the girls. They had identical twin boys, about four years old, with white blond hair. They were really naughty, but got away with it because they looked so angelic.'

Richard rubs his chin.

'Their surname was Banks, from Sheffield... I think... or somewhere up that way. I only remember because we nicknamed their father Gordon, after the famous footballer. His real name was Godfrey or Geoffrey. Something beginning with "G" but Gordon definitely suited him.'

Emily glances at Debbie. She doesn't want her to interrupt. *Please just let him talk.*

'There was talk that he and his wife – I think she may have been Sandra – got friendly with Cerys, and he in particular had shown a lot of interest in the girls. But, again, it was probably all speculation. There was so much gossip flying about after she went missing.' Richard seems much more at ease now Liz is sat next to him.

'Then there was a middle-aged couple in the tent on the other side of the girls. They were really quiet and private. I honestly don't remember their names, or anything about them.'

He shakes his head again and looks straight at Emily. 'I'm sorry, that's me done. I admire your reasons for wanting to help. I'm sure you must understand it was a truly awful time for everyone. I really can't talk about it any more. Please do excuse me.'

Pulling on his wellington boots he leaves the room, and heads off towards the barn. Liz touches his arm tenderly as he passes. Emily looks at Debbie and hurriedly finishes the last of her coffee.

Back in the privacy of the shepherd hut Emily jumps up and down, then hugs Debbie in excitement. Both are amazed at Richard's extreme reaction but at last they have some new information. A family called Banks with identical twin boys. It's going to take a lot of detective work but Emily's convinced it's an excellent start.

All she needs now is to meet George Pengelly at the Ship Inn and their weekend will have been a huge success after all.

19
JULY 2010

'Looks like you might find out who the driver was who doesn't like cyclists,' Debbie teases Emily as she spots a silver BMW in the car park at the Ship Inn. Still excited about what Richard has told them Emily is eager to see what she can glean from George too.

She had taken Debbie back to Lundy Bay earlier. Shown her the rock she hid behind. The juxtaposition of the beautiful, rugged cliff top with its spectacular view of the sea, and the awfulness of what happened there was not lost on them.

'God, I feel sick just thinking about it,' Emily has goose bumps all over.

'Me too,' Debbie says quietly. 'It was a damned good hiding place though,' she adds, to make Emily feel better.

'I can still see them. Cerys in a floaty white dress with the sun shining behind her. A cloudless sky. Her companion in the T-shirt with a slogan – three big letters – I told DI Davis about that. Have you any idea what it might be?' Emily's been racking her brains to work it out.

I'm sure it's to do with the theatre, but why? And the mark on their arm. The smiley face. What was that?

'The more I try to remember the harder it gets. Like

a flickering old cine film. Jumpy and disjointed. It's so frustrating.'

Debbie hugs Emily's shoulders.

'C'mon Em, don't beat yourself up about it. You were only six years old.' Then buoys her up. 'Everything you told the DI will be really helpful. You know the *exact* place and the *exact* date. He knows you're genuine.'

But Emily's distracted. She's already spotted what must be George leaning against the bar with a pint. He's chatting to Ben and a couple locals. Sounds like football scores and village gossip.

'Bloody hell Em, you're unstoppable,' laughs Debbie rolling her eyes. 'You're not doing anything until after we've eaten though. I forbid it. I'm absolutely starving!'

Emily eats as slowly as she can in a vain attempt to look calm. She mustn't spoil their last evening in her eagerness to speak to him. Monkfish and sea bass followed by indulgent chocolate torte with pistachio ice cream. Delicious. Politely offering their table to another couple once they have finished they grab two stools by the bar and order another bottle of wine.

Secretly shocked by the power of Richard's reaction earlier Emily is fearful of what George might do. She hopes Ben will introduce them to make it easier but the inn is so busy he's barely had a moment to acknowledge their presence.

She and Debbie enjoy the wine, reminiscing about childhood holidays and planning their next weekend trip. Emily is on edge keeping an eye on George and wondering how to make her move, but the wine is going down well.

Nothing wrong with a bit of Dutch courage, she thinks. Then he leaves the bar and she panics.

She's missed the moment.

Damn.

When he reappears she audibly breathes a sigh of relief as he makes his way back from the gents' toilet.

'Jesus, Em. Will you give it a rest. If you want to speak to him just do it. Put me out my misery. I can't sit here watching you watching him a moment longer.' Debbie knocks back the rest of her glass in one. She nudges her sister. 'Go on. Do it!'

Debbie's right. It's now or never. Emily inches towards George. Nervous about what to say but bolstered by alcohol she makes her move. Barely introducing herself or making any attempt at more general conversation she puts him on the spot. Straightaway. To Debbie's horror she blurts out how they had been reading about the story of the missing girl from 1976 and how the police had reopened the investigation.

'So, anyway, George – Ben said you were in Polzeath back then – do you remember anything about it?'

George swings round with a venomous look in his eye. Emily stumbles off the barstool she had been leaning on.

'I beg your pardon?' He bawls, mocking her. 'I'm sorry did you say something?'

He takes a huge swig of beer.

'I'll tell you what… why don't you and that snooty little sister of yours just fuck off back to your poncey city life, and leave me to get on with mine.'

He takes another swig, wiping his mouth with the back of his hand.

'How *dare* you walk in here and bring up a matter which I haven't spoken to anyone, not anyone, about for years. I may have been ill but I am still completely "*with it*" … and … and… if you are trying to accuse me of anything you had better have another think coming.'

His ruddy cheeks turn an even deeper shade of purple.

Wow. Emily tries her utmost to remain cool, calm and collected.

Leave it there. Don't move, her inner voice urges. *Don't say anything else.*

She's not that lucky. George's outburst has been heard by

everyone in the pub. Probably the whole village and beyond too. A sea of faces turn to look at her. She shuts her eyes trying to pretend it isn't happening. How she wishes the proverbial hole in the ground would appear and swallow her up. Plus they can't leave as Ben is giving them a lift home. It's too far and dark to walk back to the campsite.

After what seems like an eternity the noise levels return to normal and everyone's attention is gradually restored elsewhere. Emily sits quietly with Debbie and keeps her back to everyone. She is still aflame with embarrassment, inside and out. Ben reappears from changing a beer barrel in the cellar and is oblivious to the events of the evening. Other than noticing the scowl on his father's face.

'Don't bloody ask son,' George snarls at him. 'Just make sure you're more bloody careful what strangers you let in here in future.'

Ben has absolutely no idea what his dad is talking about but senses it has something to do with Emily and Debbie.

Please don't ask, please don't ask. Emily crosses her fingers on both hands.

'Hey, ladies!' Ben says cheerily wiping his hands on a bar towel. The pub now empty. 'Thanks for waiting, sorry it's taken me so long. Your taxi awaits… on one condition though.' He laughs as he grabs the keys. 'You must tell me what happened with Dad?'

'Ask Emily,' giggles Debbie. 'My oh-so tactful sister at her masterful best!'

'That's so unfair,' replies Emily. 'I was only asking him about *exactly* the same thing you were going to ask him but were too scared to.'

'Ooh, get you both,' laughs Ben running his hand through his hair as he pulls out the car park. He turns the music down so he can hear them. 'So what was the mysterious question?'

'I asked him about the Cerys Morgan case.' Emily admits sheepishly. 'I'm sorry.'

'Bloody hell, no wonder he was pissed off,' Ben says kindly, but in a no nonsense sort of way. 'Dad never really talked about it much, even when Mum was alive. He's bound to be over-sensitive if a stranger asks him about it.'

'I'm so sorry Ben.' Emily is contrite and wants to smooth things over. 'I was completely out of order.'

Debbie squeezes her leg hard to make sure she doesn't say any more. Emily heeds the warning with a sharp intake of breath.

God, Debbie can still pinch as hard as she did when she was a child.

'Hey, don't worry,' says Ben as he pulls up at the campsite entrance. 'Apology accepted. If you're ever back in these parts you are more than welcome at the Ship anytime. Dad has a habit of flying off the handle since his stroke. I bet he's forgotten about it already.'

Their train is due to arrive at Bristol Parkway at ten past two. Emily will be home in time to meet Marcus after work, and then they're off to her parents' house for tea with Molly and Jack. Debbie will get back to London by late afternoon.

They glide through the countryside. After a visit to the buffet car she and Debbie are like two young children on a school trip. They tuck into their sandwiches and challenge each other to see who can make a bag of crisps last the longest, or find the biggest crisp.

Debbie insists on paying but Emily is having none of it.

'Well, I'll just put the cash in your bag then so you find it later,' laughs Debbie, grabbing her sister's handbag to slip a five-pound note in.

As she does a postcard falls out.

'Oh that's nice,' she says. It's a view of Polzeath beach with Pentire Point in the background.

Emily picks it up. She is curious. She hasn't bought any postcards.

'What is it Em?' Debbie asks as Emily recoils in horror.

Emily is speechless. She places it on the table between them in silence. She is shaking.

"Greetings from Cornwall" emblazons the front. Harmless. But there is a handwritten message on the reverse. In thick, black capitals.

I KNOW WHO YOU ARE AND WHERE YOU LIVE.
RUIN MY LIFE AND I WILL RUIN YOURS.

Emily grabs it and stuffs it back in her bag.

'It's nothing,' she mumbles. 'It... it must be a mistake. It's clearly meant for someone else.'

'But what can it mean? Who on earth would have written a note like that?' asks Deb, raising her left eyebrow. Like she always does when Emily tries to avoid something.

'It must be a mistake. I haven't left my bag anywhere unattended. It can't be for me.'

'Hang on a minute, what about at the campsite yesterday morning?' suggests Deb. 'When we were talking to Richard?... or at the Ship last night?'

She's trying to be helpful but Emily doesn't even want to think about it.

'Please don't tell Marcus.' Emily pleads.

'Of course I won't,' she shakes her head in consent. 'I'd tuck it away somewhere safe though, just in case it's useful for some other reason.'

'What do you mean, for some other reason?'

'Well, you know, it might have fingerprints on it or something.'

'God, Debbie, do you think it's that serious?' Emily is scared.

'No. Probably not. To be honest I don't want you doing any more about Cerys now either. Maybe the taxi driver was right all along.'

They don't speak much for the rest of the journey. Emily's head is a merry-go-round.

'What if it's a sign Deb?' She voices her thoughts out loud as Debbie looks confused. 'I mean, really, what if it's a sign?'

Emily continues. 'It must mean there is *definitely* someone feeling guilty out there somewhere?'

'Don't be foolish Em,' Debbie thinks before she speaks. 'Be very careful. I'm talking as your big sister now. It may be sensible to take this note to the police and see what they want to do with it.'

'But they're so busy anyway Deb, what would they be able to do with this? If they're even interested in the first place?'

Debbie shrugged. 'Just saying. Do what you want.'

'Hey, Deb, don't be funny with me. I won't do anything. It's just someone being stupid. I'm going to forget all about it. Let's not let it ruin our lovely weekend.'

*

They put their differences behind them with a long, sisterly hug at Bristol. As Emily drives home she thinks about the great time they have had. They must do it again very soon. She is sure they'll laugh about the postcard in a few months' time. She just needs a bit of space to work everything out.

Emily arrives home well before Marcus is due to finish work. She unpacks her bag, has a leisurely shower and changes her clothes ready for tea at her parents. Molly and Jack are already there. She can't wait to see them all. She has bought Molly a bright pink bucket and spade for their next trip to the seaside and Jack a multicoloured, *incredibly* bouncy beach ball. They will absolutely love them.

Later, she and Marcus relax in the garden briefly to catch up on each other's news.

'Hold on a sec Marcus, I'm just going to grab a jumper.' Emily dashes upstairs.

'I'll get it!' Marcus shouts, being helpful as her mobile

buzzes in her bag. He can see it is Debbie calling. As he does the postcard catches his eye and he picks it up to have a closer look.

'What the fuck is this and what the bloody hell is it doing in your bag Emily?' He roars angrily, as he lets the phone go to voicemail.

'What's what?' She replies as innocently as she can.

'This!' He shakes it right in front of her nose. 'Where have you *really* been and what have you *really* been doing for the last three days? That's what I want to know. And has Debbie been involved too?'

'It's nothing,' Emily protests. 'It's all a mistake. I found it earlier. It must be intended for someone else. I have no idea what it's doing in my bag.'

Marcus' rage shows no sign of abating. 'I don't believe you Emily. People don't just go around leaving notes like this. Have you been messing around... you know... talking about the missing girl case again? The one I asked... *told*... you not to?'

'No. No. Really, we haven't. Debbie and I have just had a lovely, relaxing sisters' weekend.' She pleads.

'Honestly we have. Sunbathing, chatting, drinking Prosecco and... and... just doing what sisters do.' Emily's eyes fill with tears.

'Well, as we're being honest,' he says sarcastically, 'right now I really don't believe you. And you know what else? You can go to your parents on your own tonight. I'm going out for some fresh air. I'm sure you can think of a good excuse for my absence. You seem to be pretty good at lying these days'.

And he is gone.

Slamming the front door so hard it nearly falls off its hinges.

FRIDAY 25 JUNE 1976

'Oh my god, my head hurts,' wails Cerys. 'Whoever said that punch was mostly fruit juice was completely wrong!'

'Tell me about it,' Amy holds her head. 'I feel so sick… and you've been tossing and turning and whinging all night.'

True to forecast the day had dawned bright and sunny once again but the girls haven't seen any of it yet. It's midday, the campsite is deserted and they are all the worse for wear. They may try to pretend otherwise but there is no disguising the fact the punch from the night before had been far more potent than the fruity, refreshing taste had suggested.

'God I am seriously struggling,' whines Amy again. 'I've never had a proper hangover before and I am not enjoying this experience at all. You're all such a bad influence. What a waste of a lovely, sunny day. I am never going to touch a drop of alcohol again. *Ever.*'

'Yeah right, of course you won't, until the next time,' laughs Cerys. 'I tell you what though, I am never going to have a cigarette again. My throat feels like sandpaper. So much for Vicky saying we'd look glamorous and sophisticated with a packet of Silk Cut. It's obviously an acquired taste.'

'Thanks for your gratitude,' Vicky takes offence as soon as she emerges from under the canvas. 'That's the last time I buy you anything... mind you, I think you've got more than a sore throat to worry about.'

Oh god. Cerys' heart sinks. *She's only just got up and she's started already.*

'I've already told you,' Cerys says firmly. 'I'm going to sort it all out today. I didn't know John was going to kiss me and I didn't encourage him. It just happened.'

'Well, you had better sort it out,' Vicky threatens. 'Or I'll sort it out for you. I'm not scared of phoning Phil and telling him everything.'

'Like I said,' Cerys reiterates, speaking very slowly and precisely. 'There's absolutely no need for you to do that because I am going to sort it all out myself today... but thank you *so* much for your kind offer,' she adds sarcastically. Hoping and praying Vicky won't actually do anything.

Cerys strolls around the campsite with a mug of sweet tea. She's tired and miserable.

She feels awful. A horrible, metallic taste in her mouth from too much punch, and a gnawing pain in the pit of her stomach as she thinks about the reality of what she has done. She doesn't know which is worse, but the combination of the two makes her feel nauseous.

What if Vicky really does call Phil? What am I going to do? Cerys is starting to feel really guilty. And worried.

Cerys phones her mum from the usual call box on her way back. She thought it might lift her spirits. She mentions the barn dance and what a wonderful time they had but spares her the rest of the details. Like how much punch they'd really drunk and how rough they're all feeling. Or about Vicky. Some things, she decides, are better kept to herself.

Thankfully she doesn't see anything of the brothers on her stroll. What a relief. Cerys doesn't know what to say to John yet. Plus she really doesn't want them to see her in the state she is today. Avoidance seems the best tactic for now.

*

What in god's name was that? It's pitch black. Cerys is paralysed with fear. A noise. A peculiar noise. She's not sure if she actually heard it or dreamt it.

There it is again. A deep, slow, monstrous growl. In her semi-conscious state she can't even tell which direction it's coming from. Frozen to the spot, flat on her back she tries not to hyperventilate. Amy is in a very deep slumber in her sleeping bag, close enough to touch, but she's too scared to move her arm to wake her.

God, there it is again. It's like nothing she has ever heard before. It sounds like a wild animal. It must be prowling around.

She fumbles silently in the dark to find out what time it is. She doesn't want to attract the attention of whatever it is so hides the cool LED watch her parents gave her for her eighteenth birthday under the sleeping bag. The red luminous display is perfect for the job.

It's 03:23 precisely.

Phew. It'll be daylight soon. Just stay still and quiet for a bit longer and it'll go away.

All her senses are in overdrive. Blood pumps through her ears. It sounds like menacing footsteps, making her even more nervous.

Slowly she realises it could be human. It could even be coming from the tent next door.

'Amy quick, wake up, wake up.' She panics and shoves her hard in the ribs.

'My God, Cerys, what do you think you're doing. I'm asleep, leave me alone.'

'It's Vicky and Pip's tent. There's something wrong. There's something really weird going on, I don't know what to do.'

Amy rubs her eyes. She hears it for herself. 'God Cerys, that sounds like one of our ewes when they go into labour – if it's Vicky or Pip I just hope I'm wrong.'

They scrabble around for a torch and crawl out of their tent. In an instant everything becomes abundantly clear. There is vomit everywhere. It's awful.

Poor Pip.

The stench. Cerys doesn't know what to do first, and their campsite neighbours are starting to stir. The twins' parents, and the Loveshack Smythes.

Uh-huh, this is not going to be good.

Cerys and Amy try to comfort Pip. She's on her hands and knees. Her stomach is cramping so badly she can barely move an inch let alone get herself to the privacy of the bathroom.

With Amy's help Cerys finds her way to the shower block by torchlight. They grab some towels and soak them in cold water. The towels cool Pip down a little, making her feel more comfy. It seems to help the situation. For twenty minutes. Until Amy starts to feel unwell too. Cerys isn't sure if it's just the terrible smell or if she genuinely is… but then Amy too is violently struck down by whatever it is just moments later.

'Oh god,' cries Cerys looking in Vicky's direction. 'What are we going to do?'

The commotion is waking everybody up. Cerys watches as a number of tents become illuminated. Circular patches of torchlight shining through the canvas like giant fireflies in the darkness. A spectacular, mystical light show on any other day. Cows in the adjacent field start to make a noise too, keen to join in.

Cerys gets more cool, wet towels from the shower block. She's also found a bucket in the cleaning cupboard. Perhaps she can start cleaning up a bit.

'God, the stench is unbearable, I feel pretty sick myself now.'

'Me too,' says Vicky as they apologise to a few campers. Weary faces poking out of their tents, like tortoises peering from their shells. Wondering what the fuss is all about.

'I can't believe no one has offered to help us,' Cerys says, deeply upset by the sarcastic comments. 'When we were seriously tipsy last night we were really careful to be quiet and obviously *nobody* appreciated it. Now we're stone cold sober... and no one believes us.'

Cerys is the only one who isn't sick. She valiantly soldiers on providing cool, wet towels and offering sympathy as best she can. By daybreak things calm down a little but none of them get any more sleep. Pip, Amy and Vicky are pale and exhausted.

Cerys works it out. It must have been the chicken Kiev they ate the night before. The "too good to miss", two-for-one special offer. Wasn't it just. She was the only one who hadn't eaten any. She had been too hung over from the barn dance and had luckily resisted the temptation of the "golden bake" chicken. Pip and Vicky had insisted it would be just as delicious cooked over the camping stove in their makeshift saucepan rather than in a proper oven at two hundred degrees Celsius. She'd had a bowl of Smash instead.

She lets Donald and Beryl know. If it's food poisoning they don't need to worry about it spreading across the campsite. The girls just need to keep to themselves for a day or two and wait for the illness to pass. Cerys is exhausted. She's barely slept for two nights but Donald and Beryl are so kind and understanding. They make sure the girls have plenty of drinking water and fresh towels and ask their cleaner to help Cerys tidy everything up.

*

'Is this the cordon bleu restaurant we've been hearing all about?' laughs John when he and Richard pop over later in the afternoon to check they're all okay.

'Shut up John,' Richard kicks him sharply in the shin. 'It's far too soon – maybe when they're feeling better – at this moment in time it is clearly not a laughing matter!'

'They'll be fine,' John replies, trying to climb out the rather large hole he has started digging. 'I've seen far worse at Guy's… and there won't be any long-term damage.'

'Well, I have absolutely no idea who Guy is,' Cerys smiles. 'But if he's a uni friend of yours he must have some pretty crazy parties to be worse than this.'

Vicky watches as they wander away. She's sitting outside the tent fanning herself with a *Jackie* magazine trying to cool herself down. From the look on her face Cerys knows the combination of humid weather and sickness have re-ignited her rage towards her.

'I suppose you think I'm to blame for this now too? Just because Pip and I did the cooking,' Vicky snarls. 'And how very convenient that you're the only one who doesn't seem to have been taken ill.'

'That's because I didn't eat any chicken,' Cerys protests. 'I'm not glad that you're ill.

'In fact I've had a horrible day too looking after you all, just in case you hadn't noticed. It wasn't exactly much fun for me either.'

'Well, I'm sorry, how awful for you to have to be nice and kind… and look after someone else rather than just yourself for a change.' Vicky goads her. 'And don't think I've forgotten what I said yesterday – I might be ill but it won't stop me making that phone call.'

JULY 2010

Marcus has been distant and offhand for three days. Alternating between flying off the handle, at the slightest thing, to being silent and uncommunicative. Emily feels like she is treading on eggshells, wearing hobnail boots.

She's agonised about the postcard all week too. What a rubbish way to end her weekend with Debbie. She knows her parents thought it odd Marcus didn't go with her on Monday evening, although they didn't press for details. They just thought she was subdued, considering she had been away with Debbie and had such a great time. They called again on Wednesday but she brushed their concerns away.

'No, honestly, nothing's wrong. We're both fine. I'm just tired.' She'd lied, trying to sound normal.

Molly and Jack have been staying with her parents all week. They're having an absolutely fantastic time. 'Nanna and Pappa are so much fun!' they tell her on the phone, at least once a day.

Great. Just rub it in even more about what a crap week I'm having.

She's disappointed that she and Marcus have completely wasted the opportunity to have a week to themselves. The more she tries to approach him, the more he pulls away. It breaks her heart. She knows she's been foolish not telling him everything, but surely she doesn't deserve such severe treatment. She nearly lost him once before. She can't risk anything like that happening again.

By the time they leave for work on Friday he seems to have relented a little. Hoping he may be in a better frame of mind she emails him from work suggesting they go out for a bite to eat that evening. That way, if he rejects her olive branch, it'll be easier to take in writing than face to face. She'll have the rest of the working day to compose herself before going home.

She almost sobs with relief when he replies saying what a great idea to kick off their weekend. Her eyes well up with tears and she pretends to sneeze, so her colleagues won't wonder what's going on.

Brilliant! Let's just walk up to the White Horse on the edge of town. I'll book a table. Em x

Sounds perfect Mx

Phew. The rest of the day can't go quickly enough.

It's a busy Friday night but Emily's really pleased they decided to go out. She knows he'll bring the subject up at some point during the evening. She's ready for it. It'll be a relief for both of them to get the matter sorted over a nice meal and bottle of wine. Somewhere "neutral" Marcus said.

'I'm sorry Em but it's just not normal to find a note like that in your handbag.' He starts, halfway through their main course. She was surprised it took so long. 'I was shocked. Scared. I can't understand why you weren't?'

'I was. When Debbie found it – she was putting some money in my purse and the postcard fell out – I couldn't believe it. But there's no way it could have been intended for

124

me, Debbie didn't think so either, we were just having a girls' weekend.'

Emily tries to convince herself as well as Marcus. She doesn't want him worrying about it any more than he already has.

'Neither of us had any idea whatsoever how it had got in my bag, or who would even have had the opportunity to put it there.' She continues stroking the back of his hand. 'I'm so sorry you found it, I should have just thrown it away.'

'I know,' he replies leaning back on his chair and folding his arms. 'Look, if it helps, I'm sorry for being such a complete arse and storming off. I'm not very good at handling this sort of thing.' He shifts around, leaning in to her, as if he's wary someone might overhear. 'Although I'm still not sure Em. Perhaps we should go to the police or something?'

He looks at her with his huge, expressive brown eyes. Just like Molly does.

'Oh, Marcus, surely not. It can't be anything that bad... can it?'

'I don't know, I really don't. But will you promise me something, Em... promise me *faithfully* that you really will stop all this detective stuff?' He looks down at the table, wiping a minute crumb from his mat.

'I really, really mean it. I've been thinking about it all week. It'll only give you nightmares again. You spoke to the DI and did everything you can. You can't do any more and I don't want you making yourself ill. You've got to let sleeping dogs lie.'

He looks up at her again. He cares so deeply for her. She can see it in his eyes. Emily looks down at her hands as she fiddles with her new eternity ring.

'I know, so have I.' She stumbles. '... It's just that I was so certain I could help. I keep thinking about the bracelet she gave me; if Debbie and I hadn't met her that day on the beach it would be different. It just makes it all feel so *real*.

'And her poor parents. What they've gone through. I just thought if there was a chance I could help, however tiny – however *microscopic* even – then I should.'

'You did, Em. You told the police everything you saw and they will follow it up. It's not for you to do their work for them.'

'I know, you're right. I've been foolish convincing myself I'd be able to solve the mystery after all these years. You know me though, I always like to try to help.' She laughs, trying to make light of it.

'I know you do. You're way too nice, that's your trouble. Just promise me Em, I mean it, please?'

Silence.

'Please, Em?'

'OK, OK, I promise.' She smiles at him. '… On one condition though…'

'And what might that be?' He jokes, knowing what's coming.

'We settle the bill for our meal immediately and get back home for a fun, child free night before our delightful offspring make their return tomorrow!'

'Fine by me – shake hands on it – I'm not letting you renege on your promise.'

'Deal,' she says jubilantly, taking his hand.

AUGUST 2010

Emily breaks her promise three days later.

There's an article in the Sunday paper about "cold cases" various police forces are currently working on. It's fascinating. One even dates back to 1956. Using newly developed forensic techniques, especially those involving DNA, officers are investigating and solving crimes that had previously eluded them.

Her eyes devour the report. She can't believe it. Two cases have now been successfully solved and people charged, plus there are at least seven others ongoing in different parts of the country. Including Cardiff, Northumberland and Norfolk *and the disappearance of Cerys Morgan in North Cornwall in 1976.* Bodies were found in three cases, for the others nothing. Even so, for each and every one of them "the police remain ever hopeful of more plausible breakthroughs."

Emily can't stop reading, she scours the article for more detailed information. There is a quote from a police spokesperson.

"There are people alive today who know what happened in a number of these cases. There may even be people alive today who know they are guilty and have got away with their crime for all these years".

She suddenly realises her mouth is wide open and shuts it. She reads on.

"They may have perfectly normal, respectable lives with families, friends, colleagues and neighbours who have absolutely no idea about their despicable past. Our job is to pursue any credible information we are given. We never give up hope of finding the perpetrators of these crimes, some of which were particularly horrific. However, we are also ever mindful of the complexities of dealing with historic cases. They are always handled with the utmost sensitivity and professionalism for all concerned."

It concludes with a brief paragraph on the latest update for each case followed by a double page spread with the original story for some of them. Interspersed with fuzzy, black and white photos.

Emily immediately finds the piece about Cerys.

"The Cerys Morgan case received five calls following the recent television appeal. The local police are currently reviewing all the information received to ascertain if there are any fresh leads."

Wow. Five calls. Emily wonders. *Who were the other four people who called? What did they say?*

She carefully removes the pages of the newspaper and hides them in her briefcase. She doesn't really know why, it just feels preferable that Marcus doesn't see the article. She'll take it to work and read it again in private.

Emily can't imagine how anyone could live with themselves after doing something so dreadful. How could anyone lead a normal life knowing they have such a dark, evil secret?

Then the bit about sensitivity. She dwells on it. What if the police investigate and charge the *wrong* person decades later? What a living hell that would be for them and their family too. More lives ruined.

'Jesus. What a responsibility.' She thinks out loud, snapping her briefcase shut. Either way the police would need to be absolutely certain before they take action or charge anyone.

*

It's Wednesday when she's next in the office. After catching up on emails and any updates – the vast array of yellow 'Post It' notes stuck to various, random bits of paper by Jo her job share partner always amuses her – she retrieves the article to read it again in private.

And again.

And again.

She knows all the facts by rote but they still cut her to the very core. She reads the section on Cerys for a fourth time.

"The Cerys Morgan disappearance in 1976 triggered the largest search operation that Devon and Cornwall Police had ever known at the time. The constabulary drafted in extra resource from the Met and other forces to help. They asked all local residents to check their sheds and outbuildings in case she was being held somewhere against her will.

Hundreds of vehicles were stopped on the roads in and out of Cornwall to check she hadn't been abducted, or was being smuggled to another location. Hundreds of volunteers joined the search but all they found was her wristwatch. It was lying in a grass verge near the public call box she used every other day to call home.

Police interviewed dozens of people; including the campsite owner and his family, a local barman who had befriended the girls, the three girls she had been holidaying with, other campers and even the ice cream man.

But no one had any idea where she was or what had happened to her.

Her parents made two emotional TV appearances but no new leads were ever established. Eventually, after the record-breaking heatwave broke at the end of August, the search was called off and the mystery remains unsolved to this day.

The whole country had been fascinated by the story. How a beautiful young girl had literally disappeared into thin air. In the middle of a blissfully sunny afternoon, on a busy beach, crowded with people. She had offered to buy ice creams, for herself and her three girl friends. Then she walked up the path to the ice cream van and was never seen again."

It simply isn't possible.

Emily can't bear it. The look in Cerys' eyes as she saw her hiding behind the rock keeps coming back to her. How can she even think about giving up when she knows she can help? She's in agony. Deep, physical pain. Torn between the two.

She's promised Marcus faithfully that she will stop. He believes her. He trusts her.

How can she continue to help without breaking her promise? There must be a way.

After mulling over it all afternoon she hatches a plan.

Simple.

Just like formulating a product launch or press release, and she's done enough of those during her career. All she needs to do is work out the order in which to do everything. No one else need ever know. Certainly not Marcus. Or Debbie. She will – can – do it all by herself. She'll let anyone who needs to know after it's all sorted.

In the overall scheme of things she's dealt with far more complicated projects over the years. Plus they all involved zillions of other people, with a multitude of varying opinions. Discussion after discussion. Meeting after meeting. Always compromise.

This is her very own special project. She's in total control.

She's going to make sure Euan and Bronwyn Morgan know what happened to their daughter before it's too late.

*

There are lots of people she needs to make contact with. That's the first task.

So, *step one* – list everyone she needs to talk to.

Step two – find out where they now live and how to get in touch.

Step three – book meetings with them in her calendar. She knows this will involve a lot of travel; some will be quite a distance away. Emily, now getting particularly devious, makes a mental note to make them look like business meetings in her diary. Arrange them for dates and locations that look authentic. No one will ever know and Marcus will just assume she's working.

There are more than she thought. She'll need to plan carefully what order to visit them. To optimise her discussions. She mustn't miss anything important.

Emily sets up a new work file on her laptop. "Cornwall Launch".

Perfect. Looks genuine.

Then saves it in the "2010 H2 New Products" folder.

Finally, she carefully adds a password so no one can accidentally open it.

Genius.

2010 New Products
Cornwall Launch: Project Plan

STEP ONE: *ESTABLISH LIST OF PEOPLE AND THEIR CURRENT LOCATIONS*

STEP TWO: *VISIT ALL KNOWN PEOPLE AND COLLATE INFORMATION*

1. Euan and Bronwyn Morgan, Pembrokeshire

2. The girls Cerys had been camping with

  a. Pip (surname & location – tbc)
  b. Amy (ditto)
  c. Vicky (ditto)

3. The other friends and/or holidaymakers Richard (campsite owner) has told her about or from newspaper articles:

  a. 'Gordon' Banks, wife Sandra(?) and twin sons (Camper – real name & whereabouts tbc – Sheffield?)

    b. George Pengelly (Barman at the Doom Bar –
       Polzeath, Cornwall)
    c. Barry Hammett (Mechanic – George's best mate –
       Polzeath, Cornwall)
    d. Any others – tbc

4. Revisit Cornwall and talk to the following:

    a. Ben, The Ship Inn
    b. Richard, Atlantic View Campsite Owner (and brother
      John if he is there)

STEP THREE: REVIEW ALL INFORMATION

- *Decide if it is now possible to identify who was with Cerys Morgan on Tuesday 29 June 1976*
- *Let the Police know*

STEP FOUR: CASE CLOSED

She'll start tracking them down, using the internet, as soon as she can. She uses social media for her job and is becoming an expert on Facebook and Twitter with all the extra practice. It's amazing – frightening – what she has found out about people without even leaving her chair. She just needs to invest a little time. With a bit of focus she'll be away.

Emily's really excited. She'll block out time in her diary at work to do her detective work so she won't get interrupted. An hour here and there will look like genuine work meetings or teleconferences. No one will ever know.

Plus it'll only be for a while. She'll soon have all the details she needs and won't do any research at home so Marcus won't ever find out.

Win win.

Then it dawns on her. A deadline. She needs a strict deadline. The longer it takes the more chance she has of being found out. Plus it's only in the quieter summer months when her colleagues are on holiday that she can imagine getting away with doing this on top of her already challenging role.

She glances at the calendar.

Bloody hell, it's already Wednesday 4th August.

That really doesn't give her much time. She'll have to get cracking.

Emily leaves step four open. It's not one for her to decide. As long as she completes steps one, two and three before Molly goes back to school, and Jack starts his mornings only in September, it'll all be absolutely fine. Sorted.

Step One: Wed 11th August
Step Two: Fri 27th August
Step Three: Fri 3rd September
Step Four: End of September 2010

*

Later, as they prepare supper, Emily's surprisingly upbeat when Marcus asks how her day has been.

'Oh, I had a great day thanks. There's a new project that needs completing extremely quickly. I've been asked to lead it as other people are on annual leave.' She fibs, the guilt almost making her slip with the knife as she chops an onion.

'It'll mean a few extra meetings and a bit of travel – maybe even a night or two away – but I've already started working on it today. It looks like it'll be really interesting, and a great opportunity for me to prove what I'm capable of to the new department head.'

God. Listen to yourself. She cringes inside at what she is saying. *I can't believe you're already lying.*

'Wow, Em. That sounds brilliant,' he replies giving her a loving hug. 'You are so good at what you do Em, I wish they'd see that. You deliver far more in your three days a week than others do in five.'

Emily blushes a deep crimson.

'It's full on at our place too,' Marcus continues. 'But the new platform development is well ahead of schedule so I can't complain. Keeps us out of mischief, eh, being busy!'

24

SUNDAY 27 JUNE 1976

Cerys tries to wake up. It's still early morning yet unbelievably hot and sticky in her sleeping bag. She stretches her legs, as far as they can go within its limitations, and listens carefully to check if any of the others are stirring.

Nothing.

It's quiet and tranquil. Not only in their two tents but also across the whole campsite. She loves this time of day. The peacefulness. Just the birds singing to one another.

She loves the thought that she is the only person awake, even though she knows it's impossible. Half the world must be too. The sun has only just risen and she relishes the heady anticipation of another whole day before her. She wonders what excitement the next twenty-four hours will bring. She hopes the others are feeling better. Last night certainly wasn't the wild, fun, Saturday evening they had originally planned.

Cerys had hoped to get a decent night's sleep herself but it had been sporadic at best. She kept hearing noises outside the tent. Heavy breathing. It would come and go. Loud and soft. Fast and slow. At times it was literally just the other side of the canvas. Millimetres from where she lay.

She could feel it on her face and had clenched all her

muscles in fear. She knew it was probably her mind playing tricks on her, her brain still getting over the sickening events of the previous night. But then she thought about the shower incident; surely the campsite creep wouldn't be wandering around in the middle of the night? Perhaps he was stalking her? She ended up lying awake staring into the darkness and silently praying whoever – or whatever – it was would go away.

*

Pip, Amy and Vicky finally get up. Cerys can tell they're not completely recovered. They're ashen and tired with big, black shadows under their eyes. Pip has a nasty gouge on her shin too. She must have caught it on a tent peg when she was crawling around in the dark. It looks gruesome with congealed blood and a purple bruise expanding outwards.

Cerys gets the distinct feeling she will need to be chief nurse again. She makes sure they eat something, keeping it bland, and plenty of fluid in the form of sweet, milky tea. It certainly gives them a boost. Pip, ever the drama queen, wallows in the details of the past thirty-six hours to Cerys' dismay. She has obviously had the worst symptoms of anyone who had ever suffered from salmonella in the history of the world, but Cerys doesn't comment. Vicky is quiet but glad to be on the mend. Amy is angry. Angry with herself, for getting ill at all. She's never ill. What a waste of a day. What a waste of two days.

Nursing duties over Cerys goes for a walk. She'll sit on the beach, read her book, listen to some music. Phil recorded a cassette tape and gave it to her the night before she left. She thought it was such a lovely thing for him to do. She has been saving it, to play when she gets some time on her own.

She strolls along the coastal path enjoying the wonderful views. She's glad the others are getting better but she can't wait to have a few hours all to herself. The events of the last two days have worn her out.

Waiting for the girls to wake up she had been entertained for a while watching the comings and goings of the other campers. It is "change over" day today. She had secretly hoped the campsite creep would be moving on, especially after the heavy breathing in the night. She's convinced it is the twins' dad. But it looks like both their family and the Loveshack Smythes are here to stay for another week as they haven't packed anything up.

Cerys loves walking along the cliffs. It's so exhilarating. First to Rumps Point and then to Lundy Bay. She finds the most perfect rock to sit on. An ideal antidote to the previous forty-eight hours. She watches the sea and listens to Phil's cassette.

What a compilation. It must have taken him ages.

It starts with Mud's "Under the Moon of Love" which she adores. She then sings along with Dolly Parton to "Jolene", enjoying it so much she's not worried if anyone else hears.

By the third song – The Osmonds' "Love Me for a Reason" – she's starting to feel homesick. Her heart physically hurts. Then, as The Three Degrees sing "When will I see you Again" followed by Barry Manilow with "I write the Songs", tears roll uncontrollably down her cheeks.

She feels so guilty. She feels so alone. She knows she was wrong to get close to John. It must have been the sunshine, heat and punch going to her head. Vicky is right. She has behaved dreadfully.

She misses Phil. She misses his company, his sense of humour. He gets her. She gets him. They always have such a laugh together. He isn't just her boyfriend he's her best friend too.

As the cassette he has lovingly put together for her finishes with The Eagles singing "Lyin' Eyes" and "You to me are Everything" by the Real Thing she is bereft.

Bereft and resolute.

She will call him and confess. If he is to find out it must be from her, not Vicky.

That's the very least she can do.

She walks back along the cliffs to Polzeath. She thinks she sees some seals at one point, but they could have been buoys.

Postcards. She must send some postcards. If she buys some today and posts them tomorrow they'll arrive before she gets home. That'll be a nice surprise for her parents. She'll get one for Phil as well. He'll love that.

Cerys buys two postcards and sits on a bench overlooking the sea. The wooden seat is warm on the back of her legs, heated up by the sun. She can hear the chatter and laughter of the crowds on the beach below, with the background clamour of the breaking waves and seagulls.

She shuts her eyes to savour the moment.

The smell of the salty, sea air fills her nostrils. The weather forecasters are now talking about a summer-long heatwave and there's certainly no sign of a break in the sunshine anytime soon.

She starts to think about her exams and what her results might be. What it will be like to go to university. She's so excited about everything. Once the others are better they must make the most of their last week on holiday.

'Hey stranger!' a familiar voice shouts. She takes no notice, before realising it was her they were talking to.

'Hi George, how are you? Have you been let out for five minutes?' She laughs.

'Oh yes, and making the most of it. Just checking out the surf for later. Hey, you on your own? Where are all the others?'

Cerys tells him the saga of the chicken and he's horrified. He thought it strange they hadn't been around on Saturday night.

'It's such a shame George, we had a terrific time at the barn dance. It all went downhill very quickly early on Saturday morning,' she giggles pulling a face. 'I'll spare you all the vile details but I feel quite exhausted. That's why I'm having a bit of time on my own to recover too.'

'Bloody hell, what a nightmare. I don't blame you. I feel weird myself at the moment with a baby on the way and everything. It's like my life is just happening before my eyes and I don't have any control over anything anymore. I love Sue more than anything but I'm terrified of being a parent and having the responsibility of looking after them both.'

Cerys senses his anxiety and lets him talk. It won't do him any good to bottle it all up inside. He's such a gentle soul once you get past the cool, surf-dude exterior. She loves chatting with him. She can just be herself and not worry about saying the wrong thing all the time like she does with other people.

Bumping into George cheers her up immensely. She had been feeling so dreadfully homesick earlier. Phil's music cassette coupled with thoughts about her mum's wonderful home cooking and amazing chocolate cake, and their adorable spaniel Ella. How she misses playing with Ella. Dashing round the garden chasing her ball at a hundred miles an hour and her needy, puppy cuddles.

She misses her cosy bedroom where she can just lie on her bed and read her magazines, or listen to music.

'Would you like to meet again tomorrow?' George asks as if reading her thoughts. 'Same time, same bench? I get a short break after the lunchtime rush is over.'

'I would absolutely love to,' she says, and she genuinely means it. Whether the others are feeling better or not by tomorrow she will find the time to pop back in the afternoon.

'Brilliant, and thanks Cerys. Really appreciate having a chat. See you tomorrow.' He gives her a friendly shoulder hug and makes his way back to the pub.

A car toots its horn as it passes but Cerys doesn't see who it is before it disappears around the corner. She sits there for a few minutes more, her spirits lifted.

What a lovely guy. Feeling more upbeat she calls her mum from the usual phone box on her way back to the campsite. She doesn't mention the girls being ill. They're getting better and her mum will only worry. Best not to. Her mum can't worry about what she doesn't know about. She just says they're having a couple quieter days enjoying the sunshine, so it isn't actually lying.

Then she calls Phil. She almost loses her nerve then remembers the look on Vicky's face. If she doesn't call him she knows that Vicky will.

'Hi Cerys,' he sounds so happy to hear her voice. 'What a great surprise – I've literally just come in the door – don't laugh at me, like you usually do, but I've been tinkering around with my car. Your dad's been helping too.'

'You men and your cars,' Cerys teases. 'What are you like?'

'How are you?' He interrupts. 'Your mum says you're having a great time. I hope you're all behaving yourselves and not partying too hard?'

Cerys' heart skips a beat, but he's so busy chatting she can barely get a word in edgeways.

'Yes, it's great fun,' she says, silently plucking up the courage to say something. 'The campsite is amazing, the beaches are brilliant and the weather is fabulous.

'... Don't tell Mum though, Phil, but the others have all been ill. Some dodgy chicken. Luckily I didn't eat any so I've been OK. I've been spending a lot of time on my own though.' Cerys adds gently. 'I really miss you Phil.'

'I miss you too, I hope they're all OK?' He asks kindly.

'Yes, they're on the mend, hopefully they'll be back to normal for our second week.' She bites her lip.

'Phil, I love you, you know that don't you?' She goes quiet. She can't do it.

There are people waiting for the phone box. She can't do it with someone watching. She looks at her feet. Then they turn

141

away, sensing the need to give her some privacy.

'Phil… Phil…'

'Cerys… are you OK? … What's up?'

'There's something I need to tell you.' She is almost inaudible. Her lips are trembling. Phil's chatter stops abruptly; he can tell something is very wrong.

'We went to a barn dance on Thursday night and I… well, I… it was fun. We all had far too much punch… and…'

'Yes, and what?' Phil says, his voice shaking. 'What are you trying to say Cerys?'

'Phil, I love you, I miss you so much,' Cerys starts crying.

'Tell me Cerys.'

'I'm so, so sorry, I didn't mean to. I had too much to drink and I danced with someone.'

'That's it? You danced with someone?' He seems relieved. She should have stopped there.

'No, there's more,' she whispers. '… I let him kiss me.'

He's so quiet she thinks he's hung up.

'Are you still there? … Phil? I love you, I'm so, so sorry. It won't happen again. I made a big mistake. It was the punch. I won't do it again, I promise.'

The pay phone beeps to warn Cerys her money is running low.

Damn. She hits the coin box with her fist. *I don't have any more loose change to top it up.*

Tears stream down her face. There's just enough time for her to hear him sobbing. She has never heard him cry before.

'Why Cerys? Why…?' he says through angry tears. 'I thought we had something special. I never thought in a million years you would cheat on me and then be so blasé about it. You've only been gone a week.'

The phone beeps again as her money runs out and Phil's voice fades away.

'Why Cerys? I really thought you loved me.'

142

WEDNESDAY 11 AUGUST 2010

Emily is well ahead of schedule and has tracked down the Morgans, Amy and Pip. In addition, she's working on finding the Banks family and is making reasonable progress, more by process of elimination than anything else.

Today she's off to see Euan and Bronwyn Morgan. She managed to find a quiet corner of the office to call them and at first they had been, quite understandably, very reticent about who she was and why she wanted to see them.

She sensed their concern. It made her feel utterly intrusive. As if she was trespassing into their life uninvited. They were worried she might be an underhand journalist who was, yet again, simply looking to exploit their tragic story for her own gain.

It wouldn't be the first time nor would it be the last. Bronwyn had said with more than a hint of scepticism.

So Emily had told them a little about herself. She wanted to come across as a genuine, caring person who had their best interests at heart. She was acutely aware they didn't have a clue who she was and her phone call would have come completely out of the blue. How could she win their trust without even knowing them?

Keep natural, she told herself. *Just be as genuine as possible.*

Listen to what they are saying. Be considerate towards them and their feelings.

Emily explained about the news article she had seen whilst on holiday in Cornwall with her husband and children. She told them about Molly and Jack. She then – very briefly – mentioned the memories she had of her sixth birthday. She shared just enough for them to know she wanted to help. But not so much that they would jump to any false conclusions. She mustn't upset them. Nor did she want to talk about it in detail over the telephone; it would be far better to do that in person.

'We're very grateful for your phone call.' Bronwyn had said. 'We'll never, ever give up hope of finding Cerys… or finding out exactly what happened to her.'

She had a wonderfully soft Welsh accent. 'If you really do think you can help us then we would be absolutely delighted to meet up.' She had added.

Emily felt a huge sense of relief after speaking to them. She had a lump in her throat. She had half expected them to just hang up. To refuse to talk. All she had wanted was for them to know she was willing to help, that she thought she could. She didn't want Euan and Bronwyn to think she was meddling in "someone else's business" as Marcus had put it.

She decided to follow up with a short email too. Sent from work to prove she was bona fide. Their swift reply was polite and friendly.

Dear Emily,

We are so very pleased you decided to get in touch and look forward to meeting you. If it suits you then 11am on Wednesday 11th August would be a good time for us. We have attached some directions below.
Best wishes,
Euan and Bronwyn Morgan

Phew.

Emily could relax.

God knows she had agonised over her dilemma, time and time and time again.

Whether she should or shouldn't.

Whether she could or couldn't.

It was the same pattern. The recurring nightmare of Cerys would wake her in the early hours of the morning. Then, as she lay awake with so many images and thoughts swirling around in her head, solving the mystery would seem like the easiest thing in the world. Later on, in the cold light of day she would start to doubt herself all over again.

But whatever introspection and internal arguments she endured, she still had the same undeniable, overwhelming sensation. She just knew that she would be able to help them get closure. She was well aware how ridiculous that would sound to anyone else but she just *knew* it. She had no option but to believe in herself and keep resolute or they would never be released from their living nightmare.

Nor she from hers.

*

The sat nav informs Emily it is one hundred and nineteen miles with a journey time of two hours and eleven minutes. She knows it's mostly motorway and dual carriageway and sets off at quarter past eight to allow for any unexpected traffic jams.

Her £5.50 in change for the Severn Bridge toll rattles noisily in the central console, next to her mobile, as she turns the corner out of their cul-de-sac. She's told Marcus she has a work meeting at the Celtic Manor Hotel resort and needs to arrive early to set everything up.

So at least I'm not completely lying. She thinks to herself, guilt getting the better of her. *I will be in Wales.*

She makes good time and stops at some services, to stretch her legs and make sure she is presentable. Combing her hair she applies a tiny bit more bronzer on her cheekbones to give her face a healthy glow. Silly really, she tells herself, but for some reason it makes her feel more self-confident.

Emily needn't have worried. The curtains twitch in the front window as she pulls up outside and the front door opens seconds later. Both now well over seventy they looked tired, haggard and worn. Bronwyn has a silver, grey bob and straight, rather severe fringe framing her pale blue eyes. Emily can tell they had been a beautiful feature in her youth – and where Cerys no doubt got her strikingly good looks from – but were now somewhat overpowered by the dark shadows underneath. She wears no make up other than a touch of pinky red lipstick that lifts her face and brightens her skin tone a little. Emily assumes it's a special effort for today.

Euan too is grey, almost white, and tall. He must have been at least six foot two in his prime but now has a noticeable stoop. His thick hair runs in a strip around his head, under a symmetrical oval-shaped bald patch, that is leathery and suntanned.

Two pots are waiting in the immaculate lounge – one coffee the other tea – next to a plate piled high with homemade cake. They are natural hosts and Emily feels at ease. For two such kind and caring people they have been put through the most unbelievable torment for the last thirty-four years. They smile but Emily can see the profound grief and sadness behind their eyes.

Emily finds herself fascinated by all the photographs of Cerys in the room. The girl who has haunted her for years seems to now be looking at her from every angle. Pictures in all shapes and sizes next to a vase of beautiful, freshly cut flowers. It's quite disturbing. Cerys' eyes in all the photos remind her so clearly of the moment she hid behind the rock.

Then Emily spots the postcard Cerys had sent them. Propped up on the sideboard, decidedly dog-eared and faded. It had arrived after she went missing and had been lying on the doormat when they made one of their return trips from Cornwall in the relentless heatwave. Receiving it had broken their already shattered hearts into a million smaller pieces.

'You must be thirsty after your journey, would you prefer tea or coffee my dear?' Bronwyn says holding out some cake too. Delicious, home made tray bakes.

'Oh, coffee for me please, just milk no sugar,' replies Emily still fascinated by all the family mementoes. 'The cakes look out of this world.'

'Years of running a bed and breakfast,' Bronwyn explains as Emily picks a crumb from her lap. 'We used to love making sure our guests had all possible creature comforts and home baked goodies. They were easier to manage if you got them off to a good start. Welcoming them with tea and freshly baked cake generally did the trick!'

She smiles kindly, as if trying to reassure herself that Emily is genuine.

'Although we eventually stopped the B&B... you know... after Cerys. Things just didn't feel the same any more. Some people only booked out of morbid curiosity and it was awful. We decided enough was enough.'

They chat easily over coffee and more cake. Emily waits for a suitable moment to tell them about what she saw and where. She starts with her father's story and how she had believed Cerys was a mermaid. About the shell bracelet. How she had come back up the path from the beach to play hide-and-seek. How she had seen the most beautiful girl she had ever seen in a floaty summer dress. Their daughter. She knew it was Cerys and she knew exactly what day it was as it was her sixth birthday.

She articulates everything carefully. Euan and Bronwyn

listen intently. Every now and then they ask a question, like DI Davis had. What time of day was it? What did the other person look like? Who else was around?

Bronwyn sighs, reflecting quietly on their conversation.

'Have the police been in touch with you since?' asks Euan, squeezing his wife's hand.

'Not yet,' Emily shakes her head. 'But DI Davis made it clear it was going to take time for him to work through all the details, plus any new information from the recent appeal.

'I promise to let you know if he does get in touch,' she follows up kindly. 'Did Cerys mention anything to you when she called home about who she might have met down there that might help with my investigation?'

Oh God, thinks Emily. *Why did I use that word?*

'I'm sorry, that sounds so official,' she adds quickly. 'What I really mean is that I plan to track down all the people who may be able to help me, and then arrange to meet them. That way I can hopefully narrow it down or, ideally, recognise who it was I saw with Cerys that day and let DI Davis know.'

'Don't worry love, I know what you mean,' smiles Euan. 'But no, she called home a few times but never mentioned anyone in particular. We only found out names later from what we were told by the police. By the time we travelled to Cornwall she had been missing for almost forty-eight hours.'

He smiles at her again, through watery eyes.

'In hindsight, the weeks immediately after Cerys went missing were nothing more than a hideous blur. Neither of us can remember anything clearly, if anything at all really. Donald and Beryl the campsite owner and his wife were very kind and looked after us, making sure we had somewhere comfortable and private to stay.

'The police were absolutely brilliant too. Nothing too much trouble. The search was incredibly thorough and they thought of every possibility, with hundreds of locals helping. But as the scorching hot heatwave continued all we can remember now is a never-ending succession of humid, sleepless nights and feeling like zombies day in, day out.'

'I am so sorry for you both, I can't even begin to imagine what it must have been like for you.' Emily feels so helpless.

'We went through the motions, love. It's weird. I vaguely remember the two news conferences that were televised, but Bronwyn can't remember anything about them at all.'

'Would you like to see her room?' Bronwyn asks tentatively, although it's clear she wants Emily to have the opportunity. 'We haven't changed it. There's still all her favourite posters on the wall.'

Bronwyn is right. It's exactly as it was when Cerys left to go camping. Dated posters of ABBA, Queen and Starsky and Hutch on the walls. All centre pages with staple holes, now distinctly faded, from her favourite weekly *Jackie* magazine. A small selection of clothes still hang in the wardrobe; beads, jewellery and teenage knick-knacks in assorted pots adorn her dressing table alongside a photo of Ella the spaniel in a fancy silver frame.

'Her favourite photo,' says Bronwyn tearfully. 'And this is the watch we gave her for her eighteenth birthday. It was found near the phone box. It's still going, I put a fresh battery in each time it runs out just in case she comes home to wear it one day. The only other thing I do is put a fresh vase of flowers in here every week so it smells fresh. It does get musty otherwise.'

Emily is trying hard not to cry, but cannot stop her eyes welling up with tears. It really is the most poignant moment. Cerys' bedroom is literally a shrine to Euan and Bronwyn's darling daughter and they have clearly never, ever given up hope of her coming home.

'When she first went missing and we came back home I couldn't bear it. I would go to Manorbier or Stackpole, both lovely places on the coast about twenty miles from here,' Bronwyn points out the window.

'I would stand on the cliffs, and just stare across the water, for hours at a time. Poor Euan, he didn't know what to do with me. On a clear day you can see for miles and miles, and on the other side of the Bristol Channel from here is where she was staying in Cornwall.'

She holds Emily's hands tightly in both of hers.

'Do you know, it took us hours to drive to Cornwall… but if you could fly like a bird it would take no time at all.'

Bronwyn squeezes her hands even tighter.

'I used to stand on the cliffs and see the sun glinting on something in the far distance, across the water. I'd imagine it was Cerys… our beautiful Cerys, waving to me to say she was coming home. I still go there occasionally but not as often as I did. I still see the special signs. I know she is over there somewhere.'

'Oh, Mrs Morgan,' sobs Emily. 'I don't know what to say; I can't imagine what it must be like for you. I have a little girl myself and it simply doesn't bear thinking about.'

'Bronwyn, please. No need to call me Mrs Morgan.'

They embrace in silence.

Tears roll down their cheeks. Two mothers, sharing the harrowing grief and suffering of one; and the younger of them praying with all her heart that she can take some of that pain away.

WEDNESDAY 11 AUGUST 2010

Euan offers to show Emily around their garden as Bronwyn makes a fresh pot of coffee. He can see they are both upset. It's his way of giving Bronwyn some healing space.

The garden is exquisite. Emily is absolutely blown away by the beauty of it all. Euan speaks so softly she has to lean in to hear him. He tells how Cerys loved the garden from a very young age. She would tend the plants with her toy watering can, grow sunflowers and play with Ella. They used to keep the garden full of flowers, for their guests to wander around and enjoy with their morning tea. A charming, secret oasis. Only a stone's throw from the main road the trickle of water cascading into the pond and carefully positioned shrubs mask any outside noise.

After Cerys went missing the garden had been therapy for both of them. They both found an element of peace and comfort in creating a colourful, natural world that came back to provide pleasure year after year.

'Dr Green – the best doctor there is!' Euan smiles.

Emily completely understands.

They had good weeks and bad weeks. 'Still do,' he admits. But whenever the memories become too excruciatingly painful the garden soothes their pain and keeps them strong together.

Emily can't help but notice how neither of them can bear to say Cerys is gone. That Cerys is dead. Has passed away. She is always just missing.

Equally she knew if it were her daughter who had vanished she too would never, ever give up hope of finding her alive. However improbable the odds.

Returning from the garden Bronwyn starts to talk about Cerys' friends.

'Amy's married with three children – all boys – she and her husband are both vets in Somerset. I think she's Saunders now, maybe Sanders. Of course she was Jones before. Her parents still live in Narberth but sold the farm some years back when they downsized.' She takes a long breath.

'She sends photos of her boys now and then… and a long round robin letter every Christmas.' She smiles. 'I don't think Amy ever got over Cerys going missing. She really was a lovely girl. They had been "besties" for ever.'

Bronwyn picks up an old, black and white school photo. She runs her finger gently across the smiling faces.

'Now, that one is Pip… let me think… last I heard she worked for John Lewis or Marks and Spencer's… or one of the big stores. She got married quite a few years after Amy and then had a daughter almost straightaway. I don't actually know her married name, but she was Thompson.'

She points to another girl, in the middle of the back row.

'That's Vicky, I really don't know much about her now at all. Not sure anyone does. Wilson she was; she moved to France after Cerys went missing. Pretty sure she married a Frenchman and stayed out there but whereas the others kept in touch she never did.'

'Wow, thank you so much Bronwyn.' Emily's trying to take it all in. She should have brought a notebook really. Bad planning.

'That's all right love. I'm not much help really. There was Phil... Phil Williams... her boyfriend too, you know.'

'Oh?' Emily looks up. 'I don't know anything about him. Were they close?'

'Oh yes, very. Part of the family he was, round here all the time. He's settled now, still lives locally and eventually married.' Bronwyn shakes her head gently as she reminisces.

'He took it really badly; wouldn't even come down to Cornwall after it happened. I remember he was a bit moody when she was away. I thought they must have fallen out about something or were missing each other. You know what teenagers are like.

'He was visiting his cousin for a couple days around about the time it actually happened, so he wasn't in Narberth when we found out. Then, with everything going on, we didn't see him for quite a while after. He'd just passed his driving test and, after Cerys went missing, he simply hated coming round here anymore... so we never forced him to.'

Bronwyn looks sad. 'To be honest my love, we simply couldn't cope with his grief on top of our own – and he probably couldn't deal with ours – and it all just got too complicated.'

Emily feels utterly heartbroken for her; for them both. Bronwyn is so honest about her feelings. Even after all these years the grief they have endured for their beautiful daughter is unfathomable.

'How awful for him. I am so very sorry for you both, you must have missed him dreadfully afterwards too. He sounds like a lovely person.'

Bronwyn pauses as she glances at her husband.

A small grandmother clock chimes one o'clock. Emily doesn't want to outstay her welcome and she can see Euan and Bronwyn are exhausted. They've shared everything they can with her, and she with them.

Emily pulls her thoughts together as she drives home. She is exceptionally grateful to the Morgans for their openness. Knowing she has their blessing makes everything feel a million times better. She doesn't feel like she's doing anything wrong now they know.

They don't just know Emily. She tells herself. *They have positively encouraged you to keep going.*

She'll sort out her visits to Amy and Pip as soon as she's back in the office tomorrow. She's desperate to have another session online to try to find "Gordon" Banks too. He's proving tricky but she has found two – it may even be three – people with the same surname in and around the Nottingham area who have twins in their family. With another concentrated effort, and a little bit of luck, she'll soon nail it.

Not a bad day's work, she says to herself, as she daydreams on her way back.

The motorway is stop start in places but there are no particular traffic jams until she reaches Newport. Emily sings along to the radio to help ease the frustration, until "All Time Low" by The Wanted makes her eyes fill with tears so much she can hardly see where she's going. The words are so poignant for Euan and Bronwyn. She's thankful when Lady Gaga is played instead.

She sees a silver BMW in her rear view mirror and momentarily thinks of the one in Cornwall. After sitting behind her for a while it pulls out and glides past, as she tells herself not to be so stupid.

Emily taps her fingers on the steering wheel as she joins the back of the queue past road works in the Brynglas Tunnels. Emerging at the other end she can see the Celtic Manor Hotel standing proud to the north of the carriageway. What an imposing building. There are numerous banners reminding passers by that it will be hosting the 2010 Ryder Cup at the beginning of October.

A car horn toots at her as she stares at the building and fails to keep up with the slow moving traffic in front of her. A knot clenches in her gut. It's also where Marcus thinks her imaginary business meeting has taken place today. Never mind. She'll stop off at the supermarket on the outskirts of Thornbury when she gets back; pick up a bottle of wine and something tasty for supper. Some alcohol will help her relax. She and Marcus can have a lovely, chilled out evening.

As the traffic accelerates and she nears the Severn Crossing for the second time today the butterflies in her stomach return, this time in overdrive.

How can what she is doing for the Morgans feel so right when it also feels so wrong.

27

MONDAY 28 JUNE 1976

Cerys is heartbroken.

It's Monday morning. Vicky, Amy and Pip are well on the mend but Cerys has been awake all night. What a fool she has been. What if it's all over with Phil. She sobs silently into her pillow so as not to disturb Amy. She's exhausted and miserable plus the heavy breathing was there again last night too. Just before daylight broke.

'Hey Cerys, cheer up, you did the right thing you know.' Pip gives her a hug to make her feel better. 'It's always difficult over the phone. Once Phil has time to think about it I'm sure he'll be fine. It's just a shock, that's all.'

'I don't know Pip,' Cerys rubs her eyes, trying hard not to cry again. 'He sounded so upset and I didn't have any spare change to call him back. We've never argued before. I just don't know what to do.'

'Best to give him a day or two. Ask your mum how he's doing next time you call her. She'll have seen him by then and know if anything's wrong,' suggests Amy.

'At least you saved me having to make the phone call,' Vicky pipes up insensitively. 'He would have found out sooner or later.'

'Well, thanks for your concern Vicky, you're obviously feeling better,' goads Cerys.

'I'm sorry if it hurts Cerys,' Vicky adds. 'It's just that I really like John and it was so unfair that you danced with him… and then kissed him too.'

'But I didn't mean it to happen Vicky and I'm sorry that I did. I shouldn't have had so much punch and then I might have realised what I was doing. I did enjoy it, we all did, the barn dance was brilliant, but it really didn't mean anything.'

'But how can you say it didn't mean anything?' Vicky taunts again. 'He clearly fancies you, and you him, and yet you did nothing whatsoever to stop him even though you have a boyfriend at home.'

'I know and I'm sorry. How many times do I need to tell you?' Cerys loses her temper. 'Yes, he's handsome; yes, he's a good dancer and yes I had a lovely time but that was it. I did nothing in particular to encourage him. But it happened and I've confessed to Phil and I'll suffer the consequences. Does that make you happy now?'

'You just need to let people like me – who don't have a boyfriend – have just the remotest chance of dancing with someone fanciable too. You were literally throwing yourself at him and not letting me or anyone else get a look in. You're nothing but a slut.'

'So that's it, you're just jealous. Why didn't you say so before? You should have said you fancied him Vicky and we all would have helped. We'd love you to find a boyfriend of your own, it would make all of our lives a lot easier, believe me.' Cerys is livid and mocking Vicky now, putting on an artificially scornful voice. 'Just don't try to make *me* feel bad for being popular and having a good time, just because *you* can't get yourself a boyfriend.'

The others have never heard Cerys shout so loud.

'And anyway, I've told Phil and I'm actually feeling pretty crap about everything. Everything.' Cerys bursts into tears.

'Hey, hey, you two,' interrupts Amy, stretching her arms out as if getting ready to break them up. 'Enough's enough. If you want my opinion John and Richard are both fabulously gorgeous and I'd be happy with either of them too, but let's not argue over them and get into a cat fight. We've still got a week to go, there's plenty of time yet.'

'Hear, hear,' Pip joins in. 'Personally I think George is the most good looking but he's engaged to be married. His friend Barry isn't bad either.

'Let's get to the beach and plan what we're going to do this week – we've only got six days left you know and we need to make the most of it!'

*

Cerys finds a quiet spot of her own on the rocks to listen to Phil's cassette again. Sunbathing has eased the tension a little between the girls but she just wants to be on her own. Away from the bickering.

She's still tearful as she enjoys the lovely ocean scenery. Lost in her thoughts, and the song lyrics, she becomes aware of two little girls looking up at her. She smiles at them both through her watery eyes.

'My little sister thinks you're a mermaid,' says the older of the two, which makes Cerys laugh. 'But I've told her not to be so stupid as they don't really exist.'

'Are those real shells on your bracelet?' The younger one asks, clearly shy, as she drops her bucket and all the contents spill.

'Yes, I made it myself, it's a hair band really,' Cerys replies, enjoying their company. 'I make little holes in each of the shells and then thread them on – here – have a look, do you like it?'

The little girl strokes her hand and looks at the bracelet in wonder, her eyes big and wide.

'Wow… it's really beautiful.'

'Here, you can have it,' says Cerys. 'I can easily make another one.'

The little girl is over the moon. She thanks Cerys and the two of them run off again, buckets and spades aloft, to look for more fish in the rock pools.

What a chance encounter. The two little sisters have been just the tonic Cerys needed to make her feel happy again.

Maybe Amy is right too. With a bit of time Phil will calm down and forgive her for what she has done.

28
FRIDAY 13 AUGUST 2010

Emily is chuffed to bits. She's still on a high after meeting the Morgans and is well on target compared to her "project" timeline of September.

Well done girl. She tells herself. *Definitely making impressive headway.*

Feeling upbeat as she drives along the A38 towards Taunton she's also thankful Marcus, so far, seems blissfully unaware of what she is doing. She's getting used to the severe pangs of guilt, especially when he asks how her new work project is going. His support makes her deceit feel even more wicked. She plays it safe with her replies and is honest, if that's really the right word, about the progress she's making. She tells him about the "positive meetings" she's been having with her clients, their "insightful feedback" and how everything is "on track".

She's become so skilled at lying she's beginning to convince herself that it is all perfectly normal behaviour.

A couple of glasses of wine each evening help too. A nice, smooth Malbec or chilled Pinot Grigio definitely keep her calm. A bit of alcohol usually stops the recurring nightmare of the vanishing mermaid too. Not always, admittedly, and not a great habit to get into, *but what the hell, if it helps me sleep then where's the harm in it? It'll only be for a few weeks until everything is sorted.*

*

Amy welcomes her with open arms as a curious Scottish terrier sniffs gently at her ankles.

'Please don't mind Monty,' she laughs. Then explains Bronwyn has been in touch and she doesn't mind her coming to visit in the slightest. After a brief tour of the veterinary practice whilst her husband Simon deals with a variety of small animals and their doting owners they cut through a vacant consulting room to a "Private: Staff Only" area at the back of the building.

Amy switches on the kettle in a tiny kitchen and, hunting through the overhead cupboards, locates a plastic container filled with an assortment of biscuits. She's a very young looking fifty-two-year-old. Petite and slim with short dark hair. Not so much a Joanna Lumley "Purdey" hairstyle these days, though still very stylish. Probably more Annette Bening.

Amy shakes the biscuits, most of which are broken, to see if she can find any that are intact.

'Sorry about these,' she laughs. 'I have no idea who manages to break them all. They must have been playing catch with them or something, I promise you they were perfect when I put them in there.'

Amy chats easily. Monty has snuggled down at their feet. She and Simon have been in South Petherton for twenty years. Their three boys had all gone to school in Yeovil. Their two youngest are now at university and their eldest is travelling in New Zealand.

The navy blue plastic chairs remind Emily of primary school, and are distinctly hard on the buttocks, but she manages to position herself as best she can. After small talk is exhausted Amy is clearly interested to hear more from Emily. What it is she wants to know about Cerys and her reasons for getting involved. She's neither defensive nor concerned about Emily's "mission" as she calls it, but wants to fully understand what she's planning to do. If she can help in any way. She knows only too well that Bronwyn and Euan have never got over their loss and would love to help them – or Emily – find out the truth.

Amy requires little if any prompting. She's happy to tell Emily all about the camping holiday. Their teenage excitement at going away, after finishing their exams. The thrill of the train journey.

'Oh my god, you won't believe it but we listened to the Wurzels *so* many times,' she giggles again. 'I still know all the words!'

Amy tells her about the wonderful summer solstice, the warm sunny days spent lazing on the beach, the crazy barn dance, visits to Rock sailing club and the Doom Bar. She explains how they got really friendly with John and Richard at the farm, George the barman and his friend Barry. She reminisces about how lucky they were with the amazingly warm weather, not knowing at the time that it was the beginning of a record-breaking heatwave.

'We weren't ladettes,' she laughs, worried she might be giving Emily the wrong impression. 'But we certainly did do things we hadn't done before. I think everyone does on their first proper holiday without their parents. We had such a scream trying out different drinks, even smoking… which I absolutely hated and never, ever did again.' Her laugh is infectious.

'It was an absolute hoot; we so enjoyed ourselves, up until the day we fell ill. It was such a shame Vicky and Cerys had fallen out by then too.'

She stops talking briefly as she strokes Monty.

'That was on the Friday night… well, early Saturday really, as it must have been about two or three o'clock in the morning when it all kicked off,' she screws her face up as she recalls the events of that night.

'What had Vicky and Cerys fallen out about?' asks Emily.

'One of the brothers. John I think. Vicky was jealous after Cerys danced with him at the barn dance as she fancied him like mad but hadn't said… and she thought it wrong of Cerys as she had a boyfriend at home. She even threatened to phone Phil and tell him, so Pip and I tried to be peacemakers.' Amy smiles again shaking her head.

'It was such a shame, but to be fair we were all grouchy that weekend because we were feeling so rubbish. God it was truly awful, the three of us being sick everywhere. Literally. But, in hindsight, it was absolutely nothing compared to what happened the following week.' Her eyes well up with tears.

'Cerys was the only one who wasn't ill because she didn't eat the chicken,' she adds with faux jollity. Emily can see she is trying to combat the sadness she feels inside. 'And she was so kind and thoughtful looking after us all.'

Her chin wobbles as she wipes her nose.

'But that was Cerys. Always caring about others. Anyone else would've complained, but she just wanted to make sure we were all okay.'

'It must have been a tough few days for you all,' Emily says sympathetically.

'It certainly was. We were just getting back to normal, and looking forward to making the most of our final week, when she disappeared. Whatever happened she didn't deserve it.'

'What do you remember about the day she actually went missing?' asks Emily.

'We were all just taking it easy on the beach, listening to music, reading magazines, paddling in the sea. That sort of thing. Cerys had been really upset after confessing to Phil about kissing John at the barn dance. Her money ran out in the phone box. She knew she'd upset him but didn't have long enough to talk to him properly.'

'Oh, what a shame, poor girl,' Emily says softly. Ironically hearing the telephone ring on the reception desk for the umpteenth time. 'We're so fortunate to have mobile phones these days.'

'I know, it was so sad. She was completely heartbroken. We tried our best to reassure her that he would be fine by the time she went home.'

Amy looks straight at Emily. '… So it was strange really – there she was trying to cheer *us* up after we'd been ill and we were trying to cheer *her* up over Phil – that was when she offered to get us all an ice cream.'

Emily can see Amy struggling to fight her tears again.

'We said we'd help, but she insisted she was fine and would get them on her own. I still think that was strange. I've thought about it over and over… Why? How she thought she was going to carry four ice creams without dropping them. Does that sound stupid to you?'

'Not at all,' replies Emily, wondering herself. 'Why do you think she did? Did she and Vicky ever make up?'

'Not really. I think one reason why Cerys volunteered to get the ice creams was to offer an olive branch to Vicky. Either that, or just wanting to smooth everything over for all of us, and to get back to how it had been the week before.'

'Gosh,' Emily shudders. She knows so many details from the newspaper reports, but to hear Amy talk about how it *actually* was for the girls makes her shiver. 'Poor Vicky, what did she do?'

'She felt so, so bad about it all. She was the first one to go off looking for Cerys, whilst Pip and I stayed on the beach in case she came back. Looking back I'm sure it was because Vicky was worried Cerys was still angry with her. We'll never know.'

Emily sees a tear roll down Amy's cheek and takes her hand gently. She can hear a dog barking in a far room. Monty stirs but must be used to it.

'And then, when Vicky went looking for her she was gone for absolutely ages as well. We started to worry about both of them but then she – Vicky – came back to the beach to say she couldn't find her anywhere and how she had been here, there and everywhere trying to track her down. I thought about that a lot. Where did Vicky go, what did she do, whether Pip and I should have gone straight off to look for Cerys as well. Maybe we would have found her.'

'What about Pip? How did she feel about it all?' asks Emily, still holding Amy's hand tenderly.

'Much the same as me I guess,' Amy shrugs her shoulders. 'Pip and I don't think Vicky ever got over it. Vicky definitely felt guilty and blamed herself. I'm sure that's one of the reasons she moved to France and never came back.'

Amy pulls a tissue from her sleeve and blows her nose gently.

'To be truthful, we all felt really guilty about it. If we hadn't let her go off on her own to get the ice creams she would still be with us today. Who knows. I did get to the stage where I had to teach myself to let it go, so it didn't completely destroy me too.'

'It must have been dreadful, having to return home without her and then try and carry on as normal,' Emily tries to put herself in Amy's shoes.

'The first twelve months were the worst, especially our A level results. Cerys got the grades she needed for Loughborough but never knew it. She was so excited about going there.' Amy's tears are in full flow now.

'I went to Bristol and threw myself into my studies. I loved everything about it – the city, the course, the other students – which helped me enormously. I also met Simon and he was brilliant. Still is. He never once quizzed me about Cerys or made me feel bad.'

'Did people know about Cerys where you were?'

'I tried to keep it a secret but it somehow got out at uni that I was "one of the other girls"… it was strange… people were so fascinated by the whole mystery of it. Cerys' disappearance had been such a big story in the national papers for so long that I'm sure some people only befriended me out of curiosity, or plain weirdness in some cases. Simon kept me grounded. He never grilled me about it, but was always there when I needed to talk about stuff. It never goes away you know, I still have nightmares.'

'Amy, I'm so sorry, that's heartbreaking.' Emily doesn't want to interrupt, but doesn't want to upset her any more either. 'I know how hard it must have been, and still is, for her parents but I hadn't thought about how incredibly difficult it is for everyone else who was there too. To lose a close friend in such a tragic way is unimaginable. But none of you should blame yourselves for what happened. There's nothing you could have done differently. You've been put through enough pain as it is.'

'It's human nature to think "what if's" though unfortunately, we all do it,' explains Amy quietly. Her voice is fading away.

'What if I'd just done this, or said that, or whatever… oh goodness… it would be *so* good to actually know what happened. Even though part of me is terrified in equal measure. In case whatever did happen is too awful to bear.'

Emily's eyes are now filling with tears as well.

'What about John and Richard… and George and Barry… did you see much of them afterwards?'

'Not really. The brothers were both so kind and thoughtful. They had made our holiday so much fun from the moment we arrived. They took us to places we wouldn't otherwise have gone, like the sailing club.

'George was a great guy too. He worked in the Doom Bar

in Polzeath and was so handsome. Everybody loved him, he was a typical beach bum but so nice with it. Not all bigheaded and arrogant. His girlfriend was pregnant and he was getting married later that year so he was working all hours to save up money. I think he appreciated our company as the pub was always packed with holidaymakers, or emmets as they're called in Cornwall.' She chuckles as she blows her nose again.

'When Cerys first went missing Donald and Beryl took control. They were incredibly organised, they knew who to speak to, and what to do. The three of us were completely out of our depth – in total shock – whereas they liaised with the police and looked after Cerys' parents when they arrived.'

Amy pulls a fresh tissue out the box and gently dabs at her nose.

'As far as I'm aware the brothers both went back to uni at the end of the summer. John in London and, I think, Richard in Manchester. If they'd been in Bristol I would have looked to meet up, but it's probably just as well they weren't so we could all move on.'

Amy fiddles with the tissue between her finger and thumb.

'They were questioned a number of times by the police, just routine stuff. I don't think they could ever have done anything. They were such a lovely family. George was interviewed too. Likewise, apart from his fiancée all he cared about was surfing and how big the waves were. I don't think we saw him again, or Barry, afterwards.' She shakes her head.

'Did either of the brothers have a girlfriend?'

'Not that I knew of, I don't remember them mentioning any one.' Emily could see Amy trying to remember. 'John had definitely taken a shine to Cerys, but she had a boyfriend back home so it wasn't going anywhere. That's why Vicky got so upset, because she *really* fancied him.'

'What happened to Phil?' asks Emily intrigued by everything Amy is telling her.

'Couldn't cope. Went completely off the rails. He didn't even come down to help with the search. I think he probably still lives in denial. He and Cerys were very close. Everyone thought they would get married. He *did* eventually get married and has two grown up kids but he never moved away from Narberth.' She smiles at Emily.

Emily realises her coffee is only half drunk and stone cold, but continues to sip it not to appear rude. She is so engrossed in what Amy is saying the time has flown past.

'What about Vicky, do you ever hear from her anymore?'

'Not for a few years now… let me think,' Amy looks at the floor as if it will help. 'It's about four or five years. I only ever heard from her sporadically but she seemed happy enough. She and her husband don't have a family but love to travel. I seem to recall the last time I heard from her they were off on a big trip; she said she'd catch up again when they got back. Thinking about it now I don't believe she ever did.'

'Whereabouts in France does she live?'

'Somewhere near Chartres. She travelled around Europe a little intending to come back to college the following year, but the company that make Paco Rabanne and Nina Ricci had just opened a perfumery there and she got a job with them. She loved it. Then she met Xavier and was really happy. She always loved the arts and I think she still volunteers in the Museum of Fine Arts in the city too, a couple days a month.'

'What about the other campers? Did you get to know anyone else at the campsite?' asks Emily, as Amy doesn't seem to remember anything else about Vicky.

'Our tents were right in the far corner so we only had two other neighbours. There was a young family with twin boys. They seemed nice enough but we had named their father the "Campsite Creep" after he stalked Cerys in the bathroom one morning.'

'Ugh… you're joking… what happened?' says Emily, shocked. 'That sounds well out of order?'

'One morning – when she was on her own – he watched her in the shower while she got dressed and dried her hair. There was definitely something weird about him. After it happened we all kept a close eye on him, plus Cerys thought she heard someone prowling around outside our tents in the middle of the night a couple times too. He was certainly a bit of a weirdo. It freaked her out.'

Amy shudders in disgust.

'The couple on the other side to us were in their early fifties and very private. Cerys nicknamed them the "Loveshack Smythes" to spice them up a bit. They didn't have much to do with us; they were usually asleep by the time we got back in the evening, or drinking hot chocolate. But they had the smartest tent ever, it was a small bungalow.' Amy laughs as she pictures them sitting in their porch under the stars.

'I think I might know where the twins' parents are now,' confides Emily. 'I'm going to meet with them too, if I can. Somewhere near Nottingham.'

'Gosh, you have been busy playing detective,' quips Amy. 'I wish you luck, can't be easy doing what you're doing. I certainly hope that what I've said has helped you?'

'Definitely,' smiles Emily. 'I really mustn't take up any more of your time; you and Simon must have loads to do. Thank you so very much. I'm sorry if I upset you by asking so many questions.'

'Here, take this,' Amy holds out a business card for "Saunders Vets: Top Quality Pet Care for all the Family".

'Call anytime, it'd be great to hear how you get on.'

*

As Emily drives back to her office she runs through everything Amy has told her in her head. She must write everything down when she gets back so she doesn't forget anything.

Amy has been *so* helpful. Such a lovely person too. Like Cerys' parents. It's all such a mystery.

Why do such horrible things happen to such good people? Emily can't help but wonder.

Emily now knows Cerys so much better. Although she thinks it a bit strange Amy didn't ask *her* anything in particular. She had expected her to want to know what she'd seen that day, or why she was so sure she could help.

Maybe Bronwyn has already told her.

Maybe she doesn't care. Or maybe she just wants someone to end the waiting for them all, without any more heartbreak.

Emily glances at the time. Considering it's Friday the thirteenth it's been a really good day. She'll pop back to work for a few hours and then sneak off early. She's looking forward to the bottle of Pinot Grigio she put in the fridge earlier, followed by a sunny weekend of children's birthday parties and barbecues.

And getting ready for her meeting with Pip.

WEDNESDAY 18 AUGUST 2010

Emily strolls across the car park at Cribbs Causeway, the shopping mall just off the motorway on the outskirts of Bristol. She's meeting Pip in the coffee shop at John Lewis. Pip's in the store for a meeting and thought it would save Emily a trip to Swindon.

Emily wouldn't have minded a longer journey but it's actually really handy as it means she can find a wedding anniversary present for Marcus while she's there too. Plus, on a good run, it's only ten minutes from her office so she's just taking a longish lunch break if anyone asks where she's going. For her visit to Amy she'd booked it in the diary as a "mystery shopper feedback meeting" held at a "client venue" or something suitably vague. The meeting with Pip is far less obvious.

Due to meet at twelve thirty Pip is running late but Emily immediately knows it's her. She walks confidently into the coffee shop and her striking red hair gives her away. She's tall, slim and glamorous in a very natural, unselfconscious way. She's wearing a chic, charcoal grey trouser suit with a sage green blouse. Emily can picture her on their camping holiday, turning heads.

Pip has no trouble guessing who Emily is either, having also been "briefed" by Bronwyn. Like Amy, she also seems genuinely pleased to meet her. Emily has already found a corner table, away from the hustle and bustle and carefully avoiding the screened off area where invisible staff noisily sort all the used trays and crockery. At least they can hear each other speak as they sip their large cappuccinos, both with skimmed milk.

'Thanks so much for agreeing to meet today Pip, I do appreciate it.' Emily tries to get the conversation started, only too aware they now only have forty-five minutes before Pip's next appointment. Pip seems very distracted. Emily assumes she has a lot going on and is already thinking about her next meeting but trying hard not to show it.

'Oh my goodness, I don't mind at all,' smiles Pip. 'Bronwyn told me what a darling you had been going to see them both so how could I possibly refuse?'

Emily relaxes. Flattery certainly helps as she surreptitiously wipes her top lip, worried she might look a bit daft with a frothy milk and cocoa powder moustache when she's trying to have a sensible conversation.

They talk about the summer solstice, the barn dance, the girls' illness. Emily asks about Richard, John, George and Barry. What had they been like? Was Cerys really getting too close to John or was it all in Vicky's imagination? Did Pip know what happened with the twins' dad in the shower block?

The questions flow easily. Emily had prepared the key things she wanted to ask, desperate to fill in any gaps and to ensure Pip's recollections tie up with Amy's.

Pip is considered in her responses. She takes time to reflect upon everything she is asked before replying and on a couple occasions Emily begins to wonder if she will answer at all. Maybe it's just something she does. She must be used to tricky business negotiations at work and has learnt to think before she speaks so she doesn't get inadvertently caught out.

But when she does talk she is articulate and controlled. Richard and John had been great hosts, she remembered, and George… well he was *such* a cool dude… and then his mate Barry who came along to the barn dance. Pip hadn't *herself* thought about any of them as potential romances, but they were ideal holiday companions. She'd recently split up from a long-term boyfriend and just wanted to have a fantastic couple of weeks and a laugh with the girls. And they did, until everything else took over. They were having a great time socialising, drinking and catching up with Richard, John and George most evenings, plus the brothers generally drove so it meant they could go to places they wouldn't otherwise go, like the barn dance. Also the sailing club at Rock, that had been a superb day.

Emily is on a roll now. She can see the clock ticking on the wall and knows it will only be a few minutes before Pip needs to make her excuses. Much of what Pip says is the same as Amy. That's good and bad. Good as it means their recollections all tie up; bad in that she finds out nothing new.

The main difference is Pip *did* feel that Cerys had got fed up with being on her own when they were ill. Pip remembered her going for long walks, maybe three or four hours at a time. She had also been utterly heartbroken after her phone call with Phil. Although she was very kind to them all Pip had thought Cerys *was* annoyed, that they had "wasted time" being ill. She was also very secretive about what she did while they were unwell and that fuelled the fire even more with Vicky.

Vicky felt she had lost three days of her holiday and significantly reduced her opportunity for a holiday romance. All while Cerys seemed to have no trouble making friends with anybody and everybody. Or so Vicky thought.

'So where had Cerys been on those days and what did she do?' asks Emily, thinking there must be more to this.

'I wish I knew,' sighs Pip. 'Personally I'm convinced

something happened that weekend that led to her disappearance… but I just don't know what, or where, or why.'

A member of staff slowly pushes a trolley past; the piled-high crockery shakes and clatters. Pip leans in to make it easier for Emily to hear over the racket it makes.

'I just wish she'd told us more, but it was such a stressful few days. We had all been so dreadfully ill and it wasn't a good time for any of us. We weren't exactly great company. She probably didn't want to be hanging around the tents, whilst we all stank of vomit, or lay around groaning and generally feeling sorry for ourselves.'

'Ugh,' Emily recoils again. Even though it's not the first time she has heard the story now.

'Sorry to be so frank, but yes, it was horrific for all concerned,' laughs Pip. 'The trouble was it was actually me and Vicky who were in charge of cooking the chicken, so we only had ourselves to blame. Live and learn, eh.'

'So do you have any idea at all who she might have met with or seen that weekend? She must have gone somewhere?'

'None at all. Other than she bought a couple postcards. She wrote them on Sunday evening and posted them off on Monday afternoon. I only remember because that was the first day we were well enough to venture back to the beach.' Pip looks around the coffee shop, glancing briefly at the clock.

'She seemed in better spirits on *the* day… the day she went missing… gosh, how I hate saying that out loud. It still seems so unreal. Even she and Vicky seemed to be getting along a bit better.'

'Do you ever hear from Vicky anymore?' asks Emily.

'She never really stayed in touch with me. I used to find out how she was doing through Amy. As far as I'm aware she's still in France, though I really don't know. Amy may know more.'

Sure enough two minutes later Pip says she's terribly sorry but will have to get to her next appointment. She sincerely hopes she has provided some useful answers and wishes Emily every success with her search for the truth.

She hands over her business card – "Philippa Thompson, Head of Procurement, John Lewis Partnership" – and says to contact her anytime if she does have any news.

With a quick shake of her hand she is gone.

Wow, thinks Emily. *Busy lady.*

Emily has a mooch around the store, hoping to get some inspiration for a wedding anniversary present. It's hard to focus with so much going around in her head. She must type up all her notes and prepare for Friday's meeting with the rather hideous sounding, yet intriguing, Campsite Creep.

MONDAY 28 JUNE 1976

Cerys can't find her watch. She's sure she put it in her beach bag for safe keeping, so it wouldn't get sandy on her wrist.

She can't find it anywhere.

Her heart lurches – her eighteenth birthday present – what if she's lost it? Her parents would be so upset. Trying hard not to panic a little voice in her head tells her not to worry. She must have left it in the tent. Check later.

'Hey, guys, what time is it?' asks Cerys.

'Almost half past two,' Amy confirms.

'I'd better get moving then – the post goes at three – won't be long.'

Cerys feels deceitful but she can't tell them what she's *really* doing. Vicky would go berserk. Plus she's so excited about seeing George again there's no way she'll risk letting the cat out the bag, and then not be able to see him.

She's got a few minutes spare to get to the post box first, but as she nears the top of the cliff path she can see George is already sat on the bench. No problem, she'll post her cards on the way back to the beach instead.

His face lights up with a huge smile and he gives her a quick hug as she sits herself down next to him. It's really comforting.

'So how's everyone doing today?'

'Much better, thank goodness,' smiles Cerys. 'Back on the beach today, taking it very easy and all with big dark glasses on… but that's a vast improvement on yesterday so all going in the right direction. They'll be down for a pint in the Doom Bar again before you know it.'

'I hope so; it's been strangely quiet without you all the last few days. The place needs some more interesting entertainment!'

They chat easily while watching the small stick figures playing in the sea far below them. He's like a brother to her. She doesn't fancy George at all, although he is very handsome. She simply likes him as a friend, someone to confide in. She's always wondered what her own big brother would have been like. Her mum and dad had lost their precious baby boy when her mum was eight months pregnant and then she, Cerys, was born a couple years later. They had mentioned him to her a couple times *as they thought it only right she ought to know* but it wasn't something they ever spoke about. But she knew he was the reason why they more often than not wrapped her in cotton wool.

'Can I ask you something George?' Cerys looks at him. 'Promise you won't say anything to anyone?'

'Of course you can, and of course I won't, silly!' He replies laughing.

'I'm feeling awful about something and I don't know what to do.' Her eyes brim with tears again. 'I have a boyfriend at home who I've been going out with for ages. Our parents are all really close and it just sort of feels good, like we were meant to be together.'

She looks away from George, towards the sea, so he won't see her tears.

'It's just that, I had such a lovely time at the barn dance last week… but then Vicky got really nasty about it, and over the weekend I started to feel really guilty about what I did.'

'What exactly did you do?' asks George.

'I danced with John. Not just the barn dance stuff but also a couple slow dances at the end and then I… I… well, I let him kiss me. And I enjoyed it.'

She looks at the ground, unable to look him in the eye as she explains. She kicks the gravel with her toes.

'But then Vicky got really funny, it turns out she really fancies John herself, and she kept going on about it, making me feel bad and threatening to call Phil and tell him.

'Anyway, while they were ill I was on my own a lot wondering what to do. So I called him yesterday and confessed, I thought I needed to do it before Vicky did and it would be better if I told him myself too.

'He was so upset George, I've never heard him like that before. Amy says he just needs time and he'll be fine but I don't know. I just don't know.'

Silent tears roll down her cheeks.

'Gosh, it sounds complicated Cerys,' George sympathises. 'It makes my life sound easy. Seriously though, you've done the right thing telling him, otherwise he would probably have guessed something was wrong when you went home, and it would all have come out eventually.

'But to be fair, you can't string John along either if you do have someone back home… has John said anything to you about his feelings?'

'Not outright, but I get a *feeling* when I'm with him, you know, I can't explain it, but I'm sure he feels it too. I certainly sense he does,' Cerys sighs, squinting her eyes and looking far over the horizon as she thinks about what she's saying.

'Bloody hell Cerys, look at the time; sorry, I need to get back. If it would help I'm happy to meet again, what about the same time tomorrow?' George offers. 'But I do think you ought to say something to John too. It's only fair to let him know.'

'I know, you're right. It's just so hard to do.' She waves her arms to fend off an inquisitive wasp. 'But would you… I mean, meet me again tomorrow?' She smiles as he heads off.

'I don't want to get you into any trouble or anything but I would love to if you do, you're like my Cornish big brother giving me advice.'

*

The post is collected at 3.15pm. She inadvertently looks at her wrist to check the time but once again realises she doesn't have her watch. She has no idea if she's caught the post or not but crosses her fingers as she drops the cards through the slot, just to be on the safe side. As her postcards fall into the darkness a maroon coloured Morris Marina drives past. She does a double take. It's exactly the same as Phil's car. His pride and joy. He's just passed his driving test and will find any excuse to go out in it.

The homesickness she had felt the day before comes back with a vengeance. Then a car horn toots and a voice shouts 'Cerys!'

For a split second she's sure it *must* be Phil. She's overjoyed. How wonderful. He's come down to surprise her and to make up.

She spins round excitedly, only to see John waving from the farm jeep. Deflated she realises it was probably him who tooted as he passed her and George yesterday too.

He pulls up and jumps out. 'How are all the others?' he asks, genuinely interested.

'Well, I'd say they're definitely improving but not quite up to all night partying just yet.' She laughs; really pleased to see John but still disappointed it wasn't Phil.

'We're spending a quiet day on the beach while they completely recover. Then, hopefully, it'll be full on for the rest of the holiday.'

'Oh, thank goodness. We're looking forward to seeing you all again, you've got less than a week left at the campsite now.' His heartfelt relief is almost palpable. 'You look worried though, Cerys, everything alright?'

'Oh, I'm fine.' Cerys thinks on her feet. 'Apart from I've lost my watch and I'm just hoping it's back in the tent. It was a birthday present from my parents and I'll be in big trouble if I've lost it.'

'Well, borrow mine if you want,' he says, very generously handing over his watch. 'You need one more than I do at the moment. Just let me have it back when you find yours.'

Cerys is stunned by his kindness.

'Are you sure? That's very kind of you. I promise to take good care of it.' She puts it on her wrist and can see it's an expensive model.

She also realises she has missed the post by twenty minutes but not to worry, it's only Monday so her postcards will still get home long before she does.

'Did I see you with George a minute ago?' asks John, a slight quiver in his voice.

For some reason Cerys senses the question is more interrogative than friendly. She tries to be as nonchalant as possible in her answer.

'Yeah, I bumped into him on the way to the post box so we had a quick catch up.'

'Strange,' says John. 'I'm sure I saw you with him yesterday too.'

Now she does feel like she is being interrogated.

'I know, weirdly, I bumped into him yesterday too. I was out for a stroll by myself because the others were ill and he just happened to be on his break. He's been so friendly the last two days whilst the others have been ill… he really cheered me up just when I needed it.' She deliberately adds the last bit to shut John up. What does it matter to him if she did meet George yesterday?

But then she remembers the watch and how kind he has been lending her his.

'Sorry John, I didn't mean to sound rude. I did bump into George yesterday too, he was really friendly, so I stopped for a chat. It's been a difficult couple of days. I was exhausted and it was comforting to see a friendly face. We just sat on the bench over there and chatted for a bit.'

'No problem, come here,' John motions to her and gives her a hug, rubbing her back. 'You'll be fine, the others are all getting better and you've done a great job looking after them. They're lucky to have you.'

Gosh, she can feel herself going back to the barn dance all over again and tries to pull away gently. After her phone call with Phil the last thing she wants to do now is encourage John.

But he still has a way of making her feel special and she stays in his embrace a little longer than she should.

'You'd better get back to your friends. They'll be wondering where you are. Hopefully see you later, or if not tomorrow?' John climbs back into the jeep, pulling himself in with one hand on the canvas roof.

'Oh yes, that would be wonderful. Pip, Amy and Vicky all want to make up for lost time and we only have six days left – we'll definitely sort something out.'

FRIDAY 20 AUGUST 2010

Emily wakes with a start. Her heart is pounding. A car has pulled up in their peaceful cul-de-sac, right outside their house. It's 2am. The engine is running and the headlights are on full beam.

Oh my god they've come to get me. She lies flat on her back, all her muscles rigid.

Debbie said be careful who you talk to… and then the silver BMW that nearly knocked me off my bike.

Oh shit. Maybe it was them who left the postcard note in my bag too. Now they've found out where I live.

Marcus is fast asleep, his gentle breathing rhythmic and soft as if he doesn't have a care in the world.

Don't panic, keep calm.

She mustn't wake him. Paranoid, she slides slowly out of bed so he won't notice, and carefully peers from behind an inch of curtain. She shakes all over, not sure if it's relief or hysteria, and only just manages to stop herself from laughing out loud. Marcus will think she's completely insane if he wakes to find her giggling hysterically at two o'clock in the morning.

You bloody idiot Emily Harrison, she thinks, as sobs take over.

It's your neighbours returning from their holiday in Mexico.

Sure enough it is. Their flight delayed by five hours, their weary faces glow in the car lights as the taxi drops them off and they struggle to cope with four huge suitcases on top of jet lag. The tiny wheels on their luggage scrape across the driveway to their front door.

Fool, she says, almost audibly. *What the hell did you think it was going to be? A sniper come to shoot you as you looked out the window, or someone about to throw a Molotov bomb through the letterbox? You stupid girl. Stupid, stupid girl.*

She falls back onto the pillow, her head spinning wildly. Emily has told more lies in the last few weeks than in her entire life. Being so secretive is alien to her and incredibly stressful, even if it is all for the greater good.

Just who had that person been with Cerys? That was the million dollar question. The billion, trillion, zillion dollar question. All she needs to do is work it out. She's convinced one of her visits will provide the break through she so desperately wants. Surely it's only a matter of time before it all falls into place.

*

Four hours later and Emily is up bright and early. Early definitely, perhaps not so bright. Not only had she been disturbed in the middle of the night, following her meeting with Pip on Wednesday she had sneaked a delicious New Zealand Sauvignon Blanc home and secreted it in the fridge where Marcus would never spot it.

It had been so delicious she enjoyed a couple large glasses whilst preparing supper, then, as Marcus was at football practice, she thought she might as well enjoy the rest of the bottle and remove the evidence immediately to the recycling bin.

Since starting her new project a glass of wine or two each evening helps her to sleep. Without it she lies awake for hours going over all the details again and again. The image of Cerys swimming around, forever in her head.

She was fine yesterday but now, two days later, the alcohol has caught up with her. Helped no doubt by three oversized gin and tonics on Thursday evening with her job share Jo at their monthly catch up. She knows she's drinking too much, but without any wine or gin it isn't so much what she *can* remember that keeps her awake, as the details she *can't* remember.

Her head thumping, she sorts out cereal for Molly and Jack, and does her best to make sensible conversation over breakfast. She's very grateful Marcus is taking them to summer camp today. After swallowing two paracetamol and putting the rest of the packet in her handbag, in case they're needed later, she sets off for the Donington Park Services on the A42. She's meeting Gary Banks at ten o'clock. Sat nav says it's 115.7 miles and will take her one hour and fifty-seven minutes to get there.

Precisely.

Emily is in two minds about this meeting. He seems polite enough in his emails, but she can't get rid of a niggling doubt deep inside about how it will go when she meets him in person. It's probably what Amy and Pip said about him stalking Cerys in the shower room.

Campsite Creep, ugh, gross. Emily thinks. *Especially with two young children.*

She knows she needs to be careful not to prejudge him. She has absolutely no concrete evidence whatsoever on which to assume this is even true and if she doesn't keep an open mind she might end up going down *completely* the wrong track.

That would be awful. Imagine it. She thinks she's found the person, goes to the police and wham. Someone's life ruined because of her. Just like that.

Play it cool. Keep calm and gather all the facts first. She tells herself. *Deep breaths. Deep breaths.* As her fingers tap on the steering wheel in time to the radio.

Tracking down Gary "Gordon" Banks had been problematic but she had finally succeeded. She knew he and his wife had twin boys and their approximate age, otherwise it would have been a tiny needle in a giant haystack. Half a tiny needle in a supergiant haystack. She'd had some weird telephone calls with people she thought might have been him as she tried to whittle down her "potential Gordons" list. She just hoped she hadn't unsettled them too much in her due diligence.

When she had finally spoken to the real Gary Banks he was a little offhand but more confused than unpleasant. Or so she thought.

'… I'm sorry, who did you say you were… hang on a minute, is this a sick wind up?' He reacted, his voice quivering a little. 'Is that you Jackie… it is, isn't it… it's you putting on some stupid voice and thinking I'll fall for it?'

'No Mr Banks. I am very sorry if I have startled you but I am completely genuine. My name is Emily Harrison and I have been working with the police on the case of a missing girl – Cerys Morgan – dating back to 1976 and would very much like to meet with you to run through a few details.

'I understand you were camping at the site where Cerys and her friends had been staying and may be able to help with the ongoing inquiries.' Emily spoke very formally. To reassure him it wasn't a joke.

It went uncomfortably quiet but she knew he was still there. She heard heavy breathing at the end of the phone, not in a threatening way but as if he was quite literally catching his breath before he said anything else. She gave him the opportunity to respond but then decided to assist.

'I appreciate this has come out of the blue for you Mr

Banks. Please take a moment. If you would find it easier I can take a note of your email address and then send you a message for you to read and respond in your own good time.'

That seemed to work.

'Uh... gosh, yes... you have caught me unawares to be honest... uh... yes, please. That is, if you really don't mind, I would find that a lot easier. So sorry. What did you say your name was again?'

'Emily Harrison.'

'OK. Thanks. Well, Emily, yes, no problem.' He reads his email address out to her twice. 'I have to put the asterisk in as there are obviously too many Gary Banks if you use anything else.'

Don't I know it. Emily thinks, but just manages to stop herself from saying out loud. He's being helpful and she doesn't want to lose him, just as soon as she had tracked him down.

A couple, very brief, emails later and the date and time had been arranged. He lives in Long Eaton, which although only seven miles from Nottingham is actually in Derbyshire, which is one of the reasons her search had taken so long. She had wrongly assumed he was still in Nottinghamshire.

It was his suggestion to meet at the services. 'Plenty of parking and easy to find.'

Made good sense to Emily too, so outside the newsagents at ten o'clock it is.

FRIDAY 20 AUGUST 2010

Emily looks around for the "Made in Derbyshire" hessian bag
Gary Banks said he would be carrying.

'One of those environmentally friendly reusable shopping
bag thingies,' as he put it. He'd given her a brief description to
help with the identification process too. Six foot, thinning hair
and slim, most likely wearing jeans and a T-shirt.

OK. Should be able to spot him. She thinks as she loiters
outside the newsagent, bored shoppers milling around,
looking aghast at the overpriced sweets and chocolates whilst
trying to get in and out of the services as quickly as possible.
*The jeans and T-shirt won't be a give away, but the bag at least
should help.*

She's found out lots about him on Facebook since she
tracked him down, although he's posting far fewer updates
now than he originally did. He's just celebrated his sixty-fourth
birthday with a "bash" in the local pub, fake oak beams and
real ale in the background.

A postman for over forty years he met Sandra his wife
in the sorting office where she also worked. Two children –
identical twins Steven and Simon – now grown up. Steven is a
BT engineer; Simon has his own plumbing business.

She's curious too about a Jackie tagged in one of his photos, his wife's sister. That must be who he thought she had been winding him up on the phone. He obviously loves fishing too, lots of posts with various catches, in amongst family weddings and the arrival of grandchildren. All perfectly ordinary, family stuff.

Emily's amazed at what she has found out about people, without them even knowing. She feels like a clandestine, furtive individual. A stalker. But if people post so many personal things about themselves online they must realise it's there for anyone, and everyone, to see. And will be forever. So it's not her fault. So much stuff stored eternally in the great big, humongous data warehouse of the IT universe, she reasons with herself. Then immediately thinks about who might be looking at her own Facebook page. Not that she uses it that much any more. Just the other mums from her antenatal group who still keep in touch. She doesn't want to miss out on anything.

He's late. She'd got here with twenty minutes to spare and now she's waiting. She hates it when people are late. The journey had been a clear run but she knows by the afternoon it will get extremely busy. The usual Friday vehicular migration to the South West will soon be cranking up for another summer holiday weekend. She really wants to see him and start making her way back as soon as she can.

Marcus thinks she has a client meeting in Bromsgrove. She regularly holds events at a small hotel there, conveniently located adjacent to the motorway. He believes her – it doesn't sound out of the ordinary and at least it's in the same general direction. That way if she does get caught up in the traffic getting home it will sound plausible.

She's getting more and more devious. At times she loathes herself for what she's doing, but at the same time it's like an addiction. She just can't stop.

Fifteen minutes late. Just as she's starting to get agitated she sees him. As with Pip she spots him a mile off. He isn't slim though. He's positively scrawny, with weedy arms falling from his baggy T-shirt sleeves. Not so much thinning hair either, probably closer to bald, but who is she to be so pedantic. He'd only been trying to help with his description.

She smiles at him as he gets closer so that he'll hopefully acknowledge her and confirm her assumption is correct. Sure enough he reaches out a wiry hand and says sharply, 'Emily Harrison?'

'Hello, yes I am – you must be Gary Banks,' she replies, trying to be as friendly yet professional as she can.

Emily dislikes very few people but she has to admit she takes an instant aversion to this man. His expression is sour. His eyes are narrow and the lines around his mouth suggest he has spent most of his time scowling or moaning, probably both.

'Well that's good, hate to be kept waiting.' His voice is still curt. 'Why don't we grab a coffee or something? Get this over and done with as soon as we can.'

'Totally agree,' replies Emily, fighting the urge to comment on the fact it was him who was late. 'Coffee sounds like a great idea.'

They wander into the cafeteria and join the back of the queue for "Hot Beverages – Please Queue Here". The menu on the wall sounds amazing. Every variety of coffee you could ever possibly imagine from cappuccino to flat white, latte to mocha. But then Emily spots the machine where a waitress presses the relevant button and realises it isn't the proper barista type. Just an old-fashioned vending machine with frothy white stuff of some description.

Oh well, she can't have everything. It is hot and coffee-ish so will give her the much-needed caffeine boost she's looking for. They sit down at an empty plastic table with a black and white checked Formica surface, sliding sideways onto the matching plastic stools that run along the opposite sides. They look awkwardly at one another, over the top of a sticky laminated menu propped up in a plastic holder and a tomato sauce bottle, both of which have seen better days.

'So what is it you need to know?' he asks, straight to the point and definitely wanting to get on with things.

'I just need to ask a few questions about the summer of 1976.' Emily explains. 'The holiday you spent in Cornwall with your wife and twin sons, and in particular what you were doing around the time of Cerys Morgan's disappearance.'

'I am sure you know I was interviewed at length at the time so I don't know what more I can add after all these years.' His tone is gruff and he has a nervous twitch in his neck. 'One of the girls even claimed I stalked the missing girl in the shower, so I was arrested and taken in for questioning. Nice one that. Apart from the fact that I had nothing to do with the girl it caused huge problems between me and Sandra – she even threatened a divorce – encouraged by her sister Jackie who I'd always got on really well with before.'

He folds his arms defensively.

'Luckily they released me without charge, but it still got out when we returned home. Even our previously friendly neighbours treated me like a leper. It took years for us to get back to normal because it was always there, festering away in the background. The doubt. The gossip.'

He grunts with disapproval.

'It would have been so much easier for me if your guys had found her... and who ever did do it. It still makes me furious even after all these years, the way I was treated. No apology or nothing. Nothing,' he says angrily.

'So, what's today all about? Is it another interview or what?' he asks, a look of mistrust in his eyes.

'Oh no, gosh, how do I explain... I'm just interested. I was there on holiday with my parents and sister and I think I may be able to help with the investigation. I saw a TV article a few weeks ago where they were talking about the case so I have been checking a few things out.' Emily knows she's waffling, she wishes she'd worded that differently. It all sounds too vague.

'Hang on a minute,' he snaps violently. 'Are you telling me that you aren't the police?'

'Er, no?' Emily replies, unable to conceal her surprise.

'So you've dragged me all the way here on false pretences… and made me think I was needed to help with the police enquiry again after all these sodding years? Dragging all that crap back up again… and you're nothing of the sort?' His voice gets louder.

'So who the fuck are you?' He shouts. Heads turn.

'Like I said, my name is Emily Harrison and I'm investigating the case of the missing girl from 1976.'

'Well, *Emily fucking Harrison,*' he says, deliberating overemphasising the syllables of her name loud enough for everyone to hear. 'You can piss off. Who the hell do you think you are… thinking you can do this to someone?'

Spittle is now forming at the sides of his nasty, long thin mouth.

'Yes, I *was* at the campsite. Yes, I *did* know who the girl was. But I'll tell you now that I had ABSOLUTELY NOTHING – and I mean ABSOLUTELY FUCKING NOTHING – to do with her murder… or whatever it was that happened to her. So you can get that into your thick skull right now and leave me well alone. I don't want to hear from you ever again.'

He pushes himself angrily back along the plastic stool. It isn't easy. Much of the impact of his rage is lost, as he has to take a few sideways bum steps to get to the end. Then he knocks his coffee flying in a dramatic cascade across the floor and all over his "Made in Derbyshire" shopping tote.

Oops, thinks Emily.

He storms out of the cafeteria to the bewilderment and amusement of other customers, obviously eager to know what the commotion is all about.

Emily keeps her head down and decides to remain where she is and casually finish her drink, aware people are looking at her. Unsure what to do next, she very slowly sips the remainder of her "hot beverage" to give herself some valuable thinking time.

What a nasty, horrible, repugnant man.

TUESDAY 29 JUNE 1976

It's well past eleven and the girls still aren't up. They hadn't been particularly late retiring to their sleeping bags the night before but are not yet over their post-sickness fatigue.

When they eventually crawl from their tents they decide to do the same again. Spend another relaxing day on the beautiful beach at Polzeath to recharge their batteries. Then they're going to be reckless and venture out somewhere rather more exciting than the campsite in the evening. Come hell or high water they're going to make the very most of their last five days and nights.

Cerys still hasn't found her watch. She's quite fraught about it, although the others haven't noticed she's wearing a different one. She mustn't draw attention to it, the last thing she wants to do is upset Vicky again. If she finds out it's John's watch she'll go crazy again.

The weather is getting hotter and hotter, and sunnier and sunnier. The heatwave is not just a possibility any more but a certainty. Record-breaking temperatures are expected during the next week. Not that Cerys minds. Rain would have ruined their holiday. Getting cold and wet in a tent and being unable to dry her clothes is not her idea of fun. The amazing sunshine just adds to the atmosphere and the beach is absolutely packed with holidaymakers.

She lies on her back on her towel. With her eyes shut to block out the brightness she loves the feel of the sun on her skin. All she can smell is baby oil. She's nearly used all hers but she's sure Pip won't mind lending her some if she runs out. There's a young family playing ball next to them. She jumps every time it lands with a thud on the sand next to her, convinced it's going to hit her on the head or in the stomach with the next throw.

The girls are feeling unequivocally better and swim in the sea in between sunbathing, chatting and listening to their music. Cerys can still sense some deep, silent tension between herself and Vicky but she's putting on a strong front for the sake of the others. They're all having fun and she's relieved to have everything more or less back to normal. They're excited about going out to eat. Scampi and chips in a basket at the Doom Bar most likely. Certainly not chicken. Having an appetite is a good sign, they must have recovered now after three days of exceptionally boring food. They certainly don't want to cook for themselves any more. Only five nights left so they can eat out every night if they're careful with their money.

Cerys can't wait to see George again. She has been secretly trying to think of an excuse all morning; so that she can get away on her own early afternoon without raising anyone's suspicions. She doesn't fancy him in the slightest, she just enjoys chatting with him. Someone she can relax and be herself with. He really is like the big brother she never met. She doesn't want the others to find out about their meeting though, just in case. Especially Vicky after the fuss she made about John. Cerys silently panics, she really can't leave it much longer or she'll miss him.

She has a brainwave.

'Anyone fancy an ice cream?' She volunteers, getting an immediate response.

'Ooh, yes please,' wails Pip. 'That sounds wonderful. With a flake and all the trimmings for me!'

'Someone's feeling better,' laughs Cerys. 'OK, no problem, I'll get four the same.'

'They're on me,' she adds. 'I'll be as quick as I can so they don't melt in the heat.'

'I'll give you a hand, you'll never manage on your own?' offers Amy, forever practical.

'No, no. Honestly, I'll be fine,' insists Cerys. Thinking on her feet. 'It's my treat. You all just wait here then I know where to find you. I'll be straight back.'

The ice cream van is conveniently parked at the top of the cliff path that leads up from the beach.

Pip, Amy and Vicky watch in eager anticipation as Cerys walks up the slope and disappears from view.

34

FRIDAY 20 AUGUST 2010

Emily's head is starting to throb again and she's confused.

Could Gary "Horrible" Banks have been the person? To be honest she thinks not, his build is all wrong for a start. Although she knows it is perfectly possible he might have had a bit more flesh on his skinny bones all those years ago. As a six-year-old it probably wouldn't have been that easy to distinguish, most grown ups look pretty similar to a child of that age.

On the other hand the person she saw that day had been remonstrating strongly with Cerys and definitely seemed angry or annoyed about something. She remembered their arms waving about all over the place. So that would fit with his general demeanour and altogether foulness.

Plus he's the only person she has come across so far who says Cerys had been murdered. How very interesting. Everyone else just says she's "missing" or "disappeared".

Emily finishes her cappuccino, which actually tastes far better than she ever expected, and plucks up the courage to make a move. A lot of customers have come and gone in the time it took her to spoon out the final bits of frothy milk. She doesn't think there is anyone left who witnessed

her confrontation with Gary Banks. After visiting the ladies'
restroom to compose herself she returns to her car, all the time
checking he is nowhere to be seen.

The other three meetings had all gone so well.

One bad visit out of four isn't bad. She convinces herself.
At least she's met him. She now knows what he's really like
and what he looks like. She'll set off for home, and think about
what to do next, whilst she's driving.

Bad mistake. Her mind elsewhere, she pulls out of the slip
road onto the motorway in front of a juggernaut. Hooting at
full volume the driver gestures angrily and swerves into the
outside lane to avoid her. Luckily there aren't many vehicles
around but he's far from happy and makes sure she knows it.

Shaking, Emily waves a pathetic apology to him that she
knows he won't be able to see. At least she's said sorry. She just
wants to get home now.

The weather is turning and heavy rain is setting in. Her
windscreen wipers squeak annoyingly, she must get that sorted.
The scraping noise grates on her already sore head. Friday
afternoon traffic is starting to build and she feels increasingly
tired as she makes her way southwards. As if that isn't enough
she's noticed a silver BMW a couple cars behind her. It's been
there a long time. It isn't making any attempt to overtake and
looks just like the one in Cornwall. Emily knows she is being
completely paranoid but really wishes she had made a note
of the number plate now. All she can remember is WL59 or
something similar.

She sees the sign for the Strensham services and has a flash
of inspiration. If she stops there she can sort out her itinerary
for the following week and also get a closer look at the car and
its driver as they go past. Or, if they pull in to the services as
well, she can check it out in the car park. Ideal.

Gary "Horrible" Banks may have been rude and shaken
her up, but, looking on the bright side, meeting him has

helped her to see more clearly what she needs to do next. It's also increased her motivation to get it all over and done with as soon as she can.

She needs to do three things.

First and second is to find out where Phil and Vicky are and, if possible, meet with them. If Vicky is still in France they can always talk over the phone.

Then, thirdly, she must go back to Cornwall. She'll pretend to Marcus that she has a work conference for two or three days and sort out some accommodation. Somewhere near to where she saw Cerys. She'll visit all the key locations again, plus she *must* find out more about John. She feels frustrated that she met Richard but somehow managed to just miss his brother. By minutes. Seconds. This time she'll go on her own and take her time. That way she'll be able to fit all the pieces of the jigsaw together.

Emily indicates her intention to turn off to the services as late as she can, she doesn't want to give the BMW too much warning. As she decelerates carefully it passes her and she can see it's a male driver. Probably in his forties or early fifties wearing a shirt and tie, loosened slightly as if he's glad to have finished for the day. There's a smart suit jacket hanging in the back.

There you go. She decides. *Absolutely nothing to worry about.* A typical salesman making his way home, he doesn't even glance in her direction. She makes a mental note of the number plate this time just to be on the safe side. WL59XMJ. Then tries to think of a pneumonic to make it easy to remember. The best she can come up with is wavy line fifty-nine and a kiss for Molly and Jack, so that will have to do.

*

She orders a latte grande this time, with an indulgent millionaire shortbread. Delicious, one of her favourites. She has just forty miles left to drive and the heady combination of caffeine, chocolate and caramel will keep her alert for the final stint.

She sips it slowly and cuts the biscuit into bite size pieces; savouring every mouthful, as she logs on remotely to her work laptop to check her emails and sort out her diary for the following week.

Firstly, she emails the Atlantic View campsite to see if they have any of their wonderful shepherd huts available. She knows it is highly unlikely given it's the week before the August bank holiday, but worth a try. An automated response pings back almost immediately.

"Sincere apologies but we are fully booked for the required dates. Thank you for your valued enquiry, we hope to hear from you again soon. Please click here if you would like to sign up to our quarterly newsletter or join our mailing list."

Not right now. She thinks, mulling over the alternative options. *Too many other things to do.*

Other things to do being emailing Ben at The Ship Inn. She knows he also has a few rooms so it's worth checking the availability. An ideal location too. Fingers crossed. She finds the website and sends a quick email for the dates in question. Then she texts Marcus to let him know she had a tough meeting but she's on her way home and making good progress.

"Hi Gorgeous. Hope you've had a good day. Meeting was rubbish but, hey, at least it's Friday! On way home, just at M5 services. See you very soon Em xx"

Ben must be online as she has hardly pressed send on her text to Marcus when her laptop pings again.

"Hi Mrs Emily Harrison, Senior PR Executive. My, doesn't that sound grand! Good to hear from you again. Thank you for your enquiry and yes, due to a late cancellation, we do have one room available for Wednesday 25th to Friday 27th August either on a B&B (£50 pn) or DB&B basis (£65 pn)"

Cheeky so and so she thinks. But flattered he remembers her. The message continues.

"It would be great to see you again but let me know asap if you do want to reserve the room as it is likely to be booked again very quickly given it's just before the bank holiday weekend. Thanks, hopefully see you soon, Ben"

It's too good to be true. She replies quickly to confirm her reservation for two nights, including dinner to make it easier, and breathes an audible sigh of relief.

Sorted.

She'll wait until Tuesday evening the following week to let Jo her job share partner know. She'll say she isn't feeling well and feign illness of some sort. That'll give her three days grace if she's got something contagious. No one will want her in the office anyway, especially before a bank holiday. They won't want to risk catching anything, and Marcus will just think she's attending the final round of meetings for the new product launch.

One way or another she's determined to revisit the spot where it all happened. She'll sit there on her own and contemplate for as long as it takes, until she solves the mystery. She *has* to get it finished. Then she won't have to tell any more lies.

She'll be able to sleep again.

Laugh again.

Relax again.

Play with her children again.

Without her mind being somewhere else all the time. She's so exhausted at the moment she could weep; her sleep deprivation is almost as bad as when Molly and Jack had been grizzly, teething babies. She needs to give her liver a rest from all the alcohol too. She's looking, and feeling, haggard and tired.

'Just busy, but thanks for your concern,' she dismissively replies, whenever friends or colleagues ask if she's OK. Secretly knowing it has to come to an end soon or it will make her ill. Or insane. Probably both.

Her phone beeps with another message.

"Hi Em, sorry about your mtg, I'll get a bottle of fizz for in the garden. Then you can forget all about it and enjoy the w/e Big hugs Mxx"

How lovely. What a great idea. At least she won't have to drink in secret tonight.

"Thanks Gorgeous, sounds fabulous, can't wait to see you xxx"

Her spirits lifted once more, Emily is overjoyed to have got everything sorted rather than leaving it until after the weekend.

Looking ultra-carefully in her mirror this time she rejoins the ever-growing line of southbound holiday traffic for the last bit of her journey and tries to put Gary "Horrible" Banks to the back of her mind.

By this time next week she will have nailed it.

WEDNESDAY 25 AUGUST 2010

It takes a few days – and Phil is by far the easier of the two – but Emily does eventually track down both Cerys' boyfriend and Vicky.

Not wanting to waste any time she's annoyed to receive a terse, matter-of-fact response from him. "To manage her expectations," as he so kindly puts it. 'I really have no intention whatsoever of speaking about this matter with you and would be very grateful if you would refrain from ever contacting me again. Otherwise I may need to take legal action.'

Emily's curious. Why such a strong reaction? Why is he so dead set against her contacting him? Is it because he simply doesn't want to talk about it any more – she could understand that – or is it for other reasons? She wonders whether she should pursue this further just in case.

In the end she decides to focus on finding Vicky instead. It'll be a better use of her time. Bronwyn Morgan told her Phil had been away when Cerys went missing so she could understand his reticence if he wasn't even there.

On the other hand, what she definitely does know, after meeting with Amy and Pip, is that to complete all the pieces of her jigsaw it's essential to locate Vicky, and ideally talk to her as well. She also knows she must do this before her next – and final – trip to Cornwall.

Amy told her Vicky was living in France, somewhere near Chartres, and worked at a perfumery. So this is where Emily concentrates her search.

The perfumery is easy to find. Built by the Spanish company Puig in 1976, it owns numerous famous brands and is still going strong. The Musee des Beaux Arts, where Vicky volunteers, sounds wonderful too. Housed in a former palace adjacent to the amazing Gothic Cathedral. With Vicky's love of the arts she knows that must be a perfect pastime for her.

Emily is irritated, she can't find anything about Vicky on Facebook. She only knows her maiden name so that might be the problem. There are plenty of Victoria or Vicky or Vikki Wilsons, but none that seem remotely like the one she is looking for.

She's only got fifteen minutes before her next meeting as she searches on the internet, over and over again, getting impatient as she repeatedly presses "enter".

She keeps checking over her shoulder to make sure no one is watching as she tries different combinations, hoping something will pop up.

Then she spots something. A short paragraph catches her eye; she's not even sure why. A brief extract from the local newspaper, the *Journal De Chartres* dated July 2005.

Emily uses her basic O level grade B French to translate as best she can, but knows what it says almost instantaneously, without even reading a word. Her eyes fill with tears and she slumps forward, her heart heavy on her rib cage.

"The body of a forty-seven-year-old female was found in a house in a leafy suburb of Chartres on 1st July 2005. It is believed to have been there for at least twenty-four hours. Named locally as Victoria

Dubois-Wilson, the deceased was originally from the U.K. and had been living in France for almost thirty years. A post-mortem is due to take place."

Emily reads it again. Surely it can't be a coincidence. The name is too similar. The length of time she'd lived there is too similar. How awful. How unbelievably awful.

She closes the lid of her laptop down, not wanting to look, and stares out the window. Then slowly pulls it up again.

July 2005. Five years ago.

No, surely not. That would be why Amy hadn't heard from her "… let me think, not for four or five years now" she remembers her saying.

Emily refines her search to see if she can find any other articles. She needs to be quick; she only has ten minutes now. Maybe an obituary or later report that will confirm if it definitely was Vicky.

She finds one in the same journal dated about five weeks later. It says the deceased worked at the Puig perfumery where she held a senior management position in the creative design department. Her husband Xavier Dubois had been away on business for three days and returned home to find her unresponsive. A post-mortem revealed she died of a significant overdose of paracetamol and her blood alcohol level would have been roughly three times the legal limit at the time of death. A verdict of suicide was recorded, although she had not left any note, and her husband had not noticed anything unusual before he went.

Emily is mortified. Tears, a blend of sadness and frustration, stream down her cheeks. Tears for a girl, now a grown woman, even though she never actually met her in person. Had she really been as happy as everyone had thought in France, or was she just pretending?

What had made her kill herself – did something happen

while her husband was away? Or was it simply living with the guilt she had felt about Cerys for all those years? The argument they had which led to Cerys confessing to Phil and breaking her heart... and which Vicky never got a chance to apologise properly for? The confession that no doubt broke Phil's heart too, then Cerys went missing before they could make up.

It certainly seems more than a strange coincidence that Vicky died around the end of June. It's perfectly possible she decided to end her life on the anniversary of the date when Cerys went missing.

Emily never met Vicky, but over the last few weeks she has got to know her – and Amy and Pip – so well. Should she tell them? Surely Amy would have said something if she'd known. And what about Cerys' parents – they clearly don't know either.

Pull yourself together Emily. Her inner voice kicks in. *It's not your job to tell them. You've got to draw some boundaries somewhere.*

She's still surprised the news never reached Vicky's hometown of Narberth, but she had lived in France for three decades and her parents were no longer alive, so she didn't really have any current connections there.

Emily can't stop thinking about the possibility that Vicky had known more about what happened to Cerys than the other two girls. Pip said Vicky was gone for a very long time when she first went searching for Cerys. So long that she and Amy had started to worry about her too. Maybe there was more to it.

Realising she now has less than five minutes before her meeting she pulls out her make up bag to check her mascara quickly.

God Emily, you look a mess, she tells herself. *No wonder people keep asking if you're okay.*

Wiping her eyes, and dabbing a bit of lipstick on to make herself look more presentable, she can't stop thinking that she's getting herself in deeper than she had ever expected.

Maybe the taxi driver was right all along when he warned her and Debbie not to go poking their noses in.

She can't give up now though. She just can't. She's promised herself. More importantly she's promised Euan and Bronwyn Morgan.

'Who are you? Where are you?' She asks herself out loud as she snaps her laptop shut with a satisfying click.

One more trip to Cornwall and I'll get it sorted. One way or another I'm going to find you.

TUESDAY 29 JUNE 1976

Cerys doesn't come back with the ice creams.

At first Amy, Pip and Vicky assume there must be a long queue.

Then they think she must have bumped into someone she knows or be chatting with someone. She'll be back any minute.

After forty minutes they decide one of them ought to go and find her. She had refused any help but maybe she's having difficulty carrying all four ice creams after all. Vicky runs up the path following in Cerys' footsteps, leaving the others where they are just in case Cerys went to a different van and has returned to the beach from the other direction.

Vicky's happy to look for her. She's worried Cerys may still be upset with her. She has been so horrid and knows Cerys will have taken it to heart. When she finds her she'll apologise properly. Without Pip and Amy listening it'll be easier to find the right words.

Vicky's puffed out when she gets to the top. As she stops to catch her breath she realises there are only two people waiting to be served ice creams. Neither is Cerys.

There's no sign of Cerys anywhere.

Vicky asks the ice cream man, giving a brief description

of her long blond hair and floaty white beach dress. He's very kind but doesn't remember anyone of that description buying four ice creams.

'… and if she really is that pretty I'm sure I would!' He winks at her.

Vicky is starting to feel worried. It doesn't feel right. She looks frantically around. She isn't sure whether to keep searching on her own, or go back and get the others. She thinks about popping in the Doom Bar to ask George – it's only a few hundred yards down the road – but Cerys wouldn't have gone there without the others in the middle of the afternoon.

Maybe she's gone to call her mum and is in the telephone box. Maybe she's called Phil again. That must be it. She runs up the road only for her heart to sink as she realises the call box is empty.

Vicky runs down to the grocery store where they go most evenings to buy their supper bargains. The lady on the till recognises her.

'You're early today,' she calls out as Vicky hurtles in, holding the door handle to steady herself.

'Hi there,' Vicky struggles to make any more conversation. 'You haven't seen Cerys by any chance? She's the one with the long blond hair?'

'Sorry, love. Yes I'd recognise Cerys anywhere, but she's not been in yet this afternoon, probably see you all later on though.'

Without stopping to explain Vicky shouts 'Thank you,' and darts back up the hill.

She must keep looking. Cerys must be somewhere. She *must* be somewhere.

Not sure what to do next she goes back to the others, only too aware of their puzzled looks as she walks down the path without Cerys or any ice creams.

'What's going on?' stutters Pip. 'Where is she? And where have you been? You've been gone ages.'

'I honestly don't have a clue,' Vicky's voice trembles. 'I've been all over the place. She's vanished. The ice cream man hasn't seen her, and no one even remotely like her has even asked for four ice creams.'

'But that's crazy Vicky, he must have seen her,' Amy replies.

'Right. Let's not panic but think things through logically,' advises Pip, trying to sound in control.

'If she didn't get any ice creams, then something must have happened. Either on her way there, which means she's gone somewhere else to get the ice creams, or on her way back. Maybe she didn't have enough cash and went back to the campsite for some more?'

The others point out that, even if she had, she would surely be back by now. Perhaps the best thing is to walk back along their usual route to the campsite, keeping an eye out for her all the way. She's bound to be there.

If she isn't they'll come up with a plan B.

They keep their eyes peeled. But she isn't there. They ask the campsite creep and his wife if they have seen her. They haven't. They ask the Loveshack Smythes. They haven't.

All three girls are worried sick. They check the bathroom block, the kiosk and then the campsite office where Richard is manning the phones.

Nothing.

John is elsewhere he says, busy repairing a fence on the farm but Richard offers to help. He can see how worried they are. He offers to drive around Polzeath, if Vicky comes with him she can be the look out whilst he concentrates on driving. They reappear thirty minutes later with no sightings.

He phones the Doom Bar to ask George if he has seen her at all but he says he hasn't.

'Sorry Rich,' Vicky hears him say, his deep voice booming through the handset. 'I bumped into her yesterday by the bench, but I didn't see her today. It's been so busy in the bar

209

I haven't had a break. Sorry I can't be more help, mate,' he continues. 'I really hope she's OK, I'll keep an eye out and call you straightaway if she does come in.'

By 7.30pm they cannot think of any more options or ideas.

'I think we need to call the police or the coastguard,' says Pip. 'She could have had an accident or be in serious trouble somewhere. If we call now they still have a few hours of daylight left to start looking.'

Richard's dad, Donald, is now involved too and offers to make the call for them.

He dials 999. After being asked what the emergency is he's swiftly put through to the duty sergeant at Wadebridge police station, PS Clifford Watts.

'Clifford,' he exclaims. 'How the devil are you? Long time no see!' It turns out he and the policeman had gone to school together.

Whilst the others listen intently, he tells the sergeant that Cerys has not been seen for approximately five hours after going to buy ice creams in Polzeath just before two o'clock that afternoon. The three girls have searched the beach and looked all around the village, asking the ice cream man and in the grocery store, but no one remembers seeing her and they can't find her anywhere.

Sergeant Watts takes a few details. Where she was last seen plus a brief description of what she looks like and what she is wearing.

'OK Donald, that's really helpful. I'll pass all the details to the patrol cars that are covering the area this evening. However, I must reassure you that, as she has only been missing for a relatively short time, there is a high chance she may have just bumped into someone she knows. Perhaps be drinking in a local bar somewhere, and will more likely than not reappear later on this evening.

She's eighteen years old and, in my many years of

experience, it really isn't unusual for persons of her age – who are reported missing – to turn up safe and well after deciding to have a few hours to themselves.'

He reassures Donald again. 'No, there's nothing more you can do at this point in time; other than let us know if and when she turns up, or gets in touch with anyone. The PCs who are on patrol will keep an eye out in all the most likely places and pop into the local pubs to check too. They know what they're doing. If they see anyone fitting her description, or have any potential sightings, I will call you. I must say again though – in the vast majority of cases – people who have not been seen for a few hours do, eventually, reappear and there is always a very logical explanation so please don't worry yourself unduly.'

'But what happens if you don't find her anywhere... or she doesn't?' asks Donald.

'The formal procedure, if she has not turned up or been in contact with anyone, commences after twenty-four hours. So if there's nothing by two o'clock tomorrow afternoon, as you say that was when she wandered off to get the ice creams. Then, and only then, we will need to raise a formal missing persons report.'

The girls shiver as Donald heaves a sigh at the end of the line.

'If that does end up being the case we will work with you and her friends. We'll gather all the details and information that is necessary, and then decide the most appropriate course of action.'

'OK Clifford, that makes sense. Let's just hope, like you say, she turns up soon. I will let you know if she does come back to the campsite or we do hear anything. Thank you.'

Donald replaces the handset as gently as possible. The others have heard most of the conversation and got the gist of what the sergeant has said. That most people come back after a few hours. That it isn't unusual. It doesn't stop them worrying though.

Beryl invites the girls to join them for supper. John will soon be finished on the farm and she has made a huge quiche and a bowl of salad large enough to feed an army. They'll need some help to finish it.

What a lovely, kind lady thinks Amy. All day the girls had been looking forward to going out somewhere to eat. *For a proper meal.* They had laughed. The thought of going to the pub or somewhere lively seemed completely wrong now if Cerys isn't there. Plus they have completely lost their appetite. Sitting with Beryl, Donald, John and Richard around a cosy, farmhouse kitchen table would be perfect in the circumstances even if they don't eat anything. And when Cerys arrives back at the campsite they'll be there to welcome her.

The girls pick at their food, eating a little out of politeness. Beryl understands. She knows they're not going to get much sleep again either, even though they're desperately in need of some proper rest after the salmonella shenanigans of the weekend.

They round off the meal with a cup of cocoa and sit around the table in silence. They're all staring at the phone. Waiting and hoping, *willing*, it to ring. But it doesn't. At half past nine Beryl suggests they all go to bed. Whatever transpires overnight they'll all need to be up early in the morning and full of energy.

Beryl's right. The girls thank her again and reluctantly head back to their tents. Amy doesn't want to be on her own, without Cerys in their tent. She's teased Cerys endlessly about her snoring, which in reality is nothing more than heavy breathing. Now she just wishes Cerys would magically reappear in the tent so she can be soothed by it.

They wrestle all three sleeping bags into one tent and squeeze in for the night. The closeness of one another a relief as darkness falls. Their stoicism and optimism being severely tested. Of course Sergeant Watts knows what he's talking about. He's got many years of experience he said. She'll soon be back.

But, with sleep proving elusive, they lie quietly, side by side. The horror of what is happening unfolds before them. The moon shines brightly through the canvas, highlighting the salty tears running down their cheeks. The owls hoot, masking the sound of their gentle weeping.

They hold hands and silently pray they'll wake up in the morning to find it's all been a bad dream.

37

WEDNESDAY 25 AUGUST 2010

'Hi little sis,' Debbie's cheery voice is far too loud on speakerphone. Emily answers with one hand, trying not to spill her takeaway coffee on her lap. She's on her way back to Port Isaac for her final trip to Cornwall and has pulled over at a very welcoming snack van on a lay-by next to the A30.

'I was beginning to get worried about you,' she continues, slightly quieter.

'Hi Deb, how are you… What do you mean?' Emily replies, delighted to hear from her.

'Well, I've rung so many times and you never answer. I've even tried your office, but you're never there. You always seem to be in a meeting, or at a conference or something!' Debbie laughs.

'Oh I'm sorry, it's so lovely to hear from you Deb,' Emily replies, sipping her coffee slowly. 'But you don't need to worry, I'm absolutely fine. We're all fine. Just super busy. I've been working on a new project at work and it's been pretty intense… all good though.'

'As long as you're okay. I was worried you might be doing more stuff on that missing girl again and not telling anyone… I really hope you're not, Em?' Debbie adds, genuine concern in her voice.

'No, honestly, don't worry, I'm so busy Deb I literally wouldn't have time anyway.' Emily hopes she sounds truthful.

'Although I'd be lying if I said I hadn't thought about it. I do wonder if they'll solve it this time. I really hope they do. It still gives me nightmares now and then, but keeping busy helps to take my mind off it. Just about to check in now for another conference as it happens.'

'Well, don't let me hold you up... I mean it though Em, I'm here if you need me, you know that? You would tell me wouldn't you?'

'Of course, you take care too big sis, I'm sure you work too hard too. I'll ring you when I'm home again in a few days. Love you.'

God, thinks Emily, finishing the last of her coffee in one large, noisy gulp. *I'm sure she knows, she can read me like a book.*

She carefully throws the empty cardboard mug into an almost overflowing waste bin and jumps back in her car. She's going to check in, drop off her luggage as quickly as she can, and then park at the beautiful little fishing hamlet of Port Quin. From there she'll walk along the coastal path in a westerly direction towards Lundy Bay and the rock she hid behind as a child. She's brought her map this time.

Then, tomorrow, she'll walk to Lundy Bay again but from Polzeath instead. So she can approach it from a different viewpoint. It might trigger different memories.

She wants to give herself every possible chance. By – literally – trying all angles she's sure she'll be more likely to remember. All she needs are just one or two crucial details that will reveal the person's identity to her.

*

When she arrives at the Ship Inn there are a few holidaymakers chatting at the bar where they balance, legs dangling, on the high stools. It seems like a lull in proceedings before the post seaside rush come in again later. Ben is busy unpacking the dishwasher and putting glasses back in neat rows on the shelves behind the bar.

'Well hello there,' he shouts as she strolls into the bar. It's so dark after the bright sunshine outside that she can barely see where she is going, let alone where his voice is coming from.

'Room three is all yours,' he hands over an enormous brass key. It looks as old as the building itself.

'I'm not going to lose that in a hurry,' she laughs, still blinking as her eyes continue to adjust. 'It weighs a ton!'

'Would you like a hand with your luggage?'

'No, that's really kind of you but I'm fine thanks Ben, I've travelled light for once so I should be able to manage it.'

'No probs, you go up the stairs, turn right and it's the second room on your right hand side.' He continues to stack glasses. 'Make yourself at home and let me know if you need anything. There's tea, coffee, milk and biscuits in the room but shout if you need any top ups. What time would you like to book for supper? I've provisionally put you in for 7.30pm at the moment.'

'That sounds ideal, thanks. I'm going to drop my bags in the room and pop right out again so I'll see you later.'

Emily is so glad she booked the Ship Inn. It makes everything easier coming somewhere familiar and with such a warm welcome, especially when she knows what she is doing is so deceitful. It almost makes it feel acceptable. Plus Ben is still just as handsome as she had remembered. Possibly even more so.

Some work conference. But she's brought her laptop to keep up with emails so she isn't entirely lying.

Why do I have to keep convincing myself? she wonders.

*

The stroll to Lundy Bay from Port Quin is simply stunning. Emily wanders past Doyden Castle, a captivating 19th century fortress, now rented out as a compact and bijou holiday home.

Wouldn't that be a wonderful place to stay, she thinks, although not suitable for her two youngsters at the moment. You have to walk about a mile to get to it – with your entire luggage – and it is literally metres from the cliff edge, with a sheer drop down to the sea. But with uninterrupted views of the ocean from every one of its stone mullioned windows it would be a magical place to spend a vacation.

The sea is a beautiful turquoise blue and the sky ablaze with sunshine as the salty breeze gently kisses her cheeks. It's so relaxing. She's hoping a couple days of fresh sea air might make her feel a bit healthier. Even Marcus commented on how tired and thin she is looking the previous weekend.

A variety of people walk past. Ramblers with rucksacks and binoculars, or dog walkers just soaking up the wonderful scenery and escaping from the modern world.

It's heavenly.

Emily can see Rumps Point in the distance, with the coastal path meandering along the ins and outs of the cliffs, before dropping down and up again. Emily feels like she could stretch her arms out and almost touch the next headland, but as she walks towards it the rocky outcrop seems to get further away and takes ten times longer than she expects.

Concentrate Emily. She tells herself. *You need to be focused. These two days are your last chance to put the Cerys Morgan mystery to bed. If you can't do it now you never will.*

Half an hour later she reaches Lundy Bay, taking time to savour the view and make the most of every second. To enjoy the magical beauty of the place. She would love to come back in the depths of winter, when it's stormy and wild.

She walks down to the bay, climbing down the wooden staircase hugging the cliff, so she can recreate the afternoon of her sixth birthday. She must remember every possible detail. Every single, little, tiny detail. She sits on the beach for a while by the rock pools, then when she feels ready she slowly climbs back up the steps, taking in every sensation. Every view. Every sound. Then she sits on the grass where she had watched Cerys and her companion all those years ago.

She shuts her eyes to concentrate. The person with Cerys was definitely the taller of the two. Emily can still see their silhouette lit up from behind by the wonderful sunshine, like a halo. How ironic. They certainly didn't seem to be an angel now. Oh, how she wished she could tell if they were blond or dark. But with the baseball cap it was impossible. She didn't want to convince herself one way or the other unless she was completely, absolutely, definitely sure.

Their clothes. *Concentrate Emily. Concentrate.*

Definitely shorts and T-shirt. Three big capital letters. Why, oh why, can't she remember them?

She still keeps thinking it's theatrical but doesn't know why. *S? C? R? God it's so frustrating.*

Three middle-aged ladies walk past, puffing as they climb up the slope.

'Afternoon,' they greet her. 'Another wonderful day!'

'Sure is,' replies Emily, still immersed in her own, faraway world. 'Enjoy your walk.'

She takes her mind back to 1976. Surely it had to be someone Cerys knew? Why would she wander off with someone... unless of course she had seen them... or met them, before?

Look at the facts Emily Harrison. She tells herself. *Cerys is on the beach in Polzeath. That's over a mile from here. She's having a lovely time with her friends. Why would she suddenly decide to wander off, so far, when she was simply meant to be buying ice creams?*

She *must* have bumped into someone.

She must have bumped into someone *she knew*.

That must narrow it down. The girls hadn't met that many people in the time they had been on the campsite.

There were the brothers, Richard and John.

There was George.

There was George's friend Barry.

There was Vicky who came looking for her.

Hang on a minute, there was also the brothers' dad, the campsite owner, Donald.

And his wife Beryl.

Then there was the twins' dad – Gary "Horrible" Banks – the thoroughly nasty piece of work.

But when the police interviewed him the newspaper report said he had been out for the day in another part of Cornwall, with his family and friends who had been visiting for the day. The story all stacked up when they checked it out so there was no reason to think otherwise.

Then there were the "Loveshack Smythes" so called by the girls. Pip said they were in their fifties. So surely, even to a six-year-old, they would have looked too old?

She lies down in the grass again, shutting her eyes to listen to the sound of the birds and the insects and the gentle sea breeze. It is so relaxing.

You're getting there girl, you're getting there. Just relax and let it happen. Shut your eyes and just keep imagining you're back in time.

*

Emily wakes up with a jump as a group of children squeal and shriek their way up the steps from Lundy Bay. She must have dozed off. The tide is coming in. All the holidaymakers are gradually retracing their steps to the car park before the sea reclaims the sand during its twice-daily ritual.

She's dazed. She'd suddenly thought she was back with Marcus, Molly and Jack. The children who walked past a moment ago have disappeared and a feeling of horror runs through her body. A sense of déjà vu.

Please no, dear god, no… she panics.

Shaking her head in disbelief she can't believe her brain could play such a cruel trick. Five seconds later she almost bursts into tears when she hears their high-pitched chuckles of delight as, hidden from view behind the hawthorn hedge, they make their way back to the car park.

She's starting to lose her mind. She's desperate for the next two days to be successfully over, so she can get back home. To make it up to Marcus, Molly and Jack for all the time she has been preoccupied with Cerys.

It – she – is taking over her life. She knows it. Cerys is in her thoughts night and day. She can't keep it a secret for much longer. Debbie is worried about her. Marcus is worried about her. She's even worried about herself and what she might do. Too little sleep and too much alcohol is not a good combination for anybody.

Yet she can't stop.

The beautiful, mesmerising mermaid girl has turned into a complete obsession for her; from which there is currently no escape. She will not be free until she knows exactly what happened.

As she sits back up she realises the sun has gone in and it has become chilly with a brisk wind blowing across the cliff top. She's shivering and her back is stiff and aching from where she has been lying on the grass.

She'll go back to her room and have a nice, hot bubble bath. She's come prepared with a bottle of Chilean Merlot so will pour herself a big glass and relax in the tub whilst she thinks everything through.

WEDNESDAY 25 AUGUST 2010

A hot bath combined with a couple glasses of Merlot works wonders. Emily feels ready to face the world again. Her table is reserved for half past seven so she has just over an hour to relax and get ready for supper.

There's a small balcony, *a ridiculously tiny balcony*, she thinks to herself. Too small for a single seat let alone a table and chairs. It's obviously only there to look aesthetically pleasing from the outside, with no practical use whatsoever. It has a low, fancy ironwork balustrade that she imagines is simply to stop you accidentally falling over the edge, *should you manage to squeeze yourself into such a small space in the first place.*

The narrow French doors don't even open fully; they rest against the low railings at a forty-five degree angle. But they do have the benefit of letting in some fresh air after the hot bath – which has completely steamed up her room – without giving up too much privacy to anyone walking past.

Emily sits on the bed, to look out over the mini balcony and catch a glimpse of the ocean. A small triangle of blue. With her eyes shut it's simply lovely to hear the sound of sea birds again and the background chatter of holidaymakers strolling along the cobbles outside, reminding her she's back by the sea.

She props up the pillows behind her and flicks through the magazines that have been left in the room, feeling relaxed in the delightfully soft dressing gown. It must be brand new for this season. Fluffy and snug, not at all like the scratchy offerings you normally find in hotel rooms, and which have probably been worn and washed thousands of times. It's a revelation to have a few minutes of total peace and quiet and she's loving it.

Her room at the Ship Inn is small and quirky. An eclectic mix of shabby chic furniture, old wooden beams and creaky floorboards that slope just enough to make you feel a little unsteady, as if you are on a real ship. It's never going to be five star luxury but the finishing touches make it homely and comforting.

Totally engrossed in what she is reading a gentle knock at the door takes her completely by surprise. She thinks she must have imagined it and ignores it. Probably just someone for the room next door. Who would be looking for her?

There it is again. She reluctantly scoops herself up off the bed and makes sure her dressing gown is tied securely before opening the door, just a wide enough gap to see who it is. It's Ben.

'Hi Emily,' he smiles. 'Just wanted to check everything's OK?'

She smiles back, how thoughtful. 'Yes, it's great thanks. The room is lovely and I've just had a totally awesome bubble bath with all the wonderful toiletries in the bathroom, they smell heavenly.'

'Great, that's good, glad you like them.' He seems a little nervous, unusual for Ben.

'It's so good to see you back again Emily. I was really annoyed about the reception my dad gave you last time, I just hope it didn't spoil anything for you and your sister.'

Somehow he is now standing in her room but Emily doesn't mind, it's easier than talking around the doorpost.

'Gosh; that seems ages ago now,' Emily fibs, trying to make light of it. 'No, you don't need to worry, we had a great time and it was entirely my fault anyway for being a bit insensitive towards him, so I totally understand. I hope he doesn't mind me coming back.'

'Now why should he?' He whispers, reaching out and gently pulling her towards him. 'I certainly don't mind you coming back so my dad can just go whistle as far as I'm concerned.' He lets out a quiet laugh. 'He probably doesn't even know you're here yet anyway, so we'll see if he recognises you later.'

He's acting a bit weird. Emily thinks. *He keeps moving closer and he's smiling nervously, lopsided.*

'So why have you come back, Emily Harrison, Senior PR Executive? Is it really for work or were you missing me?'

Emily is confused. Is Ben flirting with her? She thinks so, and after two large glasses of merlot she's quite enjoying it. She has been so stressed and paranoid lately it's good to be able to relax and unwind.

He's also extremely handsome. As he offers her a friendly, heartfelt hug it's impossible to resist. With her head resting on his shoulder he strokes the back of her head, tenderly running his fingers through her hair and places a gentle kiss on the top of her head.

It feels so good. No, she's wrong, it feels *more* than good. It feels absolutely amazing. It's exactly what she needs, to enjoy the warmth and security of being held by someone for as long as she can. The last few weeks have been so hard. She hates all the pretence and secrecy. She is completely discombobulated, plus she and Marcus haven't been as close as they normally are. She's so preoccupied all the time, even if she's trying her best to hide it.

Ben's hug is firm and strong. Tender and comforting. She just wants to be in his arms, to forget about anything else that is going on in the world.

Just for a moment or two.

More than anything she wants to forget all about Cerys Morgan.

Cerys. The vanishing mermaid girl and the mysterious, impenetrable and increasingly terrorising web of intrigue she has got herself mixed up in.

WEDNESDAY 30 JUNE 1976

There were no sightings of Cerys on Tuesday night or Wednesday morning.

The police patrols neither saw nor heard anything. Donald, Richard and John went for a drive around Polzeath and Rock after milking the cows but they too found nothing.

The girls want to do something constructive so set off early to walk along the beach, from one end to the other, and speak to anyone they think might be able to help. They take a photo of the four of them together at the barn dance, in case someone should recognise Cerys.

Most of the people they ask are exceptionally polite and friendly. They're horrified to think their friend is missing and "of course we'll look out for her and let you know if we see anything." They take the campsite telephone number and promise to call if they do.

But as the morning wears on they become increasingly disheartened. In the early afternoon they gather again in Donald and Beryl's office, to decide what to do.

At three o'clock Donald decides they cannot put it off any longer. It's good timing as PS Watts has just started his late shift, due to finish at eleven, and it's easier to talk to him than start all over again with someone else.

'Hello Clifford,' greets Donald. 'Not good news this end I'm afraid, unless you have?'

'I'm afraid not, but the patrols have been actively looking,' he replies. 'It's over twenty-four hours now so we will need to log the details, fill out all the necessary MISPER forms and then arrange for her parents to be contacted. Just so you're aware there's quite a lot of paperwork needed… I'll ask one of the PCs to come over to you as soon as they can.'

'Thanks Clifford, appreciate your help. It's all a complete mystery to be honest and the other three girls are at a loss. They're utterly fearful of what might have happened to Cerys, it's so out of character'.

*

PC Martin arrives within the hour. Donald shows the wiry, young policeman into the office and the bundle of papers he has brought with him lands with a thump on the desk.

Beryl, as efficient as ever, produces a pot of tea within minutes. All laid out neatly on a tray with milk, sugar and chocolate digestive biscuits. She thinks he looks like he could do with building up a bit, as he thanks her profusely and asks for three spoonfuls of sugar. Either that, or he thought her tea looks so awful the sweetness will take the taste away.

Sure enough there are dozens of forms covering a whole host of questions.

PC Martin needs all the contact details for Cerys' family. As yet her parents, rightly or wrongly, haven't been told. The girls simply can't do it. To their enormous relief PC Martin says they are not to worry, he'll arrange for a colleague from the Dyfed-Powys Police Force to visit them in person at their home in Pembrokeshire. They will fully inform them of the situation once he has all the necessary details.

He requests information about the people Cerys has been

in contact with over the last three days. Plus any unusual events, or things she might have done or said, that might have been at odds with her usual behaviour. They could possibly give a clue to her whereabouts. Any phone calls she has made. Have they been with her at all times or are there any gaps in their accounts. The list goes on.

He asks for a recent photograph. Pip had taken some with her Polaroid camera at the barn dance the previous Thursday so gives him a couple of those with Cerys in. They're not particularly good quality but will hopefully help people to recognise her.

They give all the answers they can as accurately as possible. PC Martin then explains that he will need to talk to all the people she had been with immediately before she went missing. This is to further establish all possible facts. He'll make the necessary arrangements to do this over the next two days. In the meantime he and his colleagues will "step up" the search and see what leads transpire by the end of the week.

'You have to remember there is still a very strong possibility that she will turn up safe and well… so, as hard as it is, you must all keep positive. You will see an increased police presence in the immediate area. This is perfectly normal and absolutely nothing to be alarmed about.' He continues, rubbing his chin, in a very matter-of-fact sort of way.

After finishing his last drop of tea, tipping the cup up as if his life depends on it, he bids them farewell. His next step is to return to the station, file the official report and start contacting all the individuals the police will speak to in the next forty-eight hours.

He gives Donald, Beryl and the girls his direct telephone number and asks them to call immediately if they have any news. He will also confirm to them as soon as Mr and Mrs Morgan have been apprised of the situation.

WEDNESDAY 25 AUGUST 2010

The buzz of Emily's phone brings both her and Ben back to reality with a jolt. She has no idea how long they have been holding each other. It vibrates on the bedside table and rings a virtual bell. The ringtone she has deliberately selected for her family diary reminders.

Oh shit. Shit. Shit. Holy shit. Emily panics.

As she is roused from their deep, peaceful hug she realises it is Ben – not Marcus – holding her close. The stark reality of the situation dawns on her. The effect of the wine she drank earlier in the bath has now well and truly worked off. Her phone buzzes again and she knows exactly what the reminder is for. It's to remind her to call home so she can talk to Molly and Jack before they go to bed.

'You need to go,' she says very quietly. Unable to look at him as she focuses on the bedside table where the phone spins on its back like an upturned beetle.

There's no response.

'I'm sorry, but you need to go – *now*,' she repeats. Almost a shout and with more urgency.

'What's the rush?' Ben asks. 'I can move your table reservation if you want more time?'

'You need to go. Ben, I'm sorry. I need to call my children; it's their bedtime. They'll be wondering where their mum is.'

Silence.

'Of course. I understand.' He gently strokes her shoulder, where her dressing gown has slipped down her arm. '... And you don't need to worry. Nothing happened.'

'What do you mean *nothing happened*?'

'We had a hug. You enjoyed it, I enjoyed it. End of.' He smiles at her kindly.

'You look so exhausted Emily, and I was so looking forward to seeing you again after getting your email when you said the same. It's really nice having you here and I'm OK with it if you still are.'

Emily doesn't know what to say. She is too bewildered to move.

'... Hang on a minute... what do you mean? You're OK with what... If I still am?'

'Well, the email you sent me last week. After you'd reserved the room... *Thanks gorgeous, sounds fabulous, can't wait to see you xxx*... I thought you meant you were coming down especially to see me? I've been so looking forward to your visit, and on your own this time.' He gently strokes her shoulder again.

Holy cow. She remembers now. She thought she had been so efficient multi-tasking at the motorway services after that dreadful conversation with Gary "Horrible" Banks.

Somehow she must have emailed to Ben the text she had meant to send to Marcus.

Oh, Jesus. Emily thinks. *You're going to have to be much more careful. You have almost just got yourself into one right hideous mess. You might not be so lucky next time.*

WEDNESDAY 25 AUGUST 2010

Emily almost doesn't bother going down for dinner. Embarrassed – and confused – about what happened she doesn't want to make the situation any worse.

It sounds busy in the bar, she can hear the constant chatter of people; the clinking of plates and glasses reminding her that she hasn't eaten. The smell of delicious food wafting up from the kitchen begins to make her feel hungry.

She eventually goes downstairs at about nine o'clock. It's packed with holidaymakers so it's easy to avoid making eye contact with Ben. She places her order for a "light bite" with the young waitress and plans to get back to the sanctuary of her room as quickly as she can. It soon arrives and the cod mornay looks divine, although she can barely touch it. What she had mistakenly thought was hunger is just her insides churning with guilt and her faux-appetite disappears in a nanosecond.

She sits quietly, not wanting to be conspicuous. She can see George is once again sat at the bar, propped up with a pint of ale and a group of locals. She guesses they're all sixty something with beer fed bellies of varying shapes and sizes. Emily isn't sure if he has recognised her or not, but grabs the moment to pop up to the bar to sign for her uneaten meal with the waitress when Ben disappears to the kitchen.

'Such a shame. Can't believe it's been ten years now' she hears one of George's pals say, shaking his head.

'I know. Ten years. Ten years yesterday; incredible. Where's that gone? Such a nice guy. Do anything for anybody. Loved his cars. Still don't know how he came off the road that night, there was nothing else around and it wasn't as if it was raining. Conditions would have been really good.'

'Yeah, but you knew Barry as well as we all did. He always drove way too fast,' George replies, staring into his pint. 'Everyone knew that. He scared the living daylights out of me on more than one occasion.'

'George is right, doesn't take a rocket scientist to work out what happened,' chips in another.

'Truth is, after what happened I don't think he really cared anymore,' George says quietly to Emily, or anyone else close enough to hear. He's consumed at least four pints and clearly hasn't recognised her from her previous visit. 'Brave lad though... oh yes. Mark my words; he was braver than anyone I knew. Then all that other silly business when he was younger. He had such wild moments, he would temporarily lose control and do something stupid just for the hell of it.'

He's rambling now.

'Trouble is, he never meant for anything to happen, but it did. He regretted what he did for the rest of his short life. His poor dad having to cover up for him. He made me promise I'd take his secret to my grave too, and so I will.'

Bloody hell. It must be *the* Barry they're talking about. Barry the car mechanic who had been to the barn dance with Cerys and the girls the Thursday before she went missing. George's very handsome best friend Barry. Ben's dad George's best friend Barry. The one Amy told her about.

Emily's ears feel like they are stood up on end, she knows

this is important. Despite desperately wanting to avoid Ben and get back to the comfort of her room she knows she must stay to hear what else they say. She hopes the waitress doesn't strike up a conversation with her now and stop her hearing.

'No, that'll be all, thanks very much,' she says politely but quickly. The girl smiles, then looks at her oddly as she loiters at the bar pretending to tidy the receipts in her purse.

She mustn't ask George any awkward questions this time, or make him lose his temper again. She will tread carefully.

Just listen. Deep breaths. Her mantra. *Deep breaths. Don't worry what the waitress thinks.*

George is definitely more melancholy this evening although she is aware, only too well, he could turn in an instant.

She's in luck. George continues without any prompting, fuelled by the local ale. Barry had been pulled unconscious from the wreckage of his car. It had rolled over several times on a notorious corner, now nicknamed locally as "Barry's Bend". The ambulance got there really quickly but he never made it to hospital. His injuries were too severe and he died on the way. He and George had been best of friends since they were about eight years old.

George, getting emotional, pulls a scruffy old black and white photo from his wallet that he must have carried around for years. He shows it to Emily. The others have obviously seen it before and he's happy to show it to someone new.

'There he is, we were best mates from school. Such a laugh, miss him every day.'

Emily studies the photo. They're like chalk and cheese. Even in black and white she can see clearly the much younger blond, good looking surf-dude George. His remarkable likeness to Ben makes her tremble inside. Then the handsome, dark haired, athletic Barry. Both posing happily in almost matching shorts, T-shirts. Barry in a baseball cap, with his sunglasses balanced on top of his head.

'I'm so sorry to hear what happened to him, but what a lovely photo,' Emily exclaims, keeping very composed. 'When was that taken?' She tries to look even closer at it without making her interest too obvious. Barry seems so familiar, but she must not jump to any hasty conclusions.

'Oh, that was another mate's stag do. We would have been about twenty then, so at least thirty years ago.'

'Wow. I'm so sorry for your loss, it must have been really hard for you.'

Emily suddenly realises she has to chance it; she may not get such a golden opportunity again. 'I don't mean to pry but were you and Barry around when the young girl went missing from the campsite all those years ago then?'

George looks at her sideways, with suspicious eyes. '… You know there was someone else asked me about that in here not so long ago. Couldn't understand why it had come up again after all these years, then I saw the TV news appeal with her old mum and dad. Tragic.'

'Do you remember much about it?' she pushes, he seems more accommodating today. She's not going to let on that she knows he was the barman in Polzeath. She wants to give him the chance to say something of his own free will.

'Oh yes. Even with my poor memory I can still remember that summer very well,' he sighs. 'Barry and I went to a barn dance with the girls the week before. I'd got to know them as they came in the bar where I worked pretty much every night. Richard and John from the campsite thought it would be fun for the eight of us to go.'

He takes a long sip of beer.

'Cerys was such a lovely girl. I really liked her. Didn't fancy her mind, just liked her. I was engaged to be married and had a baby on the way. She was fun, you know, kind and thoughtful and we just talked a lot. Like brother and sister. In fact that's exactly what she said; that I was her Cornish big brother. Especially when all the others took ill and she was on her own for a bit.'

'Gosh, how awful for you when she went missing.' Emily tries to be calm, to not show how excited she is about the information he is sharing.

'It was. We were all questioned and gave statements. I had bumped into her a couple times just before she went missing. On the bench. I was working at the Doom Bar and used to pop out for a break in the afternoon to check out the surf.' He fiddles with the photo as he talks.

'But the day it happened, I don't know if she made it there or not. I couldn't get away from work as we were too busy. I only found out later that she had gone missing.' He bites his lip.

'We all helped with the search. Everyone who lived here helped for weeks and weeks. I still can't believe she was never found. Someone, somewhere *must* have known something.'

'What about Richard and John from the campsite? What happened to them?' She knows she's taking a risk now. She crosses her fingers behind her back.

'Didn't see them much after. I got married and had a kid, they went back to college.' He scratches his head. 'Nice blokes though. Clever too. Loved sailing if I remember. Richard took over from his father at the farm and I'm pretty sure John's a doctor, or a dentist, or something.'

Emily can't pad out the conversation with George much longer without making it seem weird or like she's interrogating him; plus she's struggling to hold her own emotions together having seen the similarity of Ben to his dad.

Just one last question. She thinks. *Just one more, then disappear.*

'It's so mysterious. To think so many people helped and they never found anything. Do you have any idea at all what might have happened to her?'

'Wouldn't like to say. Not fair on the dead to speculate.' He shrugs his shoulders and looks her straight in the eye. As if he wants to say something but can't.

She looks away.

She's feeling ghastly inside and can't press him any further as he clams up. She wishes him a good night and hastily retreats to her room.

She lies on the bed, content with her unexpected sleuthing work for the evening. Staring at the ceiling she thinks it all through.

George and Barry had definitely spent a lot of time with Cerys and the girls. George obviously met Cerys a few times on her own. Plus she now knows exactly what Barry looked like.

Interesting about Richard and John too. She must try and find John.

Note to self for the morning.

Emily shuts her eyes and pictures the black and white photo of George and Barry again.

She is exhausted. What a rollercoaster of a day. She needs to do a bit more work on this. So many thoughts are whizzing around her head.

As she starts to fall asleep her brain still can't switch off.

Just what was Barry's secret?

That his dad covered up for him?

A secret so big George promised never to tell?

And why wouldn't he speculate about "the dead"… did he mean Barry… or Cerys… or someone else?

THURSDAY 1 JULY 1976

Euan and Bronwyn Morgan arrive at the campsite just after ten o'clock in the morning. The heatwave is not abating and it's another gloriously hot and sunny day in Cornwall. Hours earlier, when they set off from Narberth, there had been a gloomy, sea mist that perfectly mirrored how they were feeling. The contrast now seemed cruel. How could something so awful be happening on such a beautiful day?

Pip's mum Janie had kindly driven them after hearing the dreadful news. The journey was made in silence other than Radio Two playing quietly in the background; until the hourly headlines mentioned the student who had gone missing in Cornwall and Janie quickly turned it to mute as surreptitiously as she could.

Amy, Pip and Vicky are out when they arrive. They are busy putting up some "Have you seen this girl?" posters in and around Polzeath. It had been Pip's idea initially then Vicky, the artistic one, quickly drew up an eye-catching A4 size design to get printed. They need to keep themselves busy to take their minds off the reality of the situation so they'd clubbed together their remaining holiday money and used a photo of Cerys in the floaty white sundress. The one she was wearing when she disappeared. It's uncanny. She looks exactly as she had as she strolled up the sandy path to buy the ice creams.

The girls are constantly fighting back tears, avoiding any conversations about Cerys that will set them off. They scrounged a lift from John to the library in Wadebridge where they had one hundred colour photocopies of the poster printed. He'd waited patiently in the car and the assistant, who was so wonderfully understanding, only charged them for fifty. She had felt so sorry for them as they counted out their spare change in between sobs.

Richard and John have also offered to drive them round Rock, St Minver, Port Isaac and Port Gaverne later so they can put up more posters in all the prominent locations.

When they return to the campsite and meet Cerys' parents they are completely overcome with emotion. Euan and Bronwyn cannot hold back their tears, or Donald and Beryl. Bronwyn cried all the way in the car and is finding it impossible to come to terms with what is happening.

Pip, Vicky and Amy each hold them tight but can find no words to articulate what they are thinking or feeling. All they can do is silently hug them and hope their presence will make Cerys reappear.

Pip was worried they might be angry. Angry with them for "losing" Cerys. But they aren't. Their hearts reach out to the girls who they can see are in as much shock as they are.

Donald and Beryl have sorted out accommodation for the Morgans and they can stay there as long as they want. A friend of theirs has been renovating a small cottage with the intention of renting it out as a holiday let. It isn't completely finished, but near enough, and he is more than happy to offer it free of charge to the distraught parents. It's a homely retreat for them in between all the police activity.

Janie books into a local bed and breakfast for a few nights to give Cerys' parents a bit of privacy. She'll make sure they're being looked after, but give them space as well. The police have drafted in extra officers who are patrolling various locations in pairs. They're on the beach, along the coastal path, in and around the villages. The local inspector is co-ordinating the search and, as more information is gathered from people Cerys spent time with over the last few days, he'll use it to refine their approach.

PC Martin has already spoken to Vicky, Amy and Pip. Their accounts are all very similar but he has become acutely aware they didn't spend much time with Cerys over the weekend, immediately prior to when she went missing. While they were poorly they couldn't say for certain who she had been with, or where she had been. All they did know is she went walking on her own a lot. She hadn't mentioned anyone, or anything, in particular.

PC Martin speaks to Donald and Beryl. They too tell the story of the girls being unwell and seeing a lot of Cerys spending time on her own. She had gallantly looked after the others; the only thing she had mentioned to them was a lovely walk she did along the coastal path on her way to choose some postcards. Beryl had been in Truro choosing an outfit for a wedding but returned late afternoon.

Methodical and meticulous he speaks to John and Richard, only to find much the same version of events. Both had been busy on the farm on Tuesday afternoon when she was last seen. John had been milking the cows, later than usual because of a technical problem with the equipment, and Richard putting up a new fence. John then helped him later in the afternoon once he had finished elsewhere. Sports mad he'd stopped for a sandwich and to check the latest news from Wimbledon on his way.

John, however, did remember seeing Cerys, he thought, the afternoon before when he drove through Polzeath. It might even have been the day before that, he recalled. He thought she was with George Pengelly and he tooted his horn. But that was at least a whole day, if not two, before she went missing so he didn't think it would be of much help to the police.

Neither he nor Richard had seen any of the girls on Monday evening as they were still not fully recovered from their sickness and had spent a quiet evening in their tents. But they had planned to meet up with them and go out somewhere, most likely the Doom Bar, on the Tuesday evening. That was, before they knew Cerys had gone missing.

A local lad himself and fiercely proud of his role in this case PC Martin speaks to George Pengelly at the Doom Bar. In a different year he vaguely remembers him from school. As well as the comment from John, the girls said they got to know him well and he joined them at the barn dance the previous week with his friend Barry. When he questions him, George tells PC Martin that, yes, he had bumped into Cerys on the days she was on her own. He had popped out for a few minutes' fresh air on those days, to check out the surf, and spotted her sat on the bench. They had chatted, but he didn't see her on Tuesday afternoon as he was busy behind the bar and didn't manage to get out that afternoon.

One thing PC Martin is interested in is the shower block incident. Pip, Vicky and Amy have all told him about it. How Cerys had been extremely upset after Gary Banks, the twins' father, spied on her. She had been really shaken up. He takes him in for questioning and gossip spreads like wildfire. But he and Sandra have a strong alibi and he's released without charge. They remembered seeing Cerys on Tuesday morning and were both delighted to see all the girls looking so much better. Gary and Sandra had then met up with some old friends in Padstow for a "spot of lunch" before returning to the campsite late afternoon. The next they knew was when the other girls came back. They were getting the twins changed out of their sandy beach clothes. The girls were all desperately looking for Cerys and had hoped she was going to be in her tent when they got back but clearly she wasn't. The "red haired one" was asking everyone if they had seen her but no one had.

Finally he speaks to Stephen and Pauline Rogers a.k.a. The Loveshack Smythes. He can tell they are a very private couple. Enjoying a peaceful walking holiday, on the Tuesday in question they had been following a circular route around Watergate Bay. They were honest in admitting when they first saw the girls arrive their immediate reaction had been annoyance; worried they would be disturbed by raucous teenagers. However, apart from a couple evenings where they had come home rather giggly – which they actually found quite entertaining – and a couple noisy arguments, they had been delightful campsite neighbours. They had felt very concerned about them when they were poorly at the weekend but the girls had apologised to them profusely for disturbing them. So, again, although they had relatively little interaction with them they had just thought them to be good campsite neighbours.

PC Martin tries to piece all the bits of information together to see what he can follow up. He will need to speak to Barry and the ice cream man too. He'll go to Hammett's Garage, he knows it well, having been there many times before. He and the other PCs will then visit all the local shops and bars again to see if there have been any new sightings or possible leads.

For now all he can do is write up his report and see what news comes in from the patrols.

43

THURSDAY 26 AUGUST 2010

Luckily Ben isn't around at breakfast.

He's been so gentlemanly about *the situation* as she keeps silently referring to it in her head, in an attempt to make it seem less distressing. Emily on the other hand is mortified. She tried to explain to Ben the email was not meant for him but it had sounded like a half-baked excuse, made up on the spot, to get her out of a disgraceful corner. After her phone buzzed Ben had quickly returned to work downstairs as if nothing had happened. All the time maintaining his chivalry. Not for a second did he make her believe she had behaved badly.

Quite the opposite. He said he had enjoyed every second. She was a special person and he had thoroughly enjoyed spending time with her. Just her. She didn't need to feel guilty. He was a grown man and knew what he was doing. He certainly did not want to lose her friendship as a result.

But nothing he said would stop her feeling guilty about what she had done.

Ben's Aunt Lisa is busy juggling the preparation of every possible variation of a full English. With sausage but no bacon; with bacon but no mushrooms; just tomatoes; no tomatoes;

poached egg; scrambled eggs; runny fried eggs; white toast; brown toast. Emily isn't sure how she pulls it off with such good grace, especially first thing in the morning. Emily doesn't feel like eating any herself so at least that will save Aunt Lisa a bit of time and effort.

She sips at an orange juice and plays around with a bowl of bran flakes, pushing them around the bowl in an anti-clockwise direction with the spoon, forcing herself to eat a little bit every so often so she doesn't feel hungry later.

*

After breakfast Emily sets off to Lundy Bay for one more time. Her final visit. She parks at the National Trust car park like she had done with Marcus and the children a few weeks before. Then walks slowly down the green, shady path overgrown with shrubs and flowers. She listens to the cacophony of field birdsong before the view opens out before her. She feels like she's standing on the edge of the world looking out over the never-ending ocean.

She's ready. Ready to once again fully immerse herself in her memories of 1976.

Today is the day. *The* day.

The day she has to solve the mystery.

She resolutely concentrates on the task in hand, not just to complete her mission but to push all sickening thoughts out of her mind of what she had done the night before. Just thinking about it makes her feel nauseous.

Plus all the lies she's been telling Marcus. This week he thinks she's at a conference in the Cotswolds. She had decided not to say Cornwall as it might make it too obvious if she was back there again. The longer her deception went on the more troubled she became about slipping up. Especially now she felt she was getting closer to a conclusion.

She'd called home after Ben left her room the previous evening and spoken to Molly and Jack, but had found it impossible to hold back the tears. Marcus could tell something was wrong and kept asking if she was OK.

'Oh I'm fine,' she'd fibbed. 'It's just been such a long day of meetings all I need is a good night's sleep. I love you Marcus, I'm so looking forward to coming home for the bank holiday weekend.'

'Me too!' he had replied. '… And it's our wedding anniversary next week too. We must do something special. I know we haven't planned anything yet, but we'll sort it out this weekend when you're back home.'

That had just made her sob even more.

'Hey, hey, Em. Don't cry, honey, don't cry. I didn't mean to upset you. That was meant to be nice. Fifteen years – we've got lots to celebrate.'

She strolls down the path towards Lundy Bay. It isn't cold but the weather has turned cloudy and feels like it might rain. She has brought a coat with her just in case. It will come in handy to sit on if nothing else.

As much as she tries to focus on Cerys she's still reeling from the events of the night before. It all feels unbelievably unreal. Perhaps it was just a bad dream. A really, awful nightmare that she will wake up from any minute now and realise it was all a figment of her imagination. If only.

Ben is so handsome, she has never denied that. He's kind and gentlemanly, she has never denied that. But why, oh why, had she let herself succumb to his affections so easily, without thinking for a moment what she was doing?

And then the photograph of Barry with George. She can't get it out of her mind. Ben looks so much like his father at the same age it is uncanny… and what was Barry's terrible secret that George had promised never to tell? It's all too much.

She walks slowly; there are fewer holidaymakers around

today. Probably sticking to the traditional hotspots like Padstow and Rock given the weather is definitely more iffy. Before settling down by the hiding rock she walks right to the end of Rumps Point. Watching the waves crash against the rocks below and listening to the roar of the ocean helps to clear her mind. Bronwyn Morgan's words had stuck with her. How, for years, she had stood on the cliffs in Pembrokeshire to look across the sea. Convinced Cerys was sending her signs and waving to her, as the sun twinkled and sparkled in the water.

Now here she is doing the same, looking back towards Bronwyn. Bronwyn said she knew her daughter was still here. Still here in Cornwall. But where?

Emily retraces her steps to exactly the same spot where she had hidden on her sixth birthday. With her back leaning against the big rock she closes her eyes and once again runs through the events from thirty-four years ago.

Cerys is in front, her companion following closely behind. Cerys doesn't seem to be talking but the other person is. They're agitated, their arms waving about, at times they grab her by the wrists. Exactly as she had told the policeman, DI Davis.

They aren't running but Cerys is walking as fast as she can, almost breaking into a jog. Trying to keep a bit of distance between them.

Emily shuts her eyes even tighter, covering them with the palms of her hands. She can't make out what they are saying; their voices are carried away on the wind, even though they are now much closer. She can see Cerys looking at her companion who is holding both her wrists now and gazing into her eyes with what looks like loving affection and confused anger in a single expression.

Then the T-shirt. Why can't she remember the three big letters? Why are they so impossible to remember? As they move further along the path, that's the moment Emily knows

Cerys has recognised her and she puts her fingers to her lips to say "shhh" so she doesn't give her hiding place away.

When she eventually plucks up enough courage to raise her head again the most beautiful girl she has ever seen, the beautiful mermaid girl who had given her the shell bracelet just the day before, in her floaty white dress and with long, wavy golden hair, has disappeared. She's gone. She's absolutely nowhere to be seen.

That's when Emily screams and ducks back down as the other person, now on their own, spins round to see what the noise is. They have their head in their hands and are stood glued to the spot, scanning in all directions and looking really worried. Emily keeps as quiet and still as she can until, after what seems an age but is probably only two minutes, she thinks it is safe to raise her head. Just as she does she hears her mum calling her name, as she climbs up the path from the beach to find her. Even though it was so long ago she can still remember the incredible sensation of relief as she saw her mum.

'Emily! I'm going to find you!' she calls.

By the time her mum reaches the top the person has walked away, heading for Rumps Point.

They're looking back and forth. Stopping every few yards to glance around, as if checking who may be there.

Watching them again now Emily thinks they must be utterly panic stricken. They're looking around either for help, or in fear. She can't really tell which. As she looks on, a silent spectator in a private screening, they gradually shrink. Reducing in both size and energy as they meander sporadically along the cliff top path, until they too vanish from sight.

Emily replays the motion picture in her head. She rewinds certain sections and then fast-forwards. Then starts again from the very beginning watching it over and over, bit by bit, frame by frame.

Still she can't get over how beautiful Cerys was. Her six-year-old self had been completely mesmerised. Sat here now she's still in awe of her natural prettiness. She keeps getting flashbacks of the photo George showed her the night before too. She's starting to think there is an uncanny resemblance to Barry in the person she's seeing walking along the path, with their baseball cap, shorts and T-shirt. Especially the way he wore his sunglasses. Emily is seriously thinking about Barry now. He had been to the barn dance with the girls the week before and George had said how wild he could be. Plus his secret. What was it he did that he regretted for the rest of his life?

She needs to think it through very carefully. If it was Barry what should she do? She's so desperate to solve the mystery, yet she keeps remembering the postcard.

Ruin my life and I'll ruin yours.

She feels so close to the answer. She's dreamt of finding the answer. But now the thought of doing anything absolutely terrifies her.

THURSDAY 26 AUGUST 2010

Emily drives slowly and thoughtfully back to the Ship Inn. She makes her way discreetly up to her room, sneaking in through the side entrance, hoping not to be seen or heard. Has she finally fathomed out the answer she has so desperately been trying to unravel?

The secret code to the safe. The final piece of the multi-dimensional jigsaw puzzle.

It horrifies her. What on earth is she meant to do next?

For the last nine weeks she has thought of nothing else. Now she thinks she has the answer she has no idea what to do with it. Her immediate thought is to run another wonderful bubble bath and relax. She mustn't rush into anything, just take her time and plan her actions carefully. Cerys has been missing for thirty-four years.

Thirty-four years, one month and twenty-eight days to be precise.

So another two hours – while she works out what to do – won't make a massive difference. She thinks to herself.

She opens the skinny French doors, pulling the curtains shut. That way the breeze can waft in but the outside world is kept exactly that. Outside.

She runs a deep, scented, luxurious bath.

Lemon verbena and rosemary. It smells mostly of the former the latter being more "a herbal hint to relax the mind". Or so says the label. She certainly needs that. The combination is blissful, along with another delicious glass of Chilean Merlot that she had left over from the night before. There's a tiny drop left in the bottle for when she manages to extract herself from the soapy bathtub.

Emily is simultaneously elated and alarmed. Happy she has the answer, but concerned her reasons for thinking it is Barry are more than a little bit flaky.

Should she go back to see DI Davis? Should she drive home and speak to Marcus? Or does she just hold tight and see what else she can find out?

She can't make up her mind. If she goes home it'll mean explaining to Marcus where she has really been for the last two days – and all the other "meetings" she has *really* had over the last few weeks – so that probably isn't the best idea. On the other hand if she goes to DI Davis what would she say to him?… *Oh, by the way, I've worked out who it is… by sitting at the top of the cliff path for two days… and I think it's Barry. Barry the mechanic.*

Would DI Davis even know who she meant? And, if Barry died ten years ago, what would they be able to do about it anyway?

She takes a long sip of the silky red wine.

Or he might just think I'm a complete crackpot. She laughs out loud. She still isn't convinced DI Davis thought her six-year-old memory was reliable anyway.

But she needs to do something. Surely Euan and Bronwyn Morgan must be told, even if the person she thinks was the last person to see Cerys alive is now himself dead.

She shuts her eyes and lets herself drift off. Delighted that she thinks she knows the answer, but trying to extinguish the next round of anxiety from her brain.

It will all work itself out. She tells herself. *Just relax, take your time and let it happen.*

*

Rejuvenated after an indulgent soak, topping up the hot water every so often to keep it beautifully warm, she calls home to catch Molly and Jack before they go to bed. Emily feels and sounds considerably more upbeat today which cheers Marcus up too. He had been worried about her the previous evening.

'So how's it all gone today Em?' he asks.

'It started off slowly but then the afternoon went really well. We're just about there.' She's doing it again. Playing with the truth.

'We're just finalising all the minor details now. Dotting all the i's and crossing all the t's.' She smiles. Comfy in the fact that, once again, she isn't entirely lying.

'A couple more conversations to be had and that'll be it. Done and dusted.'

'Wow, that's brilliant Em. Proud of you.'

'Aw, Marcus, that's sweet of you but let me get it completely finished first before you say that.' Then, trying to change the subject, 'I can't wait to come home though. Hope Molly and Jack haven't been playing you up whilst I've been away?'

'No, they've been great. We stayed up to watch *Shrek* last night and had choc ices as a special treat.'

Emily's heartstrings pull; she feels so far away and left out. She loves sitting down to watch a film together, just the four of them.

'What time are you planning to be back tomorrow Em?'

'Should be mid-afternoon, I'll set off after the final marketing session. Depends on the holiday traffic too but I certainly don't intend hanging around here any longer than I need to.' She laughs. At least that is the truth.

'Well, you have a good evening Em and drive carefully tomorrow. I've got to be in work early so just text me when you're on your way if I can't answer. We'll have a barbecue or something easy in the evening.'

'Sounds brilliant. I'll get some bits and pieces on my way. If you don't mind picking up Molly and Jack; I can whiz around the supermarket far more quickly without them.'

'Deal.'

'I love you Marcus, you know that don't you?'

'I love you too... really glad you're feeling happier tonight, one more night to go Em and it'll all be done.'

As Marcus puts the home phone down it beeps with a message. While he was talking to Emily her boss has called and left a brief voicemail.

"Hi Emily, Anne here. I'm really sorry to bother you, as I know you're off sick this week but I need to clarify something quite urgently for the PR schedules for September and I can't get hold of Jo. We need to confirm with our media contacts by close of business tomorrow and I'm pretty sure Jo has gone abroad for the bank holiday weekend. If you could call me back – tonight or in the morning – that would be wonderful. Sorry again. Hope you're feeling better. Thanks."

His hands itch to call Emily back. To find out what is going on, but he can't bring himself to do so. Surely Anne is wrong. She must be mixing Emily up with someone else. Emily isn't off sick; she's at a conference in the Cotswolds.

Leave it, he decides. Emily will call Anne to update her on the project before the bank holiday weekend anyway.

THURSDAY 26 AUGUST 2010

Emily decides what to do immediately after her phone call with Marcus.

She has to deal with her findings before she goes home, otherwise it will hang like a menacing shadow over her for evermore. She has thought it through. She can't tell Marcus; she doesn't know Richard at the campsite well enough to talk to him; she'll need to make an appointment to see DI Davis… so there's only one other option. She'll speak to Ben.

She trusts him and he's always been so helpful. Plus he said only yesterday she's a good friend. If she can eliminate all thoughts of the previous night for long enough she can talk it through with him, and get his advice on what to do next. She texts him from her room.

"It's me. Need to talk somewhere private. Is there anywhere downstairs we can go?"

At least ten minutes passes before she gets a reply. Maybe he's ignoring her. Maybe it wasn't such a good idea after all. Her hand trembles each time she checks her phone.

"Hi, not really. Bar v busy. Where r u?"

Phew, that's ok he's just busy.

"In my room"
"OK, will be up when I get a spare 2 mins"

Emily quickly finishes off the rest of the Merlot and hides the empty bottle in the pedal bin in the bathroom, disguised in a carrier bag. She doesn't know why but it makes her feel better not leaving it blatantly on show.

There's a knock at the door and Emily gingerly answers it.

It's Ben. As handsome as ever. It feels like déjà vu, minus the dressing gown.

Concentrate. Focus. You've got to do this.

Luckily Ben breaks the ice. 'Hi Emily, how are you doing?' He's friendly, normal. It's as if nothing had ever happened between the two of them. 'You OK if I come in?'

'Yes, of course… of course you can,' Emily relaxes.

He sits on the chair, one arm resting on the dressing table. She sits opposite him on the end of the bed, unsure what to say next. She runs her hands along her thighs, smoothing down the material of her skirt.

'Everything OK?' he asks.

'… Sort of. Well, yes… yes, and no, really.' Emily's talking gibberish. She knows he'll soon wonder what is going on.

'I'm sorry. I'm talking nonsense.' She giggles, her nerves getting the better of her. 'Let me start again. Thanks for coming, it's really good of you and before you ask… no, this has nothing to do with yesterday. I'm really trying to forget about that if you don't mind.'

Her eyes look down at the carpet. She feels the sea breeze as the flimsy curtains blow gently into the room and settle back again.

'No worries, understood,' he replies. He puts his arms up, as if in mock surrender, trying to make eye contact and laughing. 'Just be more careful who you send emails to.'

Emily is relieved; at least that's one good thing. He's clearly not bothered in the slightest by the previous evening but she can tell he *is* desperately trying to work out what the hell is going on. He taps his foot, getting impatient. He needs to get back to the bar that is once again packed with customers. The hustle and bustle of the inn below them rising up through the ancient floorboards.

'Well, it's like this. You know I've been trying to work out who it was I saw with Cerys when I was here on holiday with my parents back in 1976 on my sixth birthday?'

'Yep, I seem to remember you mentioning it, if not to me to my dad,' he says, almost sarcastically, but trying not to be.

'Well... I think I've worked out who it was. I've been back to the exact same spot yesterday – and today – and gone over it again and again.'

'So why do you want to talk to me about it?' He quizzes her.

'I need your help Ben. I know it all sounds pretty far fetched but I think you know – or knew – the person and I really need your advice on what to do next.'

'Go on then, hit me with it,' he says, rolling his eyes, almost bored with the conversation and finding it all rather tedious. 'Tell me who you think it was.'

'Barry. Barry the mechanic.' She looks at him. His face is motionless, as if he doesn't understand. 'You know, your dad's best friend Barry.'

'OK, OK. I know who you mean,' he snaps. His smile is gone and he's clearly agitated. 'But you had better give me the facts... what exactly are you basing your momentous statement on?'

'Well, I know it sounds daft, but the photo your dad

showed me last night. It just looks so much like the person I saw. Especially the way he wore his sunglasses balanced on top of his baseball cap.

'… And then what your dad said,' Emily continues matter-of-factly. 'About how wild Barry was and how he did things he later regretted. Plus his big secret, the one your dad promised to keep?'

Ben sits silently, his head in both hands looking at his feet as if trying to take it all in.

Finally he looks up at her, straight in the eye.

'Emily, you don't have a clue what you're saying. There was no terrible secret. If it was it was the worst kept secret in the world. My dad had a stroke and he doesn't always remember things as accurately as he used to.'

'But that's what he said Ben… and the photo. I know I may be going mad but the likeness was uncanny, surely it *has* to be him?'

'NO Emily!' He shouts. 'Stop what you're saying. … STOP RIGHT NOW!'

He waves his arms at her in exasperation.

'My dad has *not* been keeping the secret of a murderer for the last thirty-four years.'

Ben stands up angrily.

'Barry worked for his father, in his garage. Soon after he started his apprenticeship a couple that were on a road trip around Cornwall brought in their top of the range Porsche for two new tyres. Barry was young, reckless and loved fast cars. He stupidly took it out for a joyride and accidentally damaged the wing.'

Ben paces up and down the room.

'His father was absolutely furious, but somehow persuaded the owner not to report Barry to the police. I don't know how he managed to, but if he hadn't Barry would have been done for taking a vehicle without permission, driving without insurance and all the rest. The bad publicity would have ruined the family business.'

He flicks his hair out of his eyes, still pacing.

'... So, like I said, the world's worst kept secret, but he certainly wasn't a murderer.'

'... Oh,' says Emily, flummoxed by his response but still not convinced. '... So that makes him wild, but not exactly brave. What was *that* all about?'

'That was something else. Barry's wife developed kidney failure in her thirties. She was on dialysis practically every day of her life. He'd take her to Truro hospital for all her appointments. Back and forth, back and forth.'

Ben looks straight at her now. 'It turned their lives upside down. Barry was brave because he donated one of his kidneys to save her, so she could live a normal life again. But after two weeks her body rejected it, and she died of complications.'

'... But–'

'There is no *but* Emily. You've gone and barked up the wrong fucking tree... and you're accusing my dad of being a murderer's accomplice.'

'No, I am not!' She shouts back. 'I never said Barry *murdered* Cerys, I just think he was the person she was with that day.'

'Yes, the person she was with *that day*,' sneers Ben. '*That day*, as you put it. *That day*, when she went missing. Never to be seen again. So as good as the same thing, if you think he was the last person to see her alive.' Spittle collects at the corners of his mouth.

'I'm so sorry Ben...'

'No you're bloody not. You're a sanctimonious bitch who thinks she can just make up stories, and try to pass them off as the truth. Pretending you saw it all when you were just six years old. Just to make yourself feel like you're a good person.'

'I'm sorry. I shouldn't have told you what I was thinking.'

She's close to tears. 'I should have just gone back to the police and let them deal with it, all in the proper way.'

'Oh really, well, how very thoughtful of you. You just go right ahead and do that. But you're not staying here a moment longer. You can pack your bags and leave this minute.'

With a swoop of his arm he sends all her toiletries, which were neatly organised on the dressing table, flying across the room. He then wrenches open the wardrobe to grab what few clothes she had actually hung up and starts stuffing them into her suitcase.

'There you go. I'll give you a helping hand. Don't worry about paying your room bill – just get out of this building and out of my sight. Go back to your little dream world. I doubt your husband even knows you're here... you ... you... lying, conniving bitch.'

Emily covers her eyes with her hands in horror as the door slams and all she can hear are his footsteps stomping down the wooden stairs.

SUNDAY 4 JULY 1976

The peaceful, charming villages in and around Polzeath have been transported to a chaotic, tumultuous universe in a matter of days.

There are people everywhere. Not the usual holidaymakers pottering about, taking photographs and enjoying ice cream. No. These are people with serious expressions; agonised and focused on what they are doing. Time is of the essence. They're frantic to find Cerys and as each minute, hour and day passes their frenetic search intensifies.

The police have been joined by well over a hundred local residents. News of the missing girl has spread and everyone desperately wants to help. Hoping and praying she will be found safe and well.

Dozens of journalists have descended on the quiet, idyllic location. Like a swarm of locusts. Like vultures competing over a carcass. Vying for their own exclusive story about the beautiful young girl who has suddenly disappeared off the face of the earth.

They each have their own separate theory about what has happened to Cerys; but they all carry the identical, beautiful photo of her on their front pages.

National and local papers alike. Fear-mongering headlines like "Beauty and the Beast of Cornwall" where they assume she's been abducted, after police ask everyone to check their garden sheds and outbuildings in case she is being held captive.

Extra resource is drafted in from the Met for the largest operation Devon and Cornwall Constabulary has ever seen. Roadblocks stop hundreds of vehicles on the A30 – and other key routes – to make sure she hasn't been bundled into a van, or a car boot to be smuggled out of the county.

Police divers regularly check the coastline, focusing on sites renowned for being the gruesome places where bodies are washed ashore. Sometimes it takes days, or even weeks, but due to the currents and tides there are certain locations well known to them that they monitor closely.

But there is nothing.

Absolutely nothing.

Just the ongoing, extreme heat and burning sunshine. The previous day, Saturday 3rd July, was the warmest day of the year so far. So incredibly hot that Cheltenham made history; the hottest day since records began. There have now been eleven consecutive days where Heathrow has recorded temperatures of over thirty degrees Celsius. It's simply unheard of.

The severe heat is not making the heartbreaking search any easier. The ground is scorched and tinder dry from the intense sun. People helping with the search are sunburnt and dehydrated. But still they won't give up. Volunteers rally around providing water and local shops and hotels donate cold drinks and refreshments. Everyone is doing their bit to help.

On Sunday afternoon, the duty inspector receives an urgent call from one of the PCs on patrol in Polzeath. They've found her watch. It's lying in a grass verge next to a public call box. The one she had been using to telephone her parents. Euan and Bronwyn confirm it is definitely hers, the one they had given her for her eighteenth birthday just a few months ago and which she had been so delighted with. It's a little dusty but other than that unscathed.

The last known call she made was the previous Sunday afternoon, when she was out walking on her own. The other girls were still recovering and hanging around the campsite. She had been due to call her parents again on the day she went missing but never did.

The discovery of the watch is a welcome breakthrough. An overwhelming surge of new hope spreads like wildfire. She could still be found. She *will* be found. It's five days since she disappeared but the watch is still showing the correct time. Unfortunately the police can't tell how long it has been there – or how it got there – but its emergence might just help to pin down the best location in which to intensify the search.

*

Two days later there are no further leads or positive findings. The formal police search continues in the baking heat and the locals continue to gather every morning. Mobilising teams to help scour every inch of the area, or provide refreshment and moral support.

A week after Cerys went missing Euan and Bronwyn Morgan appear on television. The local paper has put up a £1,000 reward. BBC Spotlight and ITV West Country both broadcast the news conference, but Bronwyn cannot bear to even look at the cameras.

She is inconsolable. In seven days she has aged at least ten years beyond her normally youthful forty-two. It's tragic to watch. Her body shakes as tears continue to flow. Euan does his utmost best to hold himself together, but when he too is unable to take the strain of speaking, one of the policewomen who are sat each side of them takes over. On their behalf she gently and carefully says the words they had earlier prepared together.

'If anyone has any information, however big or small… or thinks they might have seen Cerys in the Polzeath area on Tuesday 29th June please, please, please just get in touch.'

She visibly squeezes Bronwyn's hand.

'Alternatively, Cerys, if you are watching this and have for some reason not been able to get in touch, please just come home or call to say you are OK. If you are in trouble or have done something wrong we will not be angry. We just want you home.'

The policewoman takes a deep breath and looks earnestly and directly at the camera, reaching out to anybody and everybody who is watching.

'We just need to know you are somewhere… somewhere safe and well. We love you with all our hearts, and more than words can ever express. We won't stop searching until you are back with us. Please, please, please come home.'

The photo of Cerys in her floaty white dress and strappy sandals, her left hand holding onto a wide brimmed sun hat, fills the entire screen. She is laughing at something as she smiles confidently at the camera. She is absolutely beautiful. If anyone has seen her surely they will remember after watching this and get in touch.

THURSDAY 26 AUGUST 2010

Tears stream down Emily's cheeks as she grabs her belongings and rescues what she can from the floor. Leaving the key in the door she slips quietly down to the car park and drives off into the semi-darkness. It's still August but the nights are closing in and it will be dark soon after eight o'clock. She pulls up in Polzeath to get her head together.

She can't drive all the way home. It's over three hours away. Apart from anything else she's most likely over the limit after the Merlot and anyway, how would she explain to Marcus if she suddenly turns up at midnight after saying she had more meetings tomorrow.

There's only one thing to do. She'll sleep in the car and drive back in the morning.

The small corner shop is open until late so she ventures there to get a bottle of water. On a whim she picks up some fruit and cereal bars too. She's barely eaten for twenty-four hours and the wine has made her thirsty, plus she'll need something in the morning.

Finding a quiet corner in the beach car park, away from some young lads and ladettes that are taking it in turns to do noisy laps in their pimped up cars with extra big exhaust pipes and oversized wheels, she huddles back into her seat. They're having fun but not really causing anyone any bother and she feels safer having a few other people around, rather than being completely on her own.

She reclines her driver's seat to make it more comfy. With the radio on very quietly to provide some distraction she decides to check her work emails on her mobile. It'll pass a bit of time before she tries to get some sleep.

It takes an age to download all the messages. All the usual stuff but it's still going, so there must be a few more.

Still paranoid about the silver BMW she looks around to check there's nothing like it in the car park. She had looked up the number plate on the DVLA site, after getting home from her Gary "Horrible" Banks meeting. To her horror she had found the first two letters "WL" meant the car had originally been registered in Truro. But managed to calm herself down by applying some logic. There would have been dozens, if not hundreds, of business people driving home that Friday evening in silver cars of a similar make and model. Statistically a reasonable percentage of those would have been registered in Cornwall, so the probability of it being *exactly* the same car is tiny. It's all just a very strange coincidence. The driver hadn't even looked at her as he drove past; there was no way he would have known who she was, or what she was doing.

She continues to convince herself as her emails finish downloading.

Emily's eyes fall out of her head. Staring at her, sat in the middle of her inbox among all her other regular work messages is an email from Cerys Morgan.

Jesus, it can't be. She does a double take; surely she's misread it. *That's not bloody possible.* It must be from someone else.

She shuts her inbox, inhales deeply and reopens it, hoping it will be gone.

But no, there it is again. Definitely Cerys Morgan. She opens the message and reads slowly.

"Haha – bet that fooled you!
I know who you are and I know where you live.
I'm going to find you.
This is your second warning. Mess things up for me
and I'll do the same for you.

Yours truly,
(Not the real) Cerys Morgan"

A spontaneous shiver runs all the way down her spine and back up again. She shuts her eyes in contemplation and realises she is trembling all over.

'Aaaaaaaaaaargh,' she screams and jumps out of her skin, as a squealing screech comes from behind and there's an almighty thump on the back of her car.

A face peers at her through the driver's door window. 'Aaaaaaaaaaaargh, go away, go away, leave me alone!' She screams at the top of her voice.

'Bloody hell miss, I'm sorry,' the poor lad is more petrified than she is. 'Sorry miss, honest. I really am. I didn't mean to frighten you; I just accidentally skidded off the kerb and couldn't stop myself in time… I'm sorry.' Then the skateboarder slides off across the car park as quickly as he can to join his mates.

Emily is shivering with fright; she cannot stop all four limbs from violently shaking. Even wrapping her arms tightly around her body doesn't help and silent tears are rolling down her face. Now she knows the taxi driver had *definitely* been right. Against all good advice, she has well and truly poked her nose in, and found out precisely what he meant.

She had already been a little bit scared about spending the night alone in her car; now she's absolutely terrified.

FRIDAY 27 AUGUST 2010

Emily does not get a wink of sleep. Even though every bone in her body aches with exhaustion she can't get comfortable. Plus the email from whoever it is pretending to be Cerys Morgan has completely unnerved her.

She isn't normally frightened of the dark but this is different. Every time there's a gust of wind and the hedge rustles she imagines there's someone hiding in it, watching her. Every time an owl hoots she jumps out of her skin. When the shadow of a mangy fox moves slowly across the pitch black tarmac it takes on the shape of the grim reaper and makes Emily tremble with fear.

As daylight gently breaks the sense of relief is immense. Her body is stiff all over yet she has never been so pleased to see the sun rise. Although that is rather an exaggeration, it's more of a faint glimmer of light through a sea fog that is rolling in fast. She can see the dense cloud wrapping itself around the rooftops as if devouring them for breakfast; moving in on the car park like some out of control ghostly monster with eerie tentacles about to grab her car.

It's like she's in a real-life horror movie. She's read and re-read the email from Cerys about fifty times, trying to work out who could possibly have sent it.

Or why.

There *must* be someone out there who is worried about what she's doing. If they're *that* worried it can only mean one thing. They have a guilty conscience. The email was received at 18:36, which was when she and Ben were arguing in her room. Maybe he is right and she has got it all dreadfully wrong.

Without some form of divine intervention there is no way Barry could have sent the email. Or George his dad. He simply wouldn't be that au fait with technology and it *must* be someone who has sufficient knowledge to be able to set up a fake email address.

Her head is as heavy as concrete due to lack of sleep and the never-ending struggle to solve the mystery. The email has made it even more fascinating and even more horrifying in equal measures. She needs to freshen up and considers going for a dip in the sea. The salty water would not help though; it would only make her feel even more unkempt.

From their family holiday a few weeks ago she remembers a hotel near Rock advertising a special summer offer for their "Spa Experiences". The facilities were all brand new and one-day passes cost just £20. It's extravagant but she could go there and have a shower, maybe even a relaxing jacuzzi and sauna, or a proper breakfast, and make sure she's fit for her drive home.

*

Her brief but thoroughly enjoyable "Spa Experience" turns out to be a brilliant idea. Emily looks and feels human again by the time she emerges. Ready to face the day. She smiles gratefully at the beautifully manicured lady on reception, who seems more than a little surprised that she is in and out so quickly as she wishes her a safe onward journey.

She texts Marcus as promised and makes a mental note to herself to remember to get the barbecue items when she's nearly home. The battery on her phone is nearly dead, probably from reading the Cerys Morgan email so many times, so she turns it off to preserve what little there is while she's driving. If she stops anywhere on the way she may need it and she can charge it up again when she gets home.

It's an uneventful drive back. Busy but moving. Most of the holiday traffic is going in the opposite direction. Emily feels her life gradually revert to normal as she leaves Cornwall and the menacing fog far behind. By the time she gets to Exeter the sun has almost burnt through the cloud; the familiarity of the M5 and the ever-congested Almondsbury interchange feel strangely comforting as she heads back to Thornbury.

It's early afternoon when she stops to get the food for their barbecue. As she mooches around the supermarket there's a keen sense of excitement in the air. Brightly dressed shoppers are busy filling their trolleys with summer treats. Everyone is optimistic about the upcoming bank holiday weekend; even strangers are more chatty and animated than usual.

Emily packs her shopping at the checkout and looks forward to getting home. She's more than ready to kick off her shoes and sit in the back garden, whether the sun comes out or not. She's made good time and Marcus will be home by now with Molly and Jack. Still extremely weary after spending the night in her car she's mentally preparing herself for an energetic evening with Molly and Jack, they'll be so excited to see her, although inwardly hoping they will be content to play while she and Marcus take it easy.

She's spent much of her journey thinking about what to do. For this weekend at least she'll put it all to the back of her mind as much as she can. There's nothing she can do before she's in the office again, and that won't be until next Wednesday.

The trouble is, the more she mulls over it, the more she thinks she has got it all completely wrong. If she has she really ought to apologise to Ben but she's reticent to do that until she's absolutely certain. What if he's just covering for his dad? The story about the kidney transplant sounded genuine but he may have been making it all up. And it still didn't explain the email.

Her head is going round and round in circles. Did whoever sent the Cerys Morgan message *really* mean it, or is it a wind up, just to make her stop what she's doing?

Either way it just isn't right. Someone, somewhere knows what happened to Cerys. And someone, somewhere is trying to stop her finding out.

She dumps her shopping in the boot of her car and switches her phone back on. Just to check there are no urgent emails from work. Or in case Marcus has texted a reminder for something else they need for the weekend.

She wishes she hadn't. Sitting amongst her unread emails is another message from Cerys Morgan. Sent at 11:06. Emily shudders with horror as she opens it.

"You silly girl. I warned you.
You'd better get home. Now.
**   Yours truly,**
**   (Not the real) Cerys Morgan"**

Emily cries in terror as her mobile drops from her grasp into the foot well. Her hands shake so much she can barely retrieve it as she desperately starts the engine. Without thinking she tosses it onto the passenger seat and reverses frantically out of her space, almost knocking someone's trolley over. She races home, nearly jumping a red traffic light, but managing to control herself just in time.

Emily's car screeches to a halt, coming to an awkward stop with one tyre hanging precariously over the kerb. Oblivious to the surprised looks in their peaceful cul-de-sac she glances again at the message on her phone lying on the passenger seat.

Why, oh why, had she turned it off just because the infuriating battery was running low?

Five hours ago. You stupid, bloody idiot. She screams silently to herself, thumping the steering wheel.

Her hands shake so much she can barely turn the key and yet her senses are on high alert. Marcus' car isn't on the drive. She chokes on her breath. Everything around her seems perfectly normal; birds singing, lawnmowers whirring. A typical Friday afternoon before a bank holiday with the afternoon sunshine making promises it probably won't keep for the weekend. Yet her whole being is telling her everything is far from normal.

Greeted by a deafening silence a spine-chilling shiver runs through her entire body and her footsteps echo eerily off the wooden floor as she runs along the hall.

'Marcus, I'm home!' The kitchen chairs are askew; three bowls of half eaten, congealed breakfast cereal on the table. Her daughter Molly's beloved but battered old teddy bear, Peanut, lies in the corner of the room. Flat on his back with all four limbs stretched out towards her as if desperate for a hug.

Oh, come here precious. She silently cries, they must have left in one almighty hurry to leave him behind. Grabbing Peanut she holds him tightly to her face. Tears roll down her cheeks as the scent of her little girl's favourite bubble bath in his tatty fur overwhelms her. A tsunami of terror rises up through her body. Frightened and alone she has no idea what to do.

Oh dear god, please, please help me, what have I done? She knew the threats had become increasingly sinister, but she didn't think whoever it was had really meant it. They were just to scare her.

'Marcus, Molly, Jack, I'm home!' She screams at the top of her voice. A surge of hope powers her up the stairs two at a time in case they are, by some miracle, having a bath or playing quietly in their bedroom.

Emily checks every room. The cumulative fatigue of two months' furtive detective work, her sleepless night in the car and the terrifying threats have finally taken their toll and crushed any remaining stamina.

She calls Marcus. "Low Battery Mode" pops up and it cuts straight through to his voicemail.

She tries again.

And again.

And again.

Then the battery dies completely.

Not knowing what else to do she curls up in a ball on the floor, hugging Peanut so tightly his innards are about to explode and sobs her heart out until she has no more tears left to cry.

SEPTEMBER 1976

As hope fades – and the chances of Cerys being found reduce further with each passing day – the number of volunteers helping with the search also begins to subside. Their valiant efforts have been so much appreciated by everyone. But even the police, and Cerys' parents, have to admit that the likelihood of her now being found is remote.

They have dealt with numerous obstacles along the way. The scorching hot heatwave had broken all records and only came to a sudden halt during the last week of August with tremendous thunderstorms and lightning.

And, while everyone focused on the search, the outside world continued. Wimbledon had come and gone with Björn Borg beating Ilie Nastase in the men's final without dropping a set. The Montreal Olympics had come and gone, with the Olympic flame being doused by rain, only to be relit by an official using his cigarette lighter. Fourteen-year-old gymnast Nadia Comaneci became the first person ever to score a perfect ten, before proceeding to achieve six more perfect tens and win three gold medals.

James Hunt won the British Grand Prix at Brands Hatch only to be disqualified weeks later when the win was given to Niki Lauda.

At the end of July there had been a massive swarm of ladybirds; estimated to be about 23 billion in number. The warm spring had led to a population explosion, but as so many plants dried up in the abnormally hot weather the aphids they ate died too and the ladybirds swarmed across the south and east of the country, looking for new food sources.

Standpipes were introduced across much of the country and the local reservoirs were running dangerously low.

*

At the end of August the police decide to scale back and eventually stop the search. The Met officers who had been helping return to London. Euan and Bronwyn, who had themselves returned to Narberth at irregular intervals to collect fresh clothes or other items they needed, know this will be their last journey home. Vicky, Amy and Pip are all back in Pembrokeshire and have received their exam results.

They do all visit Cornwall one last time, briefly. The vicar of St Enodoc organises a short service; to give thanks to everyone who helped with the search, and to pray for Cerys' safe return. It certainly helps them all to move on. Move on but never, ever forget. The tiny, quaint church is overflowing with people wanting to wish her parents and the girls well.

It's a heartbreaking time. Saying emotional, tear filled good-byes to Donald and Beryl, John and Richard, George and Barry. Everyone has been so incredibly kind to them. As they leave the police reassure them that the case isn't closed and they will be in contact immediately if there is any news at any time.

And so Euan and Bronwyn return home.

But it never feels like home again without Cerys.

50
FRIDAY 27 AUGUST 2010

Emily's tears relieve the pressure on her brain a little.

She must keep calm, think straight and charge her phone. First she checks for any missed calls. There must be a logical explanation.

Debbie left a voicemail at 12:14; Emily would have been driving then and her mobile switched off.

'Don't worry Ems, I'm in court all afternoon. I'll call again later.' So that doesn't help with anything.

She scrolls up and down the list to check again. No missed calls from Marcus. Not even a reply to her text. He always sends a few xxx's whenever she messages him or a thumbs up. That's strange. No emails either; well, none of any consequence.

Then she notices there's a message on their landline. The light isn't flashing so it must be one Marcus has already listened to and saved for her.

"Hi Emily, Anne here. I am really sorry to bother you, as I know you're off sick this week but I need to clarify something quite urgently for the PR schedules for September and I can't get hold of Jo. We need to confirm with our media contacts by close of business tomorrow

and I'm pretty sure Jo has gone abroad for the long bank holiday weekend. If you could call me back in the morning that would be wonderful. Sorry again. Hope you're feeling better. Thanks."

"Message received Thursday 28th August at 6.03pm. No more messages."

Bloody hell. That must be it. Anne has gone and blown her cover. She plays it again to double check the time it was left. Three minutes past six. When she was on the phone to Marcus last night. He must have slept on it and then set off in a mad rush this morning to come looking for her.

Shit. Double shit.

She knows only too well she's been playing with fire but has no idea how she will get herself out of this horrendous situation. Emily deletes the message. Then she can deny it had ever existed. Or, as a minimum, it'll buy her some time to work out an explanation.

Emily paces around the empty house in a complete trance. Perhaps she's wrong. The voicemail from Anne must be just a coincidence. It certainly won't have helped the situation but Marcus, Molly and Jack not being here must be something to do with the threatening emails, not just work trying to get hold of her.

Surely?

But if something has happened now, that means it definitely can't be Barry either. He's been dead for ten years. So she *will* need to apologise to Ben.

Her head is spinning. Too many thoughts. She can't sit still for a moment. Where is Marcus? And Molly and Jack? When Marcus does get back what is she going to say? What is she going to do? She tries calling his mobile but it just rings and rings. Still no messages or texts either.

Oblivious to the time, or anything else, an hour later she realises she is sat on the living room floor, unaware how she got there, with the handset still grasped in her hand. She still has absolutely no idea where Marcus is. She looks at the caller list in the phone. The last one has no number, it's just "Withheld".

Strange.

Perhaps that was Anne the night before.

Should she ask a neighbour if they have seen anything? Should she call the police? Emily's mind is in turmoil. She doesn't even know how long they've been gone and they'd probably assume she's worrying over nothing. Or think it's a domestic argument.

Marcus must have Molly and Jack with him so he can't have gone far. She's worried sick and trembling with nerves. A million and one different ideas and possible explanations are whizzing around her brain like a tumble drier on steroids. And not one of them makes any sense whatsoever.

She lies flat on the floor looking up at the ceiling. Who could have possibly sent her the emails? Maybe it's someone she doesn't even know, whose name hadn't cropped up in any articles or newspapers she had read. Perhaps the taxi driver knew. Maybe he hadn't just been friendly when warning them, but he was actually involved. Maybe it was him.

Oh my god. Emily thinks to herself, her cheeks stinging and sore from her salty tears. *You stupid idiot. You really are now completely losing the plot.*

*

It's almost six thirty when the phone suddenly rings. Piercing the silent air with its foreboding, shrill tone Emily leaps to her feet.

'Em, it's me.' Marcus is speaking too fast and his voice is full of panic. '... Em... they're not here... what do I do? I've asked everybody... but no one knows anything about them... or... or what's happened.'

'Oh Marcus,' she's shaking all over. She holds the phone with both hands so she doesn't drop it. 'Jesus. Where are you? What's going on? I've called so many times and you didn't answer... who are you talking about? Where are Molly and Jack? Are they all right?' She's panicking now and talking faster than he is. 'I got home and none of you are here... and... and everything's all over the place. I'm so worried, tell me everything's OK,' Emily cries into the handset.

'Please, Marcus, please... I am so sorry... it's all my fault.'

'Em, stop it you're scaring me now. You don't have anything to feel sorry about... and why on earth would it be your fault?'

He tries to slow down. To make sure his words came out sensibly.

'I had a phone call from the police this morning. They said my parents had been involved in a road traffic accident and taken to the Queen Elizabeth Hospital in Birmingham.'

'Oh my god no, that's dreadful, how are they?' All sorts of awful things are going through Emily's mind.

'Apparently they were in a collision near Tamworth, had both been unconscious for a short while, and had suspected broken bones, but were being checked over by the doctors in A&E. I didn't know what to do so I just threw Molly and Jack in the car with their juice and set off.' He inhales slowly in an attempt to soothe his nerves; he's out of breath from talking so fast.

'I knew you'd be getting ready for your final day of the conference and didn't want to worry you, so I left a really brief message with Debbie instead. I asked her to call you later in the morning and explain what was going on.'

'Oh, no... I missed her call...'

He continues, talking over her. 'But that's just it Em. They're not here and nobody knows anything about them, or any accident. It must have happened on their way to the airport. They were flying from East Midlands this morning, up to Edinburgh for their long weekend.'

Emily remembers now, Ron and Liz had been so excited about it.

'Are you sure it's the right hospital?'

'Yes, I'm definitely at QEH and this is the main A&E department for the area. They've been so helpful. They've checked with all the other hospitals as well and there have been no admissions in the name of Harrison, or Harris or anything remotely similar today.'

'But… how come… that all sounds crazy. Where on earth could they be?' Emily rubs her eyes.

'Hang on a minute. Have you tried calling them yourself?' Emily thinks aloud now. 'It may be worth a try? Someone may answer their phone even if they can't; at least that way you may find out where they are?'

Silence.

'I can do it if you want me to?'

'Oh Em, would you? I'm too nervous in case it's really bad news and I need to keep an eye on Molly and Jack. They're completely bewildered by everything. I'll hang up. Can you call me back in a mo. Thanks Em, you're the best, love you.'

Poor Marcus. Emily feels so bad. She'd imagined he was racing around the countryside, trying to track her down in a fit of temper after the voicemail from Anne, and it's nothing of the sort. He's out of his mind through worry about his parents. She definitely has a guilty conscience. She needs to get a grip and do what she can to help.

She calls Liz rather than Ron. She always answers her phone really quickly, whereas she can't guarantee Ron would even hear his ringing.

True to form she answers after the second ring. 'Hellooo! Liz Harrison speaking!'

Emily loves her mother-in-law's telephone voice and the way she accentuates her greeting. Pronouncing her name in exactly the same way she has done for years, even though she would be able to see on her phone that it's Emily calling.

'Hi Liz,' Emily stumbles, trying to talk normally so Liz won't think anything strange.

'How are you? Marcus and I just wanted to check you're both OK?'

'Oh, we're doing just great Emily, it's really sweet of you to phone.'

Emily is by now more than a little confused.

'The flight was on time, we've checked into the hotel and it's absolutely wonderful. They even upgraded us. We've got an enormous room and a bathroom to die for. We're just having a cocktail in a fabulous little wine bar near the castle before we decide where to go for dinner.'

AUGUST BANK HOLIDAY WEEKEND 2010

Saturday morning is strained for Marcus and Emily after a sleepless night. The immense relief of knowing his parents are well is completely eclipsed by the fact that someone was evil enough to mislead him into a frantic wild goose chase. They've not said anything to his parents. There's no need to. It would serve no benefit and they don't want to ruin their weekend.

Marcus was absolutely livid when Emily called him back. He then had the most horrendous journey home from Birmingham. The motorway was gridlocked with bank holiday traffic and there were numerous lane closures and breakdowns. Molly and Jack, luckily, fell asleep for most of it and they eventually arrived home at twenty past ten. Any thought of a barbecue having been extinguished many hours earlier.

They're all paying for it in duplicate today. Two tired, grouchy children – and two even grouchier parents – do not make a good combination.

Emily and Marcus cannot understand it. What sort of person would play a sick joke like that? No, not a joke; it's not even remotely funny. It's a depraved hoax. Dreamt up by some monstrous person to cause them extreme distress.

Emily agonises over what to do. Marcus hasn't said anything, but then he doesn't know about the two threatening emails from someone pretending to be Cerys Morgan. Nor does he know anything about all the people she's been meeting over the last two months, or her trips to various parts of the country.

Despite the chaos neither of them have forgotten about the message from her boss either. Emily had been hoping and praying Marcus wouldn't mention it; she certainly wasn't going to bring up the subject. But, when he does, she's prepared an almost plausible explanation, although she's not certain he's one hundred per cent convinced.

'Oh yes, sorry about that, Anne called my mobile just after she'd left the message here. I should have let you know.' She bluffs as she pours cereal out for Molly and Jack. 'She got it completely wrong, Jo my job share has been off sick this week and she got us mixed up. She's always doing it and it drives me mad. It's not even like our names are similar, or we even look alike.'

She laughs an empty laugh, trying to make it sound as normal as possible.

'I managed to sort out what she wanted though, so it was fine, and also reminded her it's next weekend that Jo's off to Rome. Just hope she's feeling better in time.'

That's enough. She thinks to herself. *Don't overdo it or he will think something is up.*

Marcus had seen the original threat left in her handbag and had reacted so badly that she had hidden the postcard at the back of a drawer in her dressing table for safekeeping. She didn't want to remind him about it. Neither did she want to dispose of it, just in case she should need it again. That was weeks ago now. She prays silently that he won't link what happened with his parents back to that. However hard she tries to convince herself otherwise, she knows it must all be connected. She just doesn't know how. She can't stop wondering what Marcus is *really* thinking. Is he putting two and two together?

If she comes clean she will have no choice but to tell him everything. She can't let him know about the Cerys Morgan emails without explaining about everything else. They simply won't make sense on their own. But then, if she does, he will go absolutely berserk – understandably – and she can't face that either.

She's still too exhausted. She hasn't recovered from spending the night in her car, let alone the trauma of Marcus' parents make believe accident. She would rather just spend some quality family time with Molly and Jack while she works it all out. Better to keep quiet than pour oil on troubled waters.

Debbie phones at lunchtime, just to check everything is all right and to apologise for not getting hold of her properly the day before. Emily reassures her everything is back to normal, it was all a false alarm. Emily can hear the doubt in Debbie's voice and is relieved when she doesn't press her for more of an explanation.

'Yes, I'm fine Deb, honest.' She puts on the cheeriest voice she can muster in the circumstances. 'Marcus and I are just going to have a fun weekend with the kids. We're both exhausted after a busy week, it'll be lovely having Monday off work as well.'

'Tell me about it,' laughs Debbie. 'You look after yourself Em and I'll see you soon, love and hugs to Marcus, Molly and Jack too.'

*

Sunday isn't much better. Marcus still couldn't sleep and is thoroughly confused about it all. Worried and tired he's like a bear with a sore head. He has no enemies. He has never upset anyone, which he is aware of, in his life. Why would someone do that to him? The caller had sounded perfectly genuine, but when he tried to trace the number it simply said "Withheld".

He goes over the conversation he and the fake policeman had with Emily multiple times. But with each repetition he doubts more and more what he had or hadn't actually heard – or said himself – and what he had assumed in the heat of the moment.

The caller had *definitely* said he was from the police, but Marcus can't remember which force, or if the person had even given any details like that. Or their name or rank. Or which station they were calling from. The only thing he *was* sure about was they told him his parents had been in a road traffic accident.

Marcus had known his parents were driving to the airport that morning. He begins to realise he had probably volunteered this information unwittingly during the course of the telephone call. The bogus caller then cleverly picked up on it to make the cruel story, and the location, sound more plausible.

But that still didn't explain *why*.

Emily and Marcus consider reporting it to the police, but are at a loss as to what they would be able to do to help. They have so few details to provide. They have no evidence other than a phone call had been made, with no caller name or number.

So they opt instead to have a quiet, family weekend playing with Molly and Jack in their paddling pool, in an attempt to get back to normal, happy family life.

Emily looks out the kitchen window as she pours some lemonade for them all, watching Molly and Jack play happily together. She loves to listen to their excited giggles as they splash around in the water, although more of it seems to be on the grass now than in the pool. At least they're happy; they seem oblivious to all their parents' worries.

'I'll get it!' She shouts to Marcus when the phone rings, not sure he's even heard it. He's engrossed, playing with the children.

'Hello, is it possible to speak to Mrs Emily Harrison?' enquires a polite, softly spoken male voice.

'Speaking, who's calling please?'

'Hello Mrs Harrison. I hope you enjoyed your little surprise. This is just to let you know that next time it will be for real'.

Then the line went dead.

SUNDAY 29 AUGUST 2010

Stewart Clarke is enjoying his trip along the North Cornwall shoreline. He's tried surfing but sea kayaking is way more fun. At one with the ocean he loves to watch for wildlife as he paddles beside the majestic cliffs. He's lost count of the number of dolphins, porpoises and seals he has spotted this summer. It's the perfect way to spend a summer day. Or a spring, autumn or winter day.

The weather is forecast to worsen and storms are expected overnight, so today is a short trip. Long enough to make the most of the sunny afternoon but quick enough to get back before it turns.

He and his wife of six months, Louisa, are entertaining that evening too. They've got friends coming around for dinner – mostly schoolteachers like them – before the new term starts. Tomorrow's a bank holiday so it won't matter if it's a late night. He's looking forward to a few drinks and a long lie in. Louisa offered to start getting everything ready but he'll turn round shortly, she'll need his assistance and he won't be popular if he's late.

The coast by Rumps Point is one of his favourite excursions. Newlands Island, with hundreds of resident puffins, is spectacular. On a calm day he'll circumnavigate this and the other small islands, taking care to avoid the swell from any passing tourist boats. They like to get as close as they can to the cliffs to watch the wildlife. Today he'll play it safe and keep close to the shoreline. The breeze is strengthening and he's ever mindful he must start his return journey soon.

He's meandering along, thinking about his first week back at school, when he suddenly becomes aware the sea has changed mood. The swell is increasing and the wind is brisk. He'd planned to turn around at Port Quin but he'll never make it that far now. The kayak starts to roll around, this is far earlier than forecast and the moody, dark grey sea is becoming relentless. It's throwing his kayak around all over the place and taking all his upper body strength to keep it on an even keel. He doesn't scare easily but is getting nervous. This wasn't the plan for today. He paddles furiously against the wind but isn't making any headway at all. Rumps Point appears stationary as he fights to get back, the headland then quickly disappears into a thick band of low cloud and rain.

The sky has darkened and the waves and spray fill his eyes with salt, making it hard to focus. He's angry. Angry with himself for being so foolish. He's punctilious about the weather and tide forecasts. He loves the adrenaline and adventure of kayaking but never takes unnecessary risks. This has completely caught him off guard.

He had promised to be back by five o'clock. There's no way he's going to manage that now. He panics. He's not convinced he will make it home at all. He's cold and wet. He can barely see beyond the front of the kayak and the wind roars in his ears. The waves have increased in size and severity and he's being tossed around, ever closer to the rocks.

*

Stewart doesn't make it back for five o'clock. He fights ferociously against the wind and the waves, if he can just make it around the next headland the final stretch might be more sheltered from the wind. But Mother Nature has other ideas and he has no choice but to comply with her wishes.

He's lost his sense of direction in the fog but finds himself being manoeuvred into a small cave. All the while being thrown against the barnacle studded rocks. They scratch and scrape his skin through the tough rubber of his wetsuit, making his arms hurt so much he can barely hold on to his paddle.

The crushing force of the water swirls over his head and pushes him further in. The light is fading fast but he can see an opening directly above him where the thunderous sky is scowling down at him, as if to reinforce the predicament he is in.

A sea hole. He loves them. He's explored some in the past, when the sea was calm. Caves where the sheer, ruthless power of the ocean has made the ceiling collapse some distance inland, exposing a section of the cave to the big wide world above. Literally, through a hole in the ground. Peer over the edge and you can watch the sea crashing many, many metres below you. Sometimes a small opening, sometimes a big wide crater. Either way they're usually surrounded in folklore and certainly have a magical quality.

This is certainly a piece of magic for him. If he can negotiate his way safely, he might just be able to find a suitable place to climb out the kayak and clamber up the rocks. He will need to act fast. The sea is surging in through the narrow entrance. The enormous power of each wave is like a huge, incensed dragon searching every nook and cranny of the cave for prey, before it pulls away and returns thirty seconds later with renewed urgency.

Miraculously, after waiting for the dragon to retract its

head one more time, he uses every ounce of energy he has to pull his legs out and hoist himself up onto a slippery, wet ledge. He has to sacrifice his beloved kayak, but never before has he concentrated so hard.

Pulling himself up on to the rocks the gnawing pain in all his limbs leaves him exhausted. In the dimness of the cave he finds a semi-foothold and wrenches himself up again. All the while in agony as the sea constantly drags at his legs. Huge, heavy bundles of seaweed wrap around his feet, pulling him back down.

He just needs to get a little bit higher, to be above the worst of the swell, to catch his breath and work out a route to the top.

*

Completely exhausted, it's abundantly clear there is no possible way to climb right to the top. Fortunately he manages to find a ledge wide enough to sit on and high enough to be away from the main thrust of the ocean.

Still being drenched by spray, and shivering with cold, at least he's safe for now. The grey sky torments him through the sea hole ceiling. The wind roars with laughter at his stupidity. He is so close to dry land, yet unable to scale the perilous, overhanging rocks in the dark to gain access to the outside world.

Louisa will be worried. Extremely worried. She'll have seen the weather change and he's never late without a very good reason.

The rocky shelf is cramped but offers a temporary haven and, after adjusting his position carefully so as not to fall over the edge, Stewart retrieves his phone from the watertight pocket of this wetsuit. His cold, stiff fingers struggle to keep hold of it. His mobile phone has somehow survived the thrashing from nature, although he has certainly given it a run for its money today. He's grateful he splashed out and bought a really good quality wetsuit. He will let the manufacturers know once he manages to get himself out of this hole – he laughs to himself at the irony of it – he might even get a free one.

His euphoria is short lived. There's no signal to be found on his lonely shelf. But at least he knows what time it is. 19:43. *Bloody hell. I've been gone hours.* He's heard stories where people lost in the jungle, or thousands of miles out at sea, have been found by using their mobile phone so he decides to text Louisa anyway. Perhaps a passing satellite will pick up his signal and she'll summon help to come and rescue him. Even if it takes hours it's still worth a try.

He tries to ignore the shivering cold, and the overpowering smell of salty seaweed which fills his nose and throat, reminding himself it's relatively sheltered in the sea hole compared to where he had been only a short while ago. But trembling, fat fingers make typing any message a challenging test of his hand to eye co-ordination.

He mustn't run down the battery, he'll need it when the storm passes, but uses the flashlight briefly to look closer at his surroundings. The piercing, blue tinged glow makes the rocks feel eerie. Like a huge cloak of darkness swallowing him up. At the same time it boosts his spirits. If he can keep himself warm and above the water line until morning then he'll be able to find a way out.

The ghostly, unnatural illumination throws shapes and shadows around the black walls of the cave as the sea roars and bellows below him. He marvels at the splendour of the sea cave. His shelter for the night. He thinks to himself that he's probably the only person in the world who has ever sat on this ledge.

But then something catches his eye. Astounded, he almost loses his balance and comes perilously close to slipping off the edge.

There, right beside him, is the unmistakeable shape of a human skull. The eye sockets look straight at him with a ghastly, deathly stare. The teeth grimace and the jaws are wide open as if screaming in pain.

'Dear god. No. No. No. What are you trying to do to me?' He cries out loud. His voice unheard above the crashing of the waves and the howling of the wind.

He turns off the beam, hoping it has been a cruel trick of the light. Then, after a few moments, overcomes his anxiety to tentatively switch it back on. To have another look. It is, without doubt, a human skull. Surrounded by a collection of human bones. A skeleton. Lying right next to him, on this tiny little ledge where he has no choice but to spend the night.

Jesus Christ. I wish I'd stayed at home to help Louisa. Why did I have to go for just one more paddle. I'd be tucking into a delicious meal with a glass or two of something nice.

Man up, he tells himself. *Nothing you can do about it right now and a skeleton isn't exactly going to hurt you. It's dead.*

But then something metallic glints in the ray of light and he dares to take a closer look. Lying in amongst what looks like a small pile of soaking wet, tattered old rags is a rusty buckle on a very old, worn out sandal.

And a wristwatch.

TUESDAY 1 SEPTEMBER 2010

It was August Bank Holiday Monday when a passing dog walker found Stewart. Delirious and weak, he was lying face down on the sand at Lundy Bay.

After the storm passed he waited for daylight to arrive and the tide to depart. Once both the sun and the sea had done what was needed he quickly confirmed there was no way he would be climbing to safety. Although he could see the sky above him, through the hole in the ceiling of the cave, the overhanging cliffs were crumbling and precarious. Impossible to scale even with a rope, if he had one. The ledge he had found shelter upon was completely hidden from view, tucked underneath the rocky precipice.

Instead he slowly made his way back down the rocks. He was hungry and thirsty, weak and disorientated; but knew this particular bit of the coastline well enough that, if he timed it correctly, he could follow the shoreline around to the small sandy cove at Lundy Bay.

It was only a short distance away. Every so often a larger wave would course its way back in, through the narrow entrance of the sea hole, but he kept hold of the rocks and inched himself along. Fearful of letting go, he knew he didn't have sufficient energy in reserve to swim.

He was airlifted to Truro hospital, dehydrated and hallucinating. The paramedics were fearful. When the nurse set up his intravenous drip and provided him with sincere words of encouragement he muttered incoherently about skeletons, ghouls and the monsters of the sea.

Fortunately Stewart had the nous to take some photographs of the human bones he had shared his rocky mantle with. They were grainy and blurred but he had the foresight, even in the height of the storm, to realise people might not believe such a ridiculous story when he eventually made it back. It would be so easy to dismiss it all as a terrifying delusion. His brain playing a practical joke on him as he trembled with sheer terror, facing his own mortality head on, not knowing if he would be found.

*

Today, encouraged by Louisa, he shares the photos and information with the local police. He has to do something. Then at least it can be dealt with in the proper way.

The skeleton may be hundreds of years old, perhaps even an intrepid smuggler who met a grisly end scaling the same set of rocks. But even if it isn't, they would need to be sure.

DI Davis is, as ever, extremely professional. He notes down all the details, takes copies of all the photographs, confirms the precise location with Stewart more than once, just to be sure. Then he asks Stewart to remain available in the coming days should he be needed to assist with anything.

Given the position of the bones, and the challenging nature of the immediate surroundings, the police will need to plan the operation to retrieve the skeleton and any other artefacts very carefully.

Piece by delicate piece, bone by fragile bone. Anything they find will then be subjected to DNA and toxicology tests.

THURSDAY 2 SEPTEMBER 2010

'Crystal for fifteen!' Marcus smiles, as Emily opens a beautiful pair of crystal cut champagne flutes. 'We'll crack open some bubbly in a mo – I'll just get the BBQ started.'

They've decided to celebrate their wedding anniversary twice; once at the weekend, when they'll go out for Sunday lunch with both sets of parents. Today, the actual day, they're going to have the barbecue they postponed from the previous Friday.

Marcus' parents still have absolutely no idea about the shenanigans of the week before and it's going to stay that way. Going back to work after the bank holiday had helped both Emily and Marcus find a routine of sorts again. They're feeling calmer. Although, whereas Marcus is seemingly putting the cruel hoax behind him, Emily is struggling. She's in no mood for celebrating, despite gallantly pretending to everyone she is.

*

To her surprise, Emily was summonsed into her boss's office just before she left work and is now beside herself with worry.

Everything she has been doing is silently and stealthily garnering a terrifying momentum. A crescendo, if ever there was one; all of it building up to one enormous explosion. She knows the fireworks that will ensue will surpass anything she has ever witnessed or experienced before.

She has not yet told Marcus the seriousness of it all. How can she? On their wedding anniversary. Today of all days. Anne certainly knows how to pick her moment.

Once again she decides to deploy her usual tactics. Hoping and praying. Hoping and praying it will all just blow over and he'll never need to know.

Too many lies. She's in too deep now for any resolution to be smooth. Far too deep.

What Emily didn't know is that when she was in Cornwall – and Anne phoned to request her assistance – Marcus did, in the end, err on the side of caution and call her back.

The discussion with her boss is all a blur, but she does recall Anne explaining that Marcus left her a message.

Apparently he had told her "... *Emily wasn't unwell. Anne would be able to get hold of her at the conference she was attending. In the Cotswolds. The urgent project she had been managing was going really well and he was sure Emily would need to update her before the weekend anyway...*"

Anne went on to say she had found this all rather strange. So much so, she had taken it upon herself to check out what the "urgent project" might be. When she did she unearthed a number of erroneous appointments in Emily's diary and had therefore, reluctantly, requested a high-level data check from the IT department to ensure everything was in order.

What they found had shocked her to the core. Hence why she had asked Emily into her office. The reports showed Emily had been using her email and IT equipment, *extensively* and over a *substantial* period of time – she accentuated those words as if they were important – for private and personal use, which contravenes the company security policy. She shared some examples. Emily sat on her hands demurely shaking her head. Tears welled up in her eyes as she silently pinched the back of her legs so the pain would make them go away. Anne paused in between the examples. To let Emily take it all in. All Emily could hear was the tick of the clock. Like a TV quiz. An inauspicious countdown to certain demise.

Anne went on to advise, 'I'm terribly sorry but I have no choice other than to commence formal disciplinary proceedings.'

By which, she went on to explain, the IT security team would be carrying out a meticulous review. A detailed and thorough analysis of Emily's use of email, internet and company applications over the preceding six months. To determine the *full extent* of the *misuse*. HR would separately investigate any unexplained absences.

Emily would not be suspended while the review was completed. *How kind and thoughtful.* Emily chided herself. However, a formal letter will be sent to her home address, in due course, to advise her of the date of the disciplinary hearing. At the subsequent meeting Anne will share all the findings, the outcome of the HR review and advise what actions will be taken.

Anne had then finished by saying, 'I do, however, need to stress to you the seriousness of the situation.'

She then kindly brought to her attention that, in severe cases, it was possible for employees to be instantly dismissed. As such Emily would be allowed to bring a representative with her to the hearing. A friend, relative or union member. However, due to Emily's considerable length of service – and the knowledge and expertise she brings to the department – Anne was hoping it will all be a misunderstanding and IT will find nothing of concern. None the less she must follow the correct formal procedures and she is sure Emily will understand.

Did she have any questions?

What? Emily had looked at her despairingly. *Any questions?* Her head was so fuzzy she didn't know if she had any questions or not.

She almost said 'I don't know, do I?' but it wouldn't have been appropriate. It wasn't the time to be facetious. Or sarcastic.

She had been aware of Anne sitting in front of her. Behind her large, untidy desk. Pens. Multicoloured sticky notes. Discarded papers. Family photos. Empty stapler. Half eaten pack of sandwiches. Egg and cress on brown. No mayo. She had seen her mouth moving. Heard her talking. But the words weren't registering. Just certain phrases she had zoned in on.

Disciplinary hearing.

Misuse.

HR.

Investigate.

Dismissal.

Holy cow. Dismissal?

Then Anne continued. For now it's all entirely confidential. None of her colleagues know, not even Jo her job share.

At least that's something. Emily tried to console herself as she drove home in a trance. *No one else knows.*

She had stopped off at the local service station to get her head together, before she tried to act normal with Marcus. She didn't need any fuel but it was a useful place to pull over without drawing attention to herself.

So today – their fifteenth wedding anniversary – is not quite what she had planned. Or expected.

She's also still reeling from the chilling phone call the previous weekend. She's kept that to herself as well. It makes her nauseous just thinking about it. The man's voice, so calm and yet so horrid. Evil. And the emails from Cerys Morgan. She hasn't received any more but is terrified that if she does anything else to do with Cerys, however small, something awful will happen to them all.

*

Emily bravely feigns smiles and laughter as she and Marcus play with Molly and Jack in the garden. He's in charge of cooking the sausages and pours her a glass of chilled, fizzing Prosecco.

'Cheers.' He kisses her. 'Happy Anniversary!'

Emily raises her glass in a toast and takes a huge swig.

'Cheers. Here's to the next fifteen!' She smiles.

But the clink of their glasses sounds like the beautiful, celebratory crystal is shattering into a million tiny pieces at her feet.

MONDAY 6 SEPTEMBER 2010

The story made the national news very quickly.

Monday is Emily's day for catching up on housework, tidying everything up after the weekend and before she's back in the office on Wednesday.

She turns the radio on in every room, so she can sing along to music wherever she is hoovering, without having to constantly turn them on and off. Despite her anxieties they had a fun weekend celebrating their anniversary with both sets of parents. Today she's keeping herself busy, to eliminate any thoughts about her possible dismissal.

Stay brave. She keeps telling herself, *it'll all turn out all right.* And she carries on dancing to the music as she cleans. Until the mid-day news stops her in her tracks.

> 'Police have today revealed more details about the human remains found by a kayaker stranded on the North Cornwall coast. He was miraculously saved from the ferocious bank holiday storm last week but, while taking refuge in a cave, discovered a human skeleton.
>
> 'Police deployed experienced climbers to collect the

evidence and DNA tests have positively identified the skeleton as the remains of Cerys Morgan, a young student who mysteriously went missing in 1976 when she was just eighteen years old. Specialist support officers are working with her parents, who are now in their seventies and live in Pembrokeshire, and have confirmed they will be reopening the case with immediate effect.

'And now over to Norman for the weather ...'

*

It isn't long before Emily gets a phone call from DI Davis.

'So Mrs Harrison it would be extremely helpful, in the circumstances, if you could return to Cornwall to help us with our enquiries,' he advises. 'You may, or may not, have seen the news about the remains of Cerys Morgan being found, and the information you provided at the end of June is now very important indeed to our current line of enquiry. I would very much like to make an appointment for us to meet again as soon as possible.'

Emily isn't sure. All she can hear is that voice in her head. *Next time will be for real.* She buys herself some time.

'Of course, I totally understand,' she replies, carefully and slowly. 'I'll need to discuss the logistics of any trip with Marcus, my husband. We've two small children, as you know, and Molly's new school term starts tomorrow. I really can't miss that.'

She bites her lip.

'Let me chat with Marcus this evening. Can I call you back first thing tomorrow?'

She really isn't sure how Marcus will react either. In truth Emily is utterly terrified at the thought of going back to

Cornwall. She can't stop the warning in her head… *Hope you enjoyed your little surprise. Next time it will be for real.*

She hasn't apologised to Ben yet either. He was the one ally she had in Cornwall, but as things stand he wouldn't want to see her again. She still hasn't researched Richard's brother John either. She had planned to do that when she was at the Ship Inn. Before the unexpected series of events took over. She hasn't had the time, or inclination, since.

She can't risk it.

She simply can't risk anything else happening to Marcus, Molly or Jack. If she goes back down to see DI Davis she'll be putting them all in danger.

THURSDAY 9 SEPTEMBER 2010

Three days later, Emily finds herself in Cornwall once again. Marcus had insisted. He simply couldn't understand why she was so upset at the thought of going when she had been so desperate to help before.

'Hey Em, it doesn't matter, we can make sure we're both around for Molly's first two days back at school and then you pop back down,' he had said. Trying to be helpful and giving her a hug. 'You were so keen to help, this is a perfect opportunity to do that. Once and for all. Then the horrid nightmares will stop.'

Emily knows he's right but Marcus is oblivious to what she's been doing. She can't ever tell him the real reason why she didn't want to go. Instead she convinces herself that if the police are now actively looking at the case and have further evidence, including a body, then she will be safe. Marcus, Molly and Jack will be safe. It's only a matter of time. Everything will get resolved and the matter will be out of her hands for good.

All she needs to do is make one more trip to Cornwall… then sort out the problems at work. She shudders at the thought.

Just a bit more time and it will all be over. Marcus will be none the wiser. He will *never* need to know.

Jack starts his mornings only pre-school the following Tuesday, so they agree it best he goes with her. That way Marcus only has one school night to manage on his own with Molly before Emily and Jack are back home again.

Sorted.

For convenience DI Davis has arranged for her to stay in a local hotel. It's nothing special, but close to Wadebridge police station and an ideal stopover for one night.

As she travels down the motorway she can hear Jack snoring; she smiles to herself how easily he drops off in the car. When he was tiny they often put him in his baby seat and drove around, late into the night, to get him to settle.

She's been secretly dreading the journey down to Cornwall yet again. Foolishly, almost slipping her guard, she nearly commented about how she didn't want to go back again so soon to Marcus. She managed to bite her tongue just in time. Now she's on her way it isn't as arduous as she feared. The radio is playing quietly and having Jack with her is comforting. Helping her to forget about the menacing phone call. Plus this time it is all legitimate, so far less stressful in that regard. For once she hasn't had to lie to Marcus.

Her appointment is at two thirty. That suits Emily well. A leisurely journey and quick lunch with Jack, then she can spend as long as she needs at the station to help with any details. Jack's snoring is getting louder, *Aw, bless him*. She thinks, he looks as if butter wouldn't melt in his mouth. His reflection angelic and peaceful in the rear view mirror.

As they get closer to their destination it becomes a wheeze. Jack whistles each time he inhales and then again, at a higher pitch, when he breathes out. It doesn't sound right. Emily's distracted. She frets. Marcus always tells her she always imagines the worst, but she says it's being a mum. You never stop worrying whether they're four or forty.

She needs to concentrate on her driving. As long as he's

asleep he'll be fine. She'll make sure he's OK when she arrives. She hopes he isn't coming down with anything.

*

Lunch and a few cuddles later Jack is more his usual self. DI Davis is pleased to see her and takes them both through to the same room as before at the back of the building. The same bare walls with the clock, positioned carefully for the interviewing officer to see clearly. It makes a metallic, cranking sound once a minute as the small hand moves jerkily on then falls silent again. The same small, square table and four hard, plastic chairs. Maybe that's an interview tactic she thinks. Makes people confess quicker if they're uncomfortable. The only additional item is a box of toys, clearly well used, which takes Emily by surprise. How thoughtful. She wouldn't have thought there was much call for toys in a police station. But Jack's happy, his little face lights up as he rummages in the crate for toy cars.

DI Davis goes over the details she shared on her last visit. He doesn't allude to exactly where Cerys' remains were found but implies it's very close to where Emily remembered seeing her. Hence why he's so interested in talking to her again.

Emily once again confirms where it was. The time of day. What she was doing. She explains again about the game of hide-and-seek and how she had walked back up the path from Lundy Bay after their picnic lunch, to hide behind the boulder. It all happened a little way on from the top of the steps, next to Lundy Hole. The magical hole in the ground; or so it was to a six-year old. The partially collapsed roof of a wondrous cave, where you can peek over the edge and watch the waves crashing below.

A colleague pops in with some tea and biscuits and they talk some more. Bourbons. Her favourite. She wonders if it's acceptable to dunk them. She reluctantly decides perhaps not on this occasion.

Emily likes DI Davis. She feels comfortable with him. He pulls out his notebook as she tells him about her visits. Her meetings with Euan and Bronwyn, with Amy and Pip. Her fascination with the "mermaid girl". The shell bracelet.

Once she starts she can't stop. It's such a relief to be able to talk to someone about it. Someone she can trust. Everything she has been bottling up for the last three months.

Well, not quite everything. She says about her meeting with George at the Ship Inn; how he knew Cerys from when he was younger. Then she drops Barry into the conversation, just to see if he reacts, in case he gives any inkling of what he knows about him away. Nothing. He's far too professional she decides.

She doesn't mention Ben kicking her out. Or the night in her car. She thinks that might come across as a bit too much. He might begin to think she is some weirdo.

She absentmindedly fiddles with the sleeves of her cardigan. He's genuinely interested. His brow is furrowed as he concentrates, every so often glancing up from his notes. He doesn't try to stop her talking. He doesn't interrupt. He doesn't look at the clock, or give the impression she needs to get a move on.

As he arranges another cup of tea she mulls over, silently in her head, whether to tell him about the threatening messages she has received as well. She's worried he might view her as completely insane, but equally it would be a relief to talk to someone about it.

Start with one and see how you get on. She thinks. So she tells him about the postcard. She doesn't say so, but she's actually brought it with her. It's in the car, in a small plastic freezer bag. To preserve any fingerprints. She thought that best after what Debbie had said.

He busily jots everything down, listening to her every word as if it is a matter of life and death. Jack chuckles away in the corner of the room making engine sounds as he plays with an assortment of toy cars. His nose is running and he's still extremely wheezy, but DI Davis hasn't noticed. She'll give him a warm bath later and make sure he gets an early night.

She tells him again about the T-shirt. The three capital letters, that are so clear and yet so vague. He nods encouragingly. Once again he asks her to just take her time, as long as she needs, as she sips the last of her tea. All the talking is making her throat dry. Is there anything else she can remember. Anything. However trivial it might seem.

Emily hasn't felt so at ease for weeks. Months. At last someone who isn't judging her. Telling her to stop. She doesn't have to lie. *Tell him,* a persuasive voice in her head says. *You must tell him about the emails.*

'There is one other thing. It's been quite disturbing.'

He stops writing and looks up at her.

'... I received an email from someone called Cerys Morgan.' Emily stops short, realising as she says it out loud how ominous it sounds. That she should have told him this long ago. 'Well, two actually.'

He starts to write notes again.

'They were intimidating. Threatening. The first one said they knew who I was and where I lived. That they would ruin my life if I ruined theirs. That they had warned me before. I... I can't remember the exact words but I've still got it.'

Emily's eyes are watery. She realises how much she has been holding all her emotions inside. Her fear. Now she is talking to someone, someone who is listening, the sheer awfulness of the messages hits home like a bullet.

'... The second one was a day later. The Friday before the bank holiday. It told me to get home. Now. When I got home Marcus and the kids were missing.'

It's too much. She breaks down and the tears start flowing. Jack gets upset, he doesn't understand what is happening or why his mum is crying. She picks him up and cuddles him on her lap, burying her face into the back of his head. DI Davis gently and silently moves a box of tissues in her direction.

Holding Jack makes it easier. He sucks his thumb and seems oblivious to the conversation, just happy to be with his mum. To cuddle into her.

'To cut a long story short; Marcus had a phone call in the morning while I was away. It was someone pretending to be a police officer, although he thought they were genuine at the time. Whoever it was told him his parents had been in an accident, and were in hospital in Birmingham. But they weren't. It was a cruel hoax. He spent all day chasing around trying to find them, until we eventually got hold of them in Edinburgh where they were blissfully unaware, and having a lovely weekend away.'

'Have there been any more?'

'Two days later, on the Sunday afternoon, I answered the phone at home and a man's voice asked to speak to Mrs Harrison. When I said it was me speaking he just mocked me. He said he hoped I had enjoyed "my little surprise".'

She hugs Jack again, then whispers '… and then he said that "next time it would be for real".'

She shuts her eyes.

'Mrs Harrison, you must have found this all terribly unsettling. I have to ask though, do you have any idea at all who may have either sent the emails or made the phone call? Was there anything that struck you as familiar; in the way they were written, or the way they spoke, for example?'

Emily shakes her head. Tears roll uncontrollably down her cheeks, as she remembers the awful afternoon she arrived home to find them missing.

'No. Nothing. I still have the emails but the caller's number was "withheld" so I have absolutely no idea.'

She cuddles Jack again.

'I brought my laptop with me if you want to take a look?' She looks at him through red, puffy eyes.

'Yes, I think it is important that we do. We'll need to hold it for a couple hours for the IT team to take all the necessary downloads. Your mobile phone too.'

'I'll need it tonight,' she says looking at the time. 'Can I drop it off in the morning? I could take Jack for a walk or something then pick it up again when you're finished with it?'

'That would be very much appreciated. However, I do have to ask Mrs Harrison, and I trust you understand, as part of the investigation,' he adds politely. She wonders what is coming. 'Does your husband know about any of these threats?'

Emily's shoulders shake and she can feel tears coming again, but she manages to hold herself together by holding Jack tight and biting her lip.

'No. I couldn't bear to tell him. Not after the first one. He found the postcard. He was angry. Upset. We both were. So when the others arrived I thought it best to keep them to myself.'

DI Davis looks at her with a quizzical expression, as if it doesn't all make sense. Emily looks at her lap.

'I didn't tell him *anything* after the postcard.' She adds quietly. 'He doesn't know anything about what I've been doing... or the people I've met up with.'

A great weight has been lifted from her shoulders but at the same time the guilt feels like lead in her heart. She's confessed. It's finally out in the open. DI Davis is the very first person to know her secret.

His expression is motionless. He's not judgemental. He must have seen all manner of awful things in his job, Emily decides, this is nothing.

'After I came to see you we went home, but I couldn't let it go. I had to help Cerys. I can't explain it; she was just so lovely, so kind to me. The shell bracelet she gave me. I had to repay her. I thought I was the only person who could solve the mystery. To find closure for her parents.'

'Mrs Harrison, I can only say that what you have shared with me is extremely valuable to our investigation. The emails and phone calls must have been incredibly unsettling for you and your family. Your honesty is quite commendable. As are your reasons for wanting to help the Morgans and everything you have done.'

He is sincere and genuine, she feels liberated having shared months of worry with another human being.

'I would, however, advise you from undertaking any more amateur investigations. I can reassure you that the case is in very good hands. Now we have found Cerys – and have material evidence – we will leave no stone unturned in finding out what happened to her.'

As she stands to go DI Davis shakes her hand firmly. He hands over his business card, thanking her once again.

'Do call me Mrs Harrison. Anytime. This is my direct number. If you think of anything else, or you need assistance with anything while you are in Cornwall, just let me know. I'll also let the front desk know you'll be dropping your laptop and phone in tomorrow morning. They'll try not to keep you waiting too long.'

She promises she will.

FRIDAY 10 SEPTEMBER 2010

Emily has a fitful night's sleep. Jack is definitely coming down with something. Wheezing and coughing he wakes himself up at regular intervals. She snuggles in with him to help him sleep. He settles but she doesn't. She can't stop fidgeting. She can't stop thinking about her conversation with DI Davis.

It's early. Too early to get up, but she might as well do something useful if she can't sleep. With little Jack nestled under one arm, his little body rising up and down with each breath, she gently strokes his back with her thumb. He holds on tightly to his blue blanket as she sits cross-legged on the bed and logs onto her laptop one handed. Might as well check her emails. She's swapped a couple days with Jo her job share to make the trip to Cornwall. Neither Jo nor Anne know the real reason she has come, but even so she doesn't want to fall behind on anything. She's got enough issues to deal with at work already without adding to the list.

There's nothing urgent and, confident she's keeping on top of things, she does a quick online search to see if she can find anything on John Trevelyan. She's still frustrated that he's one person who knew Cerys that she hasn't met. After telling DI Davis everything she feels much less scared. Definitely still wary but, now someone knows, she feels safe. Just knowing someone else knows is a huge relief. Someone she can trust. George said he was a doctor or a dentist One quick search will surely be okay. And if the IT team at work query it she can say she was looking for a doctor for Jack.

Bloody hell, you can't help yourself Emily. You're lying again.

She refines the search as it comes back with far too many options. She narrows it down by adding "Doctor, Cornwall, UK". Three results pop up immediately.

Dr Peter Trevelyan, Orthopaedic Consultant, Truro
Dr Robert Trevelyan, GP, Wadebridge
Dr Angela Trevelyan, Anaesthetist, Truro

Assuming he hasn't had a sex change she checks the first two. One qualified in Bristol in 1986, the other at Guy's Teaching Hospital, London in 1978. The latter is more likely as the date makes sense, but neither is called John. Jack stretches, his elbow accidentally digs into her ribs making her yelp.

Oh well. Worth a try.

She takes a closer look, clicking on his headshot under the GP practice "Our Team" page. It lists his medical qualifications but nothing more. She notices the surgery is on the same street as the police station, a little further down the road towards the river. She's curious. She'll take a stroll in that direction after she's handed her laptop in.

Emily and Jack try to enjoy a leisurely breakfast. Cereal followed by scrambled eggs on toast. She's always intrigued how Jack likes such grown up food for a four-year-old but today he's not interested in eating at all. He isn't even interested when the waitress pulls a face, trying to make him laugh, each time she offers to replenish their toast. He must be poorly. Just as she takes her very last mouthful of breakfast her phone rings.

It's Marcus. He's probably just finished the morning school run with Molly.

'My god Emily have you got some explaining to do,' he bellows. His obvious rage makes Emily jump, almost choking on her toast.

She glances around the breakfast room hoping it's not loud enough for anyone else to hear.

'I've just opened a letter from your work. I thought I'd be helpful, because it looked important. Well... what can I say... it seems it is!' He continues even louder. 'So not only have you been carrying on this stupid farce of an investigation behind *my* back, and against all *my* advice, it seems like you've been treating all your colleagues like bloody imbeciles as well.'

He takes a gulp.

'You and I need to have a very serious conversation when you get home Emily. Mark my words. I think you've completely lost your mind, I just hope you think it's all been worth it.'

Emily is stunned. As quick as he started he's gone. His words left hanging in the air. The letter about her disciplinary hearing must have arrived and for whatever reason he decided to open it.

Emily is in pieces. She always knew there was a chance Marcus would find out about everything, but today of all days.

Why oh why today? Just when it's almost over and DI Davis knows about everything.

58

Still reeling from her phone call with Marcus, Emily hands her laptop and phone in at the front desk. The duty sergeant hands her a paper receipt and, looking at the clock, advises it will be ready to collect just after eleven thirty. Two hours' time.

'DI Davis may want this as well,' she hands over the postcard still wrapped up in the plastic bag. 'He'll know what it is,' she adds, as he looks curious.

'No problem. I'll pass it on. He's not on duty today but I'll make sure he gets it when he's back in. I think he's on the late shift tomorrow.'

She heads out, and follows the road towards the river. It'll do her and Jack good to have a walk before their long drive home again. Stretch their legs, get some fresh air.

They soon reach the GP surgery. The car park is busy with people coming and going. One car catches her eye. It's the sticker in the rear window. A dog-eared sticker for the South West Air Ambulance. Then it dawns on her, she saw it at the campsite. It was in the car window, as Richard's brother pulled away.

She peers closer. It's in the area cordoned off for staff parking. She can't stop herself. She looks at the windscreen too. A staff-parking permit. Dr R J Trevelyan.

Oh my god. Perhaps it is him. The J could be for John. She checks around, to make sure no one is watching her. They may wonder what she is doing. She checks again. Yes, definitely Dr R J Trevelyan.

Keep cool, keep walking. Pretend you're just strolling through.

Emily finds a bench by the river and sits down with Jack to watch the birds. It feels autumnal today, there is a definite chill in the air and the leaves on the trees have a yellow-orange tinge to them as the sun tries to break through the cloud. Jack shivers with cold even though his forehead is warm. He really doesn't seem well and he's not his usual jolly self. She's not sure what to do. There's an hour and a half to kill before she can go back to collect her things. It's too soon for another coffee, she's only just had her breakfast.

As if in a trance, and before she is even aware of it, Emily is at the door of the surgery. She smiles at a lady who is struggling through the rotating door with tiny, baby twin girls. How unbelievably cute. All dressed in matching pink. She would help her but it's impossible; they're on opposite sides of the door.

Once inside the building she really wants to get Jack checked over. Plus she can't be so close to meeting John, or who she thinks is John, and not do anything about it. The only person she hasn't met.

The receptionist looks up and smiles.

'Can I help you?'

Emily wonders how many times a day she asks that.

'Oh. I hope so.' Emily isn't prepared, she hasn't thought this through. 'I was hoping to see Dr Trevelyan?'

'Do you have an appointment?'

'Er, no,' Emily is flustered. 'I'm not actually a patient. I'm just visiting. But my little boy, Jack, isn't well. I was hoping to see someone before I start the journey home.' She smiles, stroking Jack's hair, hoping the receptionist doesn't think she's odd.

'You know, just to check he's OK.' Then adds, 'Dr Trevelyan was recommended to me.'

'Oh, I see,' she purses her lips, scanning her screen. 'Well, it isn't really the norm, but he does have a cancellation in half an hour if you don't mind waiting?' She looks at Emily over the top of her glasses, checking her over again.

'That would be ideal, thank you,' Emily feels her cheeks reddening.

'OK, that's ten forty. I will need a few details though. Please can you fill in this form – we just need to know which surgery you are registered with, your home address, contact phone number... that sort of thing – just for our records.'

Emily nods.

'No problem at all. Thank you so much.'

She finds an empty seat in the waiting room, retrieving a pen from her handbag.

Lots of details. She rummages for her phone to find her own doctor's telephone number, then remembers she handed it in, after momentarily panicking when she can't find it. Oh well, she's got a pretty good idea what the number is, she'll just put what she thinks it is.

Emily hands her completed form back to the receptionist as she sits and watches the other patients.

Patient patients. She silently thinks. All looking at their watches, time and again, with plaintive expressions. Looking up, ever hopeful, every time a consulting room door opens, in case theirs is the next name that is called.

Ten forty comes and goes. The telephone doesn't stop ringing. The officious receptionist looks over her spectacles at everyone who comes in. Old people with walking frames, young mums with trendy buggies, pregnant ladies stroking their bulging bellies and a young man with the biggest cast on his leg Emily has ever seen. Looks like a nasty break.

She starts to doubt what she's doing here. What is she thinking of? What is she going to say to him? There's probably nothing wrong with Jack. Just a snuffle. Dr Trevelyan will be annoyed with her for wasting his time.

She has a change of heart. She can't do this. Gathering up her bag and gently taking Jack's hand she gets up to leave. Then she hears 'Mrs Harrison?' coming from room two.

Oh god, too late.

She turns around to acknowledge the person who has called her name. She pretends she's just standing up. Hoping it isn't too obvious she was on her way out. As the doctor guides her into the consulting room she knows she has seen him before, but can't place him. Her head is spinning. It's panic.

Deep breaths, deep breaths. Her mantra.

Perhaps she saw him in the Ship Inn or something, it was always packed with people. That must be it. He's dressed differently for work, so looks different.

'Hello Mrs Harrison,' he welcomes her. A strikingly handsome man in his mid-fifties, dark hair now greying at the temples. 'Do come in. This must be Jack. Jenny on reception explained you're visiting. What exactly is the concern? Let's have a chat and then I can have a look at him for you.'

It clicks.

He's the police doctor. The police doctor she saw briefly when she first visited DI Davis back in July. Dr Bob he'd call him. Of course, Dr Robert Trevelyan.

Emily explains about Jack's wheezing. That she's worried he has a temperature.

He examines Jack. His stethoscope makes Jack jump as the cold metal touches his chest. He looks in his ears and at the back of his throat for the sign of an infection. He too is concerned about his wheezing.

As Dr Trevelyan checks Jack over carefully Emily glances

around the room. Jack is cooperative at the moment, Dr Trevelyan is very gentle with him, but he'll start crying if he gets scared.

There's an eclectic mix of photos on the two wooden shelves behind him, which bow under the weight of all his medical reference books. He's obviously a keen sportsman and sailor. The obligatory graduation photo, another must be his wife and two daughters; plus an impressive collection of trophies and sporting memorabilia.

Emily inspects the photos. There's one partially hidden at the back that jumps out at her. It makes her wheeze, even louder than Jack, as she fakes a little cough to hide her shock.

There he is. Dr Trevelyan wearing a huge smile, dressed in shorts and T-shirt. He's caressing yet another trophy, on the balcony of a wooden building overlooking a small marina. Tidy rows of immaculate boats moored behind him. A very young Doctor Trevelyan. Wearing a T-shirt with three large capital letters across the front. RSC.

Emily does a double take. It can't be. R. S. C. The three letters she has been trying for months to recall. The Royal Shakespeare Company. That's why she thought it had something to do with the theatre. But she's wrong, of course it isn't. It's Rock Sailing Club.

Rock bloody Sailing Club.

She mentally kicks herself. She's seething. All the time the answer had been right on the doorstep. She had read about the sailing club in the news reports. Amy mentioned it. And Pip. How could she have been so stupid?

Her brain is taking too long to catch up with her reasoning. Her anxiety about Marcus' call, coupled with worry about Jack, is fogging her thought process. It surely isn't possible. After all this time. Yet here she is, her poorly little boy being examined by the kind doctor, and all the while she's still thinking about solving the Cerys Morgan mystery.

'Emily?' says Dr Trevelyan. 'Are you OK? You seem to have gone as white as a sheet?'

'Yes, I'm fine, sorry. Just worried about Jack. What do you think is wrong?'

Hang on a minute. How come he used her first name? It has been Mrs Harrison up until now. Odd.

'I think he has a bad case of tonsillitis. His temperature is very high and appears to be rising. It would certainly explain his wheezing and difficulty breathing.'

Jack is listless and clammy. Emily strokes his forehead as he rests on the couch. He's definitely got worse. She can feel the heat radiating from his little body.

'He is so hot, can we cool him down a little?' she asks, as Jack shivers even though he is so hot.

'I'll write him a prescription for some antibiotics to treat the tonsillitis. There's a pharmacy just up the road where you can pick it up. One dose, three times a day and you should see an improvement very quickly.'

Dr Trevelyan looks at her kindly.

'Don't worry, it won't take me long. Do you want to call your husband? I am sure you want to let him know what's going on. I can keep an eye on Jack for the moment if you want some privacy.'

Dr Trevelyan leans over the printer on the cabinet behind him to collect the prescription. His rolled up shirtsleeves reveal his forearm.

Emily fakes another cough as she gasps on her breath. There's the smiley face. The smiley face she told DI Davis about. Except it isn't a smiley face, like she had thought. It's an anchor. A very decorative tattoo of an anchor that, from a distance, would have looked exactly like a smiley face to a little six-year-old. A long, straight nose with an upturned mouth.

Oh my god. Not only is it the same T-shirt. It's him. She knows it's him.

And he knows it's her. That's why he knew her name was Emily earlier. Her throat is completely dry, she can't swallow. Then her inner voice kicks in telling her not to be so ridiculous. She's getting carried away now. Get a grip Emily; first Vicky, then Phil, then Barry, even the taxi driver, now Dr Trevelyan. Who's it going to be next?

You're getting paranoid Emily. Her inner voice says again. *It's you who needs to see the doctor. You're insane.*

What's she to do? If she steps outside the room Jack will be alone with him.

Him. The person with Cerys. The man in the T-shirt with the smiley face on his arm and the baseball cap.

The very same person who must have sent the horrible threats. Surely not? How could it be?

She steps outside to the corridor, to catch her breath. Her chest is pounding. Leaving the door slightly ajar she steadies herself with a hand on the wall. Before remembering, yet again, she doesn't have her phone with her to call Marcus anyway. Rather than have to explain she pretends he's engaged and goes back into the consulting room. Not wanting to leave Jack too long.

Too late.

Dr Trevelyan is on the phone to Jenny, his receptionist.

'Call an ambulance please we have a four-year-old male suffering a febrile convulsion due to a high temperature and suspected severe case of tonsillitis. Needs immediate attention. Thank you. Be swift.'

Emily grabs Jack and holds him tight, his body lies languid in her arms.

'What did you do… what did you do?' She sobs.

She's incensed.

Furious with herself for letting Jack out of her sight for a nanosecond. Right at the very second he needed her most.

FRIDAY 10 SEPTEMBER 2010

The ambulance arrives within minutes and Jack is blue-lighted to Truro. He is indeed suffering from a severe case of tonsillitis. The nurses manage to reduce his incredibly high temperature as quickly as they can, then start him on a course of antibiotics. They reassure Emily the treatment will take effect very quickly and as long as he gets plenty of rest he will be absolutely fine.

'He'll soon be as right as rain, my love,' the kind nurse says, squeezing Emily's arm tenderly as she sets up the monitoring equipment.

There are wires everywhere. Jack himself looks peaceful, unaware of the urgency. Oblivious to the flurry of activity going on around him.

She sits next to his bed, holding his tiny hand in hers, willing him to get better.

She needs to let DI Davis know about Dr Trevelyan. But she hasn't got her phone with her. She glances at the clock. It's gone two o'clock. She should have collected it nearly three hours ago. The desk sergeant will be wondering where she's got to.

But even if she had her phone, how on earth could she tell DI Davis? He will think she has completely lost her mind if

317

she alleges, out of the blue, it was his long-standing, respected colleague she had seen with Cerys all those years ago.

She desperately needs to tell someone. She can't talk to Marcus until he calms down. He doesn't even know about Jack yet. But if she leaves it too long Dr Trevelyan might do something to cover his tracks, yet again, and evade discovery.

She sits quietly, staring out the window but not seeing anything. As she strokes Jack's tiny hand her mind is in turmoil.

'Mrs Harrison… ' The ward sister is holding a phone aloft, the one they use to wheel around to patients. 'Mrs Harrison… sorry to disturb you, but I have a call for you. I think he said it was the Wadebridge police?'

'Hello, Emily Harrison speaking.' She tries to be calm.

'Hello, Mrs Harrison, it's PC Atkins here. I have your laptop and mobile phone from this morning. It's all ready to collect, but I noticed there had been three missed calls. I recognised the number as the local GP surgery, so I hope you don't mind, but I contacted them to see if it was urgent. It seems they have been trying to get hold of you, enquiring after your son? They said he'd been taken to Truro hospital, so I was just checking you are both all right?'

'Oh… oh… that is so very kind of you. I really don't know what to say. Jack's going to be okay, thanks.' Emily is thrown by his genuine concern. That someone she barely knows should go to so much trouble to check she is well. That Jack is well.

'It's been a bit of a day though, I'm so sorry not to have picked my things up yet.'

'No problem at all Mrs Harrison, they will all be here on the front desk whenever you're ready.'

She grasps the moment. It's an ideal opportunity.

'That's great, thank you. It may be a little while yet though. Please can I ask a favour in the meantime?'

'Of course?'

'Please can you pass a message on to DI Davis when you

see him. It's important. Just say Dr Trevelyan.' She repeats it just to be sure, 'Dr Trevelyan... he'll understand.'

'Right. Dr Trevelyan you say?' PC Atkins clarifies, clearly mystified.

Then all he hears is a thud and a crack as Emily slumps to the ground and her head hits the concrete floor.

60

DI Davis sits alone in his office, his head in his hands. He's on the verge of solving the case; acutely aware he must handle it extremely carefully. He's been working flat out for four months since being asked to lead the reopened investigation.

Initially he supported Mr and Mrs Morgan with their renewed TV appeal. Since then he's endured many long days – and even longer nights – following up potential new leads. He's reviewed every single bit of information from the original case, many times over.

All the potential suspects at the time had strong alibis, with the exception of one person. The one person he had felt a little uneasy about straight away. It wasn't anything specific, more a gut feeling. As he studiously worked through all the statements from 1976 this person's story just didn't ring true. Plus their original statement had a number of alterations, before they signed the final version.

They were vague – and at times inconsistent – about what they had been doing on Tuesday 29 June. They claimed to have watched Wimbledon on television. They had been engrossed in the women's semi-finals, when Virginia Wade lost to Evonne Goolagong Cawley. But that was the wrong day. So

320

when quizzed about this, by the DS at the time, the statement details were amended. Claiming they had got confused. Then, when asked how well they had known the girls, and how much time they had spent with them. The first version had said "a little" and "not a lot". But again, under further questioning, had been changed to "very well" and "most days".

After getting the strange message – relayed to him by PC Atkins – DI Davis had immediately driven to Truro Hospital to see Emily and Jack. To check they were okay. By the time he arrived she too had been admitted for suspected concussion after collapsing. He can only imagine the stress of the last few months, and the sinister threats, had suddenly become too much for her to bear.

He likes Emily. The first time he met her, after she had called the information line, he knew she was nervous but could see immediately what a considerate and kind person she was. Someone who simply wanted to help. To help someone she had never really known, but as long as she felt she could, she would.

To repay a random act of kindness, after Cerys gave her the shell bracelet all those years ago. He was concerned about her age. She was only six years old at the time. But there had been other recent – and successful – cases where a child had been the key witness.

Emily's recollections can also be validated. It was her birthday. The tide times at Lundy Bay on that day corroborated with her version of events. Plus a variety of much smaller, what appeared individually to be inconsequential findings, when considered together made a very powerful argument. Aristotle was definitely correct when he said the whole is greater than the sum of its parts.

DI Davis leans back in his chair and takes a huge, deep breath. His arms outstretched and his hands resting on the back of his head. He shuts his eyes. He must get it right first time. When the news gets out it will cause outrage. A scandal. To have carried such a huge secret around for so many years, never mind such an awful, tragic secret. No one would have had the remotest idea. Not even their own loyal, doting family.

He wonders how they will react. Thirty-four years. Pretending everything is "normal". Never batting an eyelid when the police questioned them, or when they helped the locals search for Cerys week after week after week.

All that summer they pretended to help, yet they knew where she was.

DI Davis never ceases to be amazed by what humans are capable of. He sees the best and worst of humankind in his role.

It was a million to one chance that, after she stumbled and fell, Cerys ricocheted off the jagged rocks and landed on the tiny ledge. There was no possible way for her to save herself from falling over the overhanging cliffs.

If she had fallen into the sea her body would have been washed up at some point and found a few days or weeks later. But she didn't.

He appeases his pain by telling himself the one good thing about the tragedy is Cerys wouldn't have known a lot about it. Her skeleton had multiple fractures to her back, legs and skull. She would have been unconscious very quickly.

It was also a million to one chance that a kayaker should end up stranded on the very same ledge thirty-four years later.

If he had stayed at home, to help his wife prepare for their guests, Cerys' bones could have been laid to rest in her rocky grave for eternity.

*

DI Davis refocuses on the task in hand.

He has worked through the implications of the case very

carefully, leaving no stone unturned. With help from the specialist crimes unit he has identified the source of the fake emails and the hoax telephone call.

Today he has urgently reviewed all the evidence one final time and referred the case to his District Commander.

He looks at the papers and files strewn across his desk. Mentally and physically he prepares himself for what is going to be the hardest interview of his career to date. He knows he has to get a confession but it isn't going to be easy. Far from it.

His phone cuts through the silence.

'Thank you, sir.'

Formal approval from the District Commander.

He's past the point of no return.

He grabs his jacket; it's time.

Time to make an arrest.

61
SEPTEMBER 2010

Dr Robert John Trevelyan is arrested by DI Davis as he leaves his home for morning surgery. Arrested on suspicion of the murder of Cerys Morgan on Tuesday 29 June 1976.

Dr Bob. His long-standing colleague. A local, well respected and admired GP and police doctor. Also known as John, especially when he was at school, and by his close family and friends. Brother of Richard. Son of Donald and Beryl.

*

Back at the station DI Davis and DS Karen Sampson are well rehearsed; they simultaneously pull up their chairs to the wooden veneer table and sit down. They've done it hundreds of times before. They know exactly how each other works. A perfectly synchronised duet without any music.

DS Sampson cautions Dr Trevelyan. She lets him know his rights and allows him a few moments to collect his thoughts.

Custody Sergeant Taylor brings them each a plastic cup of cold water, then shuts the interview room door with a very precise click as she retreats to the front desk.

Dr Trevelyan sits with his forehead resting on his arms,

which are folded in front of him on the table. He has said nothing, other than to confirm his name, and is finding it impossible to look at either of them. He's been informed he has the right to a solicitor, but has so far declined the offer.

DI Davis looks at him. He's not sure if he feels pity, anger or both. Either way he must keep his emotions private. He can't delay it any longer. A small intake of breath and he makes a start.

'Interview commenced 09:30 hours. Dr Trevelyan; can you tell us what you were doing on the afternoon of Tuesday 29 June 1976?'

The doctor sits up straight. A conscious effort to appear strong and confident.

'It would be the same as I said before. In my witness statement. I milked the cows in the morning. In the afternoon I helped my brother Richard put up some new fencing.' He speaks very precisely. Slow and calm.

'And at what time did you start and finish both those activities?'

He breathes heavily as he loosens his tie a little more.

'I milked the cows late morning. Later than usual as we'd had technical problems with the equipment. We didn't have any of the advanced computer systems they have these days. The local maintenance engineer came out to fix it. By the time he had gone it was at least eleven thirty, then milking would have taken about an hour and a half. Maybe more to see to all the cows.'

He rubs his chin.

'So, that would account for your whereabouts until approximately thirteen hundred hours. What time did you join your brother?' DI Davis probes.

'From memory it was straight after. I probably stopped for a sandwich or something, and then would've joined him. It was a two man job doing the fencing and he hated being left to do it on his own.' Dr Trevelyan continues.

'Your brother's statement says you met up with him – and I quote from his statement – "… in the far meadow at just after three o'clock." So that means you must have had a bit of time in between does it not?' DI Davis asks, wanting to be precise.

'Well I must have finished the cows much later then. I don't recall hanging around. I didn't have a watch; I must've lost it somehow working on the farm. It was difficult to keep track of things.' Dr Trevelyan is flustered.

'Did anyone help you milk the cows or join you for lunch that day?'

He shuffles around in his chair, rubbing his right knee.

'Possibly. I honestly can't remember. Dad used to pop in from time to time, but once the milking was underway I could usually manage on my own.

'… And lunch, well Mum was usually busy in the kitchen – or sorting out things for the campsite – so generally she was around. With the weather being so hot we often took our lunch outside. I guess that's what I probably did.'

'Dr Trevelyan "I guess" isn't really good enough. Either you did or you didn't.' DI Davis replies, making it clear he isn't convinced.

'Your statement from 1976 says you finished milking the cows at one o'clock, had lunch with your mother in the farmhouse kitchen and then went out to join your brother.'

DI Davis pauses. He can sense Dr Trevelyan is uncomfortable.

'But your mother said in her statement that she was in Truro that day, shopping for a wedding outfit. Plus your father's statement says the maintenance engineer was called the day before. That is Monday 28 June, *not* Tuesday 29 June.'

DI Davis looks directly at him without any change in expression. He remains silent, to see if Dr Trevelyan will respond.

'It was a long time ago. I honestly can't remember. Can *you* remember what you were doing on that day?' Dr Trevelyan is defensive. Beads of sweat glisten on his forehead.

'I'll ask the questions if you don't mind.'

Dr Trevelyan sighs noisily.

'Dr Trevelyan, how well had you got to know Cerys Morgan? I understand that you and your brother socialised with Cerys and her friends almost every day? You also took them to a barn dance at Home Farm the Thursday before she went missing?'

'Yes, Richard and I did meet up with them. They were fun. Mostly we went to the Doom Bar in Polzeath. We also celebrated the summer solstice with them, when they first arrived.'

The doctor's right leg twitches nervously. He tries to hold it still with his hand.

'So would you say you were good friends?'

'We had a laugh, yes, if that's what you mean. They were good company.'

'Did you get to know Cerys any better than the others?' DI Davis continues in his calm tone.

'Like I said, they were fun. All of them. So no, not really Cerys in particular. When we went to the barn dance George Pengelly and Barry Hammett came too. It was easier to go as a group of eight. It was fun. We all got along really well.'

'What about on the campsite? Did you and Richard spend much time with them?'

'Just in the evenings really. We'd meet up with them and go for a drink, or something, that was all.'

His leg twitches more noticeably.

'And you never asked Cerys out on her own, or spent time with her away from the others?'

'What exactly are you saying? Of course I didn't. We were just a bunch of mates.' Dr Trevelyan is clearly getting more anxious.

'What about when some of the girls were taken ill with food poisoning?'

'Yes, I do remember that. They were in a pretty bad way. Definitely salmonella from some dodgy chicken they had half-cooked on their camping stove.'

'So where were you when that happened and what did you do?'

'Richard and I worked on the farm, same as normal. But we did look out for them. Cerys wasn't ill, although she was worn out, making sure the others were all okay.'

'Did you spend any time with Cerys on her own whilst they were ill?'

'Not that I recall.'

'So how come when her remains were found they were lying next to your watch. Engraved with RJT on the back?'

'I have no idea what you're talking about.' Dr Trevelyan looks visibly concerned. The vein on the right hand side of his neck protrudes.

'Your watch. The one you just said you had mislaid. It was found with Cerys. Why would that be?'

Silence.

'Let me try a different approach. On the afternoon of Tuesday 29 June 1976 a witness remembers seeing you with Cerys on the cliff top path adjacent to Lundy Bay. Yet you say you didn't spend any time with her on her own?'

DI Davis is speaking more loudly.

'I have no idea what you are talking about.'

'The witness says the two of you appeared to be having a disagreement. That she was walking fast, as if trying to get away from you.'

'No, sorry. I have no idea what you are talking about.'

'The witness also says they were hiding behind a rock, so you wouldn't see them, but when they looked up again Cerys was gone?'

Silence.

'... And then they watched you walk away towards Rumps Point?'

Silence.

'... And all of this would have been happening around the same time you claim to have been on your own. Eating a sandwich in the kitchen back at the farm?'

Dr Trevelyan slumps his head on his hands on the table. DI Davis glances at DS Sampson. They can both see he's wavering.

They stop talking briefly. To give him time to take everything in before they start on a different round of questions.

*

'Dr Trevelyan, we need to ask questions about this year as well.' DI Davis continues. Pausing briefly to see what reaction there is.

'We have evidence that you sent an email pretending to be from someone called Cerys Morgan on Thursday 26 August 2010. Is that correct?'

'What on earth? ... I ... I ... have absolutely no idea what you are talking about.'

'I'll ask again. We have evidence that you sent an email. It was sent from a laptop – that had previously been used by a member of staff at your surgery – but not since they left on maternity leave eight months earlier.

'The message purported to be from someone called Cerys Morgan. It was sent at 18:37 on the evening of Thursday 26 August 2010. Is that correct?'

Silence.

'There is further evidence that the same laptop was subsequently used to send another email. Again purporting to be from Cerys Morgan at 14:43 the following day. That is Friday 27 August 2010.'

DI Davis pauses temporarily again. Looking directly across the table at Dr Trevelyan.

'I really don't have any idea what you are talking about.' Dr Trevelyan whispers.

He shakes his head from side to side and is still trying to stop his right leg from trembling.

'We also have evidence that you called the telephone number of a private residence in Thornbury, South Gloucestershire, at 07:13 hours on the morning of Friday 27 August 2010? Is that correct?'

Silence.

'And you then called the same number on the afternoon of Sunday 29 August 2010?'

Silence.

'Both calls were traced back to your surgery. To a spare line that is rarely used. Is that correct?'

Silence.

The small beads of perspiration that had gathered on his forehead have expanded. There are rivulets running down the side of his face. He rubs his thumbs into the palm of each hand as he holds them, fingers criss-crossed.

'Please … can … can I have another glass of water?' he asks.

'Interview adjourned at 10:30 hours, to be reconvened in five minutes.'

DS Sampson nods her head, ever so slightly, in DI Davis' direction as she buzzes PS Taylor for some fresh water.

*

'Interview resumed at 10:35 hours.' DI Davis begins.

'So, Dr Trevelyan. Let's just recap a little. You were on or around your parents' farm all day on Tuesday 29 June 1976 – the day on which Cerys Morgan went missing – but you can't *precisely* account for all your activities. In particular between one o'clock and three thirty in the afternoon.'

He pauses.

'Prior to then, you had spent a considerable amount of time with Cerys and her friends, before she went missing. She was also wearing your watch – a watch that had been a special birthday gift to you from your grandparents and engraved with your initials on the back – at the time of her disappearance.'

DI Davis looks him straight in the eye.

'Evidence shows your watch had stopped at two twenty-six on the afternoon of Tuesday 29 June. It was still showing this time and date when it was retrieved alongside the remains of Cerys Morgan, capturing the moment you were with her. This is during the period of time – on that date – that you have so far been unable to consistently explain where you were. Or what you were doing.'

Dr Trevelyan's face is ashen. He looks down at the table.

'Furthermore we have evidence, that clearly shows you sent two emails from a laptop you had access to in August this year. In both emails you pretended to be the missing girl, Cerys Morgan. These were followed by two phone calls from your surgery to a landline in Thornbury, South Gloucestershire. The recipient of the phone calls being the same recipient as the fake emails.'

Silence.

Dr Trevelyan sobs. Gentle, quiet sobs. Followed immediately by uncontrollable weeping.

'I can't do this... I really can't do this... please stop.' Dr Trevelyan is shaking. His eyes red and puffy.

'I'll tell you everything... I promise... honestly, I will. Please just stop... please.'

SEPTEMBER 2010

'Interview resumed at 11:45 hours.'

'Dr Trevelyan, please can you tell us, in your own time and words, everything that happened on Tuesday 29 June 1976.'

Dr Trevelyan pauses.

DI Davis glances at his colleague. He momentarily worries he won't talk after all.

Eventually he starts. 'I didn't mean anything to happen. I really didn't ... but you're right, I did know Cerys. She was lovely. I wanted to get to know her better, especially after we danced together at the barn dance.'

His voice is little more than a whisper. Tears slowly roll down his face, dripping onto the table from the bottom of his chin.

'She was beautiful. I fell for her from the moment they arrived. I didn't say anything to anyone else about my feelings as they were only staying for two weeks. Not even my brother Richard. Mum and Dad always teased us about holiday romances. But this was different. *She* was different.'

A little calmer now, his voice still wavers.

'We met up each evening. Mostly just going to the Doom Bar and having a laugh. The girls spent the day on the beach, while we worked on the farm. Then we'd all meet up for a few drinks.'

Dr Trevelyan's eyes are closed, silent tears continue to fall.

'On our day off Richard and I took them to the sailing club. It was such a brilliant day. They'd never sailed before… then we joined up with George and Barry to go to the barn dance at Home Farm.

'We all joined in the dancing, but she definitely flirted with me that night. I was driving but they all had a few glasses of punch. I asked her to dance, then, when they played the slow dances at the end of the evening… it was amazing… then we kissed.'

Dr Trevelyan can barely speak.

'That's when I knew. I had fallen completely head over heels in love with her. I couldn't get her out of my mind. All I could think about was when I would next get to see her. Talk to her. Be with her. I'd never felt like that before.'

Another pause.

'Do continue, Dr Trevelyan,' encourages DI Davis.

Another sob.

'The next night they were ill. Except Cerys that is. I was sorry for them, but at the same time I was pleased. Selfish. It gave me more opportunity to see Cerys on her own.

'I was obsessed. I would try to accidentally bump into her. I followed her when she went off walking on her own, without her knowing. I watched her buy postcards from the gift shop… and when she sat on the cliff top just daydreaming.

'I simply couldn't think about anyone or anything else. She was exquisitely beautiful.'

He stops. Staring directly at DI Davis now but his eyes elsewhere. Remembering how pretty she was.

'When I saw her chatting with George Pengelly, I was so jealous. They were sat on the bench in Polzeath, overlooking the beach. That was Sunday afternoon. I tooted my horn, just so they would know they had been seen, but they didn't even notice.'

He wipes his nose and sniffs.

'The next day I followed her again. Sure enough, there they were. Cerys and George, sat on the bench laughing and joking. It was all too much. I watched them in disbelief. Then they kissed – only on the cheek I know – but to me that was betrayal. He was engaged to be married and had a baby on the way. Why would she be interested in him? I knew I would be perfect for her. I wanted to make her the happiest girl in the world.'

He stops again, takes another sip of water.

'So I watched and waited. Then, as she walked to the post box I slowly drove past and hooted, then waved and jumped out the car. Made it look like I just happened to be passing by chance.'

He pauses again. Now he's started it's as if a huge burden has been lifted from his shoulders. His relief is palpable. The overbearing secret he has kept hidden for so many years is finally being released.

A tsunami of grief.

Grief. And love. For the girl who won his heart.

'Cerys was surprised to see me. She was looking for her watch. It had been an eighteenth birthday present from her parents. She was distraught to think she may have lost it. That was when I lent her mine.'

He sighs as he looks at DI Davis. So he *had* known about the watch when he denied it earlier.

'I insisted she borrow it. I was chuffed to think she would have a little bit of me with her wherever she went. Then she gave me a hug to say thank you, before heading back to the beach. I was already desperately looking forward to when I would next see her.'

DI Davis and DS Sampson are absorbed by what he is saying.

'So the next day I was more devious. I had to reach her

before she met George. I got there early, pretending I had just arrived, when she came up the path from the beach. I told her I had just seen some dolphins swimming off the coast, that the hot weather must have brought them closer to the shoreline. If we were quick they would still be there. She was so excited, she said she'd always dreamt of seeing real, live dolphins.'

He smiles. After all these years he's still pleased his ruse worked.

'I pretended they were near Lundy Bay so we walked really fast, hoping they would still be there. I took her hand, although I could sense she was wary. I was just so thrilled to be with her. On her own. I wanted to hold her; to walk with her along the cliff top looking at the amazing views and kiss her in the beautiful sunshine. To tell her how I felt about her.'

He takes another small sip of water, carefully choosing his next words. His tone deepens.

'The further we walked the more I could tell she wasn't sure. I panicked. I really wanted her to love me as much as I loved her... and then she dropped the bombshell.

'She told me she already had a boyfriend at home. A "proper" boyfriend. Just like that. Out of the blue. She said she thought it important that I knew. She really liked me as a good friend, but it could never be anything more.'

Dr Trevelyan hesitates. Longer this time. His shoulders shake uncontrollably as he wipes his nose with the back of his hand. Then he vividly recalls the moment that afternoon when his life changed forever.

'... I ... I was so angry with her, yet so in love with her at the same time. We were looking over Lundy Bay now and there were clearly no dolphins. Not wanting to miss the opportunity I tried to hold her. To kiss her. But she pulled away.'

DI Davis looks straight at him.

'She said she was scared. She told me to let her go. To leave her alone.'

Dr Trevelyan holds his head in his hands.

'So I pushed her. My anger got the better of me and I just pushed her as hard as I could.

'I heard a scream, like a child screeching behind me. I spun around but there was no one there, so I assumed it must have been a seagull. Then, when I turned back, literally a fraction of a second later, Cerys was gone.'

His sobbing turns to howls. So loud PS Taylor looks through the window on the interview room door to check all is in order.

'I never meant for anything to happen, I really didn't ... I hadn't realised we were so close to Lundy Hole. I loved her.' He wails. 'I did, I loved her.

'But I was angry... so, so angry... I had never felt such rage, not before or since. It makes me so ashamed to say it. But I did. I did want to hurt her. Just in that awful moment. For a split second. But I never, ever meant to kill her. I just wanted her to know that if I couldn't have her, then no one else was going to have her either.'

DI Davis and DS Sampson let him have a bit of time. Let his emotions flow. It must be unimaginably difficult for him. Having kept his wicked secret for so long.

'Dr Trevelyan, once you realised Cerys had fallen, what did you do about it?'

He slumps forward again, shaking his head.

'I repeat Dr Trevelyan. What did you do after you realised Cerys had fallen?'

'I looked over the edge but I couldn't see her, the overhang was too great. I couldn't hear anything either. The noise of the waves was too loud, crashing against the rocks below, and the seagulls. I assumed she must have fallen into the sea below.'

'Then I heard someone, calling their child – it sounded like "Milly" – and then I spotted a lady walking up from the cove shouting "I'm going to find you!" in a jokey sort of way, as if she was looking for someone.'

He laughs a sad, muffled laugh through his tears.

'How apt. "I'm going to find you"... Seems like their little game of hide-and-seek lasted longer than anyone would have thought. Thirty-four years later and she didn't give up trying to find me.'

He rambles into his hands.

'The stupid thing is, I found her first. I should have dealt with it there and then. Before she put two and two together...'

His voice fades away as he realises what he is saying.

'Please continue, Dr Trevelyan,' prompts DI Davis.

'I initially thought to ask the woman coming up the path for help. Or run back to the farm, to get Richard. We could rescue her and everything would be okay. But then, almost immediately, I realised no one knew I was with Cerys anyway. Someone would be bound to spot her in the water and call the lifeboat, she'd be saved. If I just went back and pretended otherwise, no one would ever know I had even been there.'

Dr Trevelyan stops to take a breath.

'So you did absolutely nothing?' asks DI Davis.

Silence.

More silence.

'... I wasn't thinking straight,' Dr Trevelyan eventually offers. 'I knew I could be in serious trouble. I didn't want that for my parents. Or for me. I was due to qualify as a doctor the following year. I was so looking forward to a career in medicine. I knew this could mess it all up... seriously mess it all up.'

He starts sobbing again.

'I couldn't throw everything away. It was a spur of the moment decision. A moment of sheer madness. I have never felt anger, or emotions, with such potency. They came over me, as if I had been taken over by a supernatural power.'

He pauses.

Then, barely audible, he slowly continues. 'Somehow, between leaving her there and getting back to the farm, I made a huge decision. The biggest decision of my life. I made a promise to myself to pretend I had done nothing. That nothing had happened. I knew it was completely wrong, and went against every grain in my body. But in the heat of the moment I couldn't think what else to do.

'Then, as time went on and she wasn't found, I persuaded myself that I had done the right thing. I actually convinced myself I hadn't even been there, that none of it had ever really happened. I even believed my own alibi.

'I know DS Watts noticed a couple of anomalies, but I thought I'd got away with them in the final statement. It was really, really hard keeping up the pretence. Trying to pretend everything was normal.'

He thinks for a moment.

'No, not normal. It was far from normal. Police everywhere, TV crews, journalists… but trying to pretend I was normal was tough. I helped the girls and the other locals every day with the search, so nobody would notice anything odd.'

He looks at DI Davis with sore, red eyes.

'Then, when the summer finally passed and Cerys was never found I went back to Guy's Hospital in London to finish my degree. To carry on living my life.'

He laughs quietly to himself as if remembering something else.

'I'm sorry. It's just that Cerys thought Guy was one of my uni friends who held crazy parties, she never realised it was where I was actually studying.'

His stifled laughter soon reverts to heavy sobs.

'After qualifying I spent two years in London. I told myself, the more time I spent saving other lives, the more it would make up for what I had done. That it all balanced out. That it was all okay.

'I moved to Vancouver to gain more experience, that's

where I met my wife Mary, a paediatrician. I knew I was the luckiest man in the world to be given a second chance. I knew I didn't deserve her.'

The sadness in his face is overwhelming, as he realises his secret will soon be known.

His wife. His daughters. His brother. Everyone will know.

'When our daughters were born we made the decision to move back to the UK. They were so, so precious to me. It became abundantly clear that I needed to do something. To protect my family. To preserve what we had created. My wife, our wonderful daughters, family and friends. To ensure the girls and my wife had the life they deserved. I couldn't risk them ever finding out what happened.

'The truth is, I could never erase the image of Cerys falling from my head. Or the thought that someone may have seen us. So, when the opportunity arose, I successfully applied for the GP vacancy in Wadebridge and then, a year later, for the police doctor role as well.

'I had an ulterior motive. I would know if anyone ever came close, even remotely close, to knowing my secret. I would be able to do something about it. To scare them away. To terrify them if necessary.'

Silent tears are still rolling down his cheeks. The puddle on the table has grown.

'I knew Emily Harrison had been to see you, after calling the police helpline. That was when I realised the woman walking up the path had been calling "Emily" not "Milly".

'You had inadvertently left some papers on your desk. I noted down her name and contact information. It was simple really. When she and her sister stayed in the shepherd hut I knew exactly who she was.'

Dr Trevelyan looks exhausted. Drained. His knee still shakes, but he's given up trying to stop it.

'I conveniently arranged for my wife and I to be there that

weekend. When I saw her handbag unattended in the office I popped the postcard in it. Nobody noticed. Foolish woman really. She made it very easy for me.'

He silently laughs through his sobs.

'The phoney email address was much harder. That took me a while to work out. But god it was clever. I still have a business interest in the campsite so I knew she was looking to book a shepherd hut again, this time on her own. So, not only did I have her work email too, I also knew what days her husband would be home alone.

'It was another perfect opportunity. I knew I could scare the living daylights out of her. I just wanted to terrorise her until she stopped. Then my secret would be safe again.'

He almost looks smug.

'... And then the phone call with her husband. That was genius. I mentioned the pretend road accident, and he let slip his parents were on their way to the airport. I hadn't intended to be so specific but he just fell into my hands.

'Then, to reinforce my message I emailed her again, telling her to get home, quick. To make her *really* panic. The only trouble was I had no way of knowing whether it had actually worked or not. Whether he had fallen for it. Or her. So, to put the final nail in the coffin, I called again on Sunday afternoon. It worked out perfectly when she answered it herself that time. I knew from the fear in her voice that it had been a huge success. That she was getting the message.'

He pauses. Trying to catch up with his own words, which are spilling out fast.

'The one thing I hadn't planned for was when she turned up at my surgery. I could see her staring at all my photos while I examined her little boy. Then she went as white as a sheet. Without saying anything we both just knew.

'I knew she'd discovered my secret. And *she* knew that I knew it was her too.'

OCTOBER 2010

Emily is anxious. It's quarter to eleven. Marcus said he'd be round at eleven and she hasn't seen him for weeks. She's excited but nervous. He said he needed some time to think it through. To decide what to do. She's terrified she really will lose him this time.

It's been traumatic. Marcus was mortified after he inadvertently opened the letter advising the date of her disciplinary hearing. He read the letter four times before it sank in. Then he remembered the phone call from her boss.

The letter itself was succinct. It gave the date, time and the name of the HR Manager who would be conducting the meeting. It was the supporting documentation that took his breath away. List upon list of internet searches and emails that had been identified as being "obtained for private use". He scanned the websites, names and contacts but didn't recognise any of them.

Until he spotted Euan and Bronwyn Morgan.

A supplementary paper also showed numerous dates where she "appeared to have some unexplained absences" from work. He immediately recognised the days Emily had travelled to meetings or conferences, away from her usual Bristol office.

Marcus was dumbfounded. This couldn't be his conscientious and loyal, loving wife. He swung from being shocked to angry. To begin with he assumed she really had lied to him all the time, about where she was and what she was doing. Then he thought it must be wrong. Emily would never do anything like that, she just wouldn't. She loved her job. She would never dream of doing anything to jeopardise it, or let her colleagues down.

Nor would she have lied to him so many times. She wouldn't have booked fake conferences or made up phoney overnight stays just for the fun of it. Not his Emily. Honest, dependable, home loving Emily. Emily, who hates being away from him or the children for a moment longer than she needs to.

Yet looking at the paperwork in front of him it looked like the last ten weeks had been one huge web of deceit.

After Jack was admitted to hospital Emily had called him from the ward. She had made no sense at all. In the end he had spoken to DI Davis. It wasn't until she got home that she was able to explain what happened during those two days. How involved she had been in solving the final stages of the mystery. How the urgency of it all had led to DI Davis visiting her in hospital, whilst Jack was fixed up to a myriad of tubes, to establish exactly what had happened.

She had broken down in tears, her entire body shaking and trembling.

Over the next few days she gradually shared the details. She told of her meetings with the Morgans in Pembrokeshire, George Pengelly's outburst, Gary "Horrible" Banks, Amy and Pip. Vicky's suicide. She even explained about the terrifying night in her car.

Marcus just let her talk. He was at a loss to know what to do or say. She needed to tell him everything, however difficult it might be, before either of them could move forward.

He tried his hardest to see it from her viewpoint. She

insisted she had only been trying to help. That she knew she could find the answer; that she was the only person who could. And as long as she felt that way then she *had* to do something about it, however foolhardy it seemed. After she met the Morgans it made her even more determined to see it through.

He tried and tried to understand. He tried and tried to accept that it was all perfectly normal behaviour.

But then the reality hit home. He wasn't sure if he knew who Emily really was anymore. That was when he decided to stay with a friend for a while to give him time. He needed "space" to think things through.

*

Five to eleven. Five minutes to go. She paces up and down the hall, listening out for his car. Molly and Jack are both at school. They agreed to meet mid-morning to give them enough time to talk properly. She looks at their children's shoes lying untidily on the rack behind the door. They still look so small. Emily spots their latest library books, Molly is such a voracious reader these days, she must remember to return them before the weekend.

She sits on the bottom step of the stairs and fiddles with her eternity ring. It's become a habit she can't stop, as she tries to quell her nerves.

She'll need to tell Marcus about her disciplinary too. It lasted three arduous hours. It took her ages to explain everything to the panel. They'd all sat in front of her. Staring. With serious looking faces. The fascinating case of the police doctor – arrested for a decades old crime – made it to the national news, but Emily had to tell them *all* the details. Right from the beginning. How else would they fully understand why she had done everything that she had done?

The HR manager was intrigued.

Never before had he been involved in such a fascinating employee hearing. There were always background stories, usually really sad or complex situations, but this had to trump them all.

After much deliberation – and due to the "highly extenuating circumstances" plus her previous, lengthy exemplary record with the company – the panel agreed to record the misdemeanours as a formal warning.

However, she would be put on a performance improvement plan for six months with her activities monitored closely. Plus she must fully reimburse the company for the time she had taken off work without permission.

Emily had been so relieved, she burst into tears on the spot. She had feared it would be instant dismissal. All she wanted now was for Marcus to give her a second chance too.

She hears footsteps walking up the drive. Her heart lurches in her chest.

How can she be so nervous about meeting her beloved husband? And yet she is.

There's a flapping sound on the other side of the door. Her heart sinks again. It's not him, it's the postman. She sees his distorted figure through the patterned glass of the door.

She jumps as a letter drops on the doormat.

She doesn't recognise the writing, it's very neat and precise. Long loops on the g's and y's. Tall t's.

Intrigued she sits on the bottom stair and gently teases it from the envelope.

Dear Emily,

It is a few weeks since we saw you and I have been meaning to write this letter for some days, but each time I tried it proved too difficult to do.

I wanted to thank you from the bottom of my heart for coming to visit us and for your selfless actions in helping the police to find out what happened to our dear, darling daughter Cerys.

When we met you it gave Bronwyn and I a huge sense of optimism in more ways than one.

Firstly, you gave us hope that there was still a possibility we would find the answer.

Secondly, you gave us joy that someone as kind and thoughtful as you would take the time to do this for an elderly couple like us.

Thirdly, you restored our faith in the human race that good things can, and do, happen.

We didn't tell you at the time - as Bronwyn had wanted to keep it private - but she was by then already very ill. She had been diagnosed with stage four, widespread secondary cancer and was subsequently admitted to the local hospice in late August.

After the kayaker found Cerys we were able to bring her home and her funeral was held at our local church. It was very moving and sad but also, in other ways, quite joyful. Bronwyn, with much support and help from the nurses, was there for the whole day. As were hundreds of friends and well wishers. We said our final good-byes to Cerys and celebrated the wonderful eighteen years we were blessed to have with her.

Sadly, Bronwyn passed away two weeks ago and we have now also laid her to rest.

This letter is just to let you know how your wonderful act of kindness made such a huge difference to Bronwyn and to me. Bronwyn is *now finally at peace knowing what happened to Cerys, and was looking forward to being reunited with our special daughter.*

Words are simply not enough but thank you once again. Wishing you, your husband and family every possible happiness.

Yours sincerely,
Euan Morgan

Tears roll down Emily's face. Small droplets land silently on the wooden floor, as Marcus pulls up outside. Dear Euan. What a wonderful man. Despite the immeasurable pain and suffering he and Bronwyn endured he still has so much kindness in his heart for others.

She'll show Marcus the letter. Perhaps it will help.

As his key turns in the lock she realises she's been helplessly trapped in a debilitating 1976 time warp for the last few months. With Marcus' help she's ready to start moving forward again. To rebuild their marriage.

It wasn't an obsession.

It was an obligation.

She *had* to find out what really happened on her sixth birthday. Surely Marcus will understand.

If only she hadn't screamed. It was always there, the bloodcurdling scream in her nightmares, over and over.

Over and over.

Over and over, as her mum walked up the path.

It was Emily's fault.

If only she hadn't screamed and distracted him. He might have been able to stop her falling.

AUTHOR'S NOTE

Emily's story was inspired by a number of things and I carried the idea around in my head for well over ten years before I actually started writing.

Firstly, I have always been curious about cases where people go missing, or are murdered, never to be found. Just the fact there *must* be someone, somewhere, who knows what happened. How do they live a normal life? How do they have a career, get married, have children – grandchildren even – without anyone ever finding out their secret?

Secondly, cases where the key witness is a young child. In my book Emily is just six years old and decades pass before she realises the terrible significance of what she saw. We all know how our memories are shaped by the passing of time. Yet there are some childhood moments, both happy and sad, that we can remember as clearly as if they were yesterday. Will anyone believe her? Does she even believe her own memories?

Finally, carefree, childhood holidays with my seven brothers and sisters. With such a large family daily life was usually a military operation but for two weeks every year we escaped to the idyllic North Cornwall coast. One place fired my imagination from a very young age. Lundy Hole. An amazing sea hole. I can vividly remember peering tentatively over the edge to watch the waves crashing against the rocks far, far below. Surrounded in local myth and legend I always knew I'd write my own story about it one day.

And so Emily's story began. I have loved every single second of writing it. From reliving the events, music, food and fashions of both 1976 and 2010, to developing believable characters and an intriguing plot full of twists and turns.

My aim was to write a story that anyone could relate to. How a seemingly ordinary family – and ordinary family holiday – could suddenly turn into something far more sinister. I wanted readers to genuinely care about the characters, and ponder long after they finish reading what would they do if they ever found themselves in the same situation?

*

Thank you for choosing my book. I sincerely hope you enjoyed reading it as much as I did writing it… and I look forward to sharing with you what Emily did next!

If you did enjoy it, I would be very grateful if you could leave a review on the website from which you bought it, please do also visit my website for more news or to subscribe to my regular newsletter:

https://www.jdpullan-author.com

Positive reviews are extremely valuable for debut authors like myself. Please excuse the pun but they provide enormous help in "spreading the word" about our books – and to build a strong support base – as they make it so much easier for other readers to find and enjoy them too.

ACKNOWLEDGEMENTS

Heartfelt thanks are owed to so many people it is impossible to name everyone. I am forever grateful to all my family and friends, who have provided endless encouragement after being subjected to various drafts, synopses and extracts.

In particular Abigail (who read numerous drafts and never once complained) and Tracey for your kind support. Plus Annette, Samantha, Nathaniel, Richard, Sarah and Shirley.

Huge thanks also to Bethany and Mia for the lovely cover photo; and braving freezing cold weather for a photo shoot in a summery dress and bare feet to make it look like a heatwave in June!

Last, but certainly not least, to my husband Andy for your never-ending love and support, even when I disappear to the "Hobby Hütte" to write for hours at a time or witter on about different ideas for characters, storylines and plot points.

I have genuinely loved every second of writing my book but couldn't have done it without you all.

ABOUT THE AUTHOR

Since a young age the author has always loved to read and write stories. A few years ago, when her parents moved from the family home where they had lived for almost half a century, she came across a book she had penned aged seven and three quarters. It started off with impeccably neat handwriting and childish illustrations then became increasingly untidy until it fizzled out altogether. She vowed there and then to finish her next one.

After qualifying as a management accountant and enjoying a varied career in Finance and HR she gave up work in 2018 to spend more time on other hobbies, including creative writing... and completing her book.

She grew up in the West Country and now lives in rural Monmouthshire with her husband Andy and their two lassie collies.

BOOK CLUB & READING GROUP DISCUSSION IDEAS

(Hopefully with no spoilers!)

1. If you were Emily would you have done anything after being reminded about what happened? If so would you have approached it in the same way?

2. What can you remember from when you were six years old? Are your memories genuine or are they fabricated from seeing photos, hearing things people have said etc? Do you think Emily really could trust her childhood memories?

3. If you were Marcus how would you have reacted? Would you have done anything differently?

4. Did you think Emily was a likeable character and someone you could empathise with? What were her key strengths and weaknesses?

5. Did you think Cerys was a likeable character? What were her key strengths and weaknesses? Do you think Vicky's accusations were justified?

6. Would you have given the book a different title? If so what would you have called it?

7. The infamous, heatwave summer of 1976 was deliberately chosen for the book, the wonderful sunshine and beautiful location contrasting with the girls' tragic holiday. Do you think this worked?

8. One key theme is how Emily never forgot the simple act of kindness Cerys showed her by giving her the shell bracelet. It is often said that every thing we do has a lasting impact on someone else, even if we don't know it – do you agree?

9. Which character and/or part of the narrative prompted the strongest emotional response for you? Why was this?

10. Do you think the perpetrator was evil? Or were they just foolish? Would you have been tempted to do the same if you had been them?

11. Would your answer to question (1) be the same before – and after – knowing the final twist?